T0143372

UNTAMED

ALSO BY P.C. CAST and KRISTIN CAST

Chosen

Betrayed

Marked

UNTAMED

A HOUSE OF NIGHT NOVEL

P.C. CAST and **KRISTIN CAST**

ST. MARTIN'S GRIFFIN

NEW YORK

This is a work of fiction. All of the characters, organizations, and events por-
trayed in this novel are either products of the author's imagination or are used
fictitiously.

UNTAMED. Copyright © 2008 by P.C. Cast and Kristin Cast. All rights reserved.
Printed in the United States of America. For information, address St. Martin's
Press, 175 Fifth Avenue, New York, N.Y. 10010.

www.stmartins.com

Library of Congress Cataloging-in-Publication Data

Cast, P.C.
    Untamed : a house of night novel / P.C. Cast and Kristin Cast. — 1st ed.
        p.   cm. — (House of night ; 4)
    ISBN-13: 978-0-312-37983-4
    ISBN-10: 0-312-37983-8
    1. Vampires—Fiction.   2. Adolescence—Fiction.   I. Cast, Kristin.
II. Title.
    PS3603.A869U58 2008
    813'.6—dc22

                                                        2008024993

10   9

This one is for the students, past and present, of South Inter-mediate High School in Broken Arrow, Oklahoma. Thanks for your enthusiasm, sense of humor, and support for the series. SIHS is the best!

Also for the ladies of Tulsa Street Cats. They're not nuns, but they do qualify as cat saints!

ACKNOWLEDGMENTS

We would like to thank our wonderful agent, Meredith Bernstein, without whom the House of Night wouldn't have been born.

A big WE HEART YOU goes to our amazing St. Martin's team: Jennifer Weis, Anne Marie Tallberg, Matthew Shear, Carly Wilkins, Brittney Kleinfelter, Katy Hershberger, Talia Ross, and Michael Storrings. It's wonderful to love working with a group of people so much.

Thank you to the fans of the House of Night—we appreciate you!

Thank you to Tulsa Street Cats for their support, sense of humor, and all they do for cats. To find out more about them and/or donate, please go to www.streetcatstulsa.org. Kristin and I heart Street Cats!

UNTAMED

CHAPTER ONE

The *caw! caw! cawing!* of one stupid crow kept me up all night. (Well, more accurately, all day—'cause, you know, I'm a vampyre fledgling and we have that whole issue of day and night being turned around.) Anyway, I got zero sleep last night/day. But my crappy nonsleep is currently the easiest thing to deal with since life *really* sucks when your friends are pissed at you. I should know. I'm Zoey Redbird, currently the undisputed Queen of Making My Friends Pissed Land.

Persephone, the big sorrel mare who I could consider mine for as long as I lived at the House of Night, craned her head around and nuzzled my cheek. I kissed her soft muzzle and went back to brushing her sleek neck. Grooming Persephone always helped me think and made me feel better. And I definitely needed help with both of those things.

"Okay, so, I've managed to avoid the Big Confrontation for two days, but that can't continue," I told the mare. "Yes, I know they're in the cafeteria right now, eating dinner while they hang out together being all buddy-buddy and totally leaving me out."

Persephone snorted and went back to munching hay.

"Yeah, I think they're being jerks, too. Sure, I did lie to them, but it was mostly by omission. And, yeah, I kept some stuff from them. Mostly for their own good." I sighed. Well, the stuff about

Stevie Rae being undead was for their own good. The stuff about me having a thing with Loren Blake—Vampyre Poet Laureate and professor at the House of Night—well, that was more for my own good. "But still." Persephone flicked an ear back to listen to me. "They're being really judgmental."

Persephone snorted again. I sighed again. Crap. I couldn't avoid them any longer.

After giving the sweet mare one last pat, I walked slowly out of her stall to the tack room and put up the array of currycombs and mane/tail brushes I'd been using on her for the past hour. I breathed deeply of the leather and horse smell, letting the soothing mixture ease my nerves. Catching my reflection in the smooth glass window of the tack room, I automatically ran my fingers through my dark hair, trying to make it look not so bedheady. I'd been Marked as a fledgling vampyre and moved to the House of Night for just over two months, but already my hair was noticeably thicker and longer. And supergood hair was only one of the many changes taking place with me. Some of them were invisible—like the fact that I had an affinity for all five of the elements. Some of them were very much visible—like the unique tattoos that framed my face in intricate, exotic swirls and then, unlike any other fledgling or adult vampyre, the sapphire design spread down my neck and shoulders, along my spine, and most recently, had moved around my waist, a little fact no one but my cat, Nala, our goddess Nyx, and I knew.

Like who could I show?

"Well, yesterday you had not one, but three boyfriends," I told the me with the dark eyes and cynical half smile that was reflected in the glass. "But you fixed that, didn't you? Today not only do you have zero boyfriends, but no one will ever trust you again for at least, I dunno, a gazillion years or so." Well, except Aphrodite, who totally freaked and took off two days ago because she might have suddenly been turned back into a human, and Stevie Rae, who was chasing said freaked re-humaned Aphrodite because she might have caused the fledgling-to-human issue when I cast a circle and turned her from creepy undead dead kid to odd-red-tattooed-vampyre-but-herself-again kid. "Either way," I told myself aloud, "you have managed to mess up just about everyone who has touched your life. Well done, you!"

My lip had actually started to quiver and I felt the sting of tears in my eyes. No. Bawling my eyes red wouldn't do any good. I mean, seriously, if it did, then my friends and I would have kissed (well, not literally) and made up days ago. I was just going to have to face them and start trying to make things right.

The late December night was cool and a little misty. The gaslights lining the sidewalk that stretched from the stable and field house area of the school to the main building flickered with little haloes of yellow light, looking beautiful and old-worldly. Actually, the whole campus of the House of Night was gorgeous, and always made me think of something that belonged in an Arthurian legend more than in the twenty-first century. *I love it here,* I reminded myself. *It's home. It's where I belong. I'll make it right with my friends, and everything will be okay then.*

I was chewing my lip and worrying about just exactly how I was going to make it right with my friends when my mental stressing was interrupted by a weird flapping noise that filled the air around me. Something about the sound sent a chill down my spine. I looked up. There was nothing above me but darkness and sky and the winter-bare limbs of the huge oaks that lined the sidewalk. I shivered, having a walking-over-my-grave moment as the night went from soft and misty to dark and malevolent.

Hang on—dark and malevolent? Well, that's just silly! What I had heard was probably nothing more sinister than the wind rustling through the trees. Jeesh, I was losing it.

Shaking my head at myself, I kept walking but had taken only a couple of steps when it happened again. The weird flapping above me actually caused the air, which seemed ten degrees colder, to flutter wildly against my skin. I automatically flailed a hand up, imagining bats and spiders and all sorts of creepy things.

My fingers passed through nothingness, but it was frigid nothingness, and an icy pain sliced through my hand. Completely freaked out, I yelped and hugged my hand to my chest. For a moment I didn't know what to do, and my body was numb with fear. The flapping was getting louder and the cold more intense when I finally managed to move. Ducking my head, I did the only thing I could think to do. I ran for the nearest door to the school.

After slipping inside, I slammed the thick wooden door behind me and, panting for breath, turned to peer through the little arched window in the center of it. The night shifted and swam before my eyes, like black paint poured down a dark page. Still, the terrible feeling of icy fear lingered within me. What was going on? Almost without realizing what I was doing, I whispered, "Fire, come to me. I need your warmth."

Instantly the element responded, filling the air around me with the soothing heat of a hearth fire. Still staring out the little window, I pressed my palms against the rough wood of the door. "Out there," I murmured. "Send your heat out there, too." With a whoosh of warmth, the element moved from me, through the door, and poured into the night. There was a hissing sound, like steam rising from dry ice. The mist roiled, thick and soupy, giving me a sense of dizzy vertigo that made me a little nauseated, and the strange darkness began to evaporate. Then the heat completely beat away the chill, and as suddenly as it had begun, the night was once again quiet and familiar.

What had just happened?

My stinging hand drew my attention from the window. I looked down. Across the back of my hand there were red welts, as though something with claws, or talons, had scraped across my flesh. I rubbed at the angry-looking marks, which stung like a curling iron burn.

Then the feeling hit me strong, hard, overwhelming—and I knew with my Goddess-given sixth sense that I shouldn't be here by myself. The coldness that had tainted the night—the ghostly something that had chased me inside and welted my hand—filled me with a terrible foreboding and for the first time in a long time, I was truly and utterly afraid. Not for my friends. Not for my grandma or my human ex-boyfriend, or even for my estranged mom. I was afraid for myself. I didn't just *want* the company of my friends; I needed them.

Still rubbing my hand, I made my legs move and knew beyond any doubt that I would rather face the hurt and disappointment of my friends than whatever dark thing might be waiting for me in the concealing night.

I hovered for a second just outside the open doors to the busy "dining hall" (a.k.a. school cafeteria) watching the other kids talk easily and happily together, and I was almost overwhelmed with the sudden wish that I could be just another fledgling—that I didn't have any extraordinary abilities or the responsibilities that went along with those abilities. For a second I wanted to be normal so bad that it was hard for me to breathe.

Then I felt the soft brush of wind against my skin that seemed warmed by the heat of an invisible flame. I caught a whiff of the ocean, even though there is definitely no ocean near Tulsa, Oklahoma. I heard birdsong and smelled new-cut grass. And my spirit quivered with silent joy within me as it acknowledged my powerful

Goddess-given gifts of an affinity for each of the five elements: air, fire, water, earth, and spirit.

I wasn't normal. I wasn't like anyone else, fledgling or vampyre, and it was wrong of me to wish otherwise. And part of my not-normal-ness was telling me that I had to go in there and try to make peace with my friends. I straightened my spine and looked around the room with eyes that were clear of self-pity, and easily found my special group sitting at our booth.

I drew a deep breath and then made my way quickly across the cafeteria, giving a little nod or small smile to the kids who said hi to me. I noticed that everyone seemed to be reacting to me with their usual mix of respect and awe, which meant that my friends hadn't been talking crap about me to the masses. It also meant that Neferet hadn't launched an all-out, open attack against me. Yet.

I grabbed a quick salad and a brown pop. Then, holding on to my tray with such abnormal tightness that it was turning my fingers white, I marched straight to our booth and took my usual seat beside Damien.

When I sat down, no one looked at me, but their easy chatter instantly died, which is something I totally hate. I mean, what's more awful than walking up to a group of your supposed-to-be friends and having them all shut up so that you knew for sure they were all talking about you? Ugh.

"Hi," I said instead of running away or bursting into tears like I wanted to.

No one said anything.

"So, what's up?" I directed the question at Damien, knowing that my gay friend was naturally the weakest link in the don't-talk-to-Zoey chain.

Sadly, it was the Twins who answered me and not gay, and therefore more sensitive and polite, Damien.

"Not shit, right, Twin?" said Shaunee.

"That's right, Twin, not shit. 'Cause we can't be trusted to know shit," Erin said. "Twin, did you know we're totally untrust-worthy?"

"Not until recently I didn't, Twin. You?" Shaunee said.

"Didn't know till recently either," Erin finished.

Okay, the Twins aren't really twins. Shaunee Cole is a caramel-colored Jamaican-American who grew up on the East Coast. Erin Bates is a gorgeous blonde who was born in Tulsa. The two met after being Marked and moving to the House of Night on the same day. They clicked instantly—it's like genetics and geography never existed. They literally finish each other's sentences. And at that moment they were glaring at me with twin looks of angry suspicion.

God, they made me tired.

They also made me mad. Yes, I'd kept secrets from them. Yes, I'd lied to them. But I'd had to. Well, mostly I'd had to. And their twin holier-than-thou crap was getting on my last nerve.

"Thank you for that lovely commentary. And now I'll try ask-ing someone who doesn't have to answer in a stereo version of hateful *Gossip Girl* Blair." I turned my attention away from them and looked directly at Damien, even though I could hear the Twins sucking air and getting ready to say something I was hop-ing they would one day regret. "So, I guess what I really wanted to ask when I said 'what's up' is if you've noticed any scary, ghost-like, flappy weirdness outside lately. Have you?"

Damien's a tall, really cute guy with excellent bone structure whose brown eyes were usually warm and expressive but were, at this moment, wary and more than a little cold. "A flappy ghost thing?" he said. "Sorry, I have no clue what you're talking about."

My heart squeezed at the strangerlike tone of his voice, but I told myself that at least he'd answered my question. "On the way here from the stables, something kinda attacked me. I couldn't really see anything, but it was cold and it put a big welt on my hand." I lifted my hand to show him—and there was no welt there anymore.

Great.

Shaunee and Erin snorted together. Damien just looked really, really sad. I was opening my mouth to explain that there had been a welt there just a few minutes ago, when Jack rushed up.

"Oh, hi! I'm so sorry I'm late but when I put on my shirt I found a ginormic stain right on the front of it. Can you believe that?" Jack said as he hurried up with his tray of food and sat at his place beside Damien.

"A stain? It's not on that lovely blue long-sleeved Armani I got you for Christmas, is it?" Damien said, scooting over to make room for his boyfriend.

"Ohmigod, no! I'd never spill anything on that one. I just love it and—" His words came to a staggering halt when his eyes flitted from Damien to me. He gulped. "Oh, uh. Hi, Zoey."

"Hi, Jack," I said, smiling at him. Jack and Damien are together. Hello. They're gay. My friends and I, along with anyone who's not narrow-minded and utterly judgmental, are cool with that.

"I didn't expect to see you," Jack babbled. "I thought you were still . . . uh . . . well . . ." He trailed off, looking uncomfortable and blushing a pretty pink.

"You thought I was still hiding in my room?" I supplied for him.

He nodded.

"No." I said firmly, "I'm done doing that."

"Well, la-te-da," Erin began, but before Shaunee could do her usual chime-in act, a blatantly sexy laugh coming from the door behind us made everyone turn and gawk.

Aphrodite twitched into the room, laughing while she batted her eyes at Darius, one of the youngest and hottest of the Sons of Erebus Warriors who protected the House of Night, and did an excellent hair flip. The girl always had been good at multitasking, but I was totally shocked at how nonchalant and utterly cool and collected she looked. Only two days ago she'd been almost dead and then utterly freaked because the sapphire-colored outline of a crescent moon—which appeared on all fledglings' foreheads, Marking them as having begun the Change that would either end in becoming a vampyre or in becoming dead—had disappeared from her face.

Which meant she had somehow turned back into a human.

CHAPTER TWO

Okay, I'd thought she'd turned back into a human, but even from where I was sitting I could see that Aphrodite's Mark had returned. Her cold blue eyes swept the cafeteria as she gave the watching kids a stuck-up sneer before turning her attention back to Darius and letting her hand linger on the big warrior's chest.

"It was ever so sweet of you to walk me to the dining hall. You're right. It shouldn't have taken two days to cut my vacation short. With all the craziness going on around here, it's best to stay on campus where we can be protected. And since you say you'll be stationed at the door of our dorm, that is definitely the most safe *and* attractive place to be." She practically purred at him. Jeesh, she was stank. Had I not been so surprised to see her, I would have made appropriate gagging noises. Loud, obvious ones.

"And I must return to my posting there. Good night, my lady," Darius said. He gave her a very sharp bow, which made him look like one of those romantic, handsome knights, minus the horse and the shining armor, from back in the day. "It is a pleasure to serve you." He smiled at Aphrodite one more time before turning neatly on his heel and leaving the cafeteria.

"And I'll just bet it would be a pleasure to service *you*," Aphrodite said in her nastiest voice as soon as he was out of earshot. Then she turned around to face the gawking, silent room.

She lifted one perfectly waxed brow and gave everyone her patented Aphrodite sneer. "What? You look like you've never seen gorgeous before. Hell, I was only gone a couple of days. Your short-term memory should be better than that. Remember me? I'm the gorgeous bitch you all love to hate." When no one said anything, she rolled her eyes. "Oh, whatever." She twitched to the salad bar and began to fill her plate as the noise dam finally broke and all the kids made rude sounds and turned back to their food dismissively.

To the uninformed, I'm sure Aphrodite looked like her usual haughty self. But I could see how nervous and tense she actually was. Hell, I understood exactly how she felt—I'd just walked through the gauntlet myself. Actually, I was currently stuck in the middle of it along with her.

"I thought she'd become human again," Damien said under his breath to all of us. "But her Mark's back."

"Nyx's ways are mysterious," I said, trying to sound wise and High Priestess in Training–ish.

"I'm thinking Nyx's ways are another M-word, Twin," Erin said. "Can you guess it?"

"Majorly messed up?" Shaunee said.

"Exactly," Erin said.

"That's three words," Damien said.

"Oh, don't be such a schoolteacher," Shaunee told him. "Plus, the point is Aphrodite is a hag, and we were kinda hoping Nyx dumped her when that Mark of hers disappeared."

"More than kinda hoping, Twin," Erin said.

Everyone stared at Aphrodite. I tried to force salad down my throat. See, here's the deal: Aphrodite used to be the most popular, powerful, bitchy fledgling at the House of Night. Since she'd crossed the High Priestess, Neferet, and been totally ostracized, she had been reduced to simply the most bitchy fledgling at the House of Night.

Of course, weirdly (and typically enough for me), she and I had kinda, sorta, accidentally become friends—or at the very least, allies. Not that we wanted the masses to know that. Nevertheless, I'd been worried about her when she disappeared, even though Stevie Rae had chased after her. I mean, I hadn't heard from either of them in two days.

Naturally, my other friends—namely Damien, Jack, and the Twins—hated her guts. So to say that they were shocked and not very pleased when Aphrodite walked directly to our booth and sat down beside me was an understatement almost as big as that knight in the *Indiana Jones* movie saying "He chose poorly" when the bad guy picked the wrong goblet to drink out of and his body disintegrated.

"Staring isn't polite, even when it's at someone as stunningly beautiful as *moi*," Aphrodite said before taking a bite of her salad.

"What in the hell are you doing, Aphrodite?" Erin asked.

Aphrodite swallowed and then blinked with fake innocence at Erin. "Eating, moron," she said sweetly.

"This is a no-ho zone," Shaunee said, finally recovering her ability to speak.

"Yeah, it's posted back here," Erin said, pointing at a pretend sign on the back of their bench.

"I hate to repeat a sentiment I've said before, but in this case I'll make an exception. So I again say: Die Dorkamese Twins."

"That's it," Erin said, barely able to keep her voice down. "Twin and I are gonna smack that damn Mark right off your face."

"Yeah, maybe it'll stay off this time," Shaunee said.

"Stop it," I said. When the Twins turned slant-eyed looks of pissed-off-ness on me, I felt my stomach clench. Did they really hate me as much as they looked like they did? It made my heart hurt to think about it, but I lifted my chin and stared right back at them. If I completed the Change to vampyre, I would someday

be their High Priestess, and that meant they had damn well better listen to me. "We've already been through this. Aphrodite is part of the Dark Daughters now. She's also part of our circle, being as she has an affinity for the element earth." I hesitated, wondering if she still had that affinity, or had she lost it when she'd gone from fledgling to human and then, apparently, back to fledgling again, but that was just too confusing, so I hurried on. "You guys know you agreed to accept her in each position, *without* name-calling and hateful remarks."

The Twins didn't say anything, but Damien's voice, sounding uncharacteristically flat and emotionless, came from the other side of me. "We agreed to that, but we didn't agree to be friends with her."

"I didn't say I wanted to be your friend," Aphrodite said.

"Ditto, bitch!" the Twins said together.

"Whatever," Aphrodite said, moving like she was going to pick up her tray and leave.

I'd opened my mouth to tell Aphrodite to sit down and the Twins to shut up when a bizarre noise echoed down the hall and through the open doors to the cafeteria.

"What the—?" I began, but didn't get the whole question out before at least a dozen cats streaked into the cafeteria, hissing and spitting like crazy.

Okay, at the House of Night, cats are everywhere. Literally. They follow us around, sleep with, and in my cat Nala's case, often complain at, the fledgling of their choice. In Vamp Soc class, one of the first cool things we learned was that cats had long been familiars of vampyres. This meant that we were all majorly used to having cats everywhere. But I had never seen them act so absolutely insane.

The Twin's huge gray tomcat, Beelzebub, jumped right up between them. He was puffed up to twice his already ginormously

large size, and he stared back through the open door to the dining hall with amber eyes slit in anger.

"Beelzebub, baby, what's wrong?" Erin tried to soothe him.

Nala leaped up on my lap. She put her little white-tipped paws on my shoulder and gave a scary, psycho-cat growl as she, too, stared at the door and the chaotic noise still coming from the hall.

"Hey," Jack said. "I know what that sound is."

And it hit me at the same time. "It's a dog barking," I said.

Then something that resembled a large yellow bear more closely than a dog burst into the cafeteria. The bear-dog was followed by a kid who was being followed by several uncharacteristically frazzled-looking professors, including our fencing master, Dragon Lankford, our equestrian instructor, Lenobia, as well as several of the Sons of Erebus Warriors.

"Got ya!" the kid yelled once he caught up with the dog and came to a skidding halt not far from us while he swooped down, snagged the barking beast's collar (which I noted was pink leather with silver metallic spikes all around it), and neatly clipped a leash to it. The instant his leash was reattached, the bear stopped barking, plopped its round butt down on the floor, and stared, panting, up at the kid. "Yeah, great. *Now* you want to act right," I heard him mutter to the obviously grinning canine.

Even though the barking had stopped, the cats in the cafeteria had definitely not stopped freaking. There was so much hissing around us, it sounded like air escaping from a punctured inner tube.

"You see, James, this was what I was trying to explain to you earlier," Dragon Lankford said as he stared, frowning, down at the dog. "The animal just won't work at this House of Night."

"It's Stark, not James," the kid said. "And like *I* was trying to explain to *you* earlier—the dog has to stay with me. It's just the way it is. If you want me—you get her, too."

I decided that the new dog kid had an unusual way about him. It wasn't like he was being openly rude or disrespectful to Dragon, but he also wasn't speaking to him with the respect, and sometimes outright fear, with which the vast majority of newly Marked fledglings spoke to vampyres. I checked out the front of his vintage Pink Floyd T-shirt. No class insignia there, so I didn't have a clue what year he was and how long he'd been Marked.

"Stark," Lenobia was saying, obviously trying to reason with the kid, "it's just not possible to integrate a dog into this campus. You can see how much he's upsetting the cats."

"They'll get used to him. They did at the Chicago House of Night. She's usually pretty good about not chasing them around, but that gray cat really did ask for it with that whole hissing and scratching thing."

"Uh-oh," Damien whispered.

I didn't need to look—I could sense the Twins puffing up like blowfish.

"My goodness, what is all this noise about?" Neferet swept into the room, looking beautiful and powerful and completely in control.

I watched the new kid's eyes widen as he took in her gorgeousness. It was soooo annoying that everybody automatically fell stupid at their first glimpse of our High Priestess and my nemesis, Neferet.

"Neferet, I apologize for the disruption." Dragon placed his fist over his heart and bowed respectfully to his High Priestess. "This is my new fledgling. He arrived only moments ago."

"That explains how the fledgling got here. It does not explain how *that* got here." Neferet pointed at the panting dog.

"She's with me," the kid said. When Neferet turned her moss-colored eyes on him, he mimicked Dragon's salute and bow. When he straightened, I was utterly shocked to see him give Neferet a lopsided grin that looked more than a little cocky. "She's my version of a cat."

"Really?" Neferet lifted one slim auburn brow. "Yet she looks oddly like a bear."

Ha! So it wasn't just me being overly descriptive.

"Well, Priestess, she's a Lab, but you're not the first person who's said she looks bearlike. Her paws are definitely big enough to be a bear's. Check it out." Disbelieving, I watched as the kid completely turned his back on Neferet and told the dog, "Gimme five, Duch." The dog obediently lifted a decidedly massive paw and slapped Stark's hand with it. "Good girl!" he said, ruffling her floppy ears.

Okay, I had to admit it. It was a cute trick.

He returned his attention to Neferet. "But dog or bear, she and I have been together since I was Marked four years ago, so that makes her cat enough for me."

"A Labrador retriever?" Neferet made a show of walking around the dog and studying her. "She's awfully large."

"Well, yeah, Duch has always been a big girl, Priestess."

"Duch? That's her name?"

The kid nodded and grinned, and even though he was a sixth-former, I was again surprised at how easily he spoke to an adult vamp, especially one who was a powerful High Priestess. "It's short for Duchess."

Neferet looked from the dog to the kid, and her eyes narrowed. "What is your name, child?"

"Stark," he said.

I wondered if anyone else saw her jaw clench.

"James Stark?" Neferet said.

"A few months ago I dropped my first name. It's just Stark," he said.

She ignored him and turned to Dragon. "He's the transfer we've been expecting from the Chicago House of Night?"

"Yes, Priestess," Dragon said.

When Neferet looked back at Stark, I saw her lips tilt up in a calculating smile. "I've heard quite a bit about you, Stark. You and I shall have to have a long talk very soon." Still studying the fledgling, Neferet spoke to Dragon. "Be sure that Stark has twenty-four-hour access to any and all archery equipment he might like to use."

I saw Stark's body do a little jerk. Obviously Neferet saw it, too, because her smile widened and she said, "Of course, news of your talent preceded you here, Stark. You mustn't get out of practice just because you've changed schools."

For the first time, Stark looked uneasy. Actually, he looked more than uneasy. At the mention of archery, Stark's expression had transformed from cute and a little sarcastic to cold and almost mean.

"I told them when they transferred me, I'd stopped competing." Stark's voice was flat, and his words barely carried the short distance to our table. "Changing schools won't change that."

"Competing? You mean that banal archery competition between the different Houses of Night?" Neferet's laughter made my skin crawl. "It matters little to me if you compete or not. Remember, I am Nyx's mouthpiece here, and I say what is important is that you don't waste your Goddess-given talent. You never know when Nyx might call on you—and it won't be for some silly contest."

My stomach flipped over. I knew Neferet was talking about her war against the humans. But Stark, being completely clueless, just looked relieved at not having to compete again, and his expression shifted back to nonchalance tinged with cockiness.

"No problem. I don't mind practicing, Priestess," he said.

"Neferet, what is it you wish us to do about the, uh, dog?" Dragon said.

Neferet paused for just a moment; then she crouched gracefully down in front of the yellow Lab. The dog's big ears pricked forward. She stuck her wet nose up, sniffing with obvious curiosity at Neferet's offered hand. Across the booth from me, Beelzebub hissed menacingly. Nala growled low in her throat. Neferet's eyes lifted and met mine.

I tried to keep my face expressionless, but I don't know how well I succeeded. I hadn't seen Neferet since two days ago when she'd followed me out of the auditorium after she'd announced the human–vampyre war she wanted to start in retribution for Loren's murder. Naturally, we'd had words. She'd been Loren's lover. So had I, but that had been inconsequential. Loren hadn't loved me. Neferet had set up the whole thing between Loren and me, and she knew I knew she had. She also knew I knew Nyx didn't approve of the things she'd been doing.

Basically, she'd seriously hurt my heart, and I hated Neferet almost as much as I feared her. I hoped none of those things showed on my face as our High Priestess strolled over to our table. With a slight hand gesture, she had Stark and his leashed dog following along behind her. The Twins' cat gave one more long hiss before streaking off. I frantically petted Nala, hoping she wouldn't totally lose her mind as the dog got closer. Neferet stopped when she reached our table. Her eyes skipped quickly from me to Aphrodite before they came to rest on Damien.

"I'm glad you're here, Damien. I'd like you to show Stark his room, and help him find his way around campus."

"I'd be happy to, Neferet," Damien said quickly, looking all sparkly-eyed when Neferet beamed her one-hundred-watt thank-you smile at him.

"Dragon will help you with the details," she said. Then her

green eyes moved to me. I braced myself. "And Zoey, this is Stark. Stark, this is Zoey Redbird, the leader of our Dark Daughters."

He and I nodded at each other.

"Zoey, as you are our High Priestess in Training, I'll leave the issue of Stark's dog with you. I trust that one of the many abilities Nyx has gifted you with will help you acclimate Duchess into our school." Her cold eyes never left mine. They told a different story than her syrupy-sweet voice. They said, *Remember that I'm in charge here and you're just a child.*

I purposefully broke eye contact with her and gave Stark a tight smile. "I'd be happy to help your dog fit in."

"Excellent," Neferet cooed. "Oh, and Zoey, Damien, Shaunee, and Erin." She smiled at my friends, and my friends grinned like utter fools right back at her. She completely ignored Aphrodite and Jack. "I've called a special Council Meeting for tonight at ten thirty." She glanced at her diamond-studded platinum watch. "It's almost ten o'clock right now, so you need to finish up eating because I expect you Prefects to be there, too."

"We will!" They trilled like ridiculous baby birds.

"Oh, Neferet, that reminds me," I said, raising my voice so that it carried across the room. "Aphrodite will be joining us. Since she's been gifted by Nyx with an earth affinity, we all agree that she should be on the Prefect Council, too." I held my breath, hoping that my friends would go along with this.

Thankfully, except for Nala's low growl at Duchess, no one said anything.

"How could Aphrodite be a Prefect? She is no longer a member of the Dark Daughters." Neferet's voice had gone cold.

I radiated innocence. "Did I forget to tell you? I'm so sorry, Neferet! It must have been because of all the horrible things that have happened recently. Aphrodite has rejoined the Dark Daughters. She swore to me, and to Nyx, to uphold our new code of conduct, and I allowed her back in. I mean, I thought that's what you'd want—to have her come back to our Goddess."

"That's right." Aphrodite sounded uncharacteristically subdued. "I've agreed to the new rules. I want to make up for my past mistakes."

I knew it would make Neferet look mean and spiteful if she publicly rejected Aphrodite after she'd made it obvious that she wanted to change. And Neferet was all about appearances.

The High Priestess smiled at the room in general, not looking at Aphrodite or me. "How very generous of our Zoey to accept Aphrodite back into the bosom of the Dark Daughters, especially as she'll be held responsible for Aphrodite's conduct. But then our Zoey seems to be comfortable with a great deal of responsibility." She did look at me then, and the hatred in her gaze made my breath catch in my throat. "Do be careful that you don't strangle under so much self-inflicted pressure, Zoey dear." Then, as if she'd thrown a switch, her face was filled with sweetness and light again, and she beamed at the new kid. "Welcome to the House of Night, Stark."

CHAPTER THREE

"Well, uh, are you hungry?" I asked Stark after Neferet and the rest of the vamps had glided out of the cafeteria.

"Yeah, I guess," he said.

"If you hurry, you can eat with us, and then Damien can show you to your room before we have to go to the Council Meeting," I said.

"I think your dog is pretty," Jack said, leaning around Damien to get a better look at Duchess. "I mean, she's big, but she's still pretty. She won't bite, will she?"

"Not if you don't bite her first," Stark said.

"Oh, eew," Jack said. "I'd get dog hair in my mouth and that'd be nasty."

"Stark, this is Jack. He's Damien's boyfriend." I decided to get the introductions and the possible *Oh, no! He's a fag!* issues out of the way.

"Hi," Jack said with a really sweet smile.

"Yeah, hi," Stark said. It wasn't a hugely warm hi, but he didn't seem to be giving off any homophobe vibes.

"And this is Erin and Shaunee." I pointed to each of them in turn. "They also answer to Twin, which will make sense once you've known them for about two-point-five minutes."

"Hey, there," Shaunee said, giving him a very obvious *look.*

"Ditto," Erin said, giving him an identical *look.*

"This is Aphrodite," I said.

His slightly sarcastic smile was back. "So you're the Goddess of Love. I've heard a lot about you."

Aphrodite was looking at Stark with a weird intensity that didn't seem particularly flirtatious, but when he spoke to her, she automatically executed a truly spectacular hair flip and said, "Hi. I like it when I'm recognized."

His smile widened and got even more sarcastic as he gave a little laugh. "It'd be hard not to recognize you—the name's pretty obvious."

I watched as Aphrodite's intense look instantly dissipated and was replaced by her much more familiar public expression of snobby disdain, but before she could verbally begin to slice up the new kid, Damien spoke. "Stark, I'll show you where the trays and stuff are." He stood up and then stopped in front of Duchess, looking more than a little confused.

"No worries," Stark said. "She'll stay put. As long as no cats do anything stupid."

His gaze had shifted to Nala, who was the only cat left close to Duchess. Nala hadn't started growling again, but she was perched on my lap, staring unblinkingly at the dog, and I could feel the tension in her body.

"Nala will be good," I said, hoping she would. I really had no control over my cat. Hell, who actually had control over *any* cat?

"All right, then." He gave me a quick nod before telling the dog, "Duchess, stay!" Sure enough, when he followed Damien over to the main line, Duchess stayed.

"You know, dogs are a lot louder than cats," Jack said, studying Duchess like she was a science experiment.

"It's all that panting they do," Erin said.

"And they're more flatulent than cats, Twin," Shaunee said.

"My mom has those ginormic standard poodles, and they are some gaseous creatures."

"Okay, well, this has really been *not* fun," Aphrodite said. "I'm out of here."

"Don't you want to stay around and make eyes at the new guy?" Shaunee asked in a too-nice voice.

"Yeah, and he seemed to like you so much," Erin said sweetly.

"I'll leave the new guy to you two, which is only right, being as he likes dogs so much. Zoey, come by my room when you're done with your nerd herd. I want to talk to you about something before the Council Meeting." And with a hair fling and a sneer for the Twins, she left the cafeteria.

"She's not actually as bad as she pretends to be," I told the Twins. They gave me disbelieving looks and I shrugged. "It's just that she pretends to be bad a lot."

"Well, we say *please*, just *please*, to her crappy attitude," Erin said.

"Aphrodite makes us understand why women have drowned their babies," Shaunee said.

"Just try to give Aphrodite a chance," I said. "She's started letting me in past that hateful crap she puts up. You'll see. She can be nice sometimes."

The Twins didn't say anything for a couple of seconds, then they looked at each other, and at the same time they shook their heads and rolled their eyes. I sighed again.

"But on to a much more important topic," Erin said.

"Yeah, the new hottie," Shaunee said.

"Check out his butt," Erin said.

"I wish he'd sag them jeans a little so I could get a better look," Shaunee said.

"Twin, sagging is seriously lame. It's so clichéd gang-wannabe circa 1990s. Hotties should just say no to it," Erin said.

"I'd still like to see his butt, Twin," Shaunee said. Then she glanced over at me and smiled. It was a reserved version of her old, friendly grin, but at least it wasn't the sarcastic wariness she'd been treating me with for the past couple days. "So, what do you think? Is he Christian Bale hot, or just Tobey Maguire hot?"

I wanted to burst into happy tears and yell, *Yea! You guys are starting to talk to me again!* Instead I acted like I had some sense and joined the Twins in checking out the new kid.

Okay, so they were right. Stark was cute. He was medium tall, not quarterback tall like my human ex-boyfriend, Heath, or abnormally gorgeous Superman tall like my fledgling-turned-vampyre ex-boyfriend, Erik. But he wasn't short, either. Actually, he was about Damien's height. He was kinda on the thin side, but I could see muscles through his old T-shirt, and his arms were definitely yummy. He had cute, messy guy hair, that sandy color between blond and brown. His face was okay, too, with a strong chin, straight nose, big brown eyes, and nice lips. So, dissected into separate parts, Stark was an okay-looking kid. As I watched him, I realized that what took him from *meh* to *hot* was his intensity and his confidence. He moved like everything he did was deliberate, but that the deliberateness was tinged with sarcasm. It was like he was a part of the world, and at the same time he was flipping it off.

And, yes, it was weird that I got that about him so quickly.

"I think he's definitely cute," I said.

"Ohmigod! I just realized who he is!" Jack gasped.

"Do tell," Shaunee said.

"He's James Stark!" Jack said.

"No shit," Erin said, rolling her eyes. "Jacky, we already know that."

"No, no, no. You don't get it. He's the James Stark who is *the* best archer in the whole world! Don't you remember reading about him online? He kicked butt in the track and field Summer Games this past year. Guys, he competed against grown vamps, actual Sons of Erebus, and he beat them all. He's a star . . ." Jack ended on a dreamy sigh.

"Well, shit! Slap me and call me impaired, Twin. Jacky's right!" Erin said.

"I knew his hotness was of major proportions," Shaunee said.

"Wow," I said.

"Twin, I'm gonna try to like his dog," Erin said.

"Of course we are, Twin," Shaunee said.

Naturally, all four of us were staring at Stark like total morons when he and Damien came back to the table.

"What?" he said, mouth filled with a bite of sandwich. He glanced from us down to Duchess. "Did she do something while I was gone? She kinda likes to lick toes."

"Eesh, that's—," Erin began, but shut up when Shaunee kicked her under the table.

"No, Duchess was a perfect lady whilst you were gone," Shaunee said, giving Stark a very, very friendly grin.

"Good," Stark said. When everyone continued to stare at him, he shifted uncomfortably in his seat. As if on cue, Duchess moved so that she could lean against his leg and gaze up at him lovingly. I watched him relax as he automatically reached a hand down and ruffled her ears.

"I remember hearing about you beating all of those vamps in archery!" Jack blurted; then he squeezed his lips shut and blushed bright pink.

Stark didn't look up from his plate. He just shrugged his shoulders. "Yeah, I'm good at archery."

"You're *that* fledgling?" Damien said, just now getting it. "Good at archery? You're amazing at archery!"

Stark looked up. "Whatever. It's just something I've been good at ever since I've been Marked." His eyes went from Damien to me. "Speaking of famous fledglings, I see the rumor about your extra Marks is true."

"It's true." I really hated these first meetings. It made me uncomfortable as hell when I met someone and all they could see about me was the uber-fledgling and not the real Zoey.

Then I got it. What I was feeling was probably a lot like what Stark was feeling.

I asked the first thing I could think of to get the subject away from how "special" he and I both were. "Do you like horses?"

"Horses?" The sarcastic smile was back.

"Yeah, well, you seem like you might be an animal lover," I said lamely, jerking my chin in the direction of his dog.

"Yeah, I guess I like horses. I like most animals. Except cats."

"Except cats!" Jack squeaked.

Stark shrugged again. "I've never really liked them. They're too bitchlike for my tastes."

I heard both the Twins snort.

"Cats are independent creatures," Damien began. I heard the schoolteacher lecture tone in his voice and knew my mission to change the subject had been successful. "We all know, of course, that they have been worshipped in many ancient cultures of the world, but did you know that they were also—?"

"Uh, guys, sorry to interrupt," I said, standing and shifting my grip on Nala so that I wouldn't drop her on Duchess's back. "But I gotta go see what Aphrodite wants before the Council Meeting. I'll see you there, 'kay?"

"Yeah, okay."

"I guess."

"Whatever."

At least I got some sort of good-bye.

I gave Stark a friendly smile. "It was nice to meet you. If you need anything for Duchess, just let me know. There's a good Southern Ag not far from here. They carry an extra lot of cat stuff, but I'll bet they have dog stuff, too."

"I'll let you know," he said.

And then, as Damien resumed his cats-are-wonderful lecture, Stark gave me a quick wink and a nod that clearly said he appreciated my not-so-subtle subject shift. I winked back at him and was halfway to the door that led outside before I realized I was grinning like a fool instead of thinking about the fact that the last time I'd been outside, something had seemed to attack me.

I was standing in front of the big oak door like a Special Needs/Special Services student when a group of Sons of Erebus Warriors poured down the stairway that led to the staff dining room on the second floor.

"Priestess," several of them said when they caught sight of me, and the entire group paused to give me respectful bows with lovely crisp salutes, hands fisted over their muscular chests.

I returned the salute nervously.

"Priestess, allow me to get the door for you," said one of the older warriors.

"Oh, uh, thank you," I said, and then with a sudden inspiration added, "I was wondering if one of you could walk back to the dorm with me and maybe give me a list of the names of the warriors who will be assigned to guard the girls' dorm. I think it would make the guys feel more at home if we knew their names."

"That's quite considerate of you, my lady," said the older warrior, who was still holding the door for me. "I would be happy to give you a list of names."

I smiled and thanked him. All the way to the girls' dorm, he chatted courteously about the warriors who would be assigned to guard us while I nodded and made the appropriate noises and tried to sneak glances up into the quiet night sky.

Nothing flapped or chilled the air, but I couldn't get rid of the frightening feeling that someone or something was watching me.

CHAPTER FOUR

I had barely touched my door handle when it was pulled open and Aphrodite grabbed my wrist. "Would you get your butt in here? Shit, you are slow as a fat kid on crutches, Zoey." She pulled me into the room and slammed the door firmly behind us.

"I'm not slow, and you have a whole hell of a lot of explaining to do," I said. "How did you get in here? Where is Stevie Rae? When did your Mark come back? What—?" My tirade of questions was cut off by a loud, insistent tapping that was coming from my window.

"First of all, you're a moron. It's the House of Night not Tulsa Public Schools. No one locks their doors, so I walked right in your room. Second, Stevie Rae is over there." Aphrodite breezed past me as she hurried to the window. I just stood there staring at her while she pulled back the thick drapes and started unlatching the heavy leaded-glass windowpane. She gave me an irritated look over her shoulder. "Hello! A little help would be nice."

Utterly confused, I joined her at the window. It took both of us to wrench it open. I gazed out from the top floor of the old raw stone building that looked more like a castle than like a dorm. The late December night was still cold and dreary, and it was now making a halfhearted attempt at rain. I could just see the east wall through the darkness and the shrouding trees. I shivered, but fledglings rarely feel cold, and it wasn't the weather giving me the chills. It was a glimpse of the east wall—a place of power and mayhem. Beside me, Aphrodite sighed and leaned forward so she could peek out the window and down the wall. "Stop messing around and get in here. You're going to get caught, and more importantly, the humidity is going to frizz my hair."

When Stevie Rae's head bobbed up into view, I almost peed on myself.

"Hi, Z!" she said cheerfully. "Check out my new ultracool climbing abilities."

"Ohmygod. Get. In. Here." Aphrodite reached through the open window, grabbed one of Stevie Rae's hands, and yanked. Like she was a balloon, Stevie Rae popped into the room. Aphrodite quickly closed the window and pulled shut the drapes.

I closed my flapping open mouth, but continued to stare as Stevie Rae stood up, brushing off her Roper jeans and retucking her long-sleeved shirt into them.

"Stevie Rae," I finally managed. "Did you just crawl up the side of the dorm?"

"Yep!" She grinned at me, nodding her head so that her short blond curls bounced around like a crazed cheerleader's. "Cool, huh? It's like I'm a part of the stones that the building's made of, and I get all weightless, and, well, here I am." She held out her hands.

"Like Dracula," I said, and knew I'd spoken my thought out loud only when Stevie Rae frowned and said, "What's like Dracula?"

I sat down heavily on the end of my bed. "In the book, *Dracula,* the old one by Bram Stoker," I explained, "Jonathan Harker says he sees Dracula crawling down the side of his castle."

"Oh, yeah, I can do that. When you said 'like Dracula,' I thought you meant I looked like Dracula—all kinda creepy and pale with bad hair and those long, nasty fingernails. That's not what you meant, was it?"

"No, you look great, actually." I was definitely telling her the truth. Stevie Rae did look great, especially compared to how she'd been looking (and acting and smelling) the past month. She looked like Stevie Rae again, *before* my best friend's body had rejected the Change and she'd died almost exactly one month ago, and then, somehow, come back from the dead. But she'd been different—broken. Her humanity had been almost completely lost, and she wasn't the only kid it had happened to. There was a pack of nasty undead dead kids lurking around the old Prohibition tunnels beneath Tulsa's downtown abandoned depot. Stevie Rae had almost become one of them—mean, hateful, and dangerous. Her Goddess-given affinity with the element earth was all that had helped her retain any bit of herself, but it hadn't been enough. She'd been slipping away. So, with the help of Aphrodite (who had also been given an affinity for the element earth), I'd cast a circle and asked Nyx to heal Stevie Rae.

And the Goddess had, but during that healing process, it seemed like Aphrodite had had to die to save Stevie Rae's humanity. Thankfully, that hadn't been true. Instead of dying, Aphrodite's Mark had disappeared as Stevie Rae's Mark had miraculously been colored in and expanded, showing that she had completed her Change into vampyre. Except to add to the general confusion, Stevie Rae's tattoo hadn't appeared in the traditional color of sapphire, as all adult vampyre Marks are colored. Stevie Rae's Mark was bright scarlet—the color of new blood.

"Uh, hello. Earth to Zoey. Anybody home in there?" Aphrodite's smart-alecky voice cut through my mental babble. "Better check your BFF. She's kinda losing it."

I blinked. Even though I'd been gawking at Stevie Rae, I hadn't been *seeing* her. She was standing in the middle of the room—what used to be *our* room up until a month ago, when her death had completely and utterly changed everything forever—staring around her with big tear-filled eyes.

"Oh, honey, I'm sorry." I hurried to her and gave Stevie Rae a hug. "It must be hard for you to be back here." She felt stiff and odd in my arms, and I pulled away a little so that I could look at her.

The expression on her face chilled my blood. The teary-eyed shock had been replaced by anger. I wondered for an instant why her anger looked familiar—Stevie Rae rarely got pissed. And then I realized what I was recognizing. Stevie Rae looked like she had *before* I'd cast the circle and she'd been given back her humanity. I took a step away from her.

"Stevie Rae? What's wrong?"

"Where's my stuff?" Her voice, like her face, was just plain mean.

"Honey," I said gently. "The vamps take a fledgling's stuff away when she, uh, dies."

Stevie Rae turned narrowed eyes on me. "I'm not dead."

Aphrodite moved so that she was standing beside me. "Hey, don't get all mental on us. The vamps think you're dead, remember?"

"But don't worry," I said quickly. "I made them give me back a bunch of your things. And I know where the rest of your stuff is. I can get it all back if you want it."

And just like that, the meanness vanished and I was looking at my best friend again. "Even my lamp made outta a cowboy boot?"

"Even that," I said, smiling at her. Hell, I'd be pissed, too, if someone had taken all my stuff.

Aphrodite said, "You'd think if someone died, at least their shitty non-fashion fashion sense would change. But no. Your bad taste is fucking immortal."

"Aphrodite," Stevie Rae told her firmly, "you really should be nicer."

"And I say *whatever* to you and your countrified Mary Poppins outlook on life," Aphrodite said.

"Mary Poppins was British. Which means she wasn't countrified," Stevie Rae said smugly.

Stevie Rae sounded so much like her old self that I gave a little happy shout and threw my arms around her again. "I'm so darn glad to see you! You're really okay now, aren't you?"

"Kinda different, but okay," Stevie Rae said, hugging me back.

I felt an amazing wash of relief that drowned out the *kinda different* part of what she'd said. I guess I was just so glad to see her, whole and herself again, that I had to hold that knowledge safe and special inside myself for a while, and that need didn't let me consider that there could be any leftover problems with Stevie Rae. Plus, I remembered something else. "Hang on," I said suddenly. "How did you guys get back on campus without the warriors going crazy?"

"Zoey, you really gotta start paying attention to the stuff that's going on around you," Aphrodite said. "I walked through the front gate. The alarm's down, which I imagine makes sense. I mean, I got the same school notification call on my cell about winter break being over I bet everyone else who was away from campus got. Neferet had to unzap this place or she'd go insane dealing with all the alarms the returning students would set off, not to mention the zillions of delicious Sons of Erebus who are descending on this place like yummy presents for us students."

"Don't you mean all the alarms would make Neferet go *more insane* than she already is?"

"Yes, Neferet is definitely batshit crazy," Aphrodite said, for an instant in complete agreement with Stevie Rae. "Anyway, the alarm's gone, even for humans."

"Huh? Even for humans? How do you know that?" I asked.

Aphrodite sighed, and with a weirdly slow motion–like movement, she brought the back of her hand up and wiped it across her forehead, causing the outline of the crescent moon to smear and partially rub off.

I gasped. "Oh, god, Aphrodite! You're . . ." My words sputtered out as my mouth refused to say it.

"Human," Aphrodite supplied for me in a flat, cold voice.

"How? I mean, are you sure?"

"I'm sure. Damn sure," she said.

"Uh, Aphrodite, even though you're human, you're definitely not a *normal* human," Stevie Rae said.

"What does that mean?" I asked.

Aphrodite shrugged. "Doesn't mean shit to me."

Stevie Rae sighed. "You know, you're lucky you turned into a human and not a wooden boy, 'cause with all the lying you're doin', your nose would be like a mile long."

Aphrodite shook her head in disgust. "Again with the bad G-rated movie analogy. I don't know why I couldn't have just died and gone to hell. At least I wouldn't be bombarded with Disney there."

"Would you just tell me what the hell's going on?" I said.

"Better explain it to her. She's almost cussing," Aphrodite said snidely.

"You're so hateful. I should have eaten you when I was dead," Stevie Rae said.

"You should have eaten your countrified mom when you were dead," Aphrodite said, bowing up like she thought she was black. "No wonder Zoey needs a new BFF. You're totally a Pollyanna pain in the ass."

"Zoey does *not* need a new BFF!" Stevie Rae yelled, turning on Aphrodite and taking a step toward her. For an instant, I thought I saw her blue eyes start to flash the ugly red that illuminated them when she was undead and out of control.

Feeling like my head was going to explode, I stepped between them. "Aphrodite, stop messing with Stevie Rae!"

"Then you better check your friend." Aphrodite walked to the mirror that was over my sink, grabbed a Kleenex, and started to wipe what was left of the smeared crescent from her forehead. I noticed that for all her nonchalant tone, her hands were shaking.

I turned back to Stevie Rae, whose eyes were once again a familiar blue.

"Sorry, Z," she said, smiling like a guilty kid. "I guess two days with Aphrodite has gotten on my nerves."

Aphrodite snorted and I looked over at her. "Just don't start again," I said.

"Fine, whatever." Our eyes met in the mirror, and I was almost sure I saw fear in Aphrodite's gaze. Then she went back to work fixing her face.

Feeling utterly confused, I tried to pick up where the conversation had gotten way weird. "So, what's the deal with you saying Aphrodite isn't normal? And I don't mean her abnormally bad attitude," I hastily added.

"Easy-peasy," Stevie Rae said. "Aphrodite still has visions, and visions aren't normal for humans." She gave Aphrodite a *so there* look. "Go ahead. Tell Zoey."

Aphrodite turned from the mirror and sat on the little stool I kept close by. She ignored Stevie Rae and said, "Yeah, I still have my visions. Whoop-tee-fucking-do. The only thing I *didn't* like about being a fledgling is the only thing I get to keep now that I'm a stupid human again."

I looked more closely at Aphrodite, seeing through the *I'm all that* façade she liked to throw up. She was pale, and there were dark circles beneath the cover-up she had slathered under here yes. Yes, she definitely looked like a girl who had just gone through a bunch of crap, and some of it could be one of her draining, life-changing visions. No wonder she was being such a bitch; I was a moron not to have noticed it before then.

"What did you see in the vision?" I asked her.

Aphrodite met my gaze with a steady one of her own and for a moment let down the steel wall of arrogance she liked to keep around her like a shield. A terrible, haunted shadow crossed her beautiful face, and her hand shook as she raised it to brush a strand of blond hair behind her ear.

"I saw vampyres slaughtering humans and humans killing vampyres right back. I saw a world filled with violence and hatred and darkness. And in the darkness I saw creatures that were so horrible, I couldn't tell what they were. I—I couldn't even keep looking at them. I saw the end of everything." Aphrodite's voice was as haunted as her face.

"Tell her the rest of it," Stevie Rae prompted her when Aphrodite paused, and I was surprised by the sudden gentleness in her voice. "Tell her why all of that was happening."

When Aphrodite spoke, I felt her words as if they had been shards of glass she'd smashed into my heart.

"I saw all of it happening because you were dead, Zoey. Your death made it happen."

CHAPTER FIVE

"Ah, hell," I said, and then my knees gave way and I had to sit down on my bed. My ears had an odd buzzing sound in them, and it was hard for me to breathe.

"You know it doesn't mean it'll come true for sure," Stevie Rae said, patting me on the shoulder. "I mean, Aphrodite saw your grandmamma, Heath, and even me dying. Well, I mean me dying a second time. And none of those things happened. So we can stop it." She looked up at Aphrodite. "Right?"

Aphrodite fidgeted uneasily.

"Ah, hell," I said for a second time. Then I forced myself to talk around the big lump of fear that had lodged in the middle of my throat. "There's something different about the vision you had of me, isn't there?"

"It could be because I'm human," she said slowly. "It's the only vision I've had since turning back into a human, so, yeah, it doesn't seem too wrong that it would feel different than the ones I had when I was a fledgling."

"But?" I prompted.

She shrugged and finally met my eyes. "But it did feel different."

"Like how?"

"Well, it felt more confusing—more emotional—more jumbled up. And I literally didn't understand some of what I saw.

I mean, I didn't recognize the horrible things that were seething around in the darkness."

"Seething?" I shivered. "That doesn't sound good."

"It wasn't. I was seeing shadows inside shadows inside darkness. It was like ghosts were turning back into living things, but the things they were turning back into were too terrible for me to look at."

"You mean like not human or vampyre?"

"Yeah, that's what I mean."

Automatically I rubbed my hand, and a skittering of fear slithered through my body. "Ah, hell."

"What?" Stevie Rae said.

"Tonight there was something that, well, kinda attacked me when I was walking from the stables to the cafeteria. It was some kind of cold shadow thing that came from the darkness."

"That can't be good," Stevie Rae said.

"You were alone?" Aphrodite asked, her voice sounding flintlike.

"Yes," I said.

"Okay, that's the problem," Aphrodite said.

"Why? What else did you see in your vision?"

"Well, you died a couple different ways, which is not something I've ever seen before."

"A—a couple different ways?" It just kept getting worse and worse.

"Maybe we should wait awhile and see if Aphrodite has another vision that'll make things clearer before we talk about this," Stevie Rae said, sitting next to me on the bed.

I didn't look away from Aphrodite's eyes, and I saw there a reflection of what I already knew. "When I ignore visions, they come true. Always," Aphrodite said with finality.

"I think some of it might already be happening," I said. My lips felt cold and stiff, and my stomach hurt.

"You're not gonna die!" Stevie Rae cried, looking upset and totally like my best friend again.

I slipped my arm through Stevie Rae's. "Go ahead, Aphrodite. Tell me."

"It was a strong vision, filled with powerful images, but it was totally confusing. Maybe because I was feeling it and seeing it from your point of view." Aphrodite paused, swallowing hard. "I saw you die two ways. Once you drowned. The water was cold and dark. Oh, and it smelled bad."

"Smelled bad? Like one of those nasty Oklahoma ponds?" I said, curious despite the horror of talking about my own death.

Aphrodite shook her head. "No, I'm almost one hundred percent sure it wasn't in Oklahoma. There was too much water for that. It's hard to explain how I can be so sure, but it just felt too big and deep to be something like a lake." Aphrodite paused again, thinking. Then her eyes widened. "I remember another thing about the vision. There was something close by the water that looked like a *real* palace on an island all its own, which means tasteful old money, probably European, and not some tacky upper middle class version of oooh-I-have-money-let's-go-buy-an-RV."

"You're seriously a snob, Aphrodite," Stevie Rae said.

"Thank you," Aphrodite said.

"Okay, so you saw me drown near a real palace on a real island maybe in Europe. Did you see anything else that might be in the least bit helpful?" I asked.

"Well, besides the fact that you felt isolated—I mean really alone in both of the visions, I saw a guy's face. He was with you not long before you died. Someone I've never seen before. At least not till today."

"What? Who?"

"I saw that Stark kid."

"He killed me?" I felt like I was going to throw up.

"Who's Stark?" Stevie Rae asked, taking hold of my hand.

"New kid who just transferred here today from the Chicago House of Night," I said. "He killed me?" I repeated the question to Aphrodite.

"I don't think so. I didn't get a good look at him, and it was dark. But it seemed like, even in the last glimpse you had of him, that you felt safe with him." She raised her brow at me. "Looks like you'll get over that whole Erik/Heath/Loren mess."

"I'm sorry 'bout all of that. Aphrodite told me what happened," Stevie Rae said.

I opened my mouth to say thanks to Stevie Rae, and then I realized that she and Aphrodite didn't know the depth of the Erik/Heath/Loren mess. They'd been away from the school, and the human media hadn't reported anything at all on Loren Blake's death. I took a deep breath. I'd almost rather hear about my deaths than talk about this.

"Loren's dead," I blurted.

"What?"

"How?"

I looked up at Aphrodite. "Two days ago. It was like Professor Nolan. Loren was beheaded and crucified and nailed to the front gate of the school with a note that quoted some terrible Bible verse about him being detestable staked through his heart." I spoke very fast, wanting to get the taste of the terrible words out of my mouth.

"Oh no!" Aphrodite turned a yucky shade of white and sat down heavily on Stevie Rae's old bed.

"Zoey, that's so awful," Stevie Rae said. I could hear the tears in her voice as she put her arm around me. "Y'all were like Romeo and Juliet."

"No!" Then because the word had come out more sharply than

I'd intended, I turned to Stevie Rae and smiled. "No," I repeated in a saner voice. "He never loved me. Loren used me."

"For sex? Ah, Z, that's crappy," Stevie Rae said.

"Sadly, no, even though I did utterly mess up and have sex with him. Loren was using me for Neferet. She told him to come on to me. She was his real lover." I grimaced, remembering the heart-ripping scene I'd witnessed between Loren and Neferet. They'd been laughing about me. I'd given Loren my heart and my body and, through our Imprint, a piece of my soul. And he'd laughed at me.

"Hang on. Go back. You said Neferet had Loren come on to you?" Aphrodite said. "Why would she do that if they were lovers?"

"Neferet wanted to get me alone." My heart froze as the pieces of the puzzle began to fit together.

"Huh? That doesn't make sense. Why would Loren acting like he was your boyfriend get you alone?" Stevie Rae asked.

"Simple," Aphrodite said. "Zoey had to sneak around to see Loren, being as he was a professor and all. My guess is she didn't tell any of the nerd herd she was playing bad little schoolgirl with *Professor* Blake. My guess is also that Neferet had something major to do with our boy Erik finding out Zoey was doing the dirty with someone who was definitely not him."

"Uh, I'm right here. You don't have to talk about me like I left the room."

Aphrodite snorted. "If my guesses are right, I'd say your good sense left the room."

"Your guesses are right," I admitted reluctantly. "Neferet made sure Erik walked in on me being with Loren."

"Damn! No wonder he acted so pissed," Aphrodite said.

"What? When?" Stevie Rae said.

I sighed. "Erik caught me with Loren. He freaked. Then I

found out that Loren was really with Neferet and he didn't care about me at all, even though we'd Imprinted."

"Imprinted! Shit!" Aphrodite said.

"So then I freaked." I ignored Aphrodite. It was already awful enough. I definitely didn't want to dwell on the details. "I was bawling when Aphrodite, the Twins, Damien, Jack, and—"

"Oh, shit, and Erik. That's when we found you crying under the tree," Aphrodite interrupted.

I sighed again, realizing I couldn't ignore her. "Yeah. And Erik announced the news about Loren and me to everyone."

"In what I would call a very mean way," Aphrodite said.

"Dang," Stevie Rae said. "It must have been *really* hateful for Aphrodite to say it was mean."

"It was. Hateful enough for her friends to feel like her sleeping around with Loren had been a slap in the face to them. So follow Erik's 'Zoey's a slut' bomb with the 'Zoey's been keeping Stevie Rae's undeadness a secret, too' bomb, and you have a gaggle of totally pissed nerds who won't want to trust Zoey again."

"Which means then Zoey is alone, just exactly as Neferet planned," I finished for her, finding it disturbing that it was so easy to fall into talking about myself in the third person.

"That's the second death I saw for you," Aphrodite said. "You're completely alone. There's no last glimpse of a cute boy and no nerd herd. Your isolation is the overriding image I got from the second vision."

"What kills me?"

"Well, that's when it gets confusing again. I get an image of Neferet as a threat to you, but the vision gets jumbled up all weird when you're actually attacked. I know this is going to sound bizarre, but at the last moment I saw something black floating around you."

"Like a ghost or something?" I swallowed hard.

"No. Not really. If Neferet's hair was black, I'd say it was her hair blowing around you in a big wind, like she's standing behind you. You're alone and you're really, *really* scared. You try to call for help, but no one answers you and you're so terrified you freeze and don't fight back. She, or whatever it is, reaches around and somehow, using something dark and hooked, slashes your throat. It is so sharp, it cuts through your neck and severs your head from your shoulders." Aphrodite shuddered and then added, "Which, in case you're wondering, bleeds. A lot."

"Gross, Aphrodite! Did ya have to go into detail?" Stevie Rae said, putting her arm back around me.

"No, it's okay," I said quickly. "Aphrodite has to give all the details she can remember—like she did when she saw visions of the deaths of you and Grandma and Heath. It's the only way we can figure out how to change things. So, what else did you see about my second death?" I asked Aphrodite.

"Just that you call for help, but nothing happens. Everyone ignores you," Aphrodite said.

"I was scared today when whatever it was came at me out of the night. So scared that for a second I just froze and didn't know what to do," I said, feeling shaky just remembering.

"Could Neferet have had something to do with whatever happened to you earlier?" Stevie Rae asked.

I shrugged. "I don't know. There was nothing for me to see but some creepy blackness."

"Creepy blackness is what I saw, too. As much as I hate to say it, you've got to make sure the nerd herd isn't pissed off at you anymore, because you being friendless is not a good thing," Aphrodite said.

"Easier said than done," I said.

"I don't see why," Stevie Rae said. "Just tell them the truth about Neferet being behind Loren and you, and tell them that you couldn't say anything about me being undead when I was dead because Neferet would . . ." Stevie Rae's words trailed off as she realized what she was saying.

"Yeah, that's brilliant. Tell them that Neferet is an evil bitch who's behind making a bunch of undead dead kids and the first time any of the nerd herd members get within the distance of a thought of Neferet, all shit will break loose. Which means our evil bitch of a High Priestess will not only know what we know, but she'll probably do something majorly nasty to your little buddies." Aphrodite paused and tapped her chin. "Hum, on second thought, some of that scenario doesn't sound too bad."

"Hey," Stevie Rae said. "Damien and the Twins and Jack already know something that is going to get them in major trouble with Neferet. They know about me."

"Ah, hell," I said.

"Well, shit," Aphrodite said. "I totally forgot about the 'Stevie Rae isn't dead' detail. Wonder why Neferet hasn't plucked that out of one of your friends' wee little brains and freaked about that already?"

"She's been too busy plotting war," I said. When Aphrodite and Stevie Rae blinked in confusion at me, I realized that Loren wasn't the only news they hadn't heard. "When Neferet was told about Loren's murder, she declared war against humans. Not an outright war, of course. She wants it to be a nasty, terrorist-style guerrilla war. God, she's so slimy. I just don't get why everyone can't see it."

"Blood and guts with the humans? Huh. That's interesting. Guess the buildup of the Sons of Erebus is supposed to be our weapon of mass destruction," Aphrodite said. "Yum, talk about a silver lining to a shitty situation."

"How can you be so whatever about this?" Stevie Rae said, exploding off the bed.

"First of all, I really don't like humans much." Aphrodite put up a hand to stop Stevie Rae's tirade. "Okay, yeah, I know. I *am* a human now. Which makes me say *ugh*. Second, Zoey's alive and well, so I'm not particularly worried about this scary little war."

"What in the hell are you talking about, Aphrodite?" I said.

Aphrodite rolled her eyes. "Would you please keep up with me? Hello—it makes perfect sense now. My vision was all about war between humans and vamps and some creepy booger-monster things. Actually, they're probably what attacked you and could very well be minions of Neferet we don't know about." She paused, looking temporarily confused, and then shrugged and continued, "But, whatever. Hopefully we won't have to find out what they are, because the war only happened *after* you'd been killed. Tragically and grotesquely, I might add. Anyway, I figure we keep you alive, we keep the war from happening."

Stevie Rae let out a big, long breath. "You have a point, Aphrodite." She turned to me. "We gotta keep you alive, Zoey. Not just 'cause we love you more than white bread, but 'cause you have to save the world."

"Oh, great. I'm supposed to save the world?" All I could think was, *And I used to stress about geometry.*

Ah, hell.

CHAPTER SIX

"Yep, you have to save the world, Z, but we'll be right there with you," Stevie Rae said, plunking herself back down on the bed beside me.

"No, dork. I'm going to be right here with her. You have to get out of here until we figure out what to tell the rest of the nerd herd about you and your hygiene-challenged friends," Aphrodite said.

Stevie Rae frowned at Aphrodite.

"Huh? Friends?" I said.

"They've been through a lot, Aphrodite. And I'll have you know bathing and decorating isn't that dang important when you're dead. Or even undead," Stevie Rae said. "Plus, you know they're better now and they're actually using the stuff you bought them."

"Okay, you guys are gonna have to back up. What friends are you—?" And then my words broke off as I realized who they must be talking about. "Stevie Rae, do not tell me you're still hanging out with those gross kids from the tunnels."

"You don't understand, Zoey."

"Translation: Yes, Zoey, I am still hangin' out with the gross tunnel rejects," Aphrodite said, mimicking Stevie Rae's Okie accent.

"Stop it," I told Aphrodite automatically before turning to Stevie Rae. "No, I don't understand. So make me understand."

Stevie Rae drew a deep breath. "Well, I think that this"—she pointed at her scarlet tattoos—"means that I need to be around the rest of the kids with the red tattoos so I can help them make the Change, too."

"The rest of those undead kids have red tattoos like yours?"

She shrugged and looked uncomfortable. "Well, sorta. I'm the only one with a finished tattoo, which I'm guessin' means I've Changed. But the outlines of the blue crescent moon on their foreheads have now all turned to red. They're still fledglings. They're just, well, a different kind of fledgling."

Wow! I sat there, speechless, trying to take in the ramifications of what Stevie Rae was saying. It was utterly amazing that there was now a whole new type of fledgling, which, of course, meant there was a whole new type of adult vampyre, and for a moment it excited me. What if it also meant that everyone who got Marked would make some type of Change, so no more fledglings would have to die! Or at least not permanently. They'd just turn into red fledglings. Whatever that meant.

Then I remembered how awful those other kids had been. They'd killed teenagers. Horribly. They'd tried to kill Heath. I was the only thing that had saved him. Hell, they would have killed me if I hadn't used my affinity with the five elements to save both of us.

I also remembered the flash of red I'd seen in Stevie Rae's eyes earlier and the meanness that had looked so out of place on her face, but seeing her now, sounding and acting like herself, it was easy to convince myself I'd been wrong—that I'd imagined or exaggerated what I'd seen.

I mentally shook myself and said, "But Stevie Rae, those other kids were awful."

Aphrodite snorted. "They're *still* awful and living in an awful disgusting place. And, yes, they're still awful rude, too."

"They're not out of control like they used to be, but they're also not what you'd call normal, either," Stevie Rae said.

"They're disgusting throwaway kids, that's what they are," Aphrodite said. "Like redheaded stepchildren."

"Yeah, some of them have problems and aren't exactly the most popular kids ever, but so what?"

"I'm just saying that it would be easier to figure out what we're going to do about you if we only had you to deal with."

"It's not always about what's easiest. I don't care what we have to do, or what I have to do. I'm not gonna let Neferet use those other kids," Stevie Rae told her firmly.

And what Stevie Rae said clicked. I shivered in horror as my gut told me my terrible new thought was right. "Oh my god! *That's* why Neferet did whatever she did to make the dying kids come back as undead dead kids. She wants to use them in the war she's declared against humans."

"But, Z, kids have been undying for a while now, and Professor Nolan and Loren were only just killed, so Neferet has only just declared the whole guerrilla war thing," Stevie Rae said.

I didn't say anything. I couldn't. What I was thinking was too awful to speak out loud. I was afraid that the syllables of the words would turn into separate little weapons, and if I put them together, they would join to destroy all of us.

"What is it?" Aphrodite was watching me too closely.

"Nothing." I shifted the words in my mind so that they became something bearable. "It's just that this whole thing makes me think that Neferet has been hoping there would be a reason to fight the humans for a long time. I really wouldn't be surprised if she did create the undead dead kids to be her private army. I saw her with Elliott not long after he was supposed to have died. It was disgusting how much control she had over him." I shivered, remembering only too clearly how Neferet had ordered Elliott around and how he had bowed and scraped in front of her, and then lapped up the offering of her blood in a disgusting and way-too-sexual manner. Watching it had been entirely nasty.

"That's why I have to go back to them," Stevie Rae said. "They need me to care about them and show them that they can Change, too. When Neferet finds out about the difference in their Marks, she'll still try to control them and keep them—well, let's just say, not so nice. I think they can be okay again, like I'm okay again."

"What about the ones who were never okay? Remember the Elliott kid Zoey was just talking about? He was a loser alive and he's a loser undead. He'll still be a loser if he manages to Change into a red whatever." Aphrodite gave an exaggerated, long-suffering sigh when Stevie Rae glared at her. "The point I'm try-ing to make is that they weren't normal to begin with. Maybe there's nothing for you to save about them."

"Aphrodite, you don't get to pick who's worth saving and who's not. I may have been a pretty normal kid before I died, but I'm not exactly normal now," Stevie Rae said. "And I was worth saving!"

"Nyx," I said, making both of them turn to look at me with question marks on their faces. "Nyx gets to pick who's worth sav-ing. Not me, not Stevie Rae, and not even you, Aphrodite."

"Guess I forgot about Nyx," Aphrodite said, turning her face away from us to hide the pain in her eyes. "It's not like the God-dess wants much to do with a human kid anyway."

"That's not true," I said. "Nyx's hand is still on you, Aphrodite. The Goddess is majorly at work here. If she didn't care about you, she would have taken away your visions when she took away your Mark." As I spoke, I got that feeling I often get when I absolutely know I'm saying the right thing. Aphrodite was a pain in the ass, but for some reason, she was important to our Goddess.

Aphrodite's eyes met mine. "Are you guessing about that, or do you *know*?"

"I *know*." I continued to meet her eyes steadily.

"Promise?" she said.

"Promise."

"Well, that's nice and all, Aphrodite," Stevie Rae said, "but you should keep in mind that you're not exactly normal, either."

"But I am attractive, properly bathed, and I do not scuttle around in really yucky old tunnels snarling and snapping my teeth at visitors."

"Which brings up another point. Why were you down in the tunnels?" I asked Aphrodite.

She rolled her eyes. "Because Miss K 95.5 FM over there just had to cowboy up and follow me."

"Well, you freaked when your Mark disappeared, and unlike some people, I'm not a witch with a capital *B*. Plus, it might have kinda been my fault you lost your Mark and it was the right thing to do to make sure you were okay," said Stevie Rae.

"You bit me, dork," Aphrodite said. "Of course it was your fault."

"I already said sorry 'bout that."

"Uh, guys, could we please stay on the subject?"

"Fine. I went down to the stupid tunnels because your stupid BFF was going to burn the hell up if we got caught out in the daylight."

"But how come you stayed away for two days?"

Aphrodite looked uncomfortable. "It took me a couple days to decide if I should come back at all. Besides that, I had to help Stevie Rae buy some stuff for the tunnels and the freaks down there. Even I couldn't just leave and let them be all"—she paused and shuddered delicately for effect—"all eeeew."

"We're really not used to having visitors yet," Stevie Rae said.

"You mean except for the people your friends like to eat?" Aphrodite said.

"Stevie Rae, you really can't let those kids eat people. Not even street people," I added.

"I know. That's another reason I need to get back to them."

"You need to bring Merry Maids and a good interior decorating team with you," Aphrodite muttered. "I'd offer you the services of my parents' help, but your buds might eat them, and as my mom would say, good illegals are really hard to find."

"I'm not gonna let the kids eat people anymore, and I'm working on getting the tunnels in order," Stevie Rae said defensively.

I remembered way too well how creepy those dark, dirty tunnels were. "Stevie Rae, isn't there someplace else we could figure out for you and your, uh, red fledglings to stay?"

"No!" she said quickly, and then smiled an apology at me. "See, the thing is that being underground feels right to me, and to them. We need to be inside the earth." She cut her eyes over at Aphrodite, who was wrinkling her nose at Stevie Rae and making an *eew* face. "Yes, I know that's not normal, but I told you I'm not normal!"

"Uh, Stevie Rae," I said. "I'm in total agreement with you about the whole nothing wrong with being not normal thing. I mean, look at me." I flailed my hand about at my many tattoos, which were decidedly *not normal*. "I'm Queen of Notnormal Land, but maybe you should explain what *you* mean by not normal."

"This should be good," Aphrodite said.

"Okay, well, I don't really know everything about myself yet. I've only been un-undead and Changed for a few days, but I do have some abilities I don't think normal adult vamps have."

"Like . . . ," I prompted when she just sat there chewing her lip.

"Like the kinda 'becomin'' part of the stones' thing I did to crawl up the side of the dorm. But I might be able to do that because of my earth affinity."

I nodded my head, considering. "It does make sense. I've found out that I can call the elements to me and I can more or less disappear as I become mist and wind and whatnot."

Stevie Rae brightened. "Oh, yeah! I remember you were all practically invisible that one time."

"Yep. So maybe having that ability really isn't that abnormal. Maybe all vamps with affinities for an element can do something like that."

"Shit, it just figures! You two get all the cool abilities. I get the pain-in-the-ass visions," Aphrodite said.

"That could be 'cause you're a pain in the ass," Stevie Rae said.

"What else?" I said before they could start bickering again.

"I'll burn up if I get out in the sun."

"Still? Are you completely sure?" I already knew the sun was a problem with her from when she had been an undead dead kid.

"She's sure," Aphrodite said. "Remember, that's why we had to go down in those nasty tunnels in the first place. The sun was coming up. We were downtown. Stevie Rae freaked out."

"I knew somethin' bad would happen if I stayed above-ground," Stevie Rae said. "So I didn't actually freak—I just was real worried."

"Yeah, well, you and I will just have to agree to disagree about your mood swings. I say you totally freaked after your arm got some sunshine on it. Check it out, Z." Aphrodite pointed at Stevie Rae's right arm.

Stevie Rae reluctantly held out her arm and pushed up the sleeve of her blouse. I could see a splotch of red skin across the top of her forearm and elbow, like she'd gotten a bad sunburn.

"That doesn't look so awful. A little sunscreen, dark shades, and a trucker cap and you'll be fine," I said.

"Uh, no," Aphrodite spoke up again. "You should have seen it *before* she drank the blood. Her arm was seriously unattractive and crispy critter. Drinking the blood made it go from third-degree nastiness to mildly annoying sunburn, but who knows how well that would work if her whole body had been fried."

"Stevie Rae, honey, let me be clear that I'm not judging, but you didn't eat a street person or anything like that after you caught on fire, did you?"

Stevie Rae shook her head back and forth so hard, her curls whipped around crazily. "Nuh-uh. On the way to the tunnels, I took the tiniest little detour and borrowed some blood from the downtown Red Cross blood bank."

"*Borrow* means 'give back when you're done,'" Aphrodite said. "And unless you're going to be the first bulimic vampyre, I don't think you'll be giving back the blood." She gave Stevie Rae a smug look. "So, actually, you stole it. Which brings us to your BFF's other new ability. This one I witnessed. More than once, actually. And, yes, it was disturbing. She is freakishly good at controlling the minds of humans. Please note that the key part of what I just said is found in the root word, *freak*."

"Are you done?" Stevie Rae asked her.

"Probably not, but you may proceed," Aphrodite said.

Stevie Rae frowned at her, then continued to explain to me. "Aphrodite's right. It's like I can reach into a human's mind and do things."

"Things?" I asked.

Stevie Rae shrugged. "Things like make them come to me, or forget they saw me. I'm not sure what else. I could sorta do it before I'd Changed, but nothing like what I can do now, and I'm really not comfortable with mind control. It just seems so, I dunno, mean."

Aphrodite snorted.

"Okay, what else? Do you still have to be invited into someone's house to enter?" And then I answered my own question.

"Wait, that must have changed, because I didn't actually invite you in here, and here you are. Not that I wouldn't have invited you in. I definitely would have," I added quickly.

"I dunno about that one. I walked right into the Red Cross place."

"You mean you walked right in after you mind-controlled that little lab tech to unlock the door for you," Aphrodite said.

Stevie Rae blushed. "I didn't hurt her or anything, and she won't remember any of it."

"But she didn't invite you in?" I asked.

"No, but the Red Cross building is a public place, and it feels different to me. Oh, and I don't think you'd have to invite me in here, Z. I used to live here, remember?"

I smiled at her. "I remember."

"If you two start holding hands and singing 'Lean on Me,' I'm going to have to excuse myself so I don't start retching," Aphrodite said.

"Can you not use some of your mind control on her and get her to stop once and for all?" I asked.

"Nope. I've already tried it. There's something about her brain that I can't get into."

"It's my superior intelligence," Aphrodite said.

"It's more like your superior annoyance," I said. "Go on, Stevie Rae."

"Let's see, what else . . ." She thought for a couple of seconds, then said, "I'm a lot stronger than I used to be."

"Regular adult vamps are strong," I said. Then I remembered she'd had to stop for blood. "So, you still have to have blood?"

"Yep, but if I don't get it, I don't think I'd go all crazy like I did before. I wouldn't like doing without it, but I don't think I'd turn into a bloodsucking monster."

"But she doesn't know for sure," Aphrodite said.

"I hate it when she's right, but she's right," Stevie Rae said. "There's just so much I don't know about what kind of vampyre I've Changed into that it's more than a little scary."

"Don't worry. We have plenty of time to figure all of this out."

Stevie Rae smiled and shrugged. "Well, y'all are gonna have to figure this out on your own 'cause I really do gotta go." Surprising the crap out of me, she started toward the window.

"Hang on. We have lots more talking to do. And what with the big announcement that winter break is over, there are going to be fledglings and vamps everywhere again, not to mention there're the Sons of Erebus and the whole war-against-the-humans thing to deal with if I try to leave campus to see you, so I don't know when I'll be able to see you." I was beginning to feel a little short of breath about the multiple issues we had going on.

"Don't worry, Z. I still got that phone you gave me. Just call, and I can sneak back in here anytime."

"You mean anytime there's no sunlight," Aphrodite said, helping me open the window for Stevie Rae.

"Yeah, that's what I mean." Stevie Rae looked at Aphrodite. "You know you can come with me if you don't want to stay here and pretend."

I blinked at my BFF in surprise. It wasn't like she could stand Aphrodite, but here she was, offering her a place to stay, and using a nice tone of voice about it, too, which was exactly like the Stevie Rae I knew and loved—and I felt like crap that somewhere in the back of my mind I'd imagined her acting undead and inhuman again.

"Really, you can come with me," Stevie Rae repeated, and when Aphrodite didn't say anything, she added something that seemed really odd to me. "I know what it's like to pretend. You wouldn't have to do that in the tunnels."

I expected Aphrodite to sneer at her and make a crack about

the red fledglings and bad hygiene, but what she actually said surprised me even more than Stevie Rae's offer.

"I have to stay here and pretend I'm still a fledgling. I'm not going to leave Zoey alone, and I don't trust the gay boy and the Dorkamese Twins to do the buddy thing right now. But thanks, Stevie Rae."

I smiled at Aphrodite. "See, you can be nice when you try."

"I'm not being nice. I'm being practical. A world filled with war isn't attractive. You know, what with all that sweaty running and fighting and killing each other. It's just not conducive to good hair or well-maintained nails."

"Aphrodite," I said wearily, "being nice is not a bad thing."

"So says the Queen of Notnormal Land," Aphrodite quipped.

"Which means she's queen of you, Vision Girl," Stevie Rae said. Then she gave me a quick hug. "Bye, Z. I'll see you soon. Promise."

I hugged her back, loving that she felt and smelled and sounded like her old self again. "Okay, but I wish you didn't have to go."

"It'll be fine. You'll see. This'll all work out." Then she crawled out the window. I watched her start to climb down the sheer side of the dorm. She looked creepily buglike until her body rippled and practically disappeared. Actually, had I not known she was there, I would never have seen her at all.

"It's like she's one of those lizards that can change the color of their bodies to match their surroundings," Aphrodite said.

"Chameleons," I said. "That's what they're called."

"Are you sure? Gecko sounds more Stevie Rae–ish to me."

I frowned at her. "I'm sure. Stop being such a smart aleck and help me close the window."

With the window closed and the drapes drawn again, I sighed and shook my head. More to myself than to her, I said, "So what are we going to do?"

Aphrodite started to paw through the chic little Coach purse she wore like decoration over her shoulder. "I don't know about you, but I'm going to use this ridiculous eyeliner pencil to draw my Mark back. Can you believe I found this shade at Target?" She shuddered. "Like, which of the fashion-challenged would even wear it? Anyway, I'm going to fix this thing, then I'm going to go to the stupid meeting Neferet called."

"I meant, *What are we going to do about all this life-and-death stuff that's going on?*"

"I don't fucking know! I don't want this." She pointed at her fake Mark. "I don't want any of this. I just want to be what I was before you showed up here and all hell broke loose. I want to be popular and powerful and dating the hottest guy in school. Now I'm none of those things, *and* I'm a human who has scary visions *and* I don't know what to do about any of it."

I didn't say anything for a second, thinking about the fact that I had been the cause of Aphrodite's losing her popularity, her power, and her boyfriend. When I did finally speak, I surprised myself by saying exactly what was on my mind.

"You must hate me."

She stared a long time at me. "I did," she said slowly. "But now it's mostly myself I hate."

"Don't," I said.

"And why the hell shouldn't I hate myself? Everyone else hates me." Her words sounded sharp and mean, but her eyes were filled with tears.

"Remember the hateful thing you said to me not too long ago when you thought I was perfect?"

A small smile tilted up her lips. "You'll have to remind me. I've said lots of hateful things to you."

"Well, this particular time you said something about the fact that power changes people and that it makes them mess up."

"Oh, yeah. It's coming back to me now. I said power changes people, but I was talking about the people around you."

"Well, you were right about them and me, and I understand that now. I also understand a lot of the stupid things you've done." I smiled and added, "Not all of the stupid things you've done, but a lot of them. Because now I've done my share of stupid things, and I kinda think I'm not done doing stupid things—as depressing as that is."

"Depressing, but true," she said. "Oh, and by the way, while we're talking about power changing people, you need to remember that when you're dealing with Stevie Rae."

"What do you mean?"

"Exactly what I said. She's changed."

"You're gonna have to do better than that," I said, getting a sick feeling in my stomach.

"Don't pretend like you didn't notice anything weird about her," Aphrodite said.

"She's been through a lot," I justified.

"My point exactly. She's been through a lot, and it's changed her."

"You've never liked Stevie Rae, so I don't expect you to suddenly start getting along with her, but I'm not going to listen to you talk crap about her—especially after she just offered to let you come with her so that you don't have to stay here and pretend to be something you're not." I was working myself up into getting really pissed, and I couldn't tell if that was because what Aphrodite was saying was hateful and wrong, or because what she was saying was a scary truth I didn't want to face.

"Did you ever think that maybe she wanted me to go with her because Stevie Rae doesn't want me to spend any time with you?"

"That's stupid. Why would she care? She's my best friend, not my boyfriend."

"Because she knows I've seen through her little act and that I'll tell you the real deal about her. The truth is that she's not what she used to be. I don't know exactly what she is now, and I don't think she knows either, but she's definitely not good ol' white-bread Stevie Rae anymore."

"I know she's not exactly like she used to be!" I snapped. "How could she be? She died, Aphrodite! In my arms. Remember? And I'm a good enough friend that I'm not going to turn my back on her just because going through something life-changing actually changed her."

Aphrodite stood there and stared at me a long time without saying anything—so long that my stomach started to hurt again. Finally she lifted one shoulder. "Fine. Believe what you want to believe. I hope you're right."

"I'm right, and I don't want to talk about it again," I said, feeling weirdly shaky.

"Fine," she repeated. "I'm done talking about it."

"Good. So finish drawing in your Mark and let's go to the meeting."

"Together?"

"Yep."

"You're not caring that people know we don't hate each other?" she said.

"Well, I look at it like this: People, especially my friends, will be thinking a whole lot of not-so-nice stuff about the possibility that you and I have suddenly become friends."

Aphrodite's eyes widened. "Which will keep their wee little brains from thinking about Stevie Rae."

"My friends do not have wee brains."

"Whatever."

"But, yes, Damien and the Twins will be busy thinking pissed-off thoughts about you, which will definitely keep their minds busy if Neferet happens to be listening in," I said.

"Sounds like the beginnings of a plan," she said.

"Sadly, it's all I have of a plan."

"Well, at least you're consistent about not knowing what the hell you're doing."

"So good of you to look on the bright side of things."

"Anything I can do to help," Aphrodite said.

When she'd put the finishing touches on her fake Mark, we headed toward the door. Just before I opened it, I glanced sideways at her. "Oh, and I don't hate you, either," I said. "Actually, you're kinda growing on me."

Aphrodite gave me one of her best sneers and said, "See, that's what I mean about you being consistent about not knowing what the hell you're doing."

I was laughing when I pulled open the door and ran smack into Damien, Jack, and the Twins.

CHAPTER SEVEN

"We want to talk to you, Z," Damien said.

"And we're glad to see she's leaving," Shaunee said, glaring at Aphrodite.

"Yeah, don't let the door hit your skinny ass on the way out," Erin said.

I saw the hurt that flashed across Aphrodite's face. "Fine. I'm out of here," she said.

"Aphrodite, you're not going anywhere." I had to wait till the Twins got over making sputtering sounds of disbelief before I could go on. "Nyx is working strongly in Aphrodite's life. Do you trust Nyx's judgment?" I asked, looking at each of my friends.

"Yes, of course we do," Damien spoke for all of them.

"Then you're gonna have to accept Aphrodite as one of us," I said.

There was a long pause during which the Twins, Jack, and Damien all shared looks, and then Damien finally said, "I suppose we do have to admit that Aphrodite is special to Nyx, but the honest truth is none of us trust her."

"I trust her," I said. Okay, maybe I didn't trust her one hundred percent, but Nyx was working through her.

"Which is ironic, because we're having trust issues with you," Shaunee said.

"Nerd herd, you make no damn sense," Aphrodite said. "In one breath, you're all 'Oh, yes! We trust Nyx!' and in the next you're saying you have trust issues with Zoey. Zoey is *the* fledgling. No one—vamp or fledgling—has ever been so gifted by Nyx. Get a clue, would ya?" Aphrodite rolled her eyes.

"Aphrodite may have a point," Damien said into the stunned silence.

"No shit?" Aphrodite said sarcastically. "Here's another news-flash for the herd of nerd—my latest vision is of Zoey being killed and the world being thrown into total chaos because of it. And guess who was responsible for your supposed friend's murder?" She paused, raising her brows at Damien and the Twins before answering her own question. "You all are. Zoey's killed because you guys turn your backs on her."

"She had a vision of your death?" Damien asked me. His face had suddenly gone very white.

"Yeah, two actually. But the visions were pretty messed up. She saw them from my point of view, which was kinda nasty. Anyway, I just have to stay away from water and—" My words broke off as I almost said *and Neferet.* Thankfully, Aphrodite chimed in.

"—She has to stay away from water, and she can't be isolated," she said. "Which means you guys need to kiss and make up. But wait till I'm not watching, 'cause it's definitely going to make me sick."

"You pissed us off, Z," Shaunee said, looking almost as pale as Damien.

"But we don't want you to die," Erin finished, looking equally upset.

"I'd just die if you died," Jack said, sniffling. Then he reached for Damien's hand.

"Well, then, you're gonna have to get over yourselves and be the buddy-buddy dork pack again," Aphrodite said.

"Since when have you cared whether Zoey lives or dies?" Damien said.

"Since I'm working for Nyx, and not myself. And Nyx gives a shit about Zoey; therefore, I give a shit about Zoey. And it's a good thing I do. You're supposed to be her best friends, and a secret or two and some stupid misunderstandings have made you freeze her out." Aphrodite looked and me and snorted, "Hell, Zoey, with friends like them, it's a good thing we're not enemies."

Damien turned from Aphrodite, shaking his head and looking more hurt than angry. "What really confuses me about all of this is that it's perfectly clear you're telling *her* the things you won't tell us."

"Oh, please, gay boy. Don't get your panties all in a big bunch over me taking your dorkish place beside Zoey. It's simple why she tells me stuff. Vamps can't read my mind."

Damien blinked in surprise. Then, eyes widening in understanding, he looked at me. "They can't read your mind either, can they?"

"No, they can't," I said.

"Oh, shit!" Shaunee said. "You mean you think telling us things is like telling everyone?"

"It can't be that easy for the vamps to read fledglings, Z," Erin said. "If it was, then a bunch of kids would be in trouble all the time."

"Wait, they overlook things like fledglings sneaking off campus or PDA," Damien said slowly, as if he were putting two and two together as he spoke. "The vamps don't really care enough about a little broken rule here and there just as long as it's only typical teenage stuff, so they don't 'listen in' or whatever you want to call their psychic eavesdropping all the time."

"But what if they thought something was going on that was

more than a little broken rule or two, and they had an idea about a certain group of fledglings who might know something," I said.

"They'd focus their thoughts on that group of fledglings," Damien concluded for me. "You really can't tell us certain things!"

"Damn," Shaunee said.

"Sucks royally," Erin said.

"Took you guys long enough," Aphrodite said.

Damien ignored her. "This has something to do with Stevie Rae, doesn't it?"

I nodded.

"Hey, speaking of," Shaunee said.

"What happened to her?" Erin asked.

"Didn't shit happen to her," Aphrodite said. "She found me. I un-freaked when I finally got my Mark back, and then I came back here."

"And she went where?" Damien asked.

"Do I look like a damn babysitter? How the hell am I supposed to know where your bumpkin friend went? All she said was she had to go because she had issues. Like that was a big shock."

"You're gonna have issues with my fist in your face if you start talking shit about Stevie Rae," Shaunee said.

"I'll hold her skinny ass for you, Twin," Erin said.

"Do you two share a brain?" Aphrodite said.

"Oh. My. God! Enough!" I yelled. "I might die. Twice. Some weird ghostly thing messed with me today, and now I'm feeling scared crapless about it. I'm not sure what the hell's going on with Stevie Rae, and Neferet has called a Council Meeting probably to go over her plans for war—a war that is totally not the right thing to do. And you guys can't stop bickering! You're giving me a headache *and* pissing me off."

"You better listen to her. I counted two real cuss words and one almost cuss in that little speech. She's serious," Aphrodite said.

I saw the Twins actually have to stifle smiles. Jeesh. Why is my not liking to cuss such a big deal?

"Okay. We'll try to get along," Damien said.

"For Zoey," Jack said, giving me a sweet smile.

"For Zoey," the Twins said together.

My heart squeezed as I looked at each of my friends. They had my back. No matter what—they would still stand beside me.

"Thanks, guys," I said, blinking back tears.

"Group hug!" Jack said.

"Ah, hell no," Aphrodite said.

"That's one thing we can agree with Aphrodite on," Erin said.

"Yeah, time to go," Shaunee said.

"Ah oh, Damien, we gotta go, too. You told Stark we'd check to be sure he was settled in before the meeting," Jack said.

"Oh, that's right," Damien said. "Bye, Z. See ya soon."

He and Jack followed the Twins out of my room. Calling goodbye to me, they filed down the hall, then went on chattering about the hottiness of Stark, leaving me with Aphrodite.

"So, my friends aren't so bad, huh?" I said.

Aphrodite turned her cool blue gaze on me. "Your friends are dorks," she said.

I grinned and butted my shoulder into her. "Then that makes you a dork."

"That's what I'm afraid of," she said. "Speaking of me being in hell—come to my room. There's something you have to help me figure out before we go to the Council Meeting."

I shrugged. "Okay by me." Actually, I was feeling pretty good about myself. My friends were speaking to me again, and it seemed that everyone might actually have a chance of getting along. "Hey," I said as we walked down the hall to Aphrodite's room. "Did you notice that the Twins said something nice to you before they left?"

"The Twins are symbiotic, and I hope very soon someone takes them away to perform science experiments on them."

"That attitude is not helping," I said.

"Could we just focus on what's really important?"

"Like?"

"Me, of course, and what I need you to help me with." Aphrodite opened the door to her room, and we walked into what I liked to think of as her palace. I mean, jeesh, the place looked like she'd decorated it out of a *Guide to Gossip Girl Design* magazine—if there was such a thing. Which, sadly, there probably was. (Not that I don't adore *Gossip Girl!*)

"Aphrodite, has anyone ever told you that you might have a personality disorder?"

"Several overpaid shrinks. Like I care." Aphrodite walked across the room and opened the door to the hand-painted (probably antique and majorly expensive) armoire that sat in front of her hand-carved (for sure antique and majorly expensive) four-poster canopy bed. As she rummaged around in it, she said, "Oh, by the way, you have got to find a way for the Council to make it okay for you and, tragically, me and—as much as I hate to say it—your nerd herd, too, to be allowed off campus."

"Huh?"

Aphrodite sighed and turned to face me. "Would you please keep up with me? We have to be able to come and go so we can figure out what the fuck is going on with Stevie Rae and her nasty friends."

"I already told you that I'm not gonna let you talk bad about Stevie Rae. Nothing is going on with her."

"That's up for discussion, but since you refuse to sanely discuss it this particular time, I'm talking about the freaks she's hanging with. What if you're right and Neferet wants to use them against humans? Not that I particularly like humans, but I definitely don't like war. So I'm thinking you need to be checking into that."

"Me? Why me? And why do I have to figure out a way to get all of us in and out of the school?"

"Because you are the superhero fledgling. I'm just your more attractive sidekick. Oh, and the herd of nerd are your dorky minions."

"Great," I said.

"Hey, don't stress about it. You'll think of something. You always do."

I blinked in surprise at her. "Your confidence in me is shocking." And I wasn't kidding. I mean, she really looked like she thought I'd figure out this mess.

"It shouldn't be." She turned back to searching through the cluttered armoire. "I know better than just about anyone else how gifted you've been by Nyx. That you're powerful, blah, blah, whatever. So you'll figure it out. Finally! God, I wish they'd let us have housekeepers in here. I can never find anything when I'm forced to clean up after myself." Aphrodite emerged with a green candle in a pretty green crystal glass and a fancy lighter.

"You need me to help you figure out something about a candle?"

"No, genius. Sometimes I *really* wonder about Nyx's choices." She handed me the little gold lighter. "I want you to help me figure out if I've lost my affinity for earth."

CHAPTER EIGHT

I looked from the green candle to Aphrodite. Her face was pale and her lips were compressed into a thin bloodless line. "You haven't tried to evoke earth since you lost your Mark?" I asked gently.

She shook her head and continued to look like her stomach hurt.

"Okay, well, you're right. I can help you figure this out. I should probably cast a circle."

"That's what I thought." Aphrodite drew in a deep shaky breath. "Let's get this over with." She walked over to the wall that was on the opposite side of the room as her bed. She stood there, holding up her candle. "This is north."

"All right." Resolutely, I went to stand in front of Aphrodite. Turning to the east, I closed my eyes and centered myself. "It fills our lungs and gives us life. I call air to my circle." Even without a yellow candle representing the element—and without Damien and his air affinity—I felt the instant response of the element as a soft breeze smoothed against my body.

I opened my eyes and turned to my right, moving deosil, or clockwise, around the circle to the south, where I stopped. "It heats us and keeps us safe and warm. I call fire to my circle." I smiled as the air around me warmed with the second element.

Moving again to my right, I stopped next in the west. "It washes us and quenches us. I call water to my circle." Right away I felt the cool of invisible waves against my legs. Smiling, I moved to stand in front of Aphrodite.

"Ready?" I asked her.

She nodded and closed her eyes and raised the green candle that represented her element.

"It sustains us and surrounds us. I call earth to my circle." I flicked the lighter and held the little flame to the candle.

"Ow, shit!" Aphrodite cried. She dropped the candle as if it had stung her. It shattered against the wood floor at her feet. When her eyes lifted from looking at the ruined glass and candle mess, I saw that they were filled with tears. "I've lost it." Her voice was little more than a whisper as the tears spilled over and down her cheeks. "Nyx took it away from me. I knew she would. I knew I wasn't good enough for her to gift me with an affinity for something as amazing as the element earth."

"I don't believe that's what's happened," I said.

"But you saw it. I'm not earth anymore. Nyx won't let me represent the element," she sobbed.

"I don't mean that you still have your earth affinity. What I mean is I don't think Nyx took it away from you because you're not worthy."

"But I'm not," Aphrodite said brokenly.

"I just don't believe that. Here, let me show you."

I took a small step back from her. This time without Aphrodite's candle, I said, "It sustains and surrounds us. I call earth to my circle."

The scents and sounds of a spring meadow instantly surrounded me. Trying to ignore the fact that what I was doing was making Aphrodite cry even harder, I walked to the center of my invisible circle and called the last of the five elements to me. "It is what we are before we're born, and what we eventually return to. I call spirit to my circle." My soul sang within me as the final element filled me.

Holding tightly to the power that always came to me when I evoked the elements, I raised my arms over my head. I tilted my head up, seeing not the ceiling over me, but imagining through it to the velvet darkness of the all-encompassing night sky. And I prayed—not the way my mom and her husband, the step-loser, pray, all filled with fake humbleness and with lots of decorative *amen*s and whatnot. I didn't change who I was when I prayed. I talked to my Goddess just like I would talk to my grandma or my best friend.

I like to believe Nyx appreciates my honesty.

"Nyx, from this place of power you have given me, I ask that you hear my prayer. Aphrodite has lost a lot, and I don't think that's because you don't care about her anymore. I think there's something else going on here, and I really wish you'd let her know that you're still with her—no matter what."

Nothing happened. I drew a deep breath and centered myself again. I'd heard Nyx's voice before. I mean, sometimes she actually talked to me. Sometimes I just got feelings about things. *Either would be okay right now,* I added that little part of my prayer silently. Then I tried to concentrate even harder. I closed my eyes and listened so hard within that I was squidging my eyes and holding my breath. Actually, I was listening so hard, I almost didn't hear Aphrodite's shocked gasp.

I opened my eyes, and my mouth flopped open along with them.

Floating between Aphrodite and me was the shimmering silver image of a beautiful woman. Later, when Aphrodite and I tried to describe to each other exactly what she'd looked like, we realized we couldn't remember any details except that we both said she'd looked like spirit suddenly made visible—which really wasn't any description at all.

"Nyx!" I said.

The Goddess smiled at me, and I thought my heart would pound out of my chest with happiness. "Greetings, my *u-we-tsi-a-ge-ya*" she said, using the Cherokee word for "daughter," just like my grandma often did. "You were right to call me. You should follow your true instinct more often, Zoey. It will never lead you wrong."

Then she turned to Aphrodite, who, with a sob, dropped to her knees before the Goddess.

"Do not weep, my precious child." Nyx's ethereal hand reached out, and like a beautiful dream given substance, she caressed Aphrodite's cheek.

"Forgive me, Nyx!" she cried. "I've done so many stupid things, and made so many mistakes. I'm sorry for all of it. I really am. I don't blame you for taking away my Mark and my earth affinity. I know I don't deserve either of them."

"Daughter, you misunderstand me. I didn't remove your Mark. It was the strength of your humanity that burned it away, just as it was the strength of your humanity that saved Stevie Rae. Whether you like it or not, you will always be more sublimely human than anything else, which is part of why I love you so deeply. But do not think that you are *only* a human now, my child. You are more than that, but exactly what that means, you must discover—and choose—for yourself." The Goddess took Aphrodite's hand and lifted her to her feet. "I want you to understand that the earth affinity was never yours, daughter. You simply held it in safekeeping for Stevie Rae. You see, the earth could not truly live within her until her humanity had been restored. You were who I trusted to keep that precious gift safe, as well as the vessel through which Stevie Rae's humanity was returned to her."

"So you're not punishing me?" Aphrodite said.

"No, daughter. You punish yourself enough without any addition from me," Nyx said gently.

"And you don't hate me?" Aphrodite whispered.

Nyx's smile was radiant and sad. "As I have already said, I love you, Aphrodite. I always will."

This time I knew the tears that washed down Aphrodite's face were tears of joy.

"You both have a long road before you. Much of it you will travel together. Depend upon one another. Listen to your instincts. Trust the still, small voice within each of you."

The Goddess turned to me. "*U-we-tsi-a-ge-ya,* there is great danger ahead."

"I know. You can't want this war."

"I don't, daughter. Though that is not the danger of which I speak."

"But if you don't want the war, why don't you just stop it? Neferet has to listen to you! She has to do what you command!" I said, not sure why I was suddenly feeling so frantic, especially when the Goddess was gazing at me serenely.

Instead of answering me, Nyx asked a question of her own. "Do you know what it is that is the greatest gift I have ever given my children?"

I thought hard, but my mind seemed to be a jumble of crossword puzzle thoughts and fragments of the truth.

Aphrodite's voice sounded strong and clear: "Free will."

Nyx smiled. "Exactly correct, daughter. And once I give a gift, I never take it away. The gift becomes the person, and were I to step in and command obedience, especially in the form of extracting affinities, I would destroy the person."

"But maybe Neferet would listen to you if you spoke to her like you're speaking to us now. She's your High Priestess," I said. "She's supposed to listen to you."

"It grieves me, but Neferet has chosen to no longer hear me. This is the danger of which I wish to warn you. Neferet has her mind tuned to another voice, one that has been whispering to her for a very long time. I hoped her love for me would drown out the other, but it has not. Zoey, Aphrodite is clever about many things. When she said that power changes, she was right. Power always changes the bearer of it and those who are closest to her, though people who believe it always corrupts think too simplistically."

As she'd been talking, I noticed waves of brightness had begun to shiver through Nyx's body, like moon-kissed mist rising from a field, and her image was getting harder and harder to see.

"Wait! Don't go yet," I cried. "I have so many questions."

"Life will reveal to you the choices you must make to answer them," she said.

"But you say that Neferet has been listening to someone else's voice. Does that mean she isn't your High Priestess anymore?"

"Neferet has left my path and has chosen chaos instead." The Goddess's image wavered. "But remember, what I have given I never take away. So do not underestimate Neferet's power. The hatred she is attempting to awaken is a dangerous force."

"This scares me, Nyx. I—I'm always screwing up," I stammered. "Especially lately."

The Goddess smiled again. "Your imperfection is part of your power. Look to the earth for strength, and the stories of your grandmother's people for answers."

"It'd be a lot safer if you just told me what I need to know and what I should do," I said.

"As with all my children, you must find your own path, and

through that discovery, you will decide what each earth child must ultimately decide—whether she chooses chaos or love."

"Sometimes chaos and love seem like the same thing," Aphrodite said. I could see that she was trying to be respectful, but there was a clear amount of exasperation in her voice.

Nyx didn't seem to mind her comment. The Goddess simply nodded and said, "Indeed, but when you look deeper, you will see that though chaos and love are both powerful and alluring, they are also as different as moonlight is from sunlight. Remember . . . I am never far from your hearts, my precious daughters . . ."

With a final flash of shimmering silver light, the Goddess disappeared.

CHAPTER NINE

"Well, crap. Chaos and love are the same, but not. Neferet still has her powers, but she's not listening to Nyx anymore. Oh, and she's trying to wake up something dangerous. What does that mean? Is it an abstract wake up, like 'waking up' danger in the form of a war with humans, or is she literally trying to wake up some horrible, scary thingie that could eat us all? Like that creepy thing that scratched me earlier, which I didn't even get a chance to ask her about. Crap again!" I babbled as Aphrodite and I hurried from the girls' dorm. Sadly, it appeared we were going to be late for the Council Meeting.

"Don't look at me. I have enough mysteries of my own to solve. I'm human, but I'm not? What does that mean? And how can my humanity be so big and bad anyway—I don't even like humans?" Aphrodite sighed and fiddled with her hair. "Shit, my hair's a mess." She turned her face to me. "Can you tell I've been crying?"

"For the gazillionth time, no. You look fine."

"Shit. I knew it. I look terrible."

"Aphrodite! I just said you look fine."

"Yeah, well, *fine* is fine for most people. For me it's terrible."

"Okay, our Goddess, the immortal Nyx, just manifested and

spoke to us and all you're thinking about is how you look?" I shook my head. That was incredibly shallow, even for Aphrodite.

"Yeah, that was amazing. Nyx is amazing. I never said she wasn't. So what's your point?"

"My point is that after experiencing a visit from the Goddess, you should, I dunno, maybe care about something more important than your already perfect hair," I said, completely exasperated. This was the kid I was supposed to battle world-shaking dangerous evil with? Jeesh, Nyx's ways were absolutely, totally mysterious. Talk about an understatement.

"Nyx knows exactly how I am and she loves me anyway. *This* is who I am." She flapped her hand up and down in front of herself. "So, you really think my hair is perfect?"

"It's as perfect as your shallow, pain-in-the-butt attitude," I said.

"Oh, good. Okay, I feel better already."

I frowned at her, but didn't say anything else as we hurried up the stairs to the Council Room that was opposite the library. I'd never been in the room before, but I'd peeked inside it often enough. When it was empty, the door was rarely closed, and the zillions of times I'd come and gone from the library, I couldn't help glancing in and gawking at the huge beautiful round table that was the predominate feature of the room. Seriously, I'd even asked Damien if that round table could have been *the* Round Table, circa King Arthur and Camelot. He'd said he didn't think so, but wasn't for sure.

Today the Council Room wasn't an empty oddity. It was filled with vamps and Sons of Erebus and, of course, the few fledglings who were on the Prefect Council. Thankfully, we slipped in as Darius was closing the door and positioning himself, all tall and muscley, beside it. Aphrodite gave him a big flirty smile, and I stifled a sigh when his eyes sparkled at her in response. She tried to hang back so she could talk to him. Instead I grabbed her arm and practically hauled her over to the two empty chairs beside Damien.

"Thanks for saving us seats," I whispered to him.

"Not a problem," he whispered back, giving me his familiar smile. It warmed me and helped ease some of my nerves.

I glanced around the table. Aphrodite and I were sitting to Damien's right. Beside Aphrodite was Lenobia, Professor of Equestrian Studies. She was talking with Dragon and Anastasia Lankford, who were beside her. To Damien's left sat the Twins. They gave me twinlike head bobs and tried to look nonchalant, but I could see that they felt as nervously out of place as I did. I knew the Council was made up of the most powerful members of the school's faculty, but along with the professors, several of whom looked familiar but I'd never been in their classes and really didn't know who the heck they were, was a heavy show of power from the Sons of Erebus, including a massive guy who had taken a chair close to the door. He was the biggest person, human or vamp, I had ever seen. I was trying not to stare at him and thinking about asking Damien, Mr. King of the Rules, if the warriors were really supposed to be allowed in a Council Meeting, when Aphrodite leaned over and whispered, "That's Ate, the Leader of the Sons of Erebus. Darius told me he was coming in today. He's one hunk of a guy, isn't he?"

Before I could answer that he was more like several hunks of many large guys, the back door to the room opened and Neferet entered.

I could tell something was wrong even before I caught sight of the woman who came into the room after her. Neferet's public face was usually implacable perfection—she more than personified calm, cool, collection. But this Neferet was shaken. Her beautiful features looked somehow tighter, as if she was straining to control herself, and the strain was a stretch for her. She took a couple steps into the room and then moved aside so we could see the vampyre who entered behind her.

As they sighted her, the shock that zapped through the vamps was immediate and obvious. The Sons of Erebus were first to their feet, but the Council followed closely. Along with everyone else, Damien, the Twins, Aphrodite, and I stood, too, automatically mimicking the vamps' respectful closed fists over their hearts and bowed heads.

Okay, I will admit that I peeked up from the head bow to get a look at the new vamp. She was tall and thin. Her skin was the color of rich, well-polished dark wood, and like mahogany, it was smooth and flawless, marred only by the intricate tattoo of her sapphire Mark, which was, incredibly, in the shape of the curving outline of the goddess figure all the vamp professors wore embroidered on their breast pockets. The female figures were mirrors of one another, their bodies stretched down her high cheekbones and along the side of her face. The inside arms were lifted, hands raised as if to cup the crescent in the middle of her forehead. Her hair was impossibly long. It fell well past her waist, in a heavy length of shining black silk. She had large dark eyes that were shaped like almonds, a long, straight nose, and full lips. She held herself like a queen, with her chin up and her gaze steady as it swept over the room. It was only when that gaze stopped briefly on me and I felt its strength that I realized she was something I'd never seen in a vamp before then—she was old. Not that she was all wrinkled, like an old human would be. This vampyre looked like she might be in her forties, which translated to ancient for a vamp. But it wasn't wrinkles and saggy skin that made her look old. It was a sense of age and dignity that she wore like a fine piece of expensive jewelry decorating her body.

"Merry meet." She had an accent that I couldn't place. It sounded Middle Eastern, but not. British, but not. Basically, it made her voice as rich as her skin. It filled the room.

We all automatically responded. "Merry meet."

Then she smiled, and the sudden resemblance between her and Nyx, who had just smiled at me moments before, made my knees feel disturbingly jellylike, so that I was relieved when she motioned for us to take our seats.

"She reminds me of Nyx," Aphrodite whispered to me.

Relieved I wasn't imagining things, I nodded. There was no time for anything else because Neferet recovered her composure enough to speak.

"I was, as I can see you all are, surprised and honored by Shekinah's rare and unannounced visit to our House of Night."

I heard Damien's sharp intake of breath and sent him a big question mark look. As per usual for Mr. Studious, he had paper and a well-sharpened number two pencil held at the ready position so he could, of course, take proper notes. He quickly wrote a few words and unobtrusively tilted the paper so I could read: SHEKINAH = HIGH PRIESTESS OF *ALL* VAMPS.

Ohmygod. No wonder Neferet looked freaked.

Shekinah continued to smile serenely while she motioned for Neferet to sit. Neferet bowed her head in a gesture that I was sure was meant to look respectful, but to me the movement seemed wooden, the respectful action forced. She sat, still holding herself with that odd rigidity. Shekinah remained standing as she began to speak.

"Were this a normal visit, I would, of course, have made the proper announcements of my coming and allowed you to prepare for it. This is far from a normal visit, which is only right because this is far from a normal Council Meeting. It is unusual enough to admit the Sons of Erebus, but I understand their presence here is needed in such a time of turmoil and danger. But even more unusual, there are fledglings present."

"They're here because—"

Shekinah raised her hand, instantly cutting off Neferet's explanation.

I couldn't figure out which freaked me out more—Shekinah's powerful, goddesslike presence, or the fact that she shut Neferet up so easily.

Shekinah's dark eyes went from the Twins to Damien, Aphrodite, and finally came to rest on me. "You are Zoey Redbird," she said.

I cleared my throat and tried not to fidget under her direct gaze. "Yes, ma'am."

"Then these four with you must be the fledglings who have been gifted with affinities for air, fire, water, and earth."

"Yes, ma'am, they are," I said.

She nodded. "I understand now why you have been included here." Shekinah tilted her head so that her eyes skewered Neferet. "You wish to use their power."

I stiffened at the same time Neferet did, although for a very different reason. Did Shekinah know what I had only begun to suspect—that Neferet was abusing her power and instigating a war between humans and vampyres?

Neferet spoke sharply, dropping all pretense of cordiality. "I wish to use every advantage the Goddess has given us to keep our people safe." The other vampyres on the Council shifted in their seats uncomfortably at her obvious lack of respect.

"Ah, and this is exactly why I am here." Completely unruffled by Neferet's attitude, Shekinah turned her gaze to the Council Members. "It was fortuitous I was making a private, unannounced visit to the House of Night in Chicago when word of your tragedies reached me. Had I been home in Venice, the news would have reached me too late to act upon, and these deaths could not have been prevented."

"Prevented, Priestess?" Lenobia spoke up. I glanced at her and saw the horse mistress looked much more relaxed than Neferet. Her tone was warm, though undeniably respectful.

"Lenobia, my dear. It is lovely to see you again," Shekinah said familiarly.

"It is always a joy to greet you, Priestess." Lenobia bowed her head, causing her unusual silver-blond hair to sweep around her like a delicate veil. "But, I think I speak for all of the Council when I say we're confused. Patricia Nolan and Loren Blake are dead. If you meant to prevent their murders, you are too late."

"I am, indeed," Shekinah said. "And their deaths make my heart heavy, but I am not too late to prevent more deaths." She paused and then said slowly and distinctly, "There will be no war between humans and vampyres."

Neferet shot to her feet, almost overturning her chair. "No war? So we are to let murderers go unpunished for their heinous crimes against us?"

I could feel more than see the tension that rippled through the Sons of Erebus as they mirrored Neferet's shock.

"Did you call in the police, Neferet?" Shekinah's question was asked in a soft, conversational tone, but I felt the power in it brush against my skin and stir something within me.

"Call in the *human* police and ask them to catch the *human* murderers so they can be taken before a *human* court? No, I did not."

"And you are so sure that you will not find justice with these humans that you are willing to begin a war."

Neferet's eyes narrowed and she glared at Shekinah, but didn't say anything in response. In the ugly silence, I thought about

Detective Marx, the cop who had helped me when Heath had been taken by the creepy undead dead kids. He'd been incredible. He'd known I'd made up the story about a street person abducting Heath and killing the other two human kids, and he'd trusted me enough to believe me when I said the danger was over, and through the whole thing he'd covered my butt. Detective Marx had explained that his twin sister had been Changed, and he'd stayed close to her, so he definitely didn't hate vamps. He was a senior homicide detective—I knew he'd do everything he could to find whoever was killing vampyres. And he couldn't be the only one in Tulsa who was real and honest.

"Zoey Redbird, what do you know about this?"

Shekinah's question was a shock. Like she'd pulled a weird string inside me that made me talk, I blurted, "I know an honest human cop."

Shekinah smiled her Nyx smile again, and my freaked nerves calmed a little. "I think we all do, or at least I thought we all did until word came to me of this declaration of war—without so much as an attempt at allowing humans to police their own."

"Don't you see how impossible that even sounds?" Neferet's moss-colored eyes were flashing. "*Police their own,* as if they would!"

"They have, many times over the decades. You know that, Neferet." Shekinah's calm words contrasted dramatically with Neferet's passion and anger.

"They killed her, then they killed Loren." Neferet's voice was almost a hiss.

Shekinah gently touched Neferet's arm. "You are too close to this. You aren't thinking rationally."

Neferet jerked away from her touch. "I'm the only one of us thinking rationally!" she snapped. "Humans have gone unpunished for their vile deeds too long."

"Neferet, very little time has passed since these murders, and you haven't given the humans even the opportunity to attempt to punish their own. Instead you instantly judge them all as dishonest. Not all humans are, despite your own personal history."

As Shekinah spoke, I remembered that Neferet had told me that her Mark had been her salvation because her father had abused her for years. She'd been Marked almost one hundred years ago. Loren had been killed two days ago. Professor Nolan only the day before that. It was obvious to me that their murders weren't the only "vile deeds" Neferet was talking about. It seemed Shekinah had come to a similar conclusion.

"High Priestess Neferet, it is my conclusion that your judgment in the matter of these deaths is skewed. Your love for our fallen sister and brother, and desire for retribution, has clouded your reason. Your declaration of war against humans has been rejected by Nyx's Council."

"Just like that!" Neferet's anger had gone from passionate to thin-lipped and steely. I was mega-glad Shekinah was the focus of that anger 'cause Neferet was just plain scary.

"Were you thinking clearly, you would realize that Nyx's Council never makes rash decisions. They weighed the situation carefully, even though word of your declaration of war did not come from you, as it should have," she said pointedly. "You know, my sister, that something of this magnitude should have been presented before Nyx's Council for their consideration."

"There was no time," Neferet snapped.

"There is always time for wisdom!" Shekinah's eyes flashed, and I had to fight the urge to cringe back in my seat. I'd thought Neferet was scary? Shekinah made her look like a bratty child. Shekinah closed her eyes briefly and drew a deep, calming breath before she continued speaking in a soothing, understanding tone. "Neither Nyx's Council nor I dispute the fact that the murders of two of our own is reprehensible, but war is unthinkable. We have lived in peace with humans for more than two centuries. We will not break that peace because of the obscene actions of a few religious zealots."

"If we ignore what is happening here in Tulsa, it will be the Burning Times again. Remember that the Salem atrocities were also begun by what you would call a few religious zealots."

"I remember well. I was born a scant century after those dark days. We are more powerful now than we were in the seventeenth century. And the world has changed, Neferet. Superstition has been replaced by science. Humans are more reasonable now."

"What will it take to make you and the almighty Council of Nyx see that we have no choice but to fight back?"

"It would take a shift in the thinking of the world, and I pray to Nyx that never happens," Shekinah said solemnly.

Neferet's eyes darted around the room until they found the Leader of the Sons of Erebus. "Are you and the Sons going to just sit by while the humans pick us off one by one?" Her voice was a cold challenge.

"I live to protect, and no Son of Erebus would allow any charge of his to be harmed. We will protect you and this school. But, Neferet, we will not stand against the judgment of the Council," Ate said solemnly in a deep, strong voice.

"Priestess, what you imply—that Ate should follow your desires rather than the Council—is unfair of you." Shekinah's tone was no longer understanding. Her gaze was fixed on Neferet, and her eyes narrowed.

Neferet said nothing for a long moment, and then a tremor passed through her body. Her shoulders slumped and she seemed to age before my eyes.

"Forgive me," she said softly. "Shekinah, you are right. I am too close to this. I loved Patricia and Loren. I am not thinking clearly. I must . . . I need to . . . please, excuse me," she finally managed. And then, looking utterly distraught, she hurried from the Council room.

CHAPTER TEN

No one spoke for what seemed like a long time, but was probably only a few tense seconds. Seeing Neferet lose it like that was bizarre, and even though I knew she had turned her back on Nyx and was into some really bad stuff, it shook me to see someone so powerful crumble so completely.

Was she nuts? Was that what was going on? Could the "darkness" Nyx warned me about be the darkness inside Neferet's crazy mind?

"Your High Priestess has been through a terrible ordeal these past days," Shekinah was saying. "I do not excuse her lapse in judgment, but I do understand it. Time will soothe her wounds, as will the actions of the local police." Her eyes moved to the huge warrior. "Ate, I would have you lead the detectives through the investigation. I understand much of the evidence has been destroyed, but perhaps modern science can still discover something." Ate nodded solemnly, and she turned her dark gaze to me. "Zoey, what is the name of this honest human detective you know?"

"Kevin Marx," I said.

"He will be contacted," Ate said.

Shekinah smiled her approval. Then she continued, "As for what the rest of us will do . . ." She paused, and her angelic smile widened. "Yes, I say *us* because I have decided to remain here, at least until your Neferet is herself again."

I glanced quickly around the table, trying to gauge the reaction of the professors to Shekinah's unexpected announcement. I saw expressions that ranged from shock to mild surprise to outright pleasure. I do believe my face was one that would have been showing the outright pleasure. I mean, how crazy could Neferet act with the leader of all vamp priestesses here?

"I think it is important, and Nyx's Council agrees with me, that we try to carry on at the school as normally as possible. Which means classes will resume tomorrow."

Several of the professors looked uncomfortable, but it was Lenobia who spoke up again.

"Priestess, we are all willing for classes to resume, but we are missing two important instructors."

"Indeed, and that is another reason I plan to remain here, for at least a little while. I will take over Loren Blake's poetry classes."

I didn't need to look at the poetry-hating Twins to know they were stifling frowns. I was actually working on trying not to smile when Shekinah's next words cut through me.

"And I was lucky enough to catch Erik Night at the airport. I know it is unusual to have a recently Changed vampyre teach so soon, but it is only temporary and we really are working under extenuating circumstances. Besides, the fledglings know Erik. He will be a good transition for them from their beloved Professor Nolan."

Ohmgod, Erik is back and I'm taking a class he's going to be teaching. I didn't know if I wanted to cheer or puke, so I settled for silence and an upset stomach.

"As for the barrier spell Neferet erected around the school—it will not be resumed. While I agree with her immediate actions in casting it—after all, there were few of the Sons of Erebus present and a murder had just been committed—those emergency actions are no longer appropriate. To seal off the school would be tantamount to the declaration of a siege state, and that is something we definitely wish to avoid. And, of course, we are fully protected by the Sons of Erebus." She nodded to Ate, who returned the gesture with a bow of acknowledgment. "All in all, I would like your lives to go on as normally as possible. Those of you with ties to the human community, exercise those relationships. Remember the lesson our ancestors learned with their precious blood: Fear and bigotry are bred from isolation and ignorance."

Okay, I do not know what the hell came over me, but suddenly I realized I had an idea, and as if of its own free will, my hand dorkishly raised over my head like it thought we were in the middle of class and we (meaning my hand and my mouth minus my brain) had just discovered a brilliant answer.

"Zoey, do you have something to add?" Shekinah asked.

Oh, hell no! is what I should have said. Instead my mouth blurted, "Priestess, I was wondering if this might be a good time to implement an idea I've had for the Dark Daughters to get involved with a local human charity."

"Go on. I am intrigued, young lady."

I gulped. "Well, I thought the Dark Daughters could contact the people who run Street Cats. It's, uh, a charity that shelters homeless cats and finds them homes. I, well, I thought it might be a good way to mix with the human community," I finished lamely.

Shekinah's smile was luminous. "A cat charity—how perfect! Yes, Zoey, I think yours is an excellent idea. Tomorrow you will be excused from your early classes so that you may begin contacting the Street Cat people."

"Priestess, I must insist the fledgling does not travel into the community alone," Ate said quickly. "Not until we know who exactly is responsible for the crimes against our people."

"But the humans won't know we're fledglings," Aphrodite said.

Everyone's eyes went to her, and I watched her spine straighten and her chin lift.

"And you are?" Shekinah asked.

"My name is Aphrodite, Priestess," she said.

I watched Shekinah closely, waiting to see a reaction that said she knew about the rumors Neferet had spread about Aphrodite—that Nyx had turned her back on her and taken away her powers, et cetera, et cetera, but the priestess's curious expression didn't change. She simply said, "What is your affinity, Aphrodite?"

I froze. Crap! She didn't have an affinity anymore!

"Earth is the element Nyx gave me," Aphrodite said. "But my greatest gift from the Goddess is my ability to see visions of future danger."

Shekinah nodded. "That's right, I have heard of your visions, Aphrodite. Go on, then. What is it you have to say?"

A huge wave of relief washed through me. Aphrodite had fielded the affinity question and, thanks to her use of tense, hadn't actually lied.

"I was just thinking that humans don't know when we leave the school anyway, because we cover our Marks. The only people who would really know that a bunch of fledglings are volunteering to help Street Cats would be the Street Cats people, and what are the chances that they're involved in the murders?" She paused and shrugged. "So we should be safe."

"She has a point, Ate," Shekinah said.

"I still believe the fledglings should be shadowed by a warrior," Ate said stubbornly.

"That would call attention to us," Aphrodite said.

"Not if the warrior covered his Mark, too," Darius said.

This time everyone turned to look at Darius, who was still standing like a very muscular and attractive mountain over by the door.

"And what is your name, Warrior?"

"Darius, Priestess." He fisted his hand over his heart and bowed to her.

"So, Darius, you are saying you would be willing to cover your Mark?" Shekinah said. I felt as surprised as she sounded. Fledglings had to cover their Marks when they left school—it was a rule of the House of Night. And it made sense. Honestly, teenagers can act stupid sometimes (especially boy teenagers), and no way would it be a good thing for a bunch of loitering fledglings (boys mostly) to be targeted by human kids (or worse—cops or overprotective parents). But once a fledgling has gone through the Change and her Mark has been filled in and expanded, no damn way is she going to ever cover it up. It was about pride and solidarity and being grown. But here was Darius, clearly young and not long Marked, volunteering to do something that most vamps, especially most vamp guys, would normally say *no way* to.

Darius hastily closed his fist over his heart again and saluted Shekinah. "Priestess, I would cover my Mark so that I might accompany the fledglings and keep them safe. I am a Son of Erebus, and protection of my people is more important to me than misplaced pride."

Shekinah's lips curved up ever so slightly as she turned to Ate. "What say you to your warrior's request?"

The vamp's answer came without hesitation, "I say that sometimes we can learn much from the young."

"Then it is settled. Zoey, you will introduce yourself to the

Street Cat people tomorrow, but I want you to choose a fledgling to go with you. Working in pairs is a good idea right now. Darius, you will accompany them with your Mark disguised."

We all made little bows to her.

"And now, if there are no more questions"—she paused, and her eyes went from Lenobia to Aphrodite, Darius, and finally, me—"or comments, I would adjourn this Council Meeting. I will be holding a schoolwide Ritual of Cleansing in the next couple of days. I felt grief and fear when I came within these walls tonight, and only Nyx's blessing can lift such heaviness." Several of the Council Members nodded in agreement. "Zoey, before you depart tomorrow, I would like you to come to me and tell me who is going to join you."

"I will," I said.

"I wish you all blessed be," she said formally.

"Blessed be," we responded.

Shekinah smiled again. With a slight motion of her hand, she gestured for Lenobia and Ate to follow her, and the three of them left the room.

"Wow," Damien said, looking more than a little starstruck. "Shekinah! That was utterly unexpected, and she was even more resplendent than I'd imagined. I mean, I wanted to say something, but I was completely flummoxed."

We were hanging around out in the hall while the room emptied of Council Members and warriors, so Damien was barely speaking above an excited whisper.

"Damien, for once we are not gonna give you a hard time about your pain-in-our-ass vocab obsession," Shaunee said.

"Yeah, 'cause it takes some seriously big words to describe Shekinah," Erin said.

"Later," Aphrodite said to me after rolling her eyes at the Twins. "I'm going to see if I can do a little flummoxing with Darius."

"Huh?" I said.

"That isn't the correct use of the word," Damien told her.

"Yeah, you were thinking of another word," Erin said.

"But it, too, starts with an *F,* which is probably what confused you," Shaunee said.

"Brain-sharers and Vocab Boy—I say a big *whatever* to you." She started to move off down the hall in the direction Darius had taken. "Oh, and I also say don't be all jealous and pissy when Zoey tells you I'm the one she's taking with her tomorrow," Aphrodite said, giving me *the look,* which clearly meant there was a definite reason she had to go with me. Then she tossed her hair and twitched away.

"Hating her," Erin said.

"Ditto, Twin," Shaunee said.

I sighed. My grandma would say that I was taking one step forward and two backward in the whole getting-my-friends-to-like-Aphrodite situation. I'd just say they were all giving me a headache.

"She seriously bugs, but my guess is you're going to take her with you to Street Cats tomorrow," Damien said.

"Yeah, your guess is right," I said reluctantly. I really didn't want to piss my friends off again, but even without knowing Aphrodite's reasons for wanting to go with me, it only made sense. Maybe she had a plan to ditch Darius and find Stevie Rae.

"You could have told us earlier about the psychic thing," Damien said as we started out of the main building and headed back toward the dorms.

"Yeah, you're probably right, but I figured the less I said about it, the less you'd think about it and the reasons I wasn't saying anything more to you guys," I said.

"Makes sense now," Shaunee said.

"Yeah, we get it now," Erin said.

"I'm glad you weren't just keeping stuff from us," Jack said.

"But you still should have told us the Loren stuff," Erin said.

"Actually, when you're done with your grief and whatnot, we'd still really like to hear the Loren details," Shaunee said.

I raised my brows at their identical looks of curiosity. "Don't count on it," I said.

They frowned.

"Give the girl some privacy," Damien said. "The Loren thing was very traumatic for her, what with the Imprint and the loss of virginity and *Erik*!"

The *Erik* part of Damien's mini-lecture had come out as a very odd squeak. I opened my mouth to ask what was wrong with him when I noticed that his eyes had gone huge and round and were fixed over my left shoulder and behind me, where I heard the distinct sound of a side door off the main school building closing. With a terrible sinking in my stomach, I, along with the Twins and Jack, turned to see Erik emerging from the wing of the school we had just been passing, which, of course, held the drama room.

"Hi, Damien, Jack." he gave Jack, his ex-roommate, a warm smile, and I could see the kid almost wriggling with pleasure as he gushed a big hello back.

My stomach, naturally, tried to turn itself inside out at this re-minder of one of the many reasons I liked Erik so much. He was popular and totally to-die-for handsome, but he was also a truly nice guy.

"Shaunee, Erin," Erik continued, nodding at them. The Twins smiled, fluttered their lashes, and said hi in unison. At last, he looked at me. "Hello, Zoey." His voice had changed from the easy, friendly tone he'd used with everyone else. He didn't sound hate-ful, though. Instead he sounded cool and polite. I thought this might be an improvement, but then I remembered what a good actor he was.

"Hi." I couldn't say anything else. I'm *not* a particularly good actor, and I was scared my voice would sound as shaky as my heart felt.

"We just heard you're going to be teaching drama class," Damien said.

"Yeah, it makes me a little uncomfortable, but Shekinah asked, and it's really not possible to say no to her," he said.

"I think Professor Nolan would be glad you're going to do it," I blurted before I could make my mouth shut up.

Erik looked at me. His blue eyes were absolutely expressionless, which felt completely wrong. Those same eyes had shown me happiness and passion and warmth and even the beginnings of love. Then they'd shown me hurt and anger. And now they showed me nothing at all? How could that even be possible?

"Did you gain a new affinity?" His tone wasn't outright hateful, but his words were definitely clipped and cold. "Can you speak to the dead now?"

I felt my face get hot. "N-no," I stammered. "I just . . . well, I just thought Professor Nolan would like it that you're here for her students."

He opened his mouth, and I saw something mean stir in his eyes, but instead of speaking he looked away from me and off into the darkness. His jaw tightened and he ran a hand through his thick, dark hair in a gesture I recognized as one that he automatically did whenever he was feeling confused.

"I hope she does like it that I'm here. She was always my favorite teacher," he finally said without looking at me.

"Erik, are we going to be roommates again?" Jack asked tentatively into the increasingly uncomfortable silence.

Erik blew out a long breath and then gave Jack a quick, easy smile. "No, sorry. They've put me in the professor building."

"Oh, that's right. I keep forgetting you've been through the Change," Jack said with a nervous little giggle.

"Yeah, sometimes I almost forget myself," Erik said. "Actually, I better get to my new place—I have boxes to unload and lesson plans to figure out. See you guys later." He paused, and then his eyes flicked to mine. "Bye, Zoey."

Bye. My lips moved, but no sound came out.

"Bye, Erik!" Everyone else called as he turned and walked quickly away from us and back toward the professors' part of the school.

CHAPTER ELEVEN

My friends babbled about nothing in particular while we walked the rest of the way to the dorms. Everyone studiously ignored the fact that we'd just run into my very ex-boyfriend and that it had been a really awkward, really awful scene. Or at least for me it had been awkward and awful.

I hated feeling like this. I'd caused Erik to break up with me, but I missed him. A lot. And I still liked him. A lot. Sure, he was acting like a butt right now, but he'd caught me having sex with another man—well, another vampyre, actually. As if that mattered. Anyway, bottom line is I'd caused this mess and it was incredibly frustrating that I couldn't fix it, because I still cared about Erik.

"What do you think of him, Z?"

"Him?" Erik? Hell, I thought he was amazing and frustrating and . . . and I realized Damien hadn't been asking me about Erik when he frowned and gave me a *get a clue* look. "Huh?" I said brilliantly.

Damien sighed. "The new kid. Stark. What do you think of him?"

I shrugged. "He seemed nice."

"Nice and hot," Shaunee said.

"Just the way we like 'em," Erin finished.

"You spent more time with him than we did. What do you think of him?" I asked Damien, ignoring the Twins.

"He's okay. But he seems distant. I suppose it doesn't help that he can't have a roommate because of Duchess. You know, that dog is really big," Damien said.

"He's new, guys. We all know how that feels. Maybe how he deals with it is being distant," I said.

"It's odd that a kid with such an amazing talent is unwilling to use it," Damien said.

"There could be more to it than we know," I said, thinking about how cool and confident Stark had acted when he'd been standing up to the vamps about his dog, but then that nonchalance had changed when Neferet made him think that she wanted him to use his talents to compete. He'd gotten weird then, maybe even scared. "Sometimes having unusual powers can be scary." I spoke more to myself than to Damien, but he smiled at me and bumped his shoulder against mine.

"Guess you'd know about being unusual," he said.

"Guess I would." I smiled at him, trying to lighten the crappy mood meeting up with Erik had gotten me in.

Shaunee's cell phone made the little bleeping sound it makes when she gets a text message, and she whipped out her iPhone.

"Oooh, Twin! That's Mr. So *Fiiiine* Cole Clifton. He and T.J. want to know if we're up for a *Bourne* movie marathon in the guys' dorm," Shaunee said.

"Twin, I was born ready for a *Bourne* marathon," Erin said. Then the Twins giggled and did a bump and grind that made the rest of us roll our eyes.

"Oh, and you guys are invited, too," Shaunee said to Damien, Jack, and me.

"Goody," Jack said. "I never did get to see the last one. What was it called?"

"*The Bourne Ultimatum,*" Damien said right away.

"That's right." Jack took his hand. "You're so smart about movies! You know all of them."

Damien blushed. "Well not *all* of them. Mostly I like the old classics. Back then is when movies had real stars in them, like Gary Cooper and Jimmy Stewart and James Dean. Today too many actors are—" Then his words came to an abrupt halt.

"What is it?" Jack asked.

"James Stark," he said.

"What about him?" I said.

"James Stark is the name of James Dean's character in the old movie, *Rebel Without a Cause.* I knew his name sounded familiar, but I thought it was just because he's so famous."

"Twin, have you ever seen that movie?" Erin asked Shaunee.

"No, Twin. Can't say that I have."

"Huh," I said. I had seen the movie—with Damien, of course—and I wondered if the name had been his before he'd been Marked. Or had he, like many kids, decided on a new name when his new life as a fledgling began. If so, that said something pretty interesting about his personality.

"So, are you coming, Z?" Damien's voice penetrated my internal babble.

I looked up to see four sets of eyes blinking questioningly at me. "Coming?"

"Jeesh, earth to Zoey! Are you coming with us to the guys' dorm to watch the *Bourne* movies?" Erin said.

I answered automatically. "Oh, that. No." I was glad my friends weren't pissed at me anymore, but I really didn't feel like hanging out. Actually, I felt kinda bruised and not myself inside. Within just a couple days, I'd Imprinted with and lost my virginity to a man/vamp who hadn't loved me, and then he'd been horribly killed. I'd broken my boyfriends' hearts. Both of them. A war had almost been started and then ended. Kind of. My best friend wasn't undead anymore, but she wasn't a "normal" fledgling or vampyre either, and neither were the kids she was living with. But I couldn't tell most of my friends, as in anyone who wasn't Aphrodite, about the weird red fledglings, 'cause it was better if Neferet didn't know what we knew. And now Erik, one of my two broken-hearted ex-boyfriends, was going to be my drama teacher—as if having him back at the House of Night wasn't drama enough. "No," I repeated more firmly. "I think I'm going to go check on Persephone." Okay, I realize I'd been in her stall not too long ago, but I could definitely use another dose of her quiet, warm presence.

"Are you sure?" Damien asked. "We really would like you to come with us."

The rest of my friends nodded and smiled, thawing the last of the knot of fear that had frozen in my stomach since they'd been mad at me.

"Thanks, guys. But I'm not really up for hanging out tonight," I said.

"Okey," said Erin.

"Dokey," said Shaunee.

"See ya," Jack said.

I thought Damien would give me his typical good-bye hug, but instead he told Jack, "You guys go on, and I'll catch up with you. I'm going to walk Z to the stables."

"Good idea," Jack said. "I'll get your popcorn ready for you."

Damien smiled. "Save me a seat, too?"

Jack grinned back at him and gave him a quick, sweet kiss. "Always."

Then the Twins and Jack took off in one direction, and Damien and I went in the opposite direction. Hopefully that wasn't an omen about where our lives were heading.

"You really don't have to walk me to the stables," I said. "It's just not that far."

"Didn't you say earlier that something attacked you and hurt your hand when you were walking from the stables to the cafeteria?"

I raised my brows at him. "I didn't think you believed me about that."

"Well, let's just say that Aphrodite's visions have converted me. So when you're done communing with your horse, if you want you can give me a call on your cell. Jack and I will pretend like we're much more butch than we are and come escort you back."

"Oh, please. You aren't what I'd call swishy and fluttery."

"Well, I'm not, but Jack is."

We laughed. I was considering arguing with him about the whole Zoey-has-to-have-an-escort issue when the crow started cawing. Actually, now that I was wide awake and listening, the cawing seemed more like weird croaking, but it wasn't any less annoying.

No, maybe *annoying* wasn't the right word for the sound. Creepy. *Creepy* was exactly the right word for the sound.

"You hear that, don't you?" I said.

"The raven? Yeah."

"Raven? I thought it was a crow."

"No, I don't think so. If I remember correctly, crows caw, but a raven's cry is more like the croaking of toads." Damien paused, and the bird croaked a few more times. It sounded closer, and its ugly voice caused goose bumps to rise on my arms. "Yep, that's definitely a raven."

"I don't like it. And why is it being so noisy? It's winter—it couldn't be mating, could it? Plus, it's night. Shouldn't it be asleep?" I peered out into the darkness as I spoke, but didn't see any of the stupid noisy birds, which wasn't so unusual. I mean, they're black and it is night. But that one raven seemed to fill the sky around me, and something about its abrasive call made my skin shiver.

"I really don't know very much about their habits." Damien paused, looked carefully at me. "Why is it bothering you so much?"

"I heard wings flapping before, when whatever it was came at me. And it just *feels* creepy. Don't you feel it?"

"I don't."

I sighed and thought he was going to tell me that maybe I needed to get a handle on my stress and my imagination, but he surprised me by saying, "But you're more intuitive than I am. So if you say the bird feels wrong, I believe you."

"You do?" We were at the steps of the stable, and I stopped and turned to him.

His smile was full of familiar warmth. "Of course I do. I believe in you, Zoey."

"Still?" I said.

"Still," he said firmly. "And I've got your back."

And just like that, the raven stopped croaking and the shivery creepiness I'd been feeling seemed to drift away with it.

I had to clear my throat and blink hard before I could manage to say, "Thanks, Damien."

Then Nala's grumpy old woman cat voice *"mee-uf-owed"* at me as my fat little orange cat padded out of the darkness to twine herself around Damien's legs.

"Hey there, little girl," he said, giving her a scratch under her chin. "Looks like she's here to take over the watch Zoey duty."

"Yep, I think you've definitely been relieved," I said.

"If you need me when you want to come back, just give me a call. I really don't mind," he said as he hugged me tight.

"Thanks," I said again.

"No problem, Z." He smiled at me once more and then, humming "Seasons of Love" from *Rent,* he disappeared back down the sidewalk.

I was still smiling when I opened the side door that led to the hallway that divided the field house and the stables. Mixed with the sweet hay and horse smell that was already wafting from the stable on my right, and the relief of knowing my friends really weren't pissed at me anymore, I could already feel myself beginning to relax. Stress—jeesh! I really needed to do some yoga or whatnot (probably more whatnot than yoga). If I kept up this tension, I'd more than likely develop an ulcer. Or worse, wrinkles.

I was just turning to my right and had my hand on the stable door when I heard a weird *thwap!* followed by a muffled *thud.* The noises were coming from my left. I glanced to the side and saw that the door to the field house was open. Another *thwap! thud* pricked at my curiosity, and as per typical for me, instead of showing some sense and going on into the stable as I'd meant to, I walked into the field house.

Okay, the field house is basically an inside football field that's not a *football* field but just the field part with a track around it. Inside it kids play soccer and do track stuff. (I'm really not into either, but I do know how the place works in theory.) It's covered so that fledglings don't have to deal with the whole sun issue, and lit along the walls by gaslights that don't bug our eyes. Tonight most of those were unlit, so it was the next *thwap!* sound and not my eyesight that drew my attention to the other side of the field.

Stark was standing there with his back to me, bow in hand, facing one of those round bull's-eye targets that have the different colors for different target areas. The red center of this particular target had been hit with a weirdly fat arrow. I squinted, but couldn't see it very well in the dim light, and the target really was way away from where Stark was standing, which meant it was way, *way* away from where I was standing.

Nala gave a little low growl, and I noticed that the blond pile of stuff beside Stark was Duchess all sprawled out, apparently asleep at his feet.

"So much for her being a watchdog," I whispered to Nala.

Stark dragged the back of his hand across his forehead, like he was wiping sweat off his face and rolled his shoulders, loosening them. Even from this distance, he looked confident and strong. He seemed so much more intense than the other guys at the House of Night. Hell, he was more intense than human teenagers in general, and I couldn't help but find that intriguing. I was standing there, trying to figure out a hot-guy scale comparison for him, when he grabbed another arrow from the quiver by his feet, turned sideways, lifted the bow, and in one blurringly fast motion, released a breath and *thwap!* let loose another arrow, which sailed like a bullet directly to the bull's-eye of the distant target. *Thud!*

With a surprised little gasp, I realized why the arrow in the center of the target looked so weirdly big. It wasn't just one arrow. It was a bunch of arrows that had hit one right over the top of each other. Every single arrow he'd shot had gone to the same center spot on the target. Utterly shocked, my eyes went back to Stark, who was still in his archer's stance. And I realized what hot-guy scale he should be on: the Bad Boy Hot Scale.

Ah, oh. Like I needed to think a bad boy was intriguing? Hell, I didn't need to think any kind of boy was intriguing right now. I'd sworn off guys. Totally. I was just starting to turn around so I could tiptoe out when his voice stopped me.

"I know you're there," Stark said without looking at me.

As if that had been her cue, Duchess got to her feet, yawned, and padded happily over to me, tail wagging while she gave me a doggie "hi" woof. Nala arched her back, but didn't spit or hiss, and she actually allowed the Lab to sniff her a little before the cat sneezed squarely in her face.

"Hi," I said to both of them while I ruffled Duchess's ears.

Stark turned to me. He was wearing his cocky almost-smile. I was beginning to understand that expression was probably his norm. I did notice he looked paler than he had at dinner. Being the new kid was hard, and it tended to wear on you—even if you were a hot bad boy.

"I was just going to the stables and I heard something in here. I didn't mean to interrupt you."

He shrugged and started to say something, and then had to stop and clear his throat, like he hadn't talked for a long time. He gave a hoarse little half cough and finally said, "No problem. Actually I'm glad you're here. Saves me from having to find you."

"Oh, do you need something for Duchess?"

"Nah, she's fine. I brought a bunch of her stuff with me. Actually I wanted to talk to you."

No. I was absolutely *not* insanely curious or flattered by his saying he wanted to talk to me. Very calmly and with total nonchalance, I said, "So, what do you want?"

Instead of answering, he asked me a question. "Do those special Marks of yours mean that you really have an affinity for all five of the elements?"

"Yeah," I said, trying not to grit my teeth. I really hated to be questioned about my gifts by new kids. They tended to either hero-worship me or treat me like I was a bomb that might explode all over them at any instant. Either way it was majorly uncomfortable and definitely *not* flattering or intriguing.

"There was a priestess at my old House of Night in Chicago

who had an affinity for fire. She could actually make things burn. Can you use the five elements like that?"

"I can't make water burn or anything bizarre like that." I avoided answering him directly.

He frowned and shook his head, wiping his hand across his brow again. I tried not to notice that he was kinda sexily sweating. "I'm not asking if you can twist the elements. I just need to know if you're powerful enough to control them."

That jerked my attention from his cuteness. "Okay, look. I know you're new, but that's really not your business."

"Which means you must be pretty powerful."

I narrowed my eyes at him. "Again, not your business. If you need me for something that *is* your business, like asking me about dog supplies, come find me. Other than that, I'm out of here."

"Wait." He took a step toward me. "It sounds like I'm being a smart-ass, but I have a good reason for asking you about this."

He'd lost his sarcastic semi-smile, and the look he was giving me wasn't an obsessive let's-see-how-weird-Zoey-really-is expression. He looked like a cute, pale new kid who seriously needed to know something.

"Fine. Yes. I'm pretty powerful."

"And you can really control the elements. Like if something bad happened, you could get them to protect you or the people you care about?"

"Okay, that's it," I said. "Are you threatening me and my friends?"

"Oh, shit no!" he said quickly, holding up one of his hands, palm out, like he was surrendering. Of course, it was hard not to notice that in his other hand, he still held the bow he'd been thunking arrows straight into the bull's-eye with. He saw my eyes glance at the bow and slowly he bent to set it on the ground at his feet. "I'm not threatening anyone. I'm just bad at explaining. Here's the deal—I want you to know about my gift."

He said the word *gift* so uncomfortably that I raised my brows and repeated it. "Gift?"

"That's what it's called, or at least that's what other people call it. It's why I'm so good with that." He jerked his chin toward the bow lying at his feet.

I didn't say anything, but raised my brows at him as I waited (impatiently) for him to continue.

"My gift is I can't miss," he finally said.

"You can't miss? So what? Why would that have anything to do with me or my affinity with the elements?"

He shook his head again. "You don't get it. I always hit my target, but that doesn't mean my target is always what I aim at."

"You're not making any sense, Stark."

"I know, I know. I told you I'm no good at this." He ran his hand backwards through his hair, which made it puff up like a duck's tail. "The best way I can say this is to give you an example. Have you ever heard of the vampyre William Chidsey?"

I shook my head. "Nope, but that shouldn't shock you. I've only been Marked for a few months. I'm not exactly up on vampyre politics."

"Will wasn't into politics. He was into archery. For almost two hundred years, he was the undisputed archery champion of all the vampyres."

"Which means of all the world, because vamps are the best archers there are," I said.

"Yeah." he nodded. "Anyway, Will kicked everyone's ass for almost two centuries. At least up until six months ago he did."

I thought for a second. "Six months ago would make it summer. That's when they have the vamp version of the Olympics, right?"

"Yeah, they call them the Summer Games."

"Okay, so this Will guy is majorly good with a bow. Seems you are, too. Do you know him pretty well?"

"Knew. He's dead. But yeah. I knew him pretty well." Stark paused and then added. "He was my mentor and my best friend."

"Oh, I'm sorry," I said awkwardly.

"So am I. I'm the one who killed him."

CHAPTER TWELVE

"Did you just say you killed him?" I was sure I'd heard him wrong.

"Yeah, that's what I said. I did it because of my gift." Stark's voice sounded cool, like what he'd said was no big deal, but his eyes said something else. The pain in them was so obvious that I had to look away. As if that pain was just as obvious to Duchess, the Lab trotted from me to her master and sat at his side, leaning heavily against him, staring up at him adoringly, and whining softly. Automatically, Stark reached down and stroked her soft head as he talked. "It happened during the Summer Games. It was right before the finals. Will and I were way in the lead, so it was for sure that the gold and silver medals were going to go to us." He didn't look as me while he talked. Instead he stared down at his bow, and his hand kept stroking Duchess's head. Weirdly enough, Nala crept quietly up to him and began rubbing herself against his leg (the one Duchess wasn't leaning on) while she purred like a lawn mower. Stark just kept talking. "We were warming up in the practice lanes. They were these long, thin areas sectioned off by white linen dividers. Will was standing to my right. I remember drawing my bow and being more focused than I'd ever been in my life. I really wanted to win." He paused again, and shook his head. His mouth twisted in self-mockery.

"That was what mattered most to me. The gold medal. So I drew the bow and thought, *No matter what, I want to hit the mark and beat Will.* I shot the arrow, seeing the bull's-eye with my eyes, but really imagining beating Will in my mind." Stark dropped his head, and he sighed deep as a storm wind. "The arrow flew straight to the target in my mind. It hit Will in his heart and killed him instantly."

I felt my head shake back and forth. "But how could that happen? Was he by the target?"

"He was nowhere near it. He was standing not more than ten paces from me to my right. We were separated only by the white linen tarp. I was facing forward when I aimed and shot, but that didn't matter. The arrow went through his chest." He grimaced with the pain the memory still caused him. "It was so fast, everything went blurry. Then I saw his blood spatter the white linen that separated us, and he was dead."

"But Stark, maybe it wasn't you. Maybe it was some kind of weird magical fluke."

"That's what I thought at first, or at least that's what I hoped. So I tested my *gift.*"

My stomach clenched. "Did you kill someone else?"

"No! I tested it on things that weren't alive. Like there was a freight train that used to go by the school every day about the same time. You know, one of those old-time-looking ones, with the big black engine and the red caboose. They still come through Chicago a lot. I printed off a picture of the caboose and put it on a target on the school grounds. I thought about hitting the caboose and shot."

"And?" I prompted when he didn't say anything.

"The arrow disappeared. Only temporarily, though. I found it again the next day when I waited by the track. It was sticking in the side of the real caboose."

"Holy crap!" I said.

"Now you see." He walked over to me so that we were standing very close. His eyes captured mine with that unique intensity of his. "That's why I had to tell you about me, and that's why I needed to know if you were strong enough to protect the people you care about."

My stomach, already clenching, flipped over. "What are you going to do?"

"Nothing!" he shouted, causing Duchess to whine again and Nala to pause in her purr/rub and stare up at him. He cleared his throat and made an obvious effort to pull himself together. "I don't *mean* to do anything. But I didn't *mean* to kill Will, and I did."

"You didn't know about your powers then, and you do now."

"I suspected," he said softly.

"Oh," was all I could think to say.

"Yeah," he said, pressing his lips tightly together before he continued. "Yeah, I knew there was something weird about my gift. I should have listened to my gut. I should have been more careful. But I didn't and I wasn't, and Will is dead. So I want you to know the real deal about me in case I mess up again."

"Hang on! If I understand what you're saying, then only *you* can know what you're really aiming at 'cause it's happening inside your head."

He snorted sarcastically. "You'd think so, wouldn't you, but that's not how it works. One time I thought it was perfectly safe for me to do a little practice shooting. I went to the park that was next to our House of Night. No one was around to distract me; I made sure of that. I found a big old oak and set up a bull's-eye in front of what I decided was the center of the tree."

He was looking at me like he expected a response, so I nodded. "You mean like the middle of the trunk?"

"Exactly! That's what I thought I was aiming at—something that was the center of the tree. But do you know what the center of a tree is sometimes called?"

"No, I really don't know too much about trees," I said lamely.

"Neither did I. I looked it up afterwards. The ancient vampyres, the ones with earth affinities, called the center of the tree its heart. They believed that sometimes animals, or even people, could represent the heart of a particular tree. So I shot, thinking about hitting the center or heart of the tree." He didn't say any more; he just stared down at his bow.

"Who did you kill?" I asked softly. Without actually thinking about it, I lifted my hand and rested it on his shoulder. I'm not even sure now why I touched him. Maybe it was because he looked like he needed the touch of another person. And maybe it was because, despite his admission and the danger he represented, I was still drawn to him.

He covered my hand with his, and his shoulders drooped. "An owl," he said brokenly. "The arrow just burst out of its chest. It was perched on one of the top inside branches of the oak. It screamed all the way to the ground."

"The owl was the heart of the tree," I whispered, fighting the insane urge I had to pull him into my arms to comfort him.

"Yeah, and I killed it." He looked up and met my eyes then. I thought I'd never seen a gaze so haunted by regret, and as the two animals at his feet comforted him and, at least for Nala, acted way more intuitively than usual, the thought flitted through my mind that Stark might very well have more gifts than just hitting whatever he aimed at, but I used some sense and didn't say anything. Like he needed more *gifts* to worry about? Stark kept talking. "See? I'm dangerous, even when I don't mean to be."

"I think I do see," I said carefully, still trying to calm him with my touch. "Maybe you should put up your bow and arrow, at least until you really have a handle on this gift of yours."

"That's what I should do. I know it is. But if I don't practice— if I stay away from shooting and try to forget about it—it's like a part of me is being ripped away. I can feel something inside me dying." He dropped his hand from mine and stepped back so that we weren't touching any longer. "You should know this part of it, too; I'm really just a coward because I can't stand that pain."

"It doesn't make you a coward to want to avoid pain," I said quickly, following the small voice that whispered in my mind. "It makes you human."

"Fledglings aren't human," he said.

"Actually, I'm not too sure about that. I think the best part of everyone is human, whether they're fledglings or vampyres."

"Are you always so optimistic?"

I laughed. "Oh, hell no!"

His smile was less sarcastic and more real this time. "You don't make me think of Debbie Downer, but I haven't known you for very long."

I grinned back at him. "I'm not exactly *that* pessimistic, or at least I didn't used to be." My smile faded. "I guess you could say that recently I haven't been as upbeat as usual."

"What happened recently?"

I quickly shook my head. "More stuff than I can go into."

He met my eyes, and I was surprised by the understanding in his. Then he surprised me even more by stepping close to me again and brushing a strand of my hair back from my face. "I'm a good listener if you need to talk. Sometimes an outsider's opinion can be a good thing."

"Wouldn't you rather not be an outsider?" I asked, trying not to be too thrown off by the nearness of his body and how easy it seemed for him to get close to me *and* under my skin.

He shrugged, and his smile turned sarcastic again. "It's easier that way. It's one reason I wasn't pissed about being moved from my House of Night."

"I wanted to ask you about that." I paused. Pretending I needed to pace to think, I moved away from him a little while my mind hopped from how attracted to him I was to trying to figure out how to frame questions that wouldn't make him think things he shouldn't think, especially around Neferet. "So you mind if I ask you something about you coming here?"

"You can ask me anything, Zoey."

I looked up and met his brown eyes and saw way more in his statement than those simple words. "Okay. Well, did they move you because of what happened with Will?"

"I think so. I don't know for sure. All the vamps at my old school would say was that the High Priestess here requested my transfer to her House of Night. It happens sometimes when fledglings have special gifts other schools need or want." His laugh was humorless. "I know for a fact our House of Night has been trying to steal that big-time actor you guys have, what's his name? Erik Night?"

"Yeah, Erik Night's his name. He's not a fledgling anymore. He's gone through the Change." I seriously didn't want to think about Erik while I was feeling so attracted to Stark.

"Oh, huh. Anyway, your House wouldn't let him go, and he didn't want to leave. My House didn't fight to keep me. And I didn't have any reason to stay. So when I found out Tulsa wanted me, I told them I wouldn't compete again, no matter what. It didn't seem to make any difference, 'cause they still wanted me, so here I am." The sarcasm in his expression faded, and for a second he just looked sweet and kinda unsure of himself. "I'm starting to be really glad Tulsa wanted me so bad."

"Yeah." I smiled, totally off balanced by how connected I was feeling to him. "I'm starting to be really glad Tulsa wanted you, too." And then my mind caught up with everything he'd said, and a terrible premonition washed over me. I had to clear my throat before I asked the next question. "Do all the vamps know how Will died?"

Pain flashed through his eyes again, and I was sorry I'd had to ask. "Probably. All the vamps at my old school knew, and you know how they are—it's hard to keep anything from any of them."

"Yeah, I know how they are," I said softly.

"Hey, did I catch a weird vibe between you and Neferet?"

I blinked in surprise. "Uh, what do you mean?"

"It just felt tense between the two of you. Is there anything I should know about her?"

"She's powerful," I said carefully.

"Yeah, I got that. All High Priestesses are powerful."

I paused. "How about I say she's also not exactly what she appears to be, and that you should be careful around her, and leave it at that for right now. Oh, and she's majorly intuitive—practically psychic."

"Good to know. I'll be careful."

Deciding to beat a hasty retreat before this new kid, who on one hand seemed all intense and confident, and on the other was obviously vulnerable and completely and utterly fascinating me and making me want to forget that I'd sworn off sex. Sex!? I meant guys. I'd sworn off guys. And sex. With them. Oh, jeesh. "I better get going. I have a horse waiting to be groomed," I blurted.

"Better not keep an animal waiting—they can be pretty demanding." He smiled down at Duchess and ruffled her ears. As I started to turn to leave, he caught my wrist and let his hand slide down so that his fingers twined through mine. "Hey," he said softly. "Thanks for not freaking about what I just told you."

I smiled up at him. "Sadly, with the kind of week I've been having, your weird gift seems almost normal."

"Sadly, that's good to hear." And then he lifted my hand and kissed it. Just like that. Just like he kissed girls' hands every day. I didn't know what to say. What's the protocol when a guy kisses your hand? Did one say thanks? I kinda wanted to kiss him back, and I was thinking about how I shouldn't be thinking that and staring into his brown eyes when he said, "Are you going to tell everyone about me?"

"Do you want me to?"

"No, not unless you have to."

"Then I won't tell unless I have to," I said.

"Thanks, Zoey," he said. He squeezed my hand, smiled, and then let me go.

I stood there for a second watching him pick up his bow and walk back to where the quiver of arrows were sitting in their leather holder. Without looking at me again, he took an arrow from the quiver, sighted, and let it fly free to the exact center of the target again. Seriously, he was totally and completely mysterious and sexy, and I was soooo out of there. I turned and, telling myself that I really needed to get a handle on my hormones, was almost out the door when I heard his first cough. I froze, hoping that if I just paused for a second, he'd clear his throat like before and then the next sound I'd hear would be another arrow hitting the bull's-eye.

Stark coughed again. This time I could hear the horrible liquid rattle in the back of his throat. And then the smell hit me—the beautiful, terrible smell of fresh blood. I gritted my teeth against my disgusting desire.

I didn't want to turn around. I wanted to run out of the building, call someone to help him, and never, ever come back. I didn't want to witness what I knew was going to come next.

"Zoey!" My name was filled with liquid and fear when it came from his mouth.

I forced myself to turn around.

Stark had already fallen to his knees. He was bent over at the waist, and I could see that he was puking up fresh blood onto the smooth, golden sand of the field house floor. Duchess was whining terribly, and even though he was choking on blood, Stark put one hand out to stroke the big dog. I could hear him whispering to her between coughs that it would be okay.

I ran back to him.

He fell as I reached him, and I was just able to grab him and pull him onto my lap. I yanked off his sweatshirt, ripping it down the middle so that he lay there only in his T-shirt and jeans. I used the sweatshirt to wipe at the blood that was pouring from his eyes and nose and mouth.

"No! I don't want this to happen now." He paused, coughing up more blood that I kept wiping away. "I just found you—I don't want to leave you so soon."

"I've got you. You're not alone." I tried to sound calm and soothing, but I was breaking apart inside. *Please don't take him! Please save him!* my mind screamed.

"Good," he gasped, and coughed again, sending fresh rivulets of blood from his nose and mouth. "I'm glad it's you. If it has to happen, I'm glad it's you here with me."

"Sssh," I said. "I'll call for help." I closed my eyes and did the first thing that popped into my mind. I called Damien. Thinking hard about air and wind and sweet, beautiful summer breezes, I suddenly felt a warm, questioning wind against my face. *Get Damien here and have him bring help!* I commanded the wind. It whirled around me, tornado-like, once, and then was gone.

"Zoey!" Stark called my name and then coughed again and again.

"Don't talk. Save your strength," I said, holding him tightly with one arm and brushing the wet hair gently back from his damp face with my free hand.

"You're crying," he said. "Don't cry."

"I—I can't help it," I said.

"I should have kissed more than your hand . . . thought I'd have more time," he whispered between liquid, panting breaths. ". . . too late now."

I looked into his eyes and completely forgot the rest of the world. In that moment, all I knew was that I was holding Stark in my arms, and I was going to lose him very, very soon.

"It's not too late," I told him. I bent and pressed my lips to his. Stark's arms went around me, still strong enough to hold me tight. My tears mixed with his blood, and the kiss was absolutely wonderful and terrible and over too soon.

He broke his lips from mine, turned his head, and coughed his life's blood onto the ground.

"Shhh," I soothed as tears washed down my face. I held him close and murmured, "I'm here. I've got you."

Duchess whined pitifully and lay down close to her master, staring with obvious fear into his bleeding face. "Zoey, listen be-fore I'm gone."

"Okay, okay. Don't worry. I'm listening to you."

"Promise me two things," he said weakly. He coughed and had to lean away from me again. I supported his shoulders, and when he lay back in my arms he was trembling and so white, he looked almost transparent.

"Yes, anything," I said.

One bloody hand reached up and touched my cheek. "Promise that you won't forget me."

"I promise," I said, turning my cheek into his hand. His thumb shakily tried to wipe at my tears, which made me cry even harder. "I couldn't forget you."

"And promise you'll take care of Duchess."

"A dog? But I—"

"Promise!" his voice was suddenly filled with strength. "Don't let them send her to strangers. At least she knows you and can tell I care about you."

"Okay! Yes, I promise. Don't worry," I said.

Stark seemed to crumple in on himself with my last promise. "Thanks. I just wish we . . ." His voice trailed off and he closed his eyes. He turned his head into my lap and put his arm around my waist. Red tears silently washed his face, and he became utterly still. The only part of him that still moved was his fluttering chest as he tried to breathe around the blood that was filling his lungs.

Then I remembered and I felt a rush of hope. Even if I was wrong, Stark had to know.

"Stark, listen to me." He showed no sign of hearing me, and I shook his shoulders. "Stark!"

His eyelids opened halfway.

"Can you hear me?"

Stark's nod was barely perceptible. His bloody lips tilted up in a ghost of his sarcastic, cocky smile. "Kiss me again, Zoey," he whispered.

"You have to listen to me." I bent my head down so that I could speak right into his ear. "This might not be the end for you. At this House of Night, fledglings die, and then they are reborn to another kind of Change."

His eyes opened farther. "I—I might not die?"

"Not for good. Fledglings have been coming back. My best friend did."

"Keep Duch safe for me. If I can, I'll come back for her, and for you—" His words ran out in a red river of blood hemorrhaging from his mouth, nose, eyes, and ears.

He couldn't talk anymore, and all I could do was hold him in my arms as his life drained away. It was as he was taking his last, gasping breath that Damien, followed by Dragon Lankford, Aphrodite, and the Twins, burst into the field house.

CHAPTER THIRTEEN

Aphrodite reached me first. She helped me to my feet as Stark's dead body slid heavily from my lap. "There's blood on your mouth," she whispered, handing me a tissue from her purse.

I wiped my lips and then my eyes, right before Damien ran up to me.

"Just come with us. We'll get you back to the dorm so you can change your clothes," Damien said. He moved to one side of me, taking my elbow firmly in one of his hands. Aphrodite was on my other side and had another viselike grip on my other elbow. The Twins had their arms wrapped around each other's waists, trying hard not to cry.

Some of the Sons of Erebus had arrived with a dark stretcher and a blanket. Aphrodite and Damien were trying to pull me from the building, but I resisted them. Instead I watched, crying silently as the warriors gently picked up Stark's blood-soaked body and laid it on the stretcher. Then they covered him with the blanket, pulling it over his face.

It was then that Duchess lifted her muzzle to the sky and started to howl.

The sound was horrible. Duchess filled the blood-soaked night with sorrow and loneliness and loss. The Twins immediately burst into tears. I heard Aphrodite say, "Oh, goddess, that's so terrible." Damien whispered, "Poor girl . . . ," and then he, too, began to cry softly. Nala had crouched close to the grief-stricken dog and was watching her with big, sad eyes as if she wasn't sure what to do.

I didn't know what to do, either. I felt weirdly numb, even though I couldn't stop crying, but I was getting ready to pull free of my friends and go to Duchess to try to figure the impossible out, when Jack rushed into the field house. He skidded to a stop. His mouth fell open in shock. One hand went to his throat, and the other pressed against his mouth, futilely trying to stop his gasp of horror. He stared from the shrouded body on the stretcher, to the bloody sand, to the mourning dog. Sniffling, Damien squeezed my arm and then let go of me to start toward his boyfriend when Jack, ignoring everyone and everything else, ran over to Duchess and dropped to his knees in front of her.

"Oh, honey! My heart is just broken for you!" he told the dog.

Duchess dropped her muzzle and looked long and steadily at Jack. I didn't know dogs could cry, but I promise you Duchess was crying. Tears were leaving dark, wet streaks from the corners of her eyes down her face and muzzle.

Jack was crying, too, but his voice sounded sweet and steady when he told Duchess, "If you come with me, I won't let you be alone."

The big blond Lab stepped forward slowly, as if she'd aged decades in the past few minutes, and laid her head against Jack's shoulder.

Through my tears, I watched Dragon Lankford touch Jack's back gently. "Take her to your room. I'll call the vet and get something that will help her sleep. Stay close to her—she is grieving just like a cat will who loses her vampyre. She's a loyal girl," Dragon continued sadly. "His loss will be hard for her."

"I—I'll stay with her," Jack said, wiping his face with one hand

and petting Duchess with his other. Then Jack wrapped both arms around the big dog's neck as the warriors carried Stark's body from the field house.

It was only as they left the building that Neferet showed up. She was looking flushed and breathless. "Oh, no! Who is it?"

"It is the new fledgling, James Stark," Dragon said.

Neferet moved to the gurney and folded the blanket back. Everyone else was looking at Stark, but I couldn't make myself see his dead face, so I didn't take my eyes from Neferet. I was the only one who saw the flash of triumph and pure, undisguisable joy that radiated from her face. Then she drew a deep breath and turned back into a concerned High Priestess, saddened by the loss of a fledgling.

I thought I might throw up.

"Bring him to the morgue. I will see that he is properly tended," Neferet said. Without looking at me, she snapped, "Zoey, be sure the boy's dog is cared for." Then she motioned for the warriors to proceed and followed them from the field house.

For a second I couldn't speak. Her heartlessness mixed with Stark's death had cut me badly. I guess some little part of me, especially at a time like this when something unspeakably awful had just happened, still wished that she was the woman I'd believed her to be when I first met her—the mother who would love me for who I am.

I watched them carry Stark's body out and wiped my eyes with the back of my hand. There were people who needed me. People I'd made promises to. It was time I faced the fact that Neferet had gone bad and stopped being so damn weak.

I turned to Damien. "Stay close to Jack tonight. He needs your help more than I do."

"You'll be okay?" Damien asked me.

"I'll take care of her," Aphrodite said.

"So will we," both Twins said together.

Damien nodded, hugged me hard, and then went to Jack. He crouched next to his boyfriend and the dog and, hesitatingly at first, then with more confidence and warmth, began to pet Duchess.

"You're real bloody, you know?" Aphrodite said, pulling my attention from the heartbreaking scene of Damien and Jack trying to comfort Stark's dog.

I glanced down at myself. I'd stopped smelling the blood after I'd kissed Stark. I'd put it out of my mind so that the sweetness of it didn't drive me crazy, and I was surprised to see that my clothes were dark and sticky with his lifeblood.

"I need to get these clothes off," I said, sounding way shakier than I'd meant to sound. "I need a shower."

"Come on. I'll let you visit the spa," Aphrodite said.

"Spa?" I asked stupidly, not able to wrap my mind around what the hell she was saying. Stark had just died in my arms and she wanted me to go to a spa?

"Didn't you know I redid my bathroom shower?"

"Maybe Z wants to shower in her own room," Shaunee said.

"Yeah, maybe she wants her own stuff around her," Erin said.

"Yeah, well, maybe she doesn't want to remember that the last time she showered off blood, alone, in her own room, was after her best friend died in her arms," Aphrodite said. Then she added smugly, "Besides, I know for damn sure she doesn't have a step-in marble Vichy shower in her room, because mine is the only one on campus."

"Vichy shower?" I said, feeling a little like I was walking through a bad dream.

Shaunee sighed. "It's like a little slice of heaven."

Erin gave Aphrodite an appraising look. "You have one in your bathroom?"

"Part of the perks of being filthy rich and very, very spoiled," Aphrodite said.

"Uh, Z," Erin said slowly, moving her gaze from Aphrodite to me. "Maybe you should go to her spa. A Vichy shower is excellent for relieving stress."

Shaunee wiped her eyes and sniffled the last of her tears. "And we all know you got you some stress to deal with tonight."

"Okay, yeah. I'll go to Aphrodite's room to clean up." I moved woodenly out the door and walked between Aphrodite and the Twins.

I felt Stark's kiss on my lips all the way back to the dorm as the surreal croaking of ravens filled the night.

A Vichy shower turned out to be four big, fat shower heads (two from the ceiling and two from the sides of Aphrodite's marble shower) that poured a gazillion tons of soft, hot water all over my body all at the same time. I stood there and let it run down my body and wash Stark's blood from me. I watched the water turn from red to pink to clear, and something about the absence of his blood made me start to cry again.

It seemed ridiculous because I'd only known him for what was really only an instant in time, but I felt Stark's absence like it was a hole in my heart. How could that be? How could I miss him so much when I hadn't really known him? Or maybe I had known him—maybe there's something that happens between some people at a level that goes beyond time measurements and what society thinks is proper. Maybe what had happened between Stark and me in those few minutes in the field house had been enough to have our souls recognize each other.

Soul mates? Was that even possible?

When my head ached from crying and my tears finally ran out,

I got wearily out of the shower. Aphrodite had a big white bathrobe hung up on the bathroom door, which I slipped on before I went out into her ritzy room. Not surprisingly, the Twins had left.

"Here, drink this." Aphrodite handed me a glass of red wine.

I shook my head. "Thanks, but I don't really like alcohol."

"Just drink it. It's more than just wine."

"Oh . . ." I took it and sipped gingerly, like I thought it might explode. And it did—all inside my body. "There's blood in it." I didn't sound accusing. She knew that I'd already known what the "more than wine" comment meant.

"It'll help you feel better," Aphrodite said. "So will this." On the end table beside the chaise longue she pointed me to was a Styrofoam to-go box opened up to show a big greasy Goldie's cheeseburger and a larger order of fries with a bottle of brown pop—fully caffeinated and sugared, waiting next to it.

I gulped the last of the blood spiked wine and, surprising myself with how starving I felt, started wolfing down the burger. "How did you know I love Goldie's?"

"Everyone loves Goldie's burgers. They're terrible for you, so I figured you needed one."

"Thanks," I said through a full mouth.

Aphrodite grimaced at me, delicately plucked a fry off my plate, and then plopped down on her bed. She let me eat for a while and then, in a voice that was uncharacteristically hesitant, she asked, "So, you kissed him before he died?"

I couldn't look at her, and the burger suddenly tasted like cardboard. "Yeah, I kissed him."

"Are you okay?"

"No," I said softly. "Something happened between us and . . ." My voice trailed away as I couldn't find the words.

"What are you going to do about him?"

I did look up at her then. "He's dead. There's nothing—" I stopped. How could I have forgotten? Of course Stark's being dead wasn't necessarily the end of things, not at this House of Night, not lately. And then I remembered the rest of it. "I told him," I said.

"About?"

"That it might not be the end for him. Before he was gone, I told him that lately fledglings have been dying and then coming back from the dead to go through a different kind of Change."

"Which means if he does come back, one of his first thoughts will be of you, and the fact that you told him that death might not be the end for him. Let's hope Neferet isn't there to hear him."

My stomach clenched, partially with hope and partially with fear. "Well, what would you have done? Let him die in your arms without saying anything to him?"

She sighed. "I don't know. Probably not. You care about him, don't you?"

"Yeah, I do. I'm not sure why. I mean, sure he is, uh I mean *was* a hot guy. But he told me stuff before he died and we kinda connected." I tried to remember exactly what all Stark had told me, but it was all jumbled up with kissing him and watching him bleed to death in my arms. I shivered and took a long drink of brown pop.

"So, what are you going to do about him?" she persisted.

"Aphrodite, I don't know! Am I supposed to march down to the morgue and ask the Sons of Erebus to let me in so I can sit with Stark until he maybe comes back alive?" As I said it, I realized that's exactly what I wished I could do.

"That's probably not a good idea," she said.

"We don't know what happens, how fast, or if it will at all." I paused, thinking. "Wait, you said you saw Stark in one of my death visions, right?"

"Yeah."

"So what was on his face? A blue crescent, a red crescent, or full red tattoos?"

She hesitated. "I don't know."

"How can you not know? You said you recognized him from your vision."

"I did. I remember his eyes and that sinfully hot mouth of his."

"Don't talk about him like that," I snapped.

She actually looked guilty. "Sorry, I didn't mean anything. He really got to you, didn't he?"

"Yes. He got to me. So try to remember what he looked like in your vision."

She chewed he lip. "I don't remember hardly anything. I just got a quick glimpse of him."

My heart was beating hard, and my head was dizzy from the sudden rush of hope that washed over me. "But that means he's not really dead. Or at least not all the way dead. You saw him in a vision of the future, so he has to be around in the future. He's coming back!"

"Not necessarily," she said gently. "Zoey, the future is fluid—it's always changing. I mean, I saw you die twice. Once alone because you were isolated from your friends. Well, they're back to being your moronic Three Musketeers." She paused and added, "Sorry. I know you've been through a bunch of shit tonight. I didn't mean to sound so hateful. But here's the deal. Because the nerd—I mean because you're not isolated anymore, the Zoey-being-killed-alone vision is probably null and void. See, the future changed. When I had the vision that Stark was in at that time he might have been going to live. That could be all changed now."

"But not necessarily?"

"Not necessarily," she agreed reluctantly. "But don't get your hopes up. I'm just Vision Girl, not an expert on stuff like fledglings coming back alive."

"Then what we need is an expert on this whole dead/undead thing." I tried not to sound too hopeful, but I could tell by the sad way Aphrodite looked at me that I wasn't hiding much from her.

"Yeah, well, I hate to say it, but you're right. You need to talk to Stevie Rae."

"I'll go back to my room and call her and have her meet us at Street Cats tomorrow. You think you can keep Darius busy while I talk to her?"

"Oh, please. I'll do more than keep him busy. I'll keep him *totally occupied*." She purred the words.

"Ugh. Whatever. I just don't want to hear it or see it." Moving on a tide of optimism, I grabbed my brown pop.

"Not a problem there. I'll be happy to keep it private."

"Again I say *ugh*." I headed to the door. "Hey, how did you get rid of the Twins tonight? Am I going to have to do damage control tomorrow?"

"Simple. I told them if they stayed that we'd be giving each other spa pedicures, and that I was first in line."

"Yeah, I see why they bolted."

Suddenly Aphrodite turned serious. "Zoey, I mean it. Don't get your hopes up about Stark. You know that even if he comes back, he might not be the same. Stevie Rae says the red fledglings are better now, and they are, but they're not *normal*, and neither is she."

"I know all of that, Aphrodite, but I still say Stevie Rae is fine."

"And I still say we're going to have to agree to disagree about her. I just want you to be careful. Stark's not—"

"Don't!" I put up my hand to cut off her words. "Let me have a little bit of hope. I want to believe there might be a chance for him."

Aphrodite nodded slowly. "I know you do, and that's what worries me."

"I'm too tired to talk about this anymore," I said.

"Okay, I understand. Just think about what I've said." I started to open the door, and she added, "Do you want to stay here tonight? You wouldn't be alone."

"Nah, but thanks. And I'm not really alone in a dorm full of fledglings." With my hand on the knob, I looked over my shoulder at Aphrodite. "Thanks for taking care of me. I do feel better. A lot better."

She waved away my thanks and looked embarrassed. Then sounding more like herself she said, "Don't worry about it. Just figure once you're queen, you'll owe me."

Stevie Rae didn't answer her phone. It went straight to her perky, countrified voice mail. I didn't leave a message. What could I say, "Hi, Stevie Rae. It's Zoey. Hey, a fledgling just bled to death in my arms tonight, and I want to know what happens now. Is he going to come back as an undead dead bloodsucking monster, or is he going to be just kinda odd like you say your fledglings are, or is he gonna stay dead? I'd like to know 'cause even though I just met him, I really care about him. Okay, so call me back!" Uh, no. That wouldn't work.

I sat heavily on my bed and had just begun to wish Nala would show up when my kitty door opened, and my grumpy girl "*mee-uf-owed*" her way across the room, jumped up on my bed, and curled up on my chest, pressing her face against my neck and purring like crazy.

"I'm really, really glad to see you." I petted her ears and kissed the white spot over her nose. "How's Duchess?" She blinked at me, sneezed, and then pressed her head against me and purred some more. I took that to mean the dog was being well taken care of by Jack and Damien.

Feeling better now that Nala was working her purr magic on me, I tried to lose myself in the book I was reading, *Ink Exchange* by my current favorite vamp author, Melissa Marr, but not even her hot fairies could keep my attention from wandering.

What was I thinking about? Stark, of course. I touched my lips, still feeling his kiss there. What was wrong with me? Why was I letting Stark affect me so much? Okay, yes. He'd died in my arms and that had been awful, truly awful. But there was more than that going on between us, or at least I thought there might be. I closed my eyes and sighed. I didn't need to care about another guy. I wasn't over Erik *or* Heath.

Okay, the truth was I wasn't over Loren.

No, I wasn't in love with Loren. What I wasn't over was the pain he'd caused me. My heart still hurt, and it wasn't ready to let another guy in.

I remembered Stark taking my hand and weaving his fingers through mine and the way his lips had felt against my skin.

"Crap. I guess no one told my heart it wasn't ready for another guy," I whispered.

What if Stark did come back?

Worse—what if he didn't?

I was tired of losing people. A tear leaked out from under my closed eyelid and I brushed it away. I curled up on my side and pressed my face against Nala's softness. I was just tired. It had been a terrible day. Tomorrow wouldn't look so bad. Tomorrow I'd talk to Stevie Rae, and she'd help me make sense out of what to do about Stark.

But I couldn't sleep. My mind kept whirring around and around, focusing on the mistakes I'd made and the people I'd hurt. Had Stark died as some kind of penalty for how badly I'd hurt Erik and Heath?

No! My rational mind told me. *That's ridiculous! Nyx doesn't work like that.* But my guilty conscience whispered darker things. *You can't hurt people as badly as you hurt Erik and Heath without a payback.*

Stop it! I told myself. *Plus, Erik didn't look so devastated today. Actually he looked like a jerk, and not like someone whose heart was broken.*

No, that wasn't right either. Erik and I had been falling in love when I messed up with Loren. What did I expect Erik to do—walk around crying and begging me to come back to him? Hell no. I'd hurt him, and he really wasn't being a jerk—he was trying to protect his heart from me.

I didn't have to see Heath to know that I'd broken his heart, too. I knew him well enough to know exactly how badly I'd hurt him. He'd been a part of my life since we'd had our first crushes on each other in grade school. He'd always been there—from the puppy love stuff to the boyfriend/girlfriend middle school phase, to the "going out" stage in high school and, finally and more recently, the I've-Imprinted-him-and-want-to-suck-his-blood-and-whatnot stage. The whatnot is a nice way of saying that Imprinting and drinking a human's blood triggers sex receptors in the fledgling and the human's brains, so I had been thinking of doing more with Heath than just sucking his blood. Yes, I know that sounds skanky, but at least I'm being honest with myself.

So, Heath and I had Imprinted, but then I'd had sex with Loren and Imprinted with *him* during the Act (it's still weird to think that I'm not a virgin anymore—weird as in disturbing and kinda scary), which broke my Imprint with Heath. Painfully and horribly, if what Loren had told me was true. And I haven't talked to Heath since.

And Stark thought he was a coward for wanting to avoid pain? Compared to me, I'd definitely say not hardly. I wondered if the connection Stark and I had felt would have lasted through him finding out about all the stuff in my past. I mean, he'd come pretty clean with me, but I hadn't told him crap about myself.

And there was a lot of crap to tell. Not to mention a lot of loose ends I hadn't tied up.

I'd been avoiding Heath because I knew I'd hurt him. And, since I was being honest with myself, I had to admit that another part of why I'd been avoiding Heath had a lot to do with being afraid of his reaction to me.

Heath was nothing if he wasn't dependable. I could depend on the fact that he was crazy about me. I could depend on the fact that he'd been my boyfriend (sometimes whether I wanted him to be or not) since third grade. I could depend on the fact that he'd always been there for me.

Suddenly I realized that I needed Heath. Tonight I felt bruised and battered and confused, and I needed to know that I hadn't lost all of them . . . that one of them really loved me, even if I didn't deserve it.

My cell phone was charging on my nightstand. I flipped it open and quickly text-messaged him before I could chicken out.

How r u?

I'd start simple, just a little message. When he answered, *if* he answered, I'd go from there.

I curled back up with Nala and tried to sleep.

After what seemed like forever, I checked the time. It was almost 8:30 A.M. Okay, so, Heath was asleep. He was still on winter break, and if the kid didn't have to get up and go to school, he slept until noon. Literally. *So he's asleep,* I repeated stubbornly to myself.

That wouldn't have mattered before, my mind lectured me right back. *Before he would have texted me back in about a second and begged me to meet him somewhere. Heath would never have slept through a text from me.*

Maybe I should call him.

And hear him tell me he doesn't ever want to see me ever again? I chewed my lip and felt sick. No. No, I couldn't do that. Not after what had happened tonight. I couldn't bear to hear him say mean things to me. Reading them would be bad enough.

If he answered.

Cuddling with Nala, I tried to focus on her purr engine and let it drown out the silence of my cell phone.

Tomorrow, I told myself as I started to drift off to restless sleep. *If I don't hear from Heath tomorrow, I'll call him.*

Right before I fell completely asleep, I swear I heard the creepy sound of a raven right outside my window.

CHAPTER FOURTEEN

I hadn't needed to set my alarm to go off at five o'clock that evening (which is really my morning—remember, a fledgling's day and night are mixed up, as in our school starts at 8 P.M. and ends at 3 A.M.). I'd been lying there wide awake, petting Nala and trying not to think about Stark or Heath or Erik when my alarm beeped at me.

Groggily I stumbled around my room, pulling on a pair of jeans and a black sweater. I stared at myself in the mirror. Okay, just ugh. I had to get some sleep tonight—the bags under my eyes had bags.

Nala had just arched her back and hissed at the door when someone pounded on it.

"Zoey! Would you hurry the hell up?"

I opened the door to see a disgruntled Aphrodite dressed in a very short (and very cute) black wool skirt, a deep purple pullover, and to-die-for black boots. She was tapping one of those boots in irritation.

"What?" I said.

"I know I've told you this before, but you are slow as a fat kid on crutches," she said.

"Aphrodite, you're mean. I know I've told you that before, too," I said, trying to blink the grogginess from my eyes and somehow think it from my mind. "And I'm not slow, I'm ready," I finally added.

"No, you're not. Your Mark isn't even covered."

"Ah, jeesh. I forgot about—" My eyes automatically went to her forehead, which was completely clear of a fledgling Mark.

"Yeah, one of the few advantages of pretending that I'm a fledgling is that I don't have to worry about covering up my Mark when I go off campus." Aphrodite's tone was flippant, but I could see the hurt in her eyes.

"Hey, remember what Nyx said. You're still special to her."

Aphrodite rolled her eyes. "Yeah, *special*. Whatever. Would you just hurry up? Darius is waiting, and you still have to tell Shekinah I'm going with you."

"And I need my bowl of cereal," I said as I slathered concealer on over the intricate tattoos of my Mark.

"No time for that," Aphrodite said while we hurried down the stairs. "We have to get to Street Cats before the stupid humans close up shop and scuttle away to their ridiculously middle class homes."

"*You're* a stupid human," I whispered.

"I'm a *special* human," she corrected me, and in an equally low voice, she continued. "When's Stevie Rae meeting us? She'll be cool if we're a little late, right?"

"Ah, crap!" I whispered. "I didn't get her last night."

"I'm not surprised. Cell service in those tunnels sucks. I'll make excuses to Darius about why you're late. You call her again. This time let's hope you get her."

"I know, I know," I said.

"Hey, Z!" Shaunee called as Aphrodite and I passed by the kitchen.

"How are ya feelin' this morning? Better?" Erin asked.

"I am—thanks, guys," I said, smiling at them. The Twins were beyond resilient. It took more than another brush with death to freak them out for very long.

"Excellent. We got your box of Count Chocula right here," Erin said.

"Hey, Dorkamese Twins, you two want to take me up on some pedicures tonight? We can do some major nerd herd bonding over the wicked bunion I have on my right foot." Aphrodite lifted up her right stiletto boot and pretended like she was going to unzip it.

"We have your breakfast ready, too, Aphrodite," Erin said.

"Yeah, we fixed you up a nice bowl of Count Skankula," Shaunee said.

"You two are so not amusing. Zoey, I'll get Darius and we'll meet you in the parking lot. Hurry up." She flipped her hair and twitched away.

"We hate her," Erin and Shaunee said together.

"I know," I sighed. "But she really was nice to me last night."

"Probably because she has a serious personality disorder," Erin said.

"Yeah, I think she's one of those split-personality people," Shaunee said. "Hey, maybe she'll get institutionalized pretty soon!"

"Excellent thinking, Twin. I like it that you always look on the bright side," Erin said.

"Here, Z. Have some cereal," Shaunee said.

I sighed at the enticing box of my favorite cereal. "I don't have time to eat. Gotta get to Street Cats and set up our community charity work."

"You should talk them into having a cool flea market sale," Erin said.

"Yeah. We need to do some serious closet cleaning to get ready for the season change, and we might as well sell the old stuff to make room for the new," Shaunee said.

"That's not a bad idea, actually. Plus, Street Cats could have the sale inside so the sun doesn't bother us," I said.

"Twin, let's go through our shoes," Shaunee said.

"Will do, Twin," Erin said. "I hear metallic is majorly in for next season."

I left the dorm on a tide of the Twins' new-shoe-purchase chatter.

The Son of Erebus warrior who was stationed outside wasn't Darius, but he was equally as big and bad looking, and he gave me a quick respectful salute. I returned it and then hurried down the sidewalk toward the main school building, nodding hi to the fledglings coming and going. Flipping open my cell phone, I punched the number of the disposable phone I'd given to Stevie Rae a few days ago. Thankfully, this time she answered on the first ring.

"Hey there, Zoey!"

"Oh, thank god." I didn't say her name, but I still kept my voice low. "I tried to call you earlier, but I couldn't get you."

"Sorry, Z. Reception down in the tunnels is crappy."

I sighed. We'd have to do something about that, but right now I couldn't take the time to think of what. "Well, never mind that. Can you meet me at Street Cats in a little while? It's important."

"Street Cats? Where's that?"

"It's at Sixtieth and Sheridan in that cute little brick building. The one behind Charlie's Chicken. Can you be there?"

"Yeah, I guess. I'll have to take the bus, so it may take me a little while. Wait, can't you come get me?"

I'd opened my mouth to explain why I couldn't give her a ride and also why it was so important I talked to her today, when the background noise of a scream followed by some truly scary-sounding laughter came through her phone.

"Um, Zoey. I gotta go," Stevie Rae said.

"Stevie Rae, what's going on?"

"Nothin'," she said too quickly.

"Stevie Rae—," I began, but she cut me off.

"They're not eatin' anybody. Really. But I gotta go make sure the pizza delivery guy doesn't remember too much of this particular delivery. See you at Street Cats—bye!"

And she was gone. I closed the phone (and wished I could close my eyes and curl into a fetal position and go back to sleep). Instead I walked through the big wooden, castlelike doors of the main entrance of the central House of Night. We don't have what you'd call a principal's office, but we do have an area manned by an attractive young vampyre named Miss Taylor. She's actually not a secretary, but an acolyte of Nyx. Damien had explained to me that part of her priestess training was to provide service for a House of Night—hence the fact she could be found busily answering phones, making copies, and running errands for the professors when she wasn't setting the chapel up for rituals and whatnot.

"Hi there, Zoey," she said with a sweet smile.

"Hi, Miss Taylor. I'm supposed to tell Shekinah who's going with me to Street Cats, but I don't have a clue where she is."

"Oh, she's made the Council Room her office when she's not teaching. And since first hour hasn't started yet, she's there right now."

"Thanks," I called as I hurried down the hall to the left and then up the circular staircase that led to the library and the Council Room across the hall from it. I wasn't sure if I should just go on in or not, and I was just raising my hand to knock when Shekinah's clear voice called, "You may enter, Zoey."

Jeesh, vamps were so scary with their weird we-know-who's-gonna-call-before-they-call thing. I straightened my shoulders and went in.

Shekinah was wearing a black dress that looked like it was made of velvet, with the silver embroidered insignia of Nyx, a woman's silhouette with her arms upraised and cupping a moon, on her breast. She smiled at me and I was struck anew at her exotic beauty and the sense of age and wisdom that surrounded her.

"Merry meet, Zoey," she said.

"Merry meet," I replied automatically.

"How are you today? I hear that one of our young fledglings died last night and that you were witness to his passing."

I swallowed. "Yes, I was with Stark when he died. And I'm as okay as I can be today."

"Do you still feel up to visiting Street Cats? You know it could be a difficult first meeting."

"I know, but I still want to go. It helps if I stay busy."

"Very well. You know yourself best."

"I'd like to take Aphrodite with me, if that's okay with you."

"She's the fledgling with the earth affinity, isn't she?"

I gave a quick, nervous nod and said, "Earth is the affinity Nyx gave her." Okay, well, it wasn't technically a lie.

"Earth is a calming influence. Usually those with an affinity for it are well grounded and dependable. You made an excellent choice as to who should accompany you today, young priestess."

I tried not to look guilty. Aphrodite grounded and dependable? As the Twins would say, please just please. "Well, she and Darius are waiting for me, so I better go."

"Just a moment." Shekinah glanced down at a paper she held in her hand and then passed it to me. "Here is your new class schedule. With my approval, Neferet has transferred you from an entrylevel of Vampyre Sociology to a sixth former level of the class." She looked pointedly at my unusual Mark, already filled in even though I am still definitely a fledgling. And of course, no vamp or fledgling has ever had the expanded tattoo Marking I have down my neck, shoulders, back, and waist. Shekinah couldn't see those, but her knowing gaze said that she was more than aware they were there. "You're too unusually developed to stay in such a simplistic level of sociology. I have a feeling, and your High Priestess agrees, that you are going to need to know details about vampyre life a normal third former would not need to know."

"Yes, ma'am," was all I could think to say.

"Putting you in the advanced class has altered your schedule somewhat. I've made sure you're excused today until after lunch. Just be sure you've returned by then, and that you attend the correct classes."

"Okay, I will. Oh, would you make sure Aphrodite is excused, too?"

"I've already done that," she said.

I swallowed hard. "Well, thanks. I mean, thank you." As usual, the uber-knowledge of the vamps made me extremely nervous. "Um, I was thinking that I would suggest to the Street Cats people that the Dark Daughters sponsor a flea market–like sale, with the money going to them. Do you think that would be okay?"

"I think it's a lovely idea. I'm sure the Dark Daughters and Sons will have some interesting items to sell."

I thought about the Twins' designer shoe horde, Erik's collection of *Star Wars* action figures (who knows—he might have grown out of them now that he's an "adult" vamp), and Damien's obsession for braided hemp choker necklaces, and I had to agree with her. "Yeah, interesting is a good way to describe the stuff."

"I'm giving you the autonomy to decide how you want to proceed with your charity work. I agree with you that more interaction with the local populace is a good idea. Segregation breeds ignorance, and ignorance breeds fear. I've already begun working with the local police about the murders, and I agree with them that it seems to be the work of a very small, very disturbed group of humans. I do have my doubts about allowing you to interact with humans right now, but I believe the good in your idea outweighs the risks."

"So do I."

"And you will be well protected in the company of Darius."

"Yeah, he reminds me of a mountain," I said without thinking, then blushed at my moronic description.

But Shekinah smiled. "He does, indeed, remind one of a mountain."

"Okay, well, I'll let you know how it goes with Street Cats."

"Please do report back to me tomorrow. Speaking of tomorrow, I've decided to call a special New Year's Ritual in which we will focus on cleansing the negative energy from the school. After the deaths of the two professors and now this poor fledgling, the grounds need a powerful, thorough cleansing. I've heard that you're very familiar with cleansing rituals, as you were raised to be aware of your Native American heritage."

"Yes!" I couldn't keep the surprise out of my voice. "My grandma still follows the Cherokee ways."

"Good. Then I'll count on you and your group of very gifted peers to perform the cleansing ritual. Tomorrow is New Year's Eve, so let's plan the ritual to begin at midnight. We will call in the new year with a schoolwide cleansing near the east wall."

"The east wall? But that's where . . ." I trailed off, feeling sick.

"Yes, that is where Professor Nolan's body was left. It is also a place of great power, and thus it should be the focal point of your cleansing."

"Isn't that what Neferet did when she performed her ritual there?" Neferet had performed a kind of funeral service for Prof Nolan at the place her body had been found. That had also been when Neferet cast a strong spell around the school that would let her know whenever anyone came or went from the House of Night.

"Cleansing and protection are two very different things, Zoey. Neferet was focusing on protection at that time, which was a perfectly admirable response to such a tragedy. There has been time for our heads to clear now, and it is time to look to the future. For that, we need to cleanse the past. Do you understand?"

"I think so," I said.

"I'll look forward to your circle," she said.

"Me, too," I lied.

"Be vigilant and wise today, Zoey."

"I'll do my best," I said. I gave her a respectful salute and a little bow as I left.

So I had to lead a cleansing ritual for the whole school tomorrow—minus my earth element—even though everyone believed Aphrodite still had her affinity for earth. Well, everyone believed Aphrodite was still a fledgling, too. Oh, jeesh. I was in serious trouble. Again.

CHAPTER FIFTEEN

Trying to keep from freaking out totally about the cleansing ritual, I checked my new schedule while I hurried toward the parking lot. Well, Shekinah had been right—switching me to an upper level of Vamp Sociology had messed up my schedule, shuffling around my first four classes and totally moving drama from second hour to fifth hour, right before the only class that had stayed the same, my Equestrian Studies class.

"Great," I mumbled to myself. "So besides a totally messed-up ritual, I have class with Erik to look forward to." I was trying to keep my empty stomach from turning inside out when I spotted Aphrodite and Darius standing beside a very cool black Lexus. Okay, actually I spotted Darius and his huge muscular self. Aphrodite was standing in his shadow, batting her eyes at him.

"Sorry I took so long," I said as I got into the backseat of the car. Aphrodite, who slid gracefully into the passenger's side, said, "Hey, no problem. Don't stress about it."

I rolled my eyes. Now it was okay for me to be late? Jeesh, she was so transparent.

"Uh, Aphrodite," I said sweetly as Darius pulled smoothly off school grounds. "Be sure to mark your calendar for midnight tomorrow."

"What?" She shot me a look over her shoulder that clearly said she wished I'd disappear into the leather upholstery so she could be alone with Darius.

"Tomorrow—midnight—you—me—Damien—the Twins— big circle casting and cleansing ritual in front of the entire school."

Her blue eyes got all round and startled looking. "That's going to be—," she began, sounding breathless and semi-hysterical.

"Fun!" I inserted the word before she could say something like *a total disaster*.

"I'm looking forward to it," Darius said, smiling warmly at Aphrodite. "The power of your circle is unique."

I could see Aphrodite pulling herself together so that when she returned Darius's smile, she sounded like her normal flirty (and slightly bitchy) self when she said, "Well, *unique* is definitely one way to describe it."

"I have never known so many powerfully gifted fledglings," Darius said.

"Honey, you have no idea how *gifted* I am," she said breathily, leaning toward him and laughing softly.

Yeah, I thought as I sat there chewing the inside of my cheek practically raw and worrying while Aphrodite flirted out-rageously and a little nauseatingly with Darius, *he and everyone else—except for Aphrodite and Stevie Rae—really have no idea about what's really going on with us.* Hell, not that the three of *us* actually knew exactly what was going on, much less what we were going to do when we had to cast a circle minus one of the five elements. I remembered what had happened when Aphrodite had tried to invoke earth in her dorm room, and I knew it would be more than obvious to anyone watching that she no longer had her earth affinity. And how were we going to explain that?

Damien and the Twins would probably get pissed at me all over again for keeping this new thing from them. Great.

What I needed was a major distraction during the circle casting so no one would notice the lack-of-an-earth-affinity detail. Okay, no. What I really needed was a vacation. Or an extra-strength Advil.

I pawed around in my purse, looking for the Advil and couldn't find any—of course, drugs don't work on fledglings very well, so it probably wouldn't help my headache anyway. Didn't look like I was going to get the distraction, either. What it looked like I was going to get was typical for me—more trouble and stress and probably a nice dose of raging diarrhea.

Darius didn't have any trouble finding the Street Cats building. It was a cozy-looking square brick building with big front windows crowded with cat stuff. I made a mental note to pick up a little something for Nala from their gift shop. My cat was grumpy enough without her thinking that I'd been cheating on her (translation: I would smell like a zillion other cats) and hadn't even brought her a present.

Darius held the door open for Aphrodite and me, and we entered the brightly lit shop area of the building. Yes, all three of us had on sunglasses, but the lights still bothered our eyes. I glanced at newly re-human Aphrodite. Well, they bothered at least two sets of our eyes.

"Welcome to Street Cats. Is this your first visit?"

I looked from Aphrodite to the—

Nun?!

I blinked in surprise and felt the urge to rub my eyes. The nun smiled up at me from her seat behind the front counter, deep brown eyes looking alive and sparkly in a pale face that was obviously old but surprisingly smooth and framed by a white-cuffed, black nun-hat thing.

"Young lady?" she prompted me, her smile not fading.

"Oh, uh, yeah. I mean, yes. This is the first time I've been to Street Cats," I said not brilliantly. My mind was racing. What was a nun doing here? Then from my side vision, I glimpsed another black-robed figure flit by and realized there were *more* nuns in the hallway off the gift shop. Nuns? Was there a whole flock of them here? Wouldn't they totally freak when they found out vampyre fledglings wanted to do charity work for Street Cats?

"Well, excellent. We always welcome first-time visitors. What is it Street Cats can do for you?"

"I didn't know the Benedictine sisters were involved with Street Cats," Aphrodite surprised me by saying.

"Why, yes. We've been running Street Cats for the past two years. Cats are very spiritual creatures, don't you think?"

Aphrodite snorted. "Spiritual? They've been killed for being witches' familiars and in league with the devil. If a black one walks across their path, people think it's bad luck. Is that what you mean by spiritual?"

I wanted to smack her for how disrespectful she sounded, but the nun wasn't ruffled at all. "Don't you think that is because cats have always been so closely associated with women? Especially those considered wise women by the general public? So, naturally, in a predominately male-dominated society, a certain type of people would see sinister things in them."

I felt Aphrodite's little start of surprise. "Yes, that's what I think. I'm surprised you think so, too, though," she said honestly. I noticed Darius had stopped pretending to shop and was listening to their exchange with obvious interest.

"Young lady, just because I have a wimple over my head, it

doesn't mean it has kept me from thinking *or* having a mind of my own. And I can guarantee you I have had many more run-ins with male domination than have you." Her smile made her words less harsh than they might have been.

"Wimple! That's what it's called," I heard my stupid mouth blurt, and then felt my cheeks burn as they turned bright red.

"Yes, that is exactly what it is called."

"I'm sorry. I've—I've never met a nun before," I said, and blushed some more.

"That's not surprising. There really aren't many of us. I'm Sister Mary Angela, prioress of our little abbey and manager of Street Cats." She turned her smile on Aphrodite. "Did you recognize our order because you're Catholic, child?"

A little burst of laughter came out of Aphrodite. "I'm definitely not Catholic. I am the daughter of Charles LaFont, though."

Sister Mary Angela nodded in understanding. "Ah, our mayor. Then, of course, you're familiar with the charitable work our order does." Then her brows lifted as she realized what else it meant that Aphrodite was the only daughter of Tulsa's mayor. "You are a vampyre fledgling."

She didn't sound overly freaked, but I decided this was as good a time as any to let the nun know Satan was in the house. I took a deep breath and held out my hand for her to shake, saying in one big rush: "Yes, Aphrodite is a fledgling and I'm Zoey Redbird, vampyre fledgling and Leader of the Dark Daughters."

Then I waited for the explosion, which didn't happen.

Sister Mary Angela took her time before responding. Then she took my hand in her firm, warm grip. "Greetings, Zoey Redbird." She looked carefully from me to Aphrodite and then to Darius, who she raised one gray brow at and said, "You look rather mature for a fledgling."

He nodded his head in a small respectful bow. "You are observant, Priestess. I am an adult vampyre, a Son of Erebus."

Oh, great. He'd called her priestess. Again I waited for a freak-out that didn't come.

"Ah, I see. You're the fledglings' escort." She turned her attention back to me. "Which means you two must be important young women to warrant such attention."

"Well, like I said, I'm the Leader of the Dark Daughters and—"

"We're important," Aphrodite interrupted me again, "but that's not the only reason Darius is with us. Two vampyres have been murdered in the past couple days, and our High Priestess wouldn't let us leave campus without protection."

I gave Aphrodite a WTF look. It really wasn't like her to have diarrhea of the mouth.

"Two vampyres have been killed? I had heard of only one murder."

"Our Poet Laureate was killed three days ago." I couldn't say his name.

Sister Mary Angela looked upset. "That is dreadful news. I will add him to our prayer list."

"You'd pray for a vampyre?" The question seemed to escape my mouth without warning me first, and I felt my cheeks get warm again.

"Of course I would, as would my sisters."

"I'm sorry. I don't mean to be rude, but don't you think that all vampyres are doomed to hell because we worship a goddess?" I asked.

"Child, what I believe is that your Nyx is just another incarnation of our Blessed Mother, Mary. I also believe devoutly in Matthew 7:1, which says 'Judge not, that ye be not judged.'"

"Too bad the People of Faith don't believe like you do," I said.

"Some do, child. Try not to paint them all with the same brush. Remember that the *judge not* goes both ways. Now, what can Street Cats do for the House of Night?"

My mind was still having trouble grasping the fact that this nun was so totally okay with vampyres, but I mentally shook myself and focused enough to say, "As the Leader of the Dark Daughters, I thought it would be a good idea if we got involved with a local charity."

Sister Mary Angela's warm smile was back. "And, naturally, you thought of cat rescue."

I returned her smile. "Yes! The truth is, I haven't been Marked very long, and I think it's weird that even though our school is smack in the middle of Tulsa, we're so isolated from the city. It just doesn't feel right to me." She was really easy to talk to, and I found myself opening up to her. "That's what brought me—" I caught Aphrodite's frown from my side vision and hastily added, "*us*—that's what brought *us* here. We thought it would be cool if we could volunteer to help with the cats, and also raised money for Street Cats. Like maybe we could sponsor a flea market and give you guys the money we make."

"We're always in need of money and experienced volunteers. Do you own a cat, Zoey?"

My grin widened. "Actually Nala owns me, and she'd tell you that if she were here."

"You do, indeed, have a cat," she said. "And what about you, Warrior?"

"Nefertiti, the most beautiful calico in the world, chose me as her own six short years ago," Darius said.

"And you?"

Aphrodite looked like she wanted to fidget, and I suddenly realized that I'd never seen a cat with her.

"No. I don't have one," Aphrodite said. When the three of us stared at her, she shrugged uncomfortably. "I don't know why, but no cat picked me."

"Do you not like them?" the nun asked.

"I like them okay, I guess. It just seems they don't like me," Aphrodite admitted.

"Huh," I said with a little too much suppressed amusement, and she glared at me.

"That's quite all right," Sister Mary Angela inserted smoothly. "We can still put a willing volunteer to work."

Jeesh, the nun wasn't kidding about putting us to work. I told her we had time to give her a couple of hours or so before we had to head back to school, and she started cracking the whip. Aphrodite automatically coupled up with Darius, clearly enjoying her part in the whole "keep the warrior busy so Zoey can rendezvous with Stevie Rae" (who had not shown yet) plan, and Sister Mary Angela sent the two of them into the cat room to clean litter boxes and brush cats with the two other nuns on duty, Sister Bianca and Sister Fatima, who Sister Mary Angela had introduced to the three of us very matter-of-factly, like it was totally normal that fledglings and vampyres (with their Marks covered) were volunteering in the community. I'm not a particularly slow learner, so by this time I'd stopped waiting for a nun freak-out, and it dawned on me that these religious women were a whole different type of "religious" than my horrid step-loser and his People of Faith sycophants. (Yes, thank Damien for my increased vocab.)

Sadly, Sister Mary Angela sent me to inventory hell. Apparently the nuns had just gotten in a shipment of various cat toys—a *big* shipment, like a massive box of more than two hundred feathery, mousey, catty toys—and Sister Mary Angela ordered me to log each separate (and annoyingly perky) cat whatnot into their computer system. Oh, and she also quickly taught me to use their "newfangled" (the nun's word for it) cash register computer system, and then she gave me a stern, "We'll stay open late tonight, and you are in charge of the store," and disappeared into the office that sat beside the boutique part of the store and across the hall from the cats waiting to be adopted.

Okay, it wasn't like she actually left me "in charge." I could see Sister Mary Angela through the big glass window that took up almost all the wall space on that side of the room, which meant that she could also see me. Yes, she was mega-busy, making calls and doing other important looking stuff, but I did feel her eyes on me pretty often.

Still, I have to admit that I thought it was cool that Sister Mary Angela—a woman who was supposed to be married to God— was so accepting of us. It made me wonder about if I really had been, to use some of the nun's words, incorrectly painting all religious folks (except for Nyx's religious folks) with the same brush. I don't particularly like to admit when I'm wrong, especially since I seem to have had to do a lot of that kind of admitting lately, but these wimpled women had definitely given me something to think about.

So I was pondering much deeper religious stuff than was my norm, and literally up to my elbows in cat stuff when the door chimed cheerily and in walked Stevie Rae.

We grinned at each other. I cannot tell you how amazing it is to see my best friend not dead. Not even undead. She looked like *my* Stevie Rae again with her short curly blond hair, her dimples, and her familiar Roper jeans with a button-up shirt (sadly) tucked into them. Yes, I love the girl. No, she doesn't have very good fashion sense. And *no,* I was not going to let what was Aphrodite being her usual bitchy self make me doubt my BFF.

"Z! Ohmygood*ness,* I've missed you! Hey, did you hear the news?" she said all in a rush in her adorable Okie twang.

"News?"

"Yeah, about the—"

But she was interrupted by a sharp rap on the window of Sister Mary Angela's office. The nun's silver brows lifted questioningly. I pointed to Stevie Rae and mouthed, *my friend.* The nun drew a little pretend crescent moon in the middle of her forehead with her finger and then pointed at Stevie Rae (who was staring at Sister Mary Angela with her mouth unattractively flopped open). I nodded vigorously. The prioress gave me a quick nod, smiled, and waved a welcome to Stevie Rae, and then went back to her phone-calling.

"Zoey!" Stevie Rae whispered. "That's a nun."

"Yes," I said in a normal voice. "I know. Sister Mary Angela runs this place. There are two more nuns back in the cat room with Aphrodite and the Son of Erebus she's keeping busy with some seriously disgusting flirting."

"Bleck! Aphrodite and her flirting is so nasty. But, more importantly, nuns?" Stevie Rae blinked in confusion. "And they know we're fledglings and stuff?"

I guessed she was referring to herself with the *and stuff* comment, so I nodded. (Well, I certainly wasn't going to try to explain to the nuns about red vamps.) "Yep. Apparently they're okay with us 'cause they think Nyx is just another form of the Virgin Mary. Plus it seems nuns are not into judging others."

"Well, I like the whole not-judging part, but Nyx and the Virgin Mary? Ohmygood*ness,* that is the weirdest thing I've heard in a long time."

"Which must make it majorly weird, 'cause I imagine being dead and then undead you heard some very weird stuff," I said.

Stevie Rae nodded solemnly and said, "So weird that, like my daddy would say, it'd knock a buzzard off a meat wagon."

I shook my head, grinned, and threw my arms around her. "Stevie Rae, you crazy kid, I've missed you!"

CHAPTER SIXTEEN

Our big hug was broken up by an annoying waterfall of Aphrodite giggles tumbling down the hall from the cat room to us. Stevie Rae and I rolled our eyes together.

"What did you say she was doin' back there, and with who?"

I sighed. "We were only allowed to leave campus with an escort from the Sons of Erebus, so this warrior named Darius—"

"He must be hot if Aphrodite is makin' such a fuss over him."

"Yeah, he's definitely hot. Anyway, Darius said he'd escort me and Aphrodite. She said she'd keep him busy so that we could talk."

"Bet that's a real hardship for her," Stevie Rae said sarcastically.

"Please—we all know she's kinda skanky," I said.

"Kinda?"

"I'm trying to be nice," I said.

"Oh, right. Okay. Me, too. So she's keeping this hot warrior busy so me and you can talk."

"Yeah, and—"

Two more raps on the window had Stevie Rae and me looking up at Sister Mary Angela, who said, "Less talk—more work!" loud enough for us to hear her through the glass.

Stevie Rae and I nodded briskly like we were scared of her. (Uh, who *isn't* scared of nuns?)

"You go through the box and pull out all of those little gray-

and-pink polka-dotted mice—the ones stuffed with catnip—and hand them to me. I'll keep clicking them into the inventory thing," I said, holding up the weird gun-looking apparatus the nun had taught me how to work. "We'll talk while I count cat toys."

"Okey-dokey." Stevie Rae began pawing through the big brown UPS box.

"So what were you saying about some news?" I asked, clicking off the mice she handed me like I was a shooter at one of those back-in-the-day arcade games.

"Oh, yeah! You will *not* believe it! Kenny Chesney is comin' in concert to the new BOK Arena!"

I looked at her. And looked at her some more. And then some more. Without saying anything.

"What? Ya know I love me some Kenny Chesney."

"Stevie Rae," I finally managed. "With all of the crap going on, I do not know how you can take time to obsess about one country music dork."

"You take that back, Z. He is so not a dork."

"Fine. I take it back. You're the dork."

"Fine," she said. "But when I figure out how to get Internet access down in the tunnels so I can get tickets online, do not ask me to get one for you."

I shook me head at her. "Computers? Down in the tunnels?"

"Nuns? At Street Cats?" she countered with.

I took a deep breath. "Okay, point made. Stuff is very weird right now. Let's start over. How have you been? I've missed you."

Stevie Rae's frown was instantly replaced by her dimpled grin. "I've been just fine. How 'bout you? Oh, and I've missed the heck outta you, too."

"I've been confused and stressed," I said. "Hand me some of those purple feather toys. I think we're all done with the gray-and-pink mice."

"Well, there're lots of purple feathers, so we're set for a while." She started handing me the long freaky-looking toys. (I definitely wasn't going to get one of those for Nala—she'd probably blow up like a big puffer fish at it.) "So, what kind of confusion and stress? The normal stuff or new-and-improved stress stuff?"

"New and improved, of course." I met Stevie Rae's eyes and, keeping my voice really low, said, "Last night a fledgling named Stark died in my arms." I paused while Stevie Rae flinched, as if what I'd just said had hurt her physically. But I had to continue. "Do you have any idea if he'll come back?"

Stevie Rae didn't say anything for a while, and I let her get her thoughts together while she handed me cat toys. Finally she looked up and met my eyes again. "I wish I could tell you that he was going to come back—that he was going to be okay. But I just don't know."

"How long does it take to know?"

She shook her head, looking really frustrated now. "I don't know! I can't remember. Back then, days didn't mean anything to me."

"What do you remember?" I asked gently.

"I remember waking up and I was hungry—so hungry, Zoey. It was terrible. I had to have blood. She was there, and she gave it to me." Stevie Rae grimaced with the memory. "From her. I fed from her first thing when I woke up."

"Neferet?" I whispered the name.

Stevie Rae nodded.

"Where were you?"

"In that terrible morgue room. You know, it's off from the side of the school by the south wall and the pine trees there. It has the cremation thing in it."

I shuddered. I did know about the cremation thing. All the

kids knew about it. That's supposedly where Stevie Rae's body had gone.

"Then what happened? I mean, after you fed?"

"She took me to the tunnels and the rest of the kids. She used to visit us a lot. Sometimes she'd even bring street people for us to eat." Stevie Rae looked away, but not before I saw the pain and guilt that filled her eyes. She was such a sweet soul—such a good girl—remembering how it was when she had been losing her humanity must be awful for her. "It's hard for me to think about it, Zoey. And it's even harder for me to talk about it."

"I know, I'm sorry, but this is important. I have to know what will happen if Stark comes back."

Stevie Rae looked me square in the eyes, and suddenly her voice was that of a stranger. "I don't know what will happen. Sometimes I don't even know what will happen to me."

"But you're different now. You're Changed."

Her expression shifted, and I saw anger in Stevie Rae's eyes. "Yeah, I've Changed, but it's not as simple as what happens to regular vamps. I still have to choose my humanity, and sometimes that choice isn't as black-and-white as you'd think it would be." Her gaze sharpened. "You said the dead kid's name was Stark? I don't remember anyone with that name."

"He was new. He'd just transferred from the House of Night in Chicago."

"What was he like before he died?"

"Stark was a good guy," I said automatically, and then I paused, realizing that I hadn't really known what kind of a guy he was, and for the first time I wondered if maybe the attraction I'd felt for him had tainted how I saw him. He had admitted to killing his mentor—how could I have overlooked that so easily?

"Zoey? What is it?"

"I was starting to like him. *Really* like him, but I didn't know him very well," I finally said, suddenly reluctant to tell Stevie Rae everything about Stark.

Her expression softened, and she looked like my BFF again. "If you care about him, you're going to have to get to the morgue and get him out of there. Keep him somewhere for a few days, and see if he comes back. And if he does, he's going to be hungry and probably a little crazy when he wakes up. You'll have to feed him, Zoey."

I passed a shaky hand over my forehead, wiping my hair from my face. "Okay . . . okay . . . I'll figure it out. I'll just have to figure it out."

"If he does wake up, bring him to me. He can stay with us," Stevie Rae said.

"Okay," I repeated, feeling utterly overwhelmed. "There's just so much stuff going on at the House of Night right now. It's different than it was before."

"Different like how? Tell me, and maybe I can help you figure this out."

"Well, for one thing, Shekinah showed up at the House of Night."

"That name sounds familiar. Like she's a big deal or somethin'?"

"She's a major big deal, as in the leader of all vamp High Priestesses. And she pretty much told Neferet right in front of the Council."

"Dang, wish I could have seen that."

"Yeah, it was great, but kinda scary, too. I mean, if Shekinah has enough power to put Neferet in her place—well, that's just plain scary."

Stevie Rae nodded. "So what did Shekinah say?"

"You know Neferet had closed the school, even though she called off winter break and made everyone come back."

"Yeah." Stevie Rae nodded again.

"Shekinah reopened the school." I leaned closer to Stevie Rae and lowered my already mostly whispery voice before I continued. "And she called off the war."

"Ooooh! I know that pissed off Neferet," Stevie Rae whispered back.

"Absolutely. Shekinah seems okay, or at least as far as I can tell. But see what I mean about her being scarily powerful?"

"Yeah, but it also looks like you might have someone on your side who is actually a bigger deal than Neferet. She did stop the war, which is a good thing."

"It is a good thing, but Shekinah also wants to have a major cleansing ritual performed for the school. I'm performing the ritual. Me with my group of uber-gifted fledglings. You know: the Twins, water and fire—Damien, who is Mr. Air—and, to top it all off, Aphrodite embodying earth, of course."

"Uh-oh," Stevie Rae said. "Uhm, Z, does Aphrodite have any affinity with earth anymore?"

"Absolutely none," I said.

"Can she fake it?"

"Absolutely not."

"She tried?"

"Yep. The green candle zaps her and flies out of her hand. She's not just minus earth, she's minus earth squared."

"That is a problem," Stevie Rae agreed.

"Yep. A problem I'm sure Neferet will somehow twist into having happened because there's something wrong with me. Or worse, something wrong with Aphrodite, Damien, and the Twins."

"Dang, that sucks. I really wish I could help." Then she brightened. "Hey! Maybe I can! What if I sneak into the ritual and hide behind Aphrodite? I'll bet if you focus on me when you call earth, and I focus on earth at the same time, the candle will light and everything will look practically normal."

I opened my mouth to say thanks but no thanks—it'd be too easy for her to get caught and then for everyone to find out about her. But then I closed my mouth. Just exactly what would be so wrong about Stevie Rae being found out? Not caught hiding and sneakily being part of a ritual, of course, but just *found out*. The warm, familiar feeling inside me told me I just might be flailing down the right path (for a change).

"Something like that might just work."

"Really? You want to hide me? Okey-dokey, just tell me when and where."

"What if we didn't hide you? What if we outed you instead?"

"Zoey, I love Damien and all, but I'm really not gay. I mean, I haven't had an official boyfriend in a really long time, but I still get kinda warm and tingly when I think about how cute Drew Partain is. Do you remember how he was likin' me before I got all dead and crazy?"

"Okay, first—yes. I remember that Drew liked you. Second, you're not dead and crazy anymore, so he would probably still like you—that is if he knew you were alive. Which brings me to my third point: When I said we should out you, I didn't mean as in you being gay. I meant as in you being *you*." I made a little figure flutter toward the colored-in scarlet tattoos on her face that she'd carefully concealed before going out in public.

Stevie Rae gaped at me for a little while, looking seriously shocked. When she finally spoke, her voice sounded choked. "But they can't know about me."

"Why not?" I asked calmly.

"Because if they find out about me, they'll find out about the others."

"So?"

"That would be bad," she said.

"Why?"

"Zoey. Like I said before, they're not normal fledglings."

"Stevie Rae, what difference does that make?"

She blinked at me. "You don't understand. They're not normal, and I'm not normal."

I looked at her for a long time, considering what I knew—that Stevie Rae had been given back her humanity, and what I half suspected but didn't want to admit—that even though she had her humanity back, she still had dark places within herself that I couldn't understand.

I knew I had to make a decision. I either trusted her, or I didn't. And when it came right down to it, that was really an easy decision to make.

"I know you're not exactly like you used to be, but I trust you. I believe in your humanity, and I always will."

Stevie Rae looked like she might cry. "Are you sure?"

"Totally."

She drew a deep breath. "Okay, then what's your plan?"

"Well, I haven't really thought this through, but it seems to me that the vamps and fledglings should know about you and the rest of the others, especially now that another fledgling has died. We don't know everything we wish we did about you, but we are pretty sure that Neferet somehow created you guys, or at least opened some kind of weird door so you could be created, right?"

"I think so. The truth is, I still worry that the fledglings might be able to be controlled, or at least influenced by her, even though they are different now and she's been leaving us alone."

"So doesn't it make sense that it's bad that Neferet is the only adult vamp who knows about you guys? Especially if she can still have some kind of control over you? Especially now that there might be a new red fledgling getting ready to wake up?" And then another thought hit me. "Stark had a special gift. He never missed what he aimed at with his bow and arrows. I mean never."

"She would for sure want to use him," Stevie Rae said. "Before my Change, she was for sure using the others, or at least trying to." She shrugged apologetically. "I'm really sorry that I can't really remember the stuff that happened before I Changed, and the rest of the kids say their memories aren't so good around then, either. I can only guess at most of this stuff."

"Well, from what little I saw, it was obvious Neferet was up to no good."

"Not a big surprise, Z," she said.

"I know. But that brings us back to other vamps knowing about you guys. If you're out in the open, it stands to reason that Neferet would have a harder time using you for her own bizarre little take-over-the-world evil plot."

"Does she have a plot like that?"

"I dunno. Sounds like something she'd have, though."

"True," Stevie Rae said.

"So? What do you think?"

She didn't answer for a while, and I kept my mouth shut and let her think. This was a big deal. As far as either of us knew, Stevie Rae and the red fledglings were something that had never before existed. If Stark didn't die, if he woke up as a red fledgling, Stevie Rae would be the first of a new kind of vampyre, and being the first of something was a serious responsibility. I definitely knew about that.

"I think you might be right," she finally said in a voice that was barely louder than a whisper. "But I'm scared. What if the normal vamps think we're freaks?"

"You're *not* freaks," I said with way more conviction than I actually felt. "I'm not gonna let anything happen to you or them."

"Promise?"

"Promise. Plus, it's perfect timing. Shekinah is more powerful than Neferet, and there's a whole buttload of Sons of Erebus warriors around the school."

"How does that help me?"

"If Neferet loses her mind, they can handle her."

"Zoey, I don't want you to use this as an excuse to openly take on Neferet," Stevie Rae said, looking suddenly kinda pale.

Her words gave me a little jolt of shock. "I'm not!" I said much too loud, and then continued in a lowered voice. "I wouldn't use you like that."

"I don't mean that you set this up on purpose to get at Neferet. I just mean that I don't think it's smart for you, or any of us, to come out against her so publicly, and I don't think it matters all that much that the Sons of Erebus and Shekinah are here. There's something more going on with Neferet than just her normal craziness. I know it deep inside me. I can't remember what I know, but she's dangerous. Really, really dangerous. Something basic has changed about her, and that change is not a good thing."

"I wish you could remember what all happened to you."

Stevie Rae grimaced. "I do, too, sometimes. And then sometimes I'm really, *really* glad I can't. What happened to me wasn't good, Zoey."

"I know," I said solemnly.

We counted cat toys silently for a while, both lost in thoughts of death and darkness. I couldn't help thinking about how awful it had been when Stevie Rae had died in my arms—and then how nightmarish the aftermath of that had been when she was undead and struggling not to let her humanity slip completely away. I looked at her and saw she was chewing her lip nervously as she searched for more purple feathered toys in the box. She looked scared and young and, despite her new powers and responsibilities, way too vulnerable.

"Hey," I said softly. "It's gonna be okay. I promise. Nyx has to be all in the middle of this."

"Which means the Goddess is on our side?"

"Exactly. So tomorrow at midnight we perform the cleansing ritual over by the east wall." I didn't need to add that it was a place of power as well as a place of death. "Think you can get on campus and hide nearby until I call earth to the circle?"

"Yeah," she said reluctantly, clearly not one hundred percent in agreement with me yet. "So if I do come, do you think I should bring the other kids with me?"

"You decide about that. If you think bringing them is best, then I'm all for it."

"I'll have to think about it. I'll have to talk to them."

"Okay, no problem. I trust your judgment on whether you decide to come and if you decide to bring the fledglings."

She grinned at me. "It's really good to hear you say that, Z."

"I mean it, too." Then—because even though she'd grinned at me, she still looked so worried and undecided about what to do—I temporarily changed the subject while she thought about it. "Hey, want to know some more of my new-and-improved stress?"

"Definitely."

"When we're done here, I have to go back to class, and since my schedule is changed around this semester, I get still get to go to drama class today, which will be taught by the ever-popular, ever-hating-my-guts, newest professor at the House of Night: Erik Night."

"Uh-oh," Stevie Rae said.

"Yeah, I'm not exactly expecting an A."

"There's one way he might give you an A, though," she said, grinning mischievously.

"Don't even start. I'm done with sex. Finished. Through. I've totally learned my lesson. Plus, it's really nasty of you to say I'd trade sex for an A."

"No, Z. I wasn't talkin' 'bout Erik givin' you an A for sex. I was talkin' 'bout him givin' you a big ol' embroidered scarlet A for your shirt."

"Huh?" I said, clueless as usual.

She sighed. "As in *The Scarlet Letter*. The heroine had to wear it on her shirt 'cause she messed up and slept around. You really need to read more, Zoey."

"Oh, yeah. And thanks for that lovely analogy. Makes me feel oh-so-better."

"Don't get mad." She threw a feathery cat toy at me. "I was just kiddin'."

I was still frowning at her when her cell phone rang. Stevie Rae looked at the number and sighed. She glanced quickly over at Sister Mary Angela, whose head was squarely in front of her computer, and then answered. "Hey there, Venus, what's up?" She sounded purposefully perky. There was a pause while she listened, during which her perkiness faded. "No! I told you I'd be back soon and *then* we'd all get somethin' to eat." Another pause—more frowning—and she said, half turning away from me and lowering her voice, "No! I said we'd get some*thing* to eat and not some*one* to eat. Y'all just be good. I'm gonna head back in a little while. Bye-bye."

Stevie Rae turned back to me with a fake smile plastered on her worried face. "So, what were we sayin'?"

"Stevie Rae, please tell me those kids are not eating people."

CHAPTER SEVENTEEN

"Of course they aren't eatin' people!" Stevie Rae put an appropriate amount of shock in her voice—so much so that we saw Sister Mary Angela's wimple lift from the computer and she turned a frown in our direction.

We waved and smiled and held up cat toys. She gave us a long look, but pretty soon her face softened into her warm smile, and she turned her attention back to the computer screen.

"Stevie Rae, what is really going on with those kids?" I whispered as I zapped more purple-feathered monstrosities into the inventory.

She shrugged way too nonchalantly. "They're just kinda hungry. That's all. You know kids—they're always hungry."

"Which means they're getting dinner from where?"

"Pizza delivery guys mostly," she said.

"They're eating pizza delivery guys?" I whispered frantically.

"No! We call on a cell and give the address of one of the downtown buildings close to the depot and the entrance to our tunnels. Mostly we say we're workin' overtime at the PAC or that we live in the Tribune Lofts, and then we wait for the pizza guy to deliver." She hesitated.

"And?" I prompted impatiently.

"And then we meet the delivery guy on his way into the build-

166

ing and take the pizzas and I make him forget he saw us and then he goes on about his business and we eat the pizza not the guy," she said all in one long rush.

"You're stealing pizzas?"

"Well, yeah, but it's better than eating the delivery guys, isn't it?"

"Uh, yeah," I said, rolling my eyes at her. "And you're also stealing blood from the downtown blood bank?"

"Again, better than eating the delivery guys," she said.

"See, these are just more reasons why we have to out you."

"'Cause we're stealing pizzas and blood? Do we really have to tell the vamps? I mean, I think we'll have enough issues to deal with without bringing up those little minor indiscretions."

"No, not 'cause you're stealing, 'cause you guys don't have money or any way to *legally*," I said, giving her a hard look, "take care of yourselves."

"Makes me wish Aphrodite would come back with me. She has major money and more than one gold card," Stevie Rae muttered.

"Then you'd have to put up with her," I said.

Stevie Rae frowned. "I really wish I could mess with the inside of her head like I do the pizza guys. I'd give her a big dose of 'be nice,' and we'd all live happily ever after."

"Stevie Rae, you really can't keep living in those tunnels."

"I like the tunnels," she said stubbornly.

"They're nasty and damp and dirty," I said.

"They're better now than they were last time you saw them, and they'd be *lots* better if they were fixed up a little more."

I stared at her.

"Okay, maybe more than a little."

"Whatever. My point is, you need the money and the power and the protection of the school behind you."

Stevie Rae met my eyes steadily, and all of a sudden she looked way older and more mature than I'd ever seen her look before. "The money and the power and the protection of the school didn't help Professor Nolan or Loren Blake or even that Stark kid."

I didn't know what to say. She was right, but I still felt deep in my gut that people—specifically vampyre people—needed to know she and the red fledglings existed. I sighed. "Okay, I know it's not a one hundred percent good plan, but I honestly believe everyone needs to know about you guys."

"Honestly, as in Nyx is giving you one of those *you need to do it* feelings?"

"Yep," I said.

Her sigh was much deeper and filled with more worry and stress than mine. (Jeesh, who knew *that* could happen?) "All right, then. I'll be there tomorrow. I'm countin' on you to make this all turn out okay, Zoey."

"I will." Silently I sent a short prayer up to Nyx: *I'm counting on you like she's counting on me . . .*

Stevie Rae and I had finished the seemingly unending cat-toy inventory about the time I glanced up at the clock and realized we were going to be late getting back to school if we didn't hurry like crazy. And of course, Stevie Rae had to get back to her group of fledglings before they committed more than petty pizza theft. So we said a quick bye, and I repeated that I'd see her the next day for her outing. She looked a little pale, but gave me a hug and promised to be there. Then I stuck my head in Sister Mary Angela's office.

"Excuse me, ma'am." I wasn't sure exactly what to call a nun when one was being ultra-respectful and needed to get her attention while she was definitely engrossed in what looked like instant messaging on her laptop.

The *ma'am* seemed to work just fine, because she looked up at me with her warm smile. "All done with the inventory, Zoey?"

"Yes, and we have to get back to school."

Sister Mary Angela glanced up at the clock, and her eyes widened in surprise. "My goodness! I had no idea it was so late. And I forget that your days are rather upside down."

I nodded. "It must seem like we keep weird hours to you."

"I'll just think of you as nocturnal—much like our lovely felines. You know they prefer the night, too. Which reminds me, how would you like it if we extend our hours on Saturday nights so that can be your volunteer day?"

"That sounds great. I'll run it by our priestess to make sure, though, and call you. Oh, and do you want me to go ahead with the flea market idea?"

"Yes. I put in a call to our Board of Church Directors, and after a slight discussion, they agreed the idea was a good one."

I noticed the hardening in her voice and the way her already straight spine seemed to grow even straighter. "Not everyone is okay with fledglings, huh?" I said.

Her hard look warmed. "That is not for you to worry about, Zoey. I've often forged my own path and am used to taking a machete to weeds and other bothersome barriers."

I felt my eyes get big and didn't doubt for a minute that this tough nun's meaning might not be only figurative. And then part of what she'd said made me ask, "When you said that you had to check with your Board of Church Directors, did you mean they were from your church, or others?"

"They aren't from our abbey, which isn't exactly a church, because our only congregation is made of Benedictine sisters. The Church Board of which I was speaking is made of several of the leaders of local churches."

"Like the People of Faith?"

She frowned. "Yes. The People of Faith have a rather large representation on the Board, which reflects their congregation size."

"Bet they were the weeds you had to chop down," I muttered.

"Pardon me, Zoey. I didn't quite catch that," she said, eyes squinting impishly with the smile she was trying (unsuccessfully) to hide.

"Oh, nothing. I was just thinking out loud."

"A terrible habit, and one that can get you in much trouble if you're not careful," she said, smiling fully.

"Don't I know it," I said. "So you're sure the flea market will be okay? You know, if it's too much hassle, we can figure out some other way to—"

Sister Mary Angela's raised hand shut me right up. She simply said, "Get with your High Priestess and see what day next month would be good for your school for the flea market. We shall accommodate ourselves to your schedule."

"Okay, good," I said, feeling proud of myself for how well my community service idea was working out. "I better get Aphrodite and go now, though. We were excused from only the first part of our classes today, and we gotta get back."

"I believe your friends have been finished for a while now, but they have been rather—" She paused, eyes twinkling again. "—distracted."

"Huh?" I was feeling kinda shocked. It was cool that Sister Mary Angela wasn't freaked about fledglings and vampyres in general, but to have her be oh-so-amused by Aphrodite's gross flirtation with Darius was totally too liberal—even for me.

Obviously the nun must have been able to guess what I was thinking by the look on my face, because she laughed, turned me around by my shoulders, and gave me a gentle push out of her office and toward the cat kennel. "Go on—you'll see what I mean," she said.

Totally confused, I walked down the short hallway to the room that held cats available for adoption. There were no nuns around, but (sure enough) Aphrodite and Darius were sitting over in the "playground for cats" corner, snuggled together like lovers with their backs turned to me. They were doing something (ugh) with their hands. Actually, it looked like they were doing a lot of something with their hands (double ugh). I cleared my throat dramatically. Instead of jumping apart guiltily as they should have, Darius glanced over his shoulder at me and grinned—Aphrodite (the ho) didn't even turn to look to see who had just walked in on them. Jeesh, I could have been a nun or someone's mom.

"Uh, I really hate to interrupt this cozy little scene, but we gotta go," I said sarcastically.

With a big sigh, Aphrodite finally turned around, saying, "Fine. Let's go. But I'm taking her with us." And I saw what it was that she and Darius had been doing with their hands.

"It's a cat!" I said.

Aphrodite rolled her eyes. "No shit? Imagine that—there's a cat at Street Cats."

"It's an ugly cat," I continued.

"Don't call her that." Aphrodite was instantly defensive as she struggled to stand up while clutching the ginormic white cat in her arms. Taking her elbow, Darius made sure Aphrodite didn't fall back on her butt. "She's not ugly. She's unique, and I'm sure quite expensive."

"She's a Street Cats cat," I said. "She only costs an adoption fee, same as all the rest of them."

Aphrodite stroked the cat absently, and it closed the beady eyes that sat in its totally smushed face and started to purr, skipping beats every now and then, like a missing engine, which probably meant she was full of hairballs. Aphrodite ignored the messed-up purring and smiled lovingly down into the cat's flat face. "Maleficent is clearly a purebred Persian who ended up in these dire circumstances because she is the sole survivor of an awful tragedy." Aphrodite wrinkled up her perfect nose, and her haughty gaze took in the neat cages that were filled with all different sizes and shapes of cats. "She definitely doesn't belong in such an ordinary place."

"Did you say her name is Maleficent? Isn't that the name of the evil witch in *Sleeping Beauty*?"

"Yes, and Maleficent was way more interesting than that sickeningly sweet, goody-goody Princess Aurora. Plus I like her name. It's powerful."

I reached out hesitantly to pet the huge cat ball of white fur. Maleficent opened her eyes to slits and growled menacingly at me. "Maleficent's root word is *malevolence*," I said, pulling my hand quickly out of her paw range.

"Yes, and *malevolence* is a powerful word," Aphrodite said, making kissing noises at the beast.

"Is she declawed?" I asked.

"Nope," Aphrodite said happily. "She could put an eye out with those big paws of hers."

"Lovely," I said.

"I think she's as unique and beautiful as her new mistress," Darius said. I noticed that when he petted Maleficent, the cat narrowed her eyes at him but didn't growl.

"And I think your judgment is impaired. But whatever. Let's go. I'm starving. I didn't get any breakfast, and we've already missed lunch, so we're gonna have to grab something quick on the way back to school."

"I'll get Maleficent's things," Darius said, striding to the side of the room to pick up a neat little bag that had *For Your New Kitty* written in lovely cursive script on the side of it.

"Did you already pay for her?" I asked.

"She absolutely did," said Sister Mary Angela from the doorway. I noticed she walked carefully around Aphrodite and Maleficent, staying well out of paw range. "It's just wonderful that the two of them have found each other like this."

"You mean no one else could touch the cat?" I asked.

"Not one single person," Sister Mary Angela said with a big grin. "At least not until lovely Aphrodite stepped through the doors of the kennel. Sister Bianca and Sister Fatima said it was nothing short of a miracle how Maleficent took to Aphrodite immediately."

Aphrodite's smile was one hundred percent authentic, and it made her look young and heartbreakingly gorgeous. "She was waiting for me," she said.

"Yes," the nun agreed. "She was, indeed. You two are a good match." Then she looked at me and Darius, including all of us in her next words. "I think Street Cats and the House of Night is a good match, too. I feel great things for us in the future." Then she raised her right hand over us and said, "Go forth under the watchful eye of our Blessed Mother."

We mumbled our thanks to Sister Mary Angela. I had the weird urge to give her a hug, but her outfit—the whole wimple and black robe/dress thing—didn't seem conducive to hugs. So instead I did a lot of what felt like overexuberant grinning and waving as we left the building.

"You were grinning and waving like a fool," Aphrodite said as she waited for Darius to open her door and help her and the tail-twitching, flat-faced Maleficent into the front seat of the Lexus.

"I was being polite. Plus, I like her," I said, opening my own door. I slid into the backseat and after strapping on my seat belt looked up into the glaring eyes of Maleficent, who was stretched out across Aphrodite's chest and over her shoulder so that she could hang halfway over the seat and stare at me. "Uh, Aphrodite, shouldn't you put her in a cat carrier or something?"

"Oh my god! Are you mean and hateful or what? Of course she doesn't ride in a cat carrier." Aphrodite stroked the beast, causing white fur to float all around us like a disgusting cat hair shower.

"Jeesh, never mind. I was just thinking of the cat's safety," I lied. Actually, I was thinking of my safety. Maleficent looked like she'd love to have a big bite of Zoey for dinner. Which reminded me. "Hey, I'm starved," I told Darius as he started the car. "We gotta stop somewhere quick so I can eat something."

"Fine with me. What do you want?" he said.

I glanced at the time on the car dash. Unbelievably, it was after 11 P.M. "Well, the time is definitely going to limit what's open." I heard Aphrodite whisper something about "stupid going-to-bed-early humans" to Maleficent, which I ignored. I looked around, trying to remember what decent fast food places (that is, Taco Bueno and Arby's versus McDonald's and Wendy's) were close by. And then a lovely and familiar aroma drifted through the cracked windows of the Lexus to me. My mouth had already started to water when I spotted the big yellow-and-red sign next door. "Oh, yum! Let's go to Charlie's Chicken!"

"It's awful greasy," Aphrodite said.

"That's part of its deliciousness. Heath and I used to eat there all the time. It fulfills all the basic food groups: grease, mashed potatoes, and brown pop."

"You're disgusting," Aphrodite said.

"I'll pay," I said.

"Done deal," she said.

CHAPTER EIGHTEEN

Darius volunteered to stay in the car and babysit Maleficent while Aphrodite and I got something to eat, which I thought was above and beyond the call of duty.

"He's way too good for you," I told Aphrodite. For as late as it was, Charlie's was really busy, and sheeplike, we jostled around with the rest of the herd animals, finally getting in line behind an obese woman who had really bad teeth and a balding guy who smelled like feet.

"Of course he's too good for me," Aphrodite said.

I blinked in surprise at her and said, "Excuse me? I couldn't have heard you right."

Aphrodite snorted. "You think I don't know I'm awful to my boyfriends? Please—I'm selfish, not stupid. Darius will probably get sick of my crap within a couple months. I'll dump him right before he dumps me, but at least it'll be a fun ride till then."

"Did you ever think about being nice and not putting him through your usual crap?"

Aphrodite met my eyes. "Actually, I have been thinking about it and may consider changing things up with Darius." She paused and added. "She chose me."

"She who?"

"Maleficent."

"Well, yeah, she chose you. She's your cat. Just like Nala chose me and Darius's cat, whatever her name is . . . uh . . ."

"Nefertiti," Aphrodite said.

"Yeah, Nefertiti, she chose him. So what's the big deal? Happens all the time. Cats choose their fledglings, or sometimes their vamps. Most every vamp eventually gets one and—"

And I suddenly realized why the cat choosing her had made such an impact on Aphrodite.

"It makes me belong," she said quietly. "Somehow I'm still a part of the whole"—she paused, talking so low, I had to lean into her to hear her—"I'm still part of the whole vamp thing. It means I'm not totally an outsider."

"You couldn't be an outsider," I whispered back. "You're part of the Dark Daughters. You're part of the school. And most important, you're part of Nyx."

"But since this happened"—she brushed her hand across her forehead where she hadn't needed any makeup to cover the Mark that no longer was there—"since this happened, I haven't really felt like I was a part of anything. But Maleficent changed that."

"Huh," I said, more than a little taken back by Aphrodite's sincerity.

Then she shook herself, shrugged, and—looking much more like the Aphrodite we all knew and couldn't stand—said, "Whatever, though. My life still sucks. And after I eat this cheap, greasy crap with you, I'll probably break out."

"Hey, a little grease is good for your hair and nails. Kinda like vitamin E." I bumped her shoulder. "I'll even order for you."

"Could I have something diet?"

"Please. There's nothing diet about Charlie's."

"They have diet pop," she said.

I sneered down at her size 6 perfectness. "Not for you."

Since it really was fast food, it didn't take long to fill our order, and Aphrodite and I found a semi-clean table and started shoving greasy fried chicken and catsup-slathered fries into our faces. Now, don't get me wrong. Even though I was shoveling in the chicken and fries 'cause we needed to get back to school and it was rude to lounge around while Darius babysat Aphrodite's cat from hell, I savored every bite. I mean, after a couple months of really nutritious, excellent food from the House of Night cafeteria, my taste buds needed a dose of disgustingly delicious and utterly not-good-for-me food. Yum. Seriously.

"So," I said between bites, "Stevie Rae and I talked."

"Yeah, I thought I heard her twang out there in the other room." Aphrodite picked delicately at a drumstick and wrinkled her nose at me when I added salt to the already totally salty fries. "You're going to bloat like a dead fish."

"If I do, I'll just wear sweats until I pee it out." I grinned around a big bite of chicken.

She shuddered. "You're so gross. I cannot believe we're friends, which proves I'm in the middle of a personal crisis. Anyway— what's up with Stevie Rae and the zoo animals?"

"Well, we didn't really talk about her or the other kids very much," I said, not willing to tell Aphrodite that Stevie Rae admitted to not being herself.

"So since you didn't talk about the crazies much, my guess is Stark was who you did talk about."

"Yeah. It's not good."

"Well, no. The kid's dead. Or possibly undead. Either isn't very good. What did Stevie Rae say about the time frame for him coming back? Or do we just wait till he starts to stink and figure he's not going to wake up."

"Don't talk about him like that!"

"Sorry, I forget that you had a thing with him. What did Stevie Rae say?"

"Sadly, she couldn't give me many specifics. Her memory of everything before she Changed is pretty sketchy. Her best advice was to steal his body and see if he wakes up. And if he does wake up, he'll need to be fed right away."

"Fed? As in a burger and some fries, or fed as in opening a vein?"

"Your second guess is the right one."

"Oh, ugh. I know you've gotten all into the bloodsucking-back-and-forth stuff, but it still squees me out."

"It squees me out, too, but there's no denying the power of it," I admitted uncomfortably.

She gave me a long contemplative look. "The Sociology book says it's a lot like sex. Maybe even better."

I shrugged.

"You're going to have to do better than that. I want details."

"Okay. Yeah. It's a lot like sex."

Her eyes widened. "And it's good?"

"Yes. But what happens because of it isn't always good." I thought about Heath and decided it was definitely time to change the subject. "Anyway, I'm supposed to figure out a way to get Stark's maybe-temporarily-dead body and hide it somewhere we can, in theory, watch it to see if he wakes up. Then we feed him—"

"Uh, don't you mean *you* feed him? I say a big *No Way* about having anything to do with that kid biting me."

"Yes, I mean I have to feed him." A fact that was more than a little appealing to me, even though I definitely wasn't going to discuss that with Aphrodite. "I'm clueless about how I can steal him or hide him."

"Well, he's going to be hard to move, especially since I'm assuming Neferet is keeping her beady eyes on him."

"You assume right—at least that's what Stevie Rae says." I took a long drink of my brown pop.

"Sounds like you need a nanny cam," she said.

"Huh?"

"You know, one of those hidden cameras rich mommies use to watch their precious babies while they're at the country club drinking martinis at eleven o'clock in the morning."

"Aphrodite, you're from a whole different world."

"Thank you," she said. "Seriously, a nanny cam would work. I could pick one up at RadioShack. Isn't that Jack kid good with electronics?"

"Yeah," I said.

"He could install it in the morgue, and you could keep the monitor in your room. Hell, I could probably even buy the kind that comes with a portable monitor, so you could carry it around with you."

"Really?"

"Totally."

"Excellent! It was freaking me more than I can say to think about putting Stark in my closet."

"Uh, puke." We chewed happily for a while, and then Aphrodite said, "So what else did the bumpkin have to say?"

"Actually, we talked about you," I said smugly.

"Me?" Aphrodite narrowed her eyes.

"Well, honestly, only a little. Mostly we talked about her stepping into the earth position during the cleansing ritual tomorrow."

"You mean like hiding behind me and trying to make it look like I'm invoking earth, but she'll really be doing it?"

"Uh, no. Not exactly. I mean like you stepping aside and letting Stevie Rae take her old place in the circle."

"In front of everybody?"

"Yep."

"You're kidding, right?"

"Nope."

"And she's going to do it?"

"Yep," I said with way more confidence than I actually felt.

Aphrodite chewed quietly for a while, and then she nodded slowly. "Okay, I get it. You're counting on Shekinah saving your ass."

"*Our* asses, actually. Which includes you, me, Stevie Rae, the red fledglings, and Stark—if he undeads. I figure if everyone knows about them, it'll be harder for Neferet to use them for her own evil means."

"Sounds very B movie."

"It might sound cheesy like that, but it's not. I'm dead serious about it. We all better be. Neferet is scary. She tried to start a war with humans, and I don't think she's done trying. Plus," I added hesitantly, "I have a bad feeling."

"Shit. What kind of bad feeling?"

"Well, honestly, I've been trying to ignore it, but I've had a bad feeling about Neferet ever since Nyx appeared to us."

"Zoey, get serious. You've had a bad feeling about Neferet for months."

I shook my head. "Not like this. This is something different. Something worse. And Stevie Rae feels it, too." I hesitated again, and then added, "And after whatever it was jumped me yesterday, the night has been scaring me."

"The night?"

"The night," I repeated.

"Zoey, we are creatures of the night. How can the night scare you?"

"I don't know! All I know is that it feels like there's something out there watching me. What do you feel?"

Aphrodite sighed. "About?"

"About the night or Neferet or whatever! Just tell me if you've noticed any new negative vibes."

"I don't know. I haven't been thinking about vibes and such. I've been kinda busy with my own issues."

I kept my hands busy with the chicken and fries so that they didn't reach over and strangle her. "Well, why don't you spend some time thinking about it? I mean, it is a little important." I lowered my voice, even though everyone was too busy ingesting their own grease to pay much attention to us. "You did have those visions about me being killed. Two of those visions, and at least one of them involved Neferet."

"Yeah, and that could account for your new 'bad feeling' about her." She air-quoted around the words *bad feeling*. "And me telling you I saw your death can't help your creep-out factor."

"It seems like more than that to me. Lots of stuff has happened to me the past couple months, and until recently I've never felt afraid. I mean honestly, make-me-want-to-cry afraid. I—" My words broke off when a familiar laugh made me glance up at the entrance to the dining room. And all the breath seemed to rush out of my body, just like someone had punched me in the gut.

He was carrying a tray filled with his favorite combo meal (the Number 3, with extra-large fries), along with a tiny kids' meal. You know, one of those meals that girls get when they're on a date so they look like they don't eat much, and then they go home and snarf down the refrigerator when they're alone. The girl with him wasn't carrying anything, but she was sticking her hand in his front pocket (front! pocket!), playfully trying to cram a wad of bills into it. But he is majorly ticklish, which is why, even though he was unnaturally pale and had bruised-looking dark circles under his eyes, he was laughing like a total moron while she smiled up at him with a flirty little grin.

"What's wrong?" Aphrodite said.

When I just sat and stared and couldn't answer, she swiveled around in her chair to see what I was gawking at.

"Hey, isn't that what's-his-name? Your old human boyfriend?"

"Heath," I said, barely able to whisper the word.

It should have been utterly impossible. We were way across the room and there's no way he could have heard me, but the moment his name left my lips, his head jerked up and his eyes instantly found me. I saw the laughter that had been on his face die. His body shuddered—actually shuddered—as if the first sight of me had caused a jolt of pain to pass through him. The girl at his side stopped playing with his pocket. She followed the direction he was looking, saw me, and her eyes got huge. Heath looked quickly from me to her, and I saw rather than heard him say, "I need to talk to her." The girl nodded solemnly, took the tray, and went to a table that was as far away from mine as she could get. Then Heath walked slowly over to me.

"Hello, Zoey," he said in a voice so strained, he sounded like a stranger.

"Hi," I said. My lips felt frozen and my face seemed to be getting hot and cold at the same time.

"So you're okay? You're not hurt or anything like that?" he said with a quiet intensity that made him look a lot older than eighteen.

"I'm fine," I managed to say.

He blew out a big puff of air like he'd been holding his breath for days, wrenched his gaze from me, and then stared off into the distance, as if he couldn't stand to see me. Pretty soon he seemed to pull himself together and turned back to me. "Something happened the other night—," he began, but broke off and pulled his gaze from me to glance meaningfully at Aphrodite.

"Oh, uh, Heath, this is my, uh, my friend from, from the, uh, House of Night, Aphrodite," I stammered, barely able to make my voice work.

Heath looked from Aphrodite to me questioningly.

When I didn't say anything, Aphrodite sighed, and with her usual sarcastic, long-suffering tone said, "What Zoey means is yes, it's okay to talk about Imprints and stuff like that in front of me." She paused, and raised her brows at me. When I still didn't say anything else, she prompted, "He *can* talk in front of me. Isn't that right, Zoey?" When I still couldn't make myself speak, she shrugged and continued, "Unless you want to talk to him alone. I'm cool with that. I'll just wait in the car and—"

"No! You can stay. Heath, you can talk in front of Aphrodite." I finally managed to break through the word dam that pain had formed in the back of my throat.

Heath nodded and looked quickly away from me, but not before I saw the flash of hurt and disappointment that shadowed his soft brown eyes.

Okay, I knew he wanted to talk to me alone.

But I couldn't. I couldn't be alone with him and his hurt feelings. Not yet. Not so soon after losing Loren and Erik and Stark. I couldn't stand hearing him tell me how much he hated me now and how sorry he was that we'd ever been together. He wouldn't say all of that in front of Aphrodite. I knew Heath. Yes, he'd break up with me, but (unlike Erik) there wouldn't be any public name-calling that might cause an ugly scene. Heath's mom and dad had raised him right. He was a gentleman, through and through, and he always would be.

When he looked back at me, his expression was carefully blank again. "Okay. Like I was saying. Something happened the other night. I think the Imprint between us is broken."

I managed to nod.

"So it's gone. For real?"

"Yes. It's gone for real."

"How?" he asked.

I drew a deep breath and said, "It was broken when I Imprinted with someone else."

He'd been looking down at me with his head kinda bowed a little, and when I spoke, his face jerked up as if I'd slapped him. "You were with another human?"

"No!"

His jaw clenched and unclenched before he said, "Then it's that fledgling you told me about? That Erik guy?"

"No," I said softly.

This time he didn't look away—didn't make any attempt to hide the pain in his eyes or his voice. "There's someone else? Someone besides the guy you already told me about?"

I opened my mouth to tell him that there *had been* someone else, but that there wasn't anymore, and that it had all been a big mistake anyway, but he didn't let me talk.

"You *did it* with him."

Heath didn't say it like a question, but I nodded anyway. He already knew—he had to. Our Imprint had been strong, and even if he hadn't felt what was going on with Loren and me through it, he would have guessed that something major had to have happened to break the bond we'd shared together.

"How could you, Zo? How could you do that to me? To us?"

"I'm sorry, Heath. I never meant to hurt you. I just—"

"No!" He raised his hand like he could hold off my words. "Didn't mean to hurt me is bullshit. I've loved you since I was in grade school. You being with someone else *hurts me*. No way it can't."

"You're with someone else tonight." Aphrodite's cool words seemed to cut the air between the three of us.

Heath's eyes flashed when he rounded on her. "I let a *friend* talk me into leaving the house for the first time in days. A *friend*," he repeated. Then he turned back to me, and I noticed again how pale and sick he looked. "It's Casey Young. Remember her? She used to be your friend, too."

I glanced over at the table where Casey was sitting by herself, looking more than a little uncomfortable. I hadn't even noticed it was her when they'd walked in. Now I recognized her thick auburn hair, pretty honey-colored eyes, and her cute, freckly complexion. Heath was right—she had been a friend of mine. Not a best friend, like Kayla, but we'd hung out. Heath had always treated her like a little sister. She'd liked him, but I'd never felt the I-wanta-steal-your-boyfriend vibe from her like I'd felt way too many times from my supposed BFF Kayla. Casey saw me looking at her, and hesitantly, she raised her hand and waved sadly at me. I managed a little wave back.

"Do you know what happens to the human when an Imprint breaks?" Heath's words snapped my attention back to him. He didn't sound cool or sad anymore. His voice was sharp, as if he'd sliced each word from his soul.

"It—it causes the human pain," I said.

"Pain? Talk about an understatement. Zoey, I thought you were dead at first. And when I thought that, I wished I was dead, too. I think part of me did die then."

"Heath," I whispered his name, utterly horrified at what I'd caused. "I'm so—"

But he wasn't done. "But I knew you weren't dead because I could feel some of what was happening to you." He grimaced. "Some of what *he* was making you feel. Then I didn't know anything except my soul had a hole in it in the place where you had been. I still feel like there's a part of me missing. A big part of me. It hurts all the time. Every day." He closed his eyes against the pain and shook his head. "You didn't even call me."

"I wanted to," I said miserably.

"Oh, wait. You did text-message me this morning. Thanks so much for that," he said sarcastically.

"Heath, I wanted to talk to you. I just couldn't. I was . . ." I paused, trying to figure out how I could possibly explain Loren to him in just a few short public sentences. But there was no way to explain. Not like this. Not here. So instead I could only say, "I was wrong. I'm sorry."

He shook his head again. "Sorry isn't good enough, Zo. Not this time. Not about this. You know how you said that I only loved you and wanted you so much because of our Imprint?"

"Yes." I braced myself for him to tell me the truth of it—that he'd never really loved me and never really wanted me, and he was glad he was rid of me and my stupid, painful Imprint.

"I told you when you said it you were wrong. You're still wrong. I fell in love with you in third grade. I loved you then. I love you and want you now; I probably will forever." Heath's eyes were bright with unshed tears. "But I don't ever want to see you again. Loving you hurts too much, Zoey."

Heath walked slowly back to Casey. When he got to her table, she said something too soft for me to hear. He nodded, and then, without one glance back at me, Casey wound her arm through his and the two of them left their food sitting uneaten on the table and Heath walked out of my life.

CHAPTER NINETEEN

I didn't say anything as Aphrodite grabbed my arm, hauled me to my feet, and led me out of Charlie's Chicken. Darius took one look at us and was out of the car in a nanosecond.

"Where is the danger!" he snapped.

Aphrodite shook her head. "Not danger—ex-boyfriend drama. Let's just get out of here."

Darius made a grunting noise and got back in the car. Aphrodite shoved me in the backseat. I didn't know I was crying until Aphrodite, juggling a grumbling Maleficent, passed a handful of Kleenex across the seat.

"You're all snotty and your makeup is seriously running," she said.

"Thanks," I mumbled, and blew my nose.

"Is she all right?" Darius asked, glancing in the rearview mirror at me.

"She'll be okay. Normal ex-boyfriend crap sucks. What happened to her in there was definitely not normal and, well, that double sucks."

"Don't talk about me like I'm not here." I sniffled and wiped my eyes.

"So you're going to be all right?" Darius repeated, this time talking to me.

"If she says no, will you go back and kill that stupid boy?" Aphrodite asked.

A little bubble of laughter escaped from my surprised mouth. "I don't want him killed, and I'm going to be okay."

Aphrodite shrugged. "Suit yourself, but I think the boy needs killing." Then she tugged on Darius's arm and pointed at the strip mall we were approaching. "Honey, would you pull in there to the RadioShack? My stupid iPod Touch has been messing up, and I want to grab a new one."

"Okay with you?" Darius asked me.

"No problem. I need some time to get myself together before we get to school. But, uh, would you stay in the car with me?"

"Of course, Priestess." Darius's kind smile in the rearview mirror made me feel guilty.

"I'll be back in like two seconds. Hang on to Maleficent for me." Aphrodite tossed the big cat at Darius and then practically ran into RadioShack.

After situating Aphrodite's hissing beast, Darius looked over the back of the seat at me. "I could speak with the boy if you'd like me to."

"No, but thanks." I blew my nose again and wiped my face. "He had every right to be pissed. I messed up."

"Humans who get involved with vampyres can be overly sensitive," Darius said, obviously choosing his words carefully. "Being the human consort of a vampyre, especially a powerful High Priestess, is a difficult path."

"I'm not a vampyre and I'm not a High Priestess," I said, feeling utterly overwhelmed. "I'm just a fledgling,"

Darius hesitated, obviously wondering how much he should say to me. It was only when Aphrodite got back into the car, clutching her bogus iPod Touch package, that he finally spoke.

"Zoey, you should keep in mind that High Priestesses aren't born overnight. They begin to come into their own even when they are fledglings. Their power builds early. Your power is building, Priestess. You are far from just a normal fledgling and you always will be. So your actions will have the ability to profoundly affect others."

"You know, I was just starting to get a handle on this 'wow I'm so different' thing, and now I feel like I'm drowning in it."

Aphrodite resituated Maleficent on her lap and then turned in her seat so that she could meet my eyes. "Yeah, being extra-special isn't as great as you'd think it would be, huh?"

I expected her to give me one of her sarcastic, bitchy "told ya so" smirks, but instead her eyes were filled with understanding.

"You're being really nice," I said.

"That's because you're a bad influence on me," she said. "But I try to look on the bright side."

"Bright side?"

"The bright side is that almost everyone thinks I'm still a terrible hag from hell," she said, smiling happily and nuzzling her cat.

"I think you're spectacular," Darius said, reaching over to pet Maleficent, who started to purr.

"And you are absolutely right." She leaned over and, smashing the complaining cat between them, kissed him noisily on the cheek.

I made gagging noises and pretended to throw up in my tissue wad, but I smiled as Aphrodite winked at me, and I did feel just a little bit better. *At least it's over*, I told myself. *Erik hates me. Stark is dead, and even if he undeads, I'm just going to help him get his feet on the undead ground. That's it. So after that nasty confrontation with Heath, I'm definitely finished with boyfriend issues for a good, long time.*

Naturally I was late for drama class. By shifting my schedule around, I'd been put in an upper-level drama class, which was really okay. I'd been in Drama II at South Intermediate High School when I'd been Marked, and I liked drama (onstage, not off). Okay, that didn't mean I was a particularly good actress, but I tried. Of course, changing hours stuck me in a class with a new group of kids. I stood in the doorway, trying to figure out where to sit and really, really not wanting to interrupt Erik (Professor Night?) in the middle of his lecture about Shakespearean plays.

"Just have a seat anywhere, Zoey." Erik spoke without even glancing in my direction. His voice was brisk and professional and even a little boring. In other words, he sounded just exactly like a teacher. No, I do not have a clue how he knew I was lurking in the doorway.

I hurried into the room and sat at the first empty desk I found. Sadly it was in the front. I nodded to Becca Adams, who was sitting right behind me. She nodded back, but was clearly distracted by her need to stare at Erik. I didn't really know Becca very well. She was blond and pretty, as per the norm for fledglings at the House of Night (there seemed to be five blondes for every "normal" kid), and she'd recently joined the Dark Daughters. I think I remember seeing her hang around with a couple of Aphrodite's old friends, but I didn't have any particular opinion of her one way or another. Of course, her craning her head around me and drooling at Erik wasn't exactly endearing her to me.

No! Erik is not my boyfriend anymore. I can't get pissed when another girl goes after him. I have to ignore it. Maybe I'll even make a point to try to be her friend to show everybody how over him I am. Yeah, I'll just—

"Hi, Z!"

Very blond, very cute, and very tall Cole Clifton, who was currently dating Shaunee (which also meant he was very brave), whispered a perky greeting to me, breaking through my inner babble. "Hi," I said back, giving him a big smile.

"Oh, hey, this is excellent. Thank you for volunteering, Zoey."

"Huh?" I blinked up at Erik.

His smile was cool. His eyes were blue ice. "You were talking, so I assumed that meant you were volunteering to read opposite me in the Shakespeare improvisation."

I gulped. "Oh. Well. I—" I started to try to beg out of doing whatever the hell a Shakespeare improvisation was, but when his cool gaze turned mocking, like he was looking forward to me totally chickening out like a giant dork, I changed my mind. Erik Night was not going to embarrass and bully me all semester. So I cleared my throat and sat up a little straighter in my seat. "I'd love to volunteer."

The quick flash of surprise that widened those gorgeous blue eyes gave me an instant of smugness. That instant evaporated as soon as he said, "Good. Then come on up here and get your copy of our scene."

Ah, crap crap crap!

"All right." Erik and I stood on the stage that faced the drama class. "As I was explaining before Zoey came in late and interrupted, Shakespeare improvisation is a great way to exercise your characterization skills. It's unusual, yes, because Shakespeare isn't usually improvised. Actors stick close to the playwright's words, which is why changing up famous scenes can be interesting." He pointed at the very short script I held in my nervously sweating hand. "That is the beginning of a scene between Othello and Desdemona—"

"We're doing *Othello*?" I squeaked, feeling my stomach clench into a nauseated fist. It was Othello's monologue that Erik had recited to me with his eyes and voice full of love in front of the entire school.

"Yes." His eyes met mine. "Do you have a problem with that?"

Yes! "No," I lied. "I just wondered, that's all." Oh, god! Was he going to make me improv one of Othello's love scenes? I couldn't tell if my stomach was getting sicker by the instant because I wanted that or because I didn't want it.

"Good. So you know the story of the play, right?"

I nodded. Of course I did. Othello, the Moor (a.k.a. a black guy), had married Desdemona (an extremely white girl). They'd been majorly in love until Iago, a crappy guy jealous of Othello, decided to make it look like Desdemona had been messing around on Othello. Othello had ended up strangling Desdemona. To death.

Ah, crap.

"Good," he repeated. "So the scene we're improv-ing is at the end of the play. Othello is confronting Desdemona. We'll start by reading the actual lines. I've copied them onto the scripts for us. When I ask if you've prayed, that's your cue to improv. Then try to stick close to the plot, but make it work in today's language. Got it?"

Sadly, I did. "Yes."

"All right. Let's start."

And then, just like I'd watched so many times before, Erik Night stepped into the character of someone else and *became* that person. He turned so that he no longer faced me and began saying Othello's lines. I noticed that he'd dropped the script and was speaking from memory:

> It is the cause, it is the cause, my soul;
> let me not name it to you, you chaste stars,
> it is the cause. I'll not shed her blood,
> nor scar that whiter skin of hers than snow . . .

I swear he changed physically, and even through my nerves and the mortification I could feel building inside me because I knew this was bound to become a very public, very embarrassing scene, I could appreciate his amazing talent.

Then he turned to me and I could barely think above the pounding of my heart when he took my shoulders in his hands.

> *. . . I know not where is that Promethean heat*
> *that can thy light relume. When I have pluck'd thy rose,*
> *I cannot give it vital growth again,*
> *It needs must wither. I'll smell thee on the tree.*

Then, utterly shocking me, Erik bent and kissed me on the lips. His kiss was rough and tender—passionate with anger and betrayal, yet it seemed he didn't want to take his lips from mine. He made me breathless. He made me nauseated. He made my head spin.

I soooo want to be his girlfriend again!

I pulled myself together as he spoke the lines that cued me to begin mine.

> *I must weep, but they are cruel tears. This sorrow's heavenly,*
> *it strikes where it doth love. She wakes.*

"Who's there? Othello?" I glanced from my paper to Erik, blinking my eyes and trying to look like his kiss had been what woke me up.

"Ay Desdemona."

Oh, jeesh! I couldn't believe what my next lines were! I gulped, which made me sound all breathy. "Will you come to bed, my lord?"

"Have you pray'd tonight, Desdemona?"

Erik's handsome face had gone all tense and scary, and I swear it wasn't much of an act for me to look freaked. "Ay, my lord," I read the last lines of my script quickly.

"Good. You'll need to have a clean soul for what's going to happen to you tonight!" he improvised, still looking like the Othello who had been driven insane with jealousy.

"What's wrong? I don't have a clue what you're talking about." Improvising to this wasn't hard. I'd forgotten about the class and all the watching eyes. All I saw was Erik as Othello, and I knew Desdemona's fear and desolation at the thought of losing him.

"Think hard!" he ground between clenched jaws. "If there's anything you're sorry for, you need to ask for forgiveness for it now. Nothing will be the same for you again, not after what happens tonight."

His fingers were digging into my shoulders so hard that I knew they were going to leave bruises, but I didn't flinch. I just kept staring into those eyes I knew so well, trying to find the Erik in there that I hoped still cared about me as my forgotten script fluttered from my numb hands.

"But I don't know what it is you want me to say!" I cried, trying to remember that Desdemona was *not* me. *She* hadn't been guilty of anything.

"The truth!" he stormed, his eyes looking wild. "I want you to admit just how much you betrayed me!"

"But I didn't!" I could feel tears stinging my eyes. "Not in my heart. I never betrayed you in my heart."

Erik's Othello blotted everything out of my world—Heath, Stark, Loren. There was only him and me and the need I had to try to make him understand that I hadn't wanted to betray him. That I still didn't want to betray him.

"Then your heart is a black, shriveled thing, because you absolutely did betray me."

His hands began to slide from my shoulders up to my neck, and I knew he could feel my pulse that pounded there like a frantically fluttering bird. "No! The things I did were mistakes! I broke my own heart, not just one time but three times."

"So you would break mine along with yours?" His fingers closed around my neck, and I could see that there were tears in his eyes, too.

"No, my lord," I said, trying to hold on to some part of Desdemona. "I just want you to forgive me and—"

"Forgive you!" he yelled, interrupting me. "How am I supposed to do that? I loved you, and you betrayed me with another guy."

I shook my head. "It was all lies."

"You're admitting that you've done nothing but lie to me?" His fingers tightened around my neck.

I gasped. "No! That's not what I meant. You're misunderstanding everything. What I had with him was the lie. *He* was the lie. You were right about him all along."

"Too late," he said thickly. "You've realized this too late."

"It doesn't have to be too late. Forgive me and give me another chance. Don't let us end like this."

I watched as several emotions played across Erik's face. I could easily see anger and even hatred, but there was also sadness and maybe, just maybe, what looked like hope waiting quietly way back in the warm summer sky blue part of his eyes.

Then all of a sudden the sadness and hope flattened from his expression. "No! You acted like a slut, so now you get a slut's reward!"

With a seriously crazy look in his eyes, he seemed to grow even taller until he towered over me. He stepped close, taking one hand from my throat so that he could use that arm to hold me locked against him. His other hand was big enough that it reached almost all the way around my neck. As he squeezed, our bodies were pressed together, and I felt a wild rush of white-hot desire for him. I knew it was wrong. I knew it was weird, but my heart was pounding with more than fear or nerves. I stared into his eyes, feeling Desdemona's terror along with my own passion, and I knew by the hardness in his body that he was feeling the same things. He was Othello—crazed with jealousy and anger, but he was also Erik—the guy who had been falling in love with me and had been hurt so badly when he'd found me with another guy.

His face was so close to mine that I could feel his breath against my skin. His scent was familiar, and it was that familiarity that decided me. Instead of pulling away from him or continuing with the improv and "fainting" in his arms to pretend I was dead, I wrapped my arms around him and pulled him into me, closing the short distance between our lips.

I kissed him with everything in me. I put all my pain and sorrow and passion and love for him into that kiss, and his mouth opened under mine, meeting me passion for passion, pain for pain, and love for love.

And then the stupid bell rang.

CHAPTER TWENTY

Oh. My. Goddess. The ringing bell was like a fire alarm. Erik broke away from me, and the class burst into cheers and a chorus of Okie "Whoo-Hoo!" and "That was hawt!" I would have fallen over if Erik hadn't kept a hold of my hand.

"Bow," he said under his breath to me. "Smile."

I did as he said, somehow bowing and forcing myself to smile like my world hadn't just exploded. As the kids filed out, Erik spoke in his teacherly voice again.

"Okay, remember to take a look at *Julius Caesar*. Tomorrow we're improv-ing from that one. And you guys did a good job today."

When the last kid had walked out the door, I said, "Erik, we have to talk."

He dropped my hand like I'd burned him. "You better get going. You don't want to be late to your next class, too." Then he turned away from me and walked into the drama office, closing the door with a *slam!* behind him.

I bit my lip hard to keep from bursting into tears as I bolted from the drama room, face burning with humiliation. What the hell had just happened? Well, I knew one thing for sure, even if it was only *one* thing, and that was that Erik Night was still interested in me. Sure, the interest might be focused mostly on wanting to strangle me. But still. At least he wasn't as all grown and unfeeling and whatever about me as he'd tried to pretend he was. My lips felt sore from the intensity of our kisses. I lifted my hand, running a finger over my bottom lip gently.

I started to walk, not looking at the fledglings that passed by me on their way to class, and didn't actually even pay attention to where I was until the croaking caw of a raven sounded from the branches of a tree beside the sidewalk.

With a shiver I came to an abrupt halt and peered up into the dark tree. As I watched, the night wavered and folded, like tallow dripping down a black candle. There was something about it—something about whatever it was in the tree that made my knees weak and my stomach hurt.

Since when had I become such a victim—such a scared little girl?

"Who are you!" I yelled at the night. "What do you want?" I straightened my shoulders, deciding that I was sick of this stupid hide-and-seek game. I might be heartbroken about Heath and confused about Stark, and I might not be able to do crap about the mess I'd made with Erik, but I could do something about this. So I was going to march over there to those trees and call wind to shake whatever it was up there watching me down so that I could kick its butt. I was tired of feeling weird and afraid and totally not myself, and—

Before I could take a step off the sidewalk, Darius seemed to materialize beside me. Jeesh, for a great big guy, he could sure move scarily fast and silent.

"Zoey, you must come with me," he said.

"What's going on?"

"It's Aphrodite."

My stomach clenched so hard, I thought I was going to be sick. "She's not dying, is she?"

"No, but she needs you. Now."

He didn't have to tell me any more. The strain in his face and the deadly seriousness of his voice said it all. She wasn't dying, so Aphrodite had to be having a vision.

"Okay, I'm coming." And I started hurrying toward the dorms, trying to keep up with Darius.

The warrior stopped for an instant, giving me a piercing look that was so intense, it made me want to squirm. "Do you trust me?" he asked abruptly.

I nodded.

"Then relax and believe you're safe with me."

"Okay." I didn't have a clue what he was talking about, but I didn't protest when he grabbed my arm.

"Remember, stay relaxed," he said.

I opened my mouth to repeat my okay (and maybe roll my eyes at him), when all the breath was pushed from my lungs as Darius exploded forward, somehow taking me with him. It was the most bizarre thing I'd ever experienced, which was saying something, because I'd had a ton of bizarre experiences in the past couple of months. But this was like being on one of those moving sidewalks at the airport, only the "sidewalk" was Darius's aura or something, and the moving was happening so fast that the world around us was one big blur.

We were in front of the girls' dorm within a couple of seconds, and I'm not exaggerating.

"Holy crap! How did you do that?" I was panting a little, and as soon as he let go of my arm, I began to frantically brush my hair back out of my face. It was like I'd just taken a supersonic ride on a Harley.

"The Sons of Erebus are mighty warriors with vast skills," he said cryptically.

"Huh. No kidding?" I was going to say that they also sounded like they should be in a *Lord of the Rings* movie, but I didn't want to be rude.

"She's in her room," he said, kinda pushing me up the stairs to the dorm while he reached ahead of me and opened the door. "She told me to get you right away."

"Well, you certainly did that," I said over my shoulder. "Oh, could you find Lenobia and tell her why I'm not in class?"

"Of course, Priestess," he said. Then he disappeared again. Jeesh. I hurried into the dorm, still feeling kinda frazzled. The main room was empty—everyone (except Aphrodite and me) was in class, so I could rush up the stairs and sprint to Aphrodite's room without having to answer a bunch of questions from way-too-curious girls. I rapped twice on Aphrodite's door before opening it.

The only light in the room was coming from one small candle. Aphrodite was sitting on her bed with her knees pulled up to her chest, her elbows resting on them, and her face buried in her hands. Maleficent was curled into a fluffy white ball beside her. The cat looked up at me when I entered the room and growled softly.

"Hey, are you okay?" I asked.

Her body shuddered, and with what was obviously a huge effort, she lifted her head and opened her eyes.

"Oh my god! What happened!" I hurried over to her, turning on the Tiffany's light that was on her bedside table. When Maleficent stirred and hissed a warning at me, I told the beast, "Try it and I will throw you out the window and call down rain to soak the crap out of you."

"Maleficent, it's okay. Zoey's hateful, but she won't hurt me," she said wearily.

The cat growled again, but subsided back into a white ball. I turned my attention to Aphrodite. Her eyes were completely bloodshot—it was so bad that the whites of them were totally red. Not pink and inflamed like she was allergic to pollen and she'd just walked through a field of it. They were *red*. As in blood. As in blood filling her eyes and staining them scarlet.

"This one was really bad." She sounded awful. Her voice was shaky, and her face was scarily white. "C-can you get me a bottle of Fiji Water from the fridge?"

I hurried over to her mini-fridge and grabbed a bottle of water from it. Then I detoured into her bathroom, where I got one of her gold-embroidered washcloths. (Jeesh, she is so darn rich!) I quickly poured some of the cold spring water onto the washcloth before hurrying back to her.

"Drink some of this, and then close your eyes and put this across your face."

"I look terrible, don't I?"

"Yep."

She took several big gulps from the Fiji bottle like she was dying of thirst, then put the cold, wet washcloth over her eyes and leaned back against her mound of designer pillows with an exhausted sigh. Maleficent watched me with mean, slitted cat eyes, which I ignored.

"Have your eyes ever done that before?"

"You mean hurt like hell?"

I hesitated and decided to just tell her. It wasn't like Aphrodite avoided mirrors. She'd see for herself soon enough. "I mean turn bright, blood red."

I saw the little jerk of surprise her body gave, and she started to reach for the washcloth, but her hand stopped and plopped back down on the bed and her shoulders slumped. "No wonder Darius freaked and ran for you like the hounds of f-ing hell were after him."

"I'm sure it'll go away. You should probably just keep your eyes closed for a while."

She sighed dramatically. "It's really going to piss me off if these damn visions start making me ugly."

"Aphrodite," I said, trying to keep my smile out of my voice. "You're too pretty to ever be ugly. Or at least that's what you've told all of us about a zillion times."

"You're right. Even with red eyes, I'm better looking than everyone else. Thanks for reminding me. It just shows how stressed this vision bullshit is making me that I'd even consider worrying about it."

"Speaking of the vision bullpoopy. You want to fill me in on this one?"

"You know, you *really* wouldn't melt or anything if you'd cuss a little. My Goddess, bull*poopy* is unbelievably lame."

"Could you please stay on the subject?"

"Fine. But don't blame me when people tell you that you sound lame and annoying. Over there on my desk there's a piece of paper with a poem written on it. Do you see it?"

I went over to her pricey vanity/desk, and sure enough, there was a single sheet of paper lying alone against the glistening wood. I picked it up. "I see it," I said.

"Good. You're supposed to read it, and I hope you understand what the hell it means. I never can figure out poetry. It's all boring bull*shit*."

She emphasized the *shit* part of the word. I ignored her and focused on the poem. As soon as I got a good look at it, my skin started to tingle and gooseflesh lifted on my arms as if a cold wind had just blown over me.

"Did you write this?"

"Oh, yeah, right. I didn't even like Dr. Seuss when I was a kid. No damn way I wrote that poem."

"I didn't mean did you compose it. I meant did you physically write it down?"

"Are you getting stupider? Yes, Zoey. I wrote down the poem that I saw in my horrid and way-too-painful vision. No, I didn't compose it. I copied it. Satisfied?"

I looked at her reclining back on her pillows in the middle of her expensive four-poster canopy bed with the gold-embroidered washcloth over her face and one hand petting her awful cat and shook my head in irritation. She looked one hundred gazillion percent diva bitch. "You know, I could smother you with your pillow and no one would miss you. By the time they found you, that hateful cat would have eaten you *and* all the evidence of my crime."

"Maleficent wouldn't eat me. She'd eat you if you tried any crap. Plus, Darius would miss me. Just read the damn poem and tell me what it means."

"You're Vision Girl. You're supposed to know what things mean." I turned my attention back to the poem. What was it about the writing that was making me feel so weird?

"That's right, I vision. I don't interpret. I'm just the very attractive oracle. You're the High Priestess in training, remember? So figure it out."

"All right—all right. Let me read it out loud. Sometimes it helps make poems understandable when you can hear them."

"Whatever. Just get to the figuring out part."

I cleared my throat and started reading.

> *Ancient one sleeping, waiting to arise*
> *When earth's power bleeds sacred red*
> *The mark strikes true; Queen Tsi Sgili will devise*
> *He shall be washed from his entombing bed*
>
> *Through the hand of the dead he is free*
> *Terrible beauty, monstrous sight*

Ruled again they shall be
Women shall kneel to his dark might

Kalona's song sounds sweet
As we slaughter with cold heat

When I was finished I paused, trying to understand what it meant and trying to figure out why it made me feel so freaked out.

"It's scary, isn't it?" Aphrodite said. "I mean, it's definitely not love and roses and happily ever after."

"It's definitely not that. Okay, let's see. What's earth's power, and when does it bleed red?"

"Don't have a clue."

"Hum." I chewed my cheek, thinking. "Well, the earth could look like it's bleeding when something is killed and the blood leaks into the ground. And maybe the power part comes from whatever is killed. Like a powerful person."

"Or a powerful vampyre. It's like when I found Professor Nolan's body." The smartass in Aphrodite's voice was subdued by the memory. "The earth looked like it was bleeding then."

"Yeah, you're right. So it might have something to do with this Queen Tsi Sgili dying or being killed because a queen is definitely a powerful person."

"Who the hell is Queen Tsi Whatever?"

"It sounds familiar to me. The name seems Cherokee. I wonder if it might—" My words were broken off by my gasp of shock as suddenly I knew why the writing had made me feel so weird.

"What?" Aphrodite sat up again, lifting the washcloth off her eyes and squinting at me. "What's wrong?"

"It's the writing," I said through lips that had gone cold. "This is my grandma's handwriting."

CHAPTER TWENTY-ONE

"Your grandma's handwriting?" Aphrodite said. "Are you sure?"

"Positive."

"But that's impossible. I wrote the damn thing just a few minutes ago."

"Look, I practically transported here with Darius, and that should have been impossible, but I definitely did it."

"Yes, dork, seeing as there is no such thing as *Star Trek*."

"You recognized the transporter reference. You're a dork, too," I said smugly.

"No, I'm just burdened with geeky friends."

· "Look, I'm positive it's Grandma's handwriting, but hang on. I have a letter from her in my room. I'll go get it. Maybe you're right . . ." I lifted my brows at her and added, ". . . for a change, and it just reminds me of her writing." I started to hurry from the room, but on second thought stopped long enough to hold the paper with the poem on it up to Aphrodite. "Is this your normal handwriting?"

She took the paper from me and blinked several times to clear her vision. I saw the shock pass over her face and knew what she'd say before she spoke. "Well, shit! This is soooo not my writing."

"I'll be right back."

I tried not to overthink what was going on while I rushed

down the hall to my room, flung open the door, and was greeted by Nala's *"mee-uf-ow!"* of disgruntled surprise as I interrupted her beauty nap.

It took me only a second to grab the last card Grandma had sent me. I had it sitting up on my desk (a much cheaper version of the one in Aphrodite's room). On the front of it was a picture of three grim-faced nuns (nuns!). The caption under them said, THE GOOD NEWS IS THEY'RE PRAYING FOR YOU. Inside it continued, THE BAD NEWS IS THERE ARE ONLY THREE OF THEM. It still made me giggle a little as I hurried back to Aphrodite's room, even as I wondered if Sister Mary Angela would think the card was funny or insulting. I'd bet on funny, and made a mental note to ask her about it sometime.

Aphrodite had her hand already out when I returned to her room. "Okay, let me check it out." I gave her the card and looked down with her as she held it open to the short note Grandma had written me. Then she held the paper that had the poem right up next to it and we looked from one to the other, comparing the handwriting.

"That is so damn weird!" Aphrodite said, shaking her head at the utter similarity of the handwriting. "I swear I wrote this poem not five minutes ago, but that's definitely your grandma's writing and not mine." She looked up at me. Her face looked ultra-white in comparison to the awful blood color of her eyes. "You'd better call her."

"Yeah, I will. First I want to know everything you remember about that vision."

"Okay with you if I shut my eyes and put the washcloth back on my face while I talk?"

"Yeah, I'll even put some fresh water on it. Speaking of, drink some more out of that bottle. You look, well, *bad*."

"No wonder. I feel *bad*." She gulped down the rest of the Fiji

Water while I rinsed out the washcloth again. After I folded it up and gave it back to her, she laid it across her eyes and settled back against her pillows again, absently stroking the purring Malefi-cent. "I wish I knew what this was all about," she said.

"I think I do."

"No shit? You have the poem figured out?"

"No, I didn't mean that. I meant I think this is all about that bad feeling Stevie Rae and I have been having about Neferet. She's up to something—something more than her usual brand of pain in the butt. I think she graduated to whatever it is that's going on now when Loren was killed."

"I wouldn't be surprised if you're right, but I have to tell you Neferet had no part of my vision."

"So explain it to me."

"Well, it was short and unusually clear for what my visions have been like lately. It was a pretty summer day. I couldn't tell who it was, but there was a woman sitting in the middle of a field or, no, it was more like a pasture or something. I could see a little cliff not far away, and I could hear water from a stream or small river close by. Anyway, the woman was sitting on a big white eye-let quilt. I remember thinking that it wasn't very smart of that woman to have a *white* quilt out there on the ground like that. It was going to get all grass stained."

"It didn't." I spoke through lips that felt numb and cold again. "It was cotton, and it washed up easily."

"So you know what I'm describing?"

"It's Grandma's quilt."

"Then it must have been your grandma who was holding the poem. I didn't see her face. I actually didn't see much of her at all. She was sitting cross-legged, and it was like I was standing behind her, peeking over her shoulder. Only, once I saw the poem, every-thing else went out of the vision and I was totally focused on it."

"Why did you copy it down?"

Her shoulders shrugged. "Don't really know. I just had to, that's all. So I wrote it down while I was still in the vision. Then I came out of it, looked up at Darius, told him to get you, and then I think I fainted."

"That's it?"

"What more do you want? I copied the whole damn poem."

"But your visions are usually warnings about majorly bad stuff getting ready to happen. So where's the warning?"

"There wasn't one. Actually, I didn't have any bad feelings at all. There was just the poem. The field place was really nice—I mean for being all out in nature. Like I said, it was a pretty summer day. Everything seemed fine and dandy until I came out of the vision and my head and my eyes hurt like hell."

"Well, I have a bad enough feeling about this for both of us," I said, pulling my phone from my purse. I glanced at the time. It was almost 3 A.M. Crap! Grandma would be sound asleep. Also I realized I was going to miss all my classes today except for that very public scene with Erik in Drama class. Great. I sighed heavily. I knew Grandma would understand—I could only hope my professors would, too.

She answered on the first ring.

"Oh, Zoeybird! I'm so glad you called."

"Grandma, I'm sorry to call you so late. I know you're sleeping, and I hate waking you up," I said.

"No, *u-we-tsi-a-ge-ya*, I was not asleep. I woke hours ago from a dream of you, and I have been awake and praying ever since."

Her familiar use of the Cherokee word for "daughter" made me feel loved and safe, and I suddenly wished so bad that her lavender farm wasn't an hour and a half outside Tulsa. I wished that I could see her now and let her hug me and tell me that everything would be okay, just like she used to do when I was lit-tle and I stayed with her after my mom married the step-loser and turned into an ultra-religious version of a Stepford Wife.

But I wasn't little anymore, and Grandma couldn't hug my problems away. I was becoming a High Priestess, and people de-pended on me. Nyx had chosen me, and I had to learn to be strong.

"Honey? What is it? What has happened?"

"It's okay, Grandma; I'm okay," I assured her quickly, hating to hear the worry in her voice. "It's just that Aphrodite has had an-other vision, and it has something to do with you."

"Am I in danger again?"

I couldn't help smiling. She'd sounded worried and upset when she thought something might be wrong with me, but when it was *just* herself that might be in danger, then she sounded all tough and ready to take on the world. I really heart my grandma!

"No, I don't think so," I said.

"I don't either," Aphrodite added.

"Aphrodite says you're not in danger. At least not at this in-stant."

"Well, that's good," Grandma said, sounding very matter-of-fact.

"That's definitely good. But, Grandma, the thing is we really don't understand what Aphrodite's vision was about this time. There's usually a big warning that's clear. This time all she saw was you holding a piece of paper with a poem on it, and she felt like she had to copy the poem." I didn't mention the part about her copying it in Grandma's own handwriting. That felt like adding super weird to already majorly weird. "So she did, but it doesn't make sense or mean anything to either one of us."

"Well, perhaps you should read the poem to me. Maybe I'll recognize it."

"Yeah, that's what we thought, too. Okay, here goes." Sightlessly

Aphrodite held up the sheet of paper with the poem on it. I took it from her and started to read:

> *Ancient one sleeping, waiting to arise*
> *When earth's power bleeds sacred red*
> *The mark strikes true; Queen Tsi Sgili will devise*

Here Grandma stopped me. "It is pronounced t-si *s-gi-li*," she said, with special emphasis on the last word. Her voice sounded strained and she spoke almost in a whisper.

"Are you okay, Grandma?"

"Go on reading, *u-we-tsi-a-ge-ya*," she commanded, sounding more like herself. I kept reading, repeating the last line with the right pronunciation:

> *The mark strikes true; Queen Tsi Sgili will devise*
> *He shall be washed from his entombing bed*
>
> *Through the hand of the dead he is free*
> *Terrible beauty, monstrous sight*
> *Ruled again they shall be*
> *Women shall kneel to his dark might*
>
> *Kalona's song sounds sweet*
> *As we slaughter with cold heat*

Grandma gasped and cried, "O Great Spirit protect us!"

"Grandma! What is it?"

"First the Tsi Sgili and then Kalona. This is bad, Zoey. This is very, very bad."

The fear in her voice was totally freaking me out. "What's a Tsi Sgili and a Kalona? Why is it so bad?"

"Does she know the poem?" Aphrodite asked, sitting up and taking the washcloth off her face. I noticed her eyes were starting to look more normal and her face had gotten some of its color back.

"Grandma, do you care if I put you on speaker phone?"

"No, of course not, Zoeybird."

I pressed the speaker button and went over to sit on the bed beside Aphrodite. "Okay, you're on speaker now, Grandma. It's just me and Aphrodite here."

"Aphrodite and me," she automatically corrected me.

I rolled my eyes at Aphrodite. "Sorry, Grandma, Aphrodite and me."

"Mrs. Redbird, do you recognize the poem?" Aphrodite asked.

"Sweetheart, call me Grandma. And, no, I don't recognize it, as in having read it before. But I've heard of it, or at least I've heard of the myth, passed down from generation to generation in my people."

"Why did you freak out about the Tsi Sgili and the Kalona part?" I asked.

"They are Cherokee demons. Dark spirits of the worst type." Grandma hesitated, and I could hear her rustling around with something in the background. "Zoey, I'm going to light the smudge pot before we speak any more of these creatures. I'm using sage and lavender. I'll be fanning the smoke with a dove's feather while we talk. Zoeybird, I suggest you do the same."

I felt an awful jolt of surprise. Smudging had been used for hundreds of years in Cherokee rituals—especially when cleansing, purifying, or protection was needed. Grandma smudged and cleansed herself regularly—I'd grown up believing it was just a way of honoring the Great Spirit and of keeping my own spirit clean. But never in my life had Grandma ever felt the need to smudge at the mention of anyone or anything.

"Zoey, you should do it now," Grandma said sharply.

CHAPTER TWENTY-TWO

As always, when Grandma told me to do something, I did it. "Okay, yeah. I'm going. I have a smudge stick in my room. I gotta run and get it." I gave Aphrodite a look and she nodded, shooing me toward the door with a hand flutter.

"Which herbs?" Grandma asked.

"White sage and lavender. It's the one I keep in my T-shirt drawer," I said.

"Good, good. That's good. It's personal to you, but its magic hasn't been released yet. Good."

I rushed back to Aphrodite's room.

"I got the pot part covered," Aphrodite said, handing me a lavender-colored bowl that was decorated with three-dimensional grapes and a vine that twined all the way around it. It was absolutely gorgeous and looked expensive and old. She shrugged her shoulders at me. "Yeah, it's expensive."

I rolled my eyes at her. "Okay, I have the bowl, Grandma."

"Do you have a feather? From a peaceful bird, like the dove, or a protective bird, like a hawk or an eagle would be best."

"Uh, Grandma, no. I don't have any feathers." I looked questioningly at Aphrodite.

"No feathers here, either," she said.

"No matter, we can make do. Are you ready, Zoeybird?"

I waved the small wandlike stick of tightly woven dried herbs until the fire went out and smoke began to waft gently from it. Then I put it in the purple bowl and set it between us. "I'm ready. It's smoking perfectly."

"Waft it around you. Girls, both of you need to concentrate on protection and positive spirits. Think of your Goddess and how much she loves you."

We did as Grandma told us. Both of us were fanning the smoke gently around with our hands as we inhaled slowly.

Maleficent sneezed, growled, and jumped off the bed to disappear into Aphrodite's bathroom. I can't say I was sorry to see her go.

"Now keep the pot close to you while you listen carefully to me," Grandma said. I heard her draw three deep cleansing breaths before she began. "First you should know that the Tsi Sgili are Cherokee witches, only do not be deceived by the title 'witch.' They do not follow the peaceful, beautiful ways of Wicca. Nor are they the wise priestesses you know and respect who serve Nyx. A Tsi Sgili lives as an outcast, separate from the tribe. They are evil, through and through. They delight in killing; they revel in death. They have magical powers granted through the fear and pain of their victims. They feed on death. They can torture and kill with the *ane li sgi*."

"I don't know what that means, Grandma."

"It means they are powerful psychics and can kill with their minds."

Aphrodite looked up at me. Our eyes met and I could tell we were thinking the same thing: Neferet is a powerful psychic.

"Who is this queen the poem talks about?" Aphrodite asked.

"I know of no Tsi Sgili queen. They are solitary beings and have no hierarchy. But I am not an authority on them."

"So is Kalona one of the Tsi Sgili?" I asked.

"No. Kalona is worse. Much worse. The Tsi Sgili are evil and dangerous, but they are human and can be dealt with as any human can." Grandma paused, and I could hear her drawing in three more deep cleansing breaths. When Grandma began to speak again, her voice was lowered, as if she was worried about being overheard. She didn't exactly sound scared. She sounded cautious. Cautious and very, very serious.

"Kalona was the father of the Raven Mockers and he was not human. We call him and his twisted offspring demons, but that's not really accurate. I guess the best way I can describe Kalona is as an angel."

A cold chill went through my body when Grandma said the words *Raven Mockers;* then I realized what else she had said, and I blinked in surprise. "An angel? Like in the Bible?"

"Aren't they supposed to be good guys?" Aphrodite asked.

"They are supposed to be. Keep in mind that the Christian tradition says that Lucifer himself was the brightest and most beautiful of the angels, but he fell."

"That's right. I'd forgotten about that," Aphrodite said. "So this Kalona was an angel who fell and turned bad guy?"

"In a way. In ancient times, angels walked the earth and mated with humans. Many peoples have stories to describe this time. The Bible called them Nephilim. The Greeks and Romans called them Olympian gods. But whatever they have been called, all of the stories agree on two points: First, that they were beautiful and powerful. Second, that they mated with humans."

"Makes sense," Aphrodite said. "If they were so hot, of course women would want to be with them."

"Well, they were exceptional beings. The Cherokee people tell of one particular angel, beautiful beyond compare. He had wings the color of night, and he could change form into a creature that looked like an enormous raven. At first our people welcomed him as a visiting god. We sang songs to him and danced for him. Our crops thrived. Our women were fertile.

"But gradually everything changed. I don't really know why. The stories are too old. Too many of them have been lost to time. My guess is that it is difficult to have a god live among you, no matter how beautiful he is.

"The song I remember my grandmother singing tells that Kalona changed when he began to lie with the maidens of the tribe. The story goes that after the first time he bedded a maiden, he became obsessed. He had to have women—he craved them constantly, and he also hated them for causing the lust and need he felt for them."

Aphrodite snorted. "I bet it was him feeling the lust, not them. No one wants a guy who's a man ho, no matter how hot he is."

"You're right, Aphrodite. My grandmother's song said that the maidens turned their faces from him, and that's when he became a monster. He used his divine power to rule our men while he defiled our women. And all the while his hatred for women grew with an intensity that was all the more frightening because of his obsession with them. I heard an old Wise Woman speak once, and she said that to Kalona the Cherokee women were water and air and food—his very life, though he hated that he needed them so desperately." She paused again, and I could easily envision the look of disgust on her face that was mirrored in her voice as she continued her story.

"The women he raped became pregnant, but most of them gave birth to dead things, unrecognizable as infants of any species. But once in a while, one of his offspring would live, though it was clearly not human. The stories say that Kalona's children were ravens, with the eyes and limbs of man."

"Eeewww, the body of a crow and the legs and eyes of a man? That's disgusting," Aphrodite said.

A shiver passed through me. "I've been hearing ravens, a lot of them. I think one of them tried to attack me. I swiped at it, and it scratched my hand."

"What! When?" Grandma snapped.

"I've been hearing them at night. I thought it was weird that they were making so much noise. And . . . and then last night something I couldn't really see flapped around me, like a nasty invisible bird. I hit at it and then ran inside the school and called fire to make the cold it brought with it go away."

"And it worked? Fire chased it away?" Grandma said.

"Yeah, but I've felt eyes on me ever since."

"Raven Mockers." Grandma's voice was hard as steel. "What you've been dealing with are the spirits of the demon children of Kalona."

"I've heard them, too," Aphrodite said, looking pale again. "Actually I've been thinking how annoying they've been the last few nights."

"Ever since Professor Nolan was killed," I said.

"I think that's when I started noticing it, too. Ohmygod, Grandma! Could they have had something to do with Professor Nolan and Loren's deaths?"

"No, I don't think so. The Raven Mockers lost their physical forms. They only have their spirits left and can do little harm except to those who are old and very near death. How badly did they hurt your hand, sweetheart?"

Automatically I looked down at my unmarked hand. "Not bad. The scratch went away in just a few minutes."

Grandma hesitated before saying, "I have never heard of a Raven Mocker being able to really hurt a vibrant young person. They are mischief makers—dark spirits that take pleasure from annoying the living and tormenting those at the cusp of death. I do not believe they could cause a healthy vampyre's death, but they could be drawn to the House of Night by the deaths of those vampyres, and have somehow become stronger because of them. Be wary. They are terrible creatures, and their presence is always an ill omen."

As Grandma had been talking, my eyes had wandered back to the poem. Over and over I kept reading the line *Through the hand of the dead he will be free.*

"What happened to Kalona?" I asked abruptly.

"It was his insatiable lust for women that eventually destroyed him. The warriors of the tribes tried for years to overpower him. They simply could not. He was a creature of myth and magic, and only myth and magic could defeat him."

"So what happened?" Aphrodite said.

"The Ghigua called a secret council of Wise Women from all tribes."

"What's a Ghigua?" I asked.

"It is the Cherokee name for the Beloved Woman of the tribe. She is a gifted Wise Woman, a diplomat, and often very close to the Great Spirit. Each tribe chooses one, and she serves on a council of women."

"Basically they're High Priestesses?" I said.

"Yes, that's a good way to think of them. So a Ghigua called the Wise Women together, and they met in secret in the only place where Kalona would not eavesdrop on them—a cave deep in the earth."

"Why wouldn't he hear them there?" Aphrodite asked.

"Kalona had an aversion to the earth. He was a creature of the heavens, which is where he belonged."

"Well, why didn't the Great Spirit or whoever make him go back to where he belonged?" I said.

"Free will," Grandma said. "Kalona was free to choose his path, just as you and Aphrodite are free to choose your paths."

"Free will sometimes sucks," I said.

Grandma laughed and the familiar happy sound made my insides relax a little. "Indeed it sometimes does, *u-we-tsi-a-ge-ya*. But in this case, the free will of the Ghigua women is what saved our people."

"What did they do?" Aphrodite said.

"They used the magic of women to create a maiden so beautiful, she would be impossible for Kalona to resist."

"Created a girl? You mean they did some kind of magical makeover on someone?"

"No, *u-we-tsi-a-ge-ya*, I mean they *created* a maiden. The Ghigua who was the most gifted potter formed a maiden's body from clay, and painted a face for her that was beautiful beyond compare. The Ghigua known as the most gifted weaver in all the tribes wove long, dark hair for her that fell in waves around her slim waist. The Ghigua dressmaker fashioned a dress for her that was the white of the full moon, and all of the women decorated it with shells and beads and feathers. The Ghigua who was the most fleet of foot stroked her legs and gifted her with speed. And the Ghigua who was known as the most talented singer of all the tribes whispered sweet, soft words to her, giving her the most pleasing of all voices.

"Each of the Ghigua cut their palms and used their own blood as ink to draw on her body symbols of power representing the Sacred Seven: north, south, east, west, above, below, and spirit. Then they joined hands around the beautiful clay figure and, using their combined power, breathed life into her."

"You've got to be kidding, Grandma! The women made what was basically a doll come alive?" I said.

"That's how the story goes," she said. "Young lady, why is that any more difficult to believe than a girl having the ability to call forth all five of the elements?"

"Huh," I said, feeling my cheeks getting warm at her mild rebuke. "I guess you have a point."

"For sure she has a point. Now be quiet and let her tell the rest of the story," Aphrodite said.

"Sorry, Grandma," I muttered.

"You must remember that magic is real, Zoeybird," Grandma said. "It is dangerous to forget that."

"I'll remember," I assured her, thinking how ironic it was that I could doubt the power of magic.

"So, to continue," Grandma said, drawing my attention back to the story. "The Ghigua women breathed life and purpose into the woman they called A-ya."

"Hey, I know that word. It means 'me,'" I said.

"Very good, *u-we-tsi-a-ge-ya*. They named her A-ya because she had a piece of every one of them within her—she was, to each Ghigua woman, *me*."

"That's pretty cool, actually," Aphrodite said.

"The Ghigua told no one about A-ya—not their husbands or daughters, sons, or fathers. With the next dawn, they led her out of the cave to a place near the stream where Kalona came every morning to bathe, all the while whispering to her what she must do.

"So it was there, sitting in a little patch of morning sunlight, combing her hair and singing a maiden's song, that Kalona saw her, and—as the women knew he would—he became instantly obsessed with possessing her. A-ya did what she had been created to do. She fled from Kalona with her magical speed. Kalona followed her. In his fierce need for her, he barely hesitated at the mouth of the cave into which she disappeared, and he did not see the Ghigua women who followed behind him, nor did he hear their soft magical chanting.

"Kalona caught A-ya deep within the bowels of the earth. Instead of screaming and struggling against him, this most beautiful of maidens welcomed him with smooth arms and inviting body. But the instant he penetrated her, that soft, inviting body changed back into what it had once been—earth and the spirit of woman. Her arms and legs became the clay that held him, her spirit the quicksand that trapped him, as the Ghigua Women's chanting called on the Earth Mother to seal the cave, trapping Kalona in A-ya's eternal embrace. And there he still is today, firmly held to the bosom of Earth."

I blinked, like I was surfacing after a long underwater dive, and my eyes found the poem lying on the bed beside the lavender pot. "But what about the poem?"

"Well, Kalona's entombment wasn't the end of the story. At the moment his tomb was sealed, each of his children, the terrible Raven Mockers, began to sing a song in a human's voice that promised Kalona would one day return, and described the horrible vengeance he would take against human beings, especially women. Today the details of the Raven Mockers' song are pretty much lost. Even my grandmother knew only snippets of what it said, and only that from words whispered by her grandmother. Few people wanted to remember the song. They thought it bad luck to dwell on such horrors, though enough of it has survived by being passed from mother to daughter that I can tell you it spoke of the Tsi Sgili and the bleeding earth, and how their father's terrible beauty would rise again." Grandma hesitated as Aphrodite and I stared in horror at the poem. Finally she said, "I'm afraid the poem from your vision is the song the ravens sang. And I think it's a warning that Kalona is about to return."

CHAPTER TWENTY-THREE

"It is a warning," Aphrodite said solemnly. "All of my visions are warnings of a tragedy that could happen. This one really wasn't any different."

"I think you're right," I said to Aphrodite and Grandma.

"And aren't Aphrodite's visions warnings that, if heeded, prevent the terrible outcomes from occurring?" Grandma said.

Aphrodite looked doubtful, so I answered for her, making my voice sound much surer than I felt. "Yes, they are. Her vision saved you, Grandma."

"And several other people who would have died on the bridge that day, too," Grandma said.

"All we had to do then was figure out how to prevent the accident from happening the way she saw it, so that's all we have to do with this warning, too," I said.

"I agree, Zoey. Aphrodite is a vessel of Nyx, and the Goddess is clearly warning you."

"She also clearly wants you to help us," Aphrodite said. "It was you who I saw reading the poem." She hesitated, looked at me, and I nodded, understanding what else she wanted to say to Grandma. "When I copied the poem, it came out in your handwriting."

I heard Grandma's small gasp of surprise. "You're quite sure of that?"

"Yeah," I said. "I even got one of your letters and double-checked. It's definitely your handwriting."

"Then I must agree that Nyx wants me to play a part in this," Grandma said.

"That's not surprising," I said. "You're the only Ghigua Woman we know."

"Oh, sweetheart! I'm not a Ghigua Woman. That's something an entire tribe votes on, and besides, there hasn't been an official Ghigua Woman for generations."

"Well, you've got my vote," Aphrodite said.

"And mine," I said. "And I'll bet Damien's and the Twins', too. Plus, we're kinda a tribe all our own."

Grandma laughed. "Well, I wouldn't think of arguing with the will of the tribe."

"You should come here," Aphrodite said suddenly.

I looked at her in surprise, and she nodded her head slowly, deadly serious. I listened to my gut instinct and knew with a sickening thud of my heart that Aphrodite was right.

"Oh, Aphrodite, thank you, but no. I really don't like to leave my lavender farm. We'll just talk on the phone or instant-message each other and figure this out."

"Grandma, do you trust me?" I said.

"Of course I trust you, daughter," came her unhesitating reply.

"You need to come here," I said simply.

The phone was silent, and I could almost see Grandma thinking. "I'll pack just a few things," she finally said.

"Bring some of those feathers," Aphrodite said. "I'm betting we're going to have to do more smudging."

"I will, child," Grandma said.

"Come now, Grandma." I hated the sense of urgency I was feeling.

"Tonight, Zoeybird? I can't wait a few hours until morning?"

"Tonight." As if to punctuate my request through the phone, Aphrodite and I heard the chilling sound of a raven's deep, creepy, croaking cry. It was so loud, it could have been in her warm, tidy living room with her. "Grandma! Are you okay?"

"They're spirit creatures, *u-we-tsi-a-ge-ya*. They can cause me real harm only if I am near death, and I can assure you—I am nowhere near death," she said firmly.

I remembered the freezing fear they'd brought with them and the stinging welt that had risen on my hand, and wasn't convinced she was one hundred percent right about that. "Just hurry, Grandma. I'll feel a lot better when you're here," I said.

"Me, too," Aphrodite said.

"I'll be there within two hours. I love you, Zoeybird."

"I love you, too," Grandma.

I was just getting ready to click the phone closed when Grandma added, "And I love you, too, Aphrodite. This might very well be twice that you are responsible for saving my life."

"Bye. See you soon," Aphrodite said.

I did click the phone closed then and was surprised to see that Aphrodite's eyes, which were now almost entirely clear blue again, had filled with tears and she was pink-cheeked. She felt me watching her and shrugged one shoulder and wiped at her eyes, looking totally uncomfortable. "What? So I kinda like your Grandma. Is that a crime?"

"You know, I'm beginning to think that somewhere inside you there's a nice Aphrodite hiding."

"Well, don't get all warm and tingly. As soon as I find her, I'm going to drown her in the bathtub."

I just laughed at her.

"Don't you think you should get going? You have a lot to do."

"Huh?" I said.

She sighed. "You have to round up the nerd herd, brief them

on the poem and whatnot, and figure out where your grandma's staying, which means you'll probably have to okay something with Shekinah, since I'll bet you don't want to have a cozy one-on-one with Neferet, and there's still the nanny cam you have to have Jack set up in the morgue. Good luck with all of that."

"Crap, you're right. While I'm doing all of that, what are you gonna be doing?"

"I am going to be resting so I can be refreshed and ready to put the scarily awesome powers of my brain to work on the poem puzzle."

"So you're gonna take a nap?"

"Basically. Hey, cheer up. We managed to skip out on a whole day of school," she said.

"*You* managed to skip out on a whole day of school. I managed to make the one class my ex-boyfriend is teaching just in time to do a really uncomfortable and more than slightly embarrassing improvisation scene with him in front of the entire class."

"Ooooh! I want to hear all about that!"

"Don't hold your breath," I said over my shoulder as I went out the door.

Damien and the Twins weren't hard to find. They were downstairs in the main room of the dorm, snarfing down bags of pretzels and baked chips. (Ugh! It was such a pain in the butt that the vamps made us eat healthy stuff.) It was obvious when everyone shut up at first sight of me and then all began to babble at once that they were also gossiping about me.

"Oh, honey. We just heard about Erik and Drama class," Damien said, giving me a little sympathetic pat on my arm.

"Yeah, but we haven't heard enough about it," Shaunee said.

"We definitely need details from the horse's mouth," Erin said.

"And you're the horse," Shaunee finished.

I sighed. "We did an improv scene. He kissed me. The class went nuts. Everyone left when the bell rang. I stayed. He ignored me. The end."

"Oh, nuh-uh. You're not getting away with just those little details," Erin said.

"Yeah, we got better dirt from Becca. You know, Twin, I do believe that girl has a crush on our Erik," Shaunee said.

"Do tell, Twin? Should we claw her eyes out for Z?" Erin said. "I haven't done a nice eye-clawing in ages."

"You two are so banal," Damien said. "Erik and Zoey are broken up, remember?"

"Yeah, well, your vocab is a ba-pain in our ba-asses," Erin said.

"Ba-exactly," Shaunee said.

"Holy crap! Would you guys stop bickering? We've got some major life stuff going on that makes my pathetic love life stuff seem even more ridiculous than it already is. Now I'm gonna get myself a brown pop and try like hell to find some *real* chips in the kitchen. While I do that, get your butts upstairs and meet me in Aphrodite's room. We have stuff we have to figure out."

"Stuff?" Damien said. "What kind of stuff?"

"The same old stuff of the scary, life-shattering, world-ending variety we're so familiar with," I said.

Damien and the Twins blinked at me for a couple of seconds; then all three muttered, "Okay, cool. We're in."

"Oh, and Damien," I said. "Get Jack. He's part of this, too."

Damien looked surprised and then happy, and then a little sad. "Z, is it okay if he brings Duchess? The dog won't let him out of her sight."

"Yeah, she can come. But warn him that Aphrodite has a new cat, and the cat is a weird furry clone of Aphrodite."

"Oh, ewww," the Twins said.

Shaking my head, I disappeared into the kitchen, determined not to let any of them give me another headache.

"Ohmigod, I feel faint!" Jack fanned himself while he looked really, really pale and kept shooting glances at the heavily draped window. Duchess, who was crammed into Aphrodite's room in the midst of all of us and her snarling cat, leaned against him and whined. Jack had been the first to speak after the long silence that followed Aphrodite and me clueing them in on her vision, the poem, and Grandma's story about the Tsi Sgili, Raven Mockers, and Kalona.

"Okay, that's the creepiest story I've heard in ages." Shaunee sounded practically breathless. "I swear it's even scarier than all of the *Saw* movies put together."

"Ohmygod, Twin. *Saw Four* scared the bejezzus right outta me," Erin said. "But you're right. This Kalona stuff is even freakier. And I think it was a good idea to get your grandma here, Z."

"Ditto, Twin," Shaunee chimed in.

"Oh, Z!" Jack cried, petting Duchess's ears frantically. "Just thinking about those disgusting raven things croaking at your sweet grandma sitting there in her little house on that lavender farm way out in the boondocks gives me the heebie-jeebies."

"Nice," Aphrodite said. "As if Zoey isn't freaked out enough without you three feeling the need to twist the knife in her gut."

"Oh, jeesh! I'm so sorry, Zoey!" Jack was instantly contrite, clutching Damien with one hand and petting Duchess with the other. He looked like he was going to cry.

I expected the Twins to puff up and hiss at Aphrodite as per usual, but instead they shared a look and then turned to me.

"Sorry, Z," Erin said.

"Yeah, the hag—I mean Aphrodite—is right. We shouldn't have freaked you out about your grandma," Shaunee said.

"Damn. Did the Dorkamese Twins just say I was right about something?" Aphrodite pressed the back of her hand against her forehead and pretended to be about to faint.

"If it makes you feel any better," Shaunee said.

"We still hate you," Erin finished.

"Uh, can we please remember that Duchess has been through a bunch of bullpoop in the past day?" Crouching in front of the big blond Lab, I took her face between my hands. Her eyes were calm and knowing, like she already understood way more than we ever would. "You're a better girl than all of us, aren't you?"

Duchess licked my face, and I smiled. She reminded me of Stark—the living, breathing, confident Stark—and I felt a rush of hope that maybe he would come back for his dog (and for me). Even though that would only add to the complexity of my life, it also somehow made me feel like maybe things weren't so scary as I'd thought they were. Then Damien shattered my illusion.

"Let me see the poem." Typical for Mr. Studious, he went right to the point, bypassing a good portion of the drama.

Feeling utterly relieved to have another brain trying to figure it out, I stood up and handed him the poem.

"First, you know calling it a poem is really a misnomer," Damien said.

"Grandma called it a song," I said.

"It's not actually that, either. Or at least in my opinion it's not."

I had some major respect for Damien's opinion, especially on anything vaguely academic, so I said, "If it's not a poem or a song, what is it, then?"

"It's a prophecy," he said.

"Well, shit! He's right," Aphrodite said.

"Sadly, I have to agree," Shaunee said.

"Gloom and doom to come put in confusing what-the-fuck language. Yep, definitely a prophecy," Erin said.

"Prophecy, like in *Lord of the Rings* about the return of the king?" Jack said.

Damien smiled at him. "Yes, just like that."

Then they all looked my way. "Feels right to me," I said lamely.

"All right. Let's get to work deciphering it." Damien studied the prophecy. "Okay, so, it's written in an *abab cdcd ee* rhyme scheme, breaking it into three stanzas."

"Is that important?" I asked. "I mean, we're calling it a prophecy now instead of a poem, so do we care about that *abab* stuff?"

"Well, I'm not one hundred percent sure, but it is written in poetic form, so my best guess is that we should use poetic rules to decipher it."

"Okay, sounds logical," I said.

"Poetic stanzas are roughly synonymous to paragraphs in prose—each one being self-contained with its own subject, even though it has to fit together as a whole."

"That's my boy!" Jack said, grinning and hugging Duchess.

"Damn, the kid is *smart*," Shaunee said.

"Seriously a brainyack," Erin said.

"Just watching him gives me a headache," Aphrodite said.

"And it means we need to look at the stanzas separately at first," I said. "Right?"

"It can't hurt," Damien said.

"Read it out loud," Aphrodite said. "It was easier to understand when Zoey read it out loud."

He cleared his throat and read the first stanza in his excellent reading voice.

> *Ancient one sleeping, waiting to arise*
> *When earth's power bleeds sacred red*
> *The mark strikes true; Queen Tsi Sgili will devise*
> *He shall be washed from his entombing bed*

"Well, it's obvious that the ancient one it's referring to is Kalona," Damien said.

"And Aphrodite and I already decided that the earth bleeding could come from someone being killed, like Professor Nolan." I paused and swallowed. I should have added Loren, but I couldn't make myself say his name.

"When I found her, there was—there was so much blood all over the grass that it—it hadn't soaked in, so it really did look like the earth had been bleeding." Aphrodite's voice was shaky with the memory.

"Yeah, it definitely could have been described as the earth bleeding," I agreed. "And if the person or vamp who had been killed was powerful, that would fit with the reference to power."

"Okay, that works, especially when you add the next two lines. Obviously this Queen Tsi Sgili devises the whole thing." Damien stopped and squidged his forehead, then added, "You know, it could be a trick reference. Tsi Sgili devises, or brings about what happens, but it's her powerful blood that makes the earth bleed and washes him from his bed."

"Ugh, nasty," Shaunee said.

"So who's the Queen of the Tsi Sgili?" Erin asked.

"We don't know for sure. Grandma had no idea. Actually, she doesn't know much about the Tsi Sgili, except that they are dangerous and feed off death," I said.

"All right, then we need to keep our eyes open for a potential queen," Damien said.

"Even though we don't have a clue who she or he could be?" Shaunee said.

"We do have a clue," Erin said. "Zoey's grandma said the Tsi Sgili feed off death, so it has to be someone who gets stronger after someone dies."

"Also Zoey's grandma said that often the Tsi Sgili have something called . . . uh . . . *ane li*—what was it, Zoey?" Aphrodite said.

"*Ane li sgi,*" I said. "It means they're majorly psychic." I took a deep breath and barreled on. "I think we all know one particular vamp who might fit into this description."

"Neferet," Damien whispered.

"Okay, we know that she's not what she appears to be," Erin said.

"But does that mean that she's as evil as it sounds like a Tsi Sgili has to be?" Shaunee said.

Aphrodite and I exchanged a look. I made the decision and nodded.

"She's chosen a different path from Nyx," Aphrodite said.

The Twins gasped. Jack hugged Duchess, and I swear he made a little doggy whining sound.

"You know that for sure?" Damien said, his voice sounding shaky.

"Yes. We know it for sure," I said.

"Then chances are Neferet is the queen the prophecy refers to."

I felt my stomach turn as more pieces of the puzzle started to fall into place. "Neferet has been different ever since the deaths of Professor Nolan and Loren."

"Oh, Goddess! Are you saying she had something to do with those horrible murders?" Jack gasped.

"I don't know whether she had something to do with them, or whether she just fed off their effects," I said. And I remembered the scene I'd witnessed between Loren and Neferet shortly before he was killed. They'd been lovers—that had been obvious. And he'd been in love with her, but she'd used him to get to me—used her lover to seduce and then Imprint me. How could she really have loved him and sent him to do that?

What if her version of love was as twisted as she had become? Did that mean she could murder what she professed to love?

"But we all thought the People of Faith had something to do with those killings," Shaunee was saying.

"Maybe that's what the Tsi Sgili queen wanted us to think," Damien said, avoiding the use of Neferet's name, which I thought was smart.

"You're right. First those murders, then Aphrodite has a couple whammy visions one right after another about me being killed—and Neferet was definitely involved in at least one of those, and then another vision and this prophecy surfaces? It's too much of a coincidence. Maybe it was supposed to look like a religious hate crime," I said, thinking about the really nice nuns I'd just met who had definitely made me think twice about believing all Christians were narrow-minded jerks out to get anyone who believed differently.

"When really it was a power crime," Aphrodite said. "Because Neferet wants Kalona to rise."

"Uh, let's just call her the queen for right now, okay?" I said quickly.

Everyone nodded—Aphrodite shrugged. "Okay with me."

"Wait, the prophecy could mean that the queen's death makes it possible for Kalona to rise. Let's just say we might know this queen, and if she's who we think she might be, no way do I see her sacrificing herself for someone else to come into power," Damien said.

"Maybe she knows only part of the prophecy. I mean, Grandma said that no one had written the Raven Mockers' song down—that it's remembered only in little tiny bits and pieces, so it's basically been lost for a zillion years."

"Uh-oh," Aphrodite said.

We all looked at her. "What?" I said.

"Okay, I might be wrong, but what if Kalona is somehow reaching out from his grave or whatever you want to call it? He's been there a long time. What if the earth that has been holding him is losing its grip? He's an immortal. Maybe he can reach from where he is and get inside people's brains. Nyx can do it. She can whisper things to us. What if he can, too?"

"Whisper! That's what Nyx said—that Neferet was listening to the whispers of someone else." I shivered at the thought and at the gut feeling that told me we were on to something.

"It would be logical that the people whose minds he could reach easiest would be those who were open to death and evil," Damien said.

"Like the Tsi Sgili," Erin said.

"Especially their queen," Shaunee said.

"Ah, crap," I said.

CHAPTER TWENTY-FOUR

"Okay, let's go on to the next stanza," Damien said. Then he read:

> Through the hand of the dead he is free
> Terrible beauty, monstrous sight
> Ruled again they shall be
> Women shall kneel to his dark might

"Then, of course, the couplet at the end concludes it." Damien finished it by reading:

> Kalona's song sounds sweet
> As we slaughter with cold heat

"Sadly, most of the rest of it isn't too tough to figure out," Erin said. We all gawked at her. "Okay, I'll admit—under duress—that I actually learned something last semester in Poetry class. So sue me. Anyway, except for the first line, it's just saying that he's gonna start raping and pillaging women again when he's free."

"But it's how he's set free that's described in the first line," Damien said. "Through the hand of the dead, and if we're keeping the first stanza in mind, that hand is going to cause something so bloody and nasty, it'll make the ground bleed."

"Yeah, and in the first stanza it sounds like the person who's gonna cause the ground to bleed is the Queen Tsi Sgili. If she's who we think it is, that doesn't fit here. She's not dead," I said.

"Couldn't it be just symbolism? 'Cause how does something that's already dead cause anything to bleed? It just doesn't make sense, which is yet another reason why I've never liked poetry," Aphrodite said. "Plus, let's say it's all jumbled up into one person and this Tsi Sgili is dead and she bleeds—dead people don't bleed. Or at least not for long after they're dead they don't."

"Oh! Oh, no!" I suddenly knew what the prophecy had to mean, and I sat down on the bed hard as my knees buckled.

"Zoey? What is it?" Damien asked, fanning me with the slip of paper.

"If you puke on my bed, I'm going to kill you," Aphrodite said.

I ignored Aphrodite and grabbed Damien's arm. "It's Stevie Rae—she was dead, and now she's undead. She bleeds. She bleeds a lot. Plus she has psychic powers, along with other major earth powers. What if she's the queen?"

"And she has a red tattoo. Just like in the story about the hot chick the Ghigua women made for Kalona," Erin said.

"That's definitely a connection," Shaunee said.

"Stevie Rae! Ohmigod! Stevie Rae!" Jack said, looking even paler than I did.

"I know, honey, I know. It's a lot to take in," Damien said.

Aphrodite met my eyes. "I gotta agree with the theory that it might be Stevie Rae."

"But no. Stevie Rae *was* horrid when she was losing her humanity," Damien said slowly, thinking it out. "But she Changed, and now she's back to her old self. I don't think she could be the queen Tsi Sgili, because Stevie Rae is definitely not evil."

Aphrodite gave me a hard look, then said, "Look, Stevie Rae isn't the same as she used to be."

"Which is only logical because she's been through a lot," I said quickly. No matter what, I wasn't willing to believe that Stevie Rae was bad. Different, yes. But bad, no way. Then I had another thought. "You know, it really makes more sense that one of those other gross kids could be the Tsi Sgili. I mean, you even said they were still—" I stopped, finally realizing that Aphrodite was making a small *Cut!* gesture while Damien and the Twins stared openmouthed at me.

"Uh, yeah. Are you remembering not everyone knows about the other kids?" Aphrodite said. Then she rolled her eyes at the dumfounded looks on my friends' faces. "Well, oopsie. Hey, I'll just let Zoey handle this one. Go ahead, explain the freaks to the geeks, Z."

Ah, crap. I forgot they don't know about the red fledglings.

I decided to be firm. Just tell the whole truth and nothing but the truth and get it over with. And if all else failed, I would burst into tears.

"Okay. Remember all those other dead kids?"

They nodded kinda woodenly at me.

"Nasty Elliot and Elizabeth No Last Name and, well, some other kids, too?"

They nodded again.

"They didn't die. They did what Stevie Rae did—only, well, different. It's really kinda awkward to explain." I hesitated, trying to find the right words. "But basically they're still alive, and their blue crescents have changed to red crescents and they live in the tunnels with Stevie Rae."

Weirdly enough, it was sweet Jack who saved me. "You mean this is more stuff you couldn't tell us 'cause you didn't want us accidentally thinking about it and having Neferet, who really isn't one of the good guys, listening in to our minds and finding out that you knew?"

"Jack, I could kiss you," I said.

"Oh, hee hees!" Jack giggled, ruffling Duchess's ears.

Then I looked from him to my other friends. Would the Twins and Damien discount another passel of lies so easily? I saw the three of them share a long look.

Damien spoke first. "Neferet is behind these undead dead kids, isn't she?"

I hesitated, wanting to save them from the truth as long as possible.

"Yes." Aphrodite took the choice away from me. "Neferet is definitely behind them. That's why Zoey didn't want to tell you guys about the other kids. Neferet is dangerous, and she wanted to keep you from that danger." She paused and looked at me. "But it's too late now. They have to know."

"Yeah," I said slowly. "You all have to know."

"Good," said Damien resolutely. He reached over and took Jack's hand that wasn't stroking Duchess. "It's time we knew everything. We're ready and we're not scared."

"At least not very much," Jack said.

"Yeah, you know how much we love us some good gossip," Erin said.

"And this is some prime, inside, good gossip," Shaunee said.

"Dorkamese Twins, you can't *tell* anybody the gossip," Aphrodite said, clearly disgusted.

"Oh, please, we know that," Shaunee said.

"Yeah, not now we can't, but in the future, this will be some wicked good gossip," Erin said.

"All right," Damien interrupted. "Tell us, Zoey."

I took a deep breath and told them everything. All about the first time I thought I'd seen "ghosts," which had ended up being that nasty Elliot kid and Elizabeth No Last Name (whom I'd had to zap with fire and make really, really dead to get Heath out of the tunnels) when they were actually undead. I told them about the tunnels and what happened when I rescued Heath. I told them about Stevie Rae, *all* about her. I even told them about Stark maybe coming back undead.

When I was finished, there was a long shocked silence from my friends.

"Wow," Jack said. He looked at Aphrodite. "So you're the only one she could tell about all this stuff because for whatever reason vamps can't read your mind?"

"Yes," she said. I could see Aphrodite draw herself up and pull that cold, haughty look over her that meant she was readying herself for them to turn on her—to tell her that now that they knew everything she wouldn't be needed anymore.

"That must have been hard, especially when we were being so mean to you," Jack said.

Aphrodite blinked in surprise.

"Yeah," Damien said. "Sorry about some of the stuff I said. You were being a good friend to Zoey, even when we weren't."

"Ditto," said Shaunee.

"Sadly, ditto here, too," said Erin.

Aphrodite looked utterly stunned. I grinned and sneaked her a quick wink. I didn't say it out loud, but it definitely looked like she was becoming one of the nerd herd.

"So, now that you guys know everything, we have a lot of work to do," I said. I had everyone's attention. "Like Stevie Rae said, we gotta make sure if Stark wakes up, he doesn't do it with Neferet there all waiting to make him into her minion."

"Ugh," Shaunee said.

"It's so damn gross, 'cause he was so damn fine," Erin said.

"He might still be fine," Jack said. Then he gasped and covered

Duchess's ears. "And if you're going to talk about *him* I think we should either just call *him* J.S. or spell his name. You know, out of respect for Duchess."

I looked into Duchess's brown eyes. For a moment I got trapped there, and I swear I saw pain and loss and a deep, limitless kindness.

"Okay, we'll just use his initials," I said, relieved because maybe if I just used Stark's initials, I wouldn't think about that it was really *him* we were discussing, and then I wouldn't remember how much we'd connected right before he died.

"So, instead of trying to snatch, uh, J.S.'s body and hiding it in Z's closet or wherever, I, of course, had a much better idea." Aphrodite paused to be sure she had everyone's attention. "I got a nanny cam."

"Oh, cool!" Jack said. "I saw that on *Dr. Phil* the other day. God, it was just awful. Some horrid and, may I say, *fat, poorly dressed* nanny was caught by one of them shaking the crap out of some poor little kid."

"Then you know about them?" Aphrodite said.

"Yep," he said.

"Good. You need to sneak down to the morgue. Install the camera, and then bring the remote monitor back to Zoey. Think you can handle that?" Aphrodite said.

Jack blanched. "The morgue? As in where they keep dead bodies?"

"Don't think of it like that," I said quickly. "J.S. might just be sleeping, only without the breathing part."

"Oh," Jack said, looking totally unconvinced.

"Can you do it?" I asked, unbelievably relieved that I knew nothing about electronics and this couldn't be my job.

"Yes. I can do it. I promise," Jack said resolutely, hooking an arm around Duchess's neck.

"Good, then that problem is dealt with." At least until he woke up, if he woke up, but I was hoping I had a couple of days before I had to deal with all the ramifications of that. Actually, it was hard for me to think about Stark at all, so I hastily changed the subject. "We need to get back to the prophecy. I'm really worried that the line that says 'through the hand of the dead' is talking about Stevie Rae."

"I still don't think Stevie Rae would be involved in raising this fallen angel," Damien said.

"But there are more of those other new kind of vampyres, right?" Jack said.

"Well, not really more of the vamps," I explained. "Stevie Rae is the only one who has completely gone through the Change. But there are quite a few fledglings."

"It makes more sense that it would be one of them," Damien said.

"Yeah, Stevie Rae is not gonna get mixed up with a bad guy," Erin said.

"Nope, not a chance," Shaunee agreed.

Aphrodite just looked at me. She and I didn't say anything.

"But Zoey said the other kids are, well, gross," Jack said.

"They are," Aphrodite said. "They're like"—she paused, and then her eyes lit up—"they're like blue collar workers. Eesh."

"Aphrodite, there is nothing wrong with blue collar workers," I said, completely exasperated.

"Huh? I hear your words, but you're making no sense."

I rolled my eyes. "Okay, the truth is that in actuality, the red fledglings might be disgusting only in Aphrodite's weird world. I haven't seen any of them since Stevie Rae Changed, and she's told me that they're under control and have their humanity back, so I'm going to try to withhold judgment."

"Well, whether they're really gross or just being class-stereotyped by Gossip Girl, I think we need to keep an eye on them," Damien said. "We need to know what they're doing. Who they're talking to. What they're thinking. If we know all of that, we'll also know if this demon guy is trying to contact one of them and use him for his nefarious means."

"Nef—what?" Shaunee said.

"Arious—who?" Erin said.

"It means 'wicked in the extreme,'" Jack whispered to the Twins.

"Well, then it's a good thing that Stevie Rae and her red fledglings are coming to the ritual tomorrow," I announced.

My friends gaped at me.

I looked at Aphrodite. She sighed. "I don't have an earth affinity anymore," she admitted. Then she reached up and with the back of her hand wiped it across her forehead, smearing the fake sapphire crescent tattoo she'd drawn there. "I'm not a fledgling anymore. I'm human again."

"Well, she's not exactly a normal human," I added. "She still has visions, as is obvious by the prophecy she just copied for us. She's also still really important to Nyx." I smiled at Aphrodite. "I heard the Goddess say so."

"Okay, that's majorly freaky!" Jack said.

"It's totally queer," Shaunee said.

"And she doesn't mean that in the gay sense," Erin input.

"So, like Stevie Rae and the red fledglings, Aphrodite is something that's never been before," Damien said thoughtfully.

"Looks like it," I said.

"Things are changing," Damien said slowly. "The world order is shifting into something new."

A cold shiver passed through me. "Is that good or bad?"

"I don't think we can know yet," he said. "But I think we will know pretty soon."

"It's scary," Jack said.

I looked at my friends. They all seemed frightened and unsure, and I knew this would not do. We had to be strong. We had to stick together and believe in each other.

"I don't think it's scary." When I started saying it, it was a big fat lie. But the more I spoke, the more I began to believe. "Change can be weird, or even *queer*." I grinned at Damien and Jack, and they smiled hesitatingly back at me. "But change has to happen for things to grow—for us to grow. Hey, if it wasn't for this change, Stevie Rae would be dead. I remember that when I start feeling overwhelmed by all of this. Plus"—I looked at each of them—"we have each other. And change isn't so bad when you're not in it alone."

Their looks of growing confidence made me think that I might, someday, become a halfway decent High Priestess.

"So what's the Plan?" Damien asked.

"Well, you and Jack have to install the nanny cam in the morgue. Think you can do that without getting caught?" I said.

"I think we might be able to create a diversion," Jack said slowly, looking from Duchess to Maleficent, who had spent the entire "meeting" growling ominously at the dog from the bathroom. "If we can count on Aphrodite's help."

"Fine. But if my cat eats that dog, I don't want to hear a word about it, even if *S-t-a-r-k* wakes up and gets testy about why his Lab's muzzle has been torn to shreds."

"Uh, try to make it just a diversion, not a bloodbath," I said.

"Deal," Damien and Jack said together.

"I'm going to go find Shekinah and tell her that my grandma is coming to visit, and that I need her to stay in a guest room," I said.

"And we're gonna stay the hell away from Neferet," Erin said.

"Ditto," Shaunee said. "And that should be ditto for all of us except Z and Aphrodite."

I was opening my mouth to agree with her when Aphrodite's loud, "No!" shocked all of us.

"What do you mean no? We have to stay away from Neferet. If she starts listening in to our minds, she'll know we all know about Stevie Rae and the other kids. And if she's really the Queen of the Tsi Sgili, she'll be warned that we know about her, the Raven Mockers, and even Kalona," Damien said, sounding totally exasperated.

"Wait a second. Tell me why you think they shouldn't avoid Neferet," I asked Aphrodite.

"Simple. If the nerd herd avoids her, Neferet is going to for sure start listening in to their thoughts. She'll listen long and hard and deep. But what if Damien and Jack and the Dorkamese Twins act like their normal, clueless selves? What if they don't avoid her, but if they even maybe seek her out and say hi to her, ask her questions about homework, and make up complaints about the food being too healthy?"

"We really wouldn't have to make that up," Jack said.

"Exactly, and while they're around Neferet, let's say Jack is thinking about nothing but how stressful it is to try to deal with a sad dog all the time. Damien's thinking about homework and how cute Jack's eyes are. And the twins are thinking about sneaking out for the end-of-season winter shoe sale at Saks, which is next week, by the way."

"No way! It starts already!" Shaunee said.

"I knew it. I knew it was going to be early this year. What with that stupid snowstorm we had, they have to increase sales, so it's thrown off the whole traditional sale schedule," Erin said.

"Tragic, Twin, just tragic," Shaunee said.

"See, if the geeks and freaks act as empty-headed as Neferet really, deep down, believes they are, she won't look farther," Aphrodite said.

"Do you really think Neferet believes we're empty-headed?" Damien said.

"Neferet consistently underestimates me. It makes sense that she underestimates you guys, too," I said.

"If that's true, we have a huge advantage," Damien said.

"Until she realizes her mistake," Aphrodite said.

"Well, let's hope that takes a while," I said. "Okay, I'm going to go find Shekinah. From here on out, I think we should all stick together as much as we can. I know Grandma said the Raven Mockers were just spirits, but I'm almost one hundred percent sure one of them attacked me yesterday—and it hurt. Plus, I have a generally creepy feeling about them. She also said they could harm old people who are close to death. Well, what if Kalona is getting stronger, and they're getting stronger, too? What if they can harm people not so old or not so close to death?"

"You're freaking me out," Jack said.

"Good," I said. "If you're scared, you'll be more careful."

"I don't want to be scared and sneaking around a morgue," Jack said.

"Remember, he might be just sleeping," Damien said. He put his arm around Jack. "Let's take Duchess back to my room and figure out our whole diversionary plan." He looked at Aphrodite. "You're coming with us, aren't you?"

She sighed. "You're going to use my cat."

It wasn't a question, but the two boys nodded and grinned.

"Well, then I'm coming with you. We'll leave Maleficent here until the deed is getting ready to be done."

"Definitely," Damien said.

I looked at the Twins. "I don't need to tell you guys to stick together, do I?"

"Nope," Erin said.

"Hey, what if we gather up some more stuff for smudge sticks," Shaunee said.

"Good idea. Smudging all of our rooms couldn't hurt," I said.

"Okey," Shaunee said.

"Dokey," Erin said.

"But wait on that," Jack said. "You guys might be able to help in our diversionary action, too."

"You know Beelzebub isn't nice," Shaunee said.

Jack grinned and nodded. "Exactly why he's so perfect."

"Poor Duchess," Erin said.

"Hey, what are you gonna do, Z?" Jack asked.

"Go see Shekinah and ask about Grandma staying here." I glanced at my clock. "Actually, she should be here pretty soon."

"Okay, we all know what we're doing. So let's get to it," Damien said.

As we all headed out the door, Aphrodite hung back. "Hey, I'll meet you back here pretty soon. Looks like you and I will be sticking together for a while."

I smiled at her. "You got yourself into some crap this time, didn't you?"

She rolled her eyes, pulled a mirror out of her purse, and expertly reapplied her fake tattoo, and as I followed her out the door, I walked in a trail of her muttering, "Yeah . . . yeah . . . yeah . . . stupid red-eye-causing visions, dorky friends, ancient evil . . . I can hardly wait to see what's next . . ."

CHAPTER TWENTY-FIVE

Walking down the sidewalk that ran from the girls' dorm to the main school building, I decided that it wouldn't be smart to see Shekinah all tense and stressed out, so I took several deep cleansing breaths to calm myself, collect my thoughts, and told myself to relax and appreciate the beautiful, unseasonably warm night. Gaslights made pretty shadows against the winter trees and hedges, and there was a soft wind blowing the scent of cinnamon and earth from the fallen leaves that carpeted the grounds. Groups of kids walked back and forth between the buildings, mostly heading to the dorms or the near end of the school that held the cafeteria. They were talking and laughing together. Several of them called hellos to me, and many of them saluted me respectfully. Despite the problems facing me, I realized I was feeling optimistic. I wasn't alone in this. My friends were with me, and for the first time in a long time, they knew everything. I wasn't lying or evading. I was telling the truth and really, *really* happy about it.

Nala padded out of the shadows and up to me, *"mee-uf-owing"* and giving me a reproachful look. With barely a pause, she hurled herself up and into my arms and I had to scramble to catch her.

"Hey! You could warn me, ya know!" I said, but ended up kissing the white spot over her nose and tickling her ears. We walked down the shadowy sidewalk, heading away from the kid-filled part of campus to the quieter section that held the library and eventually the professors' rooms. The night really was pretty, with a clear Oklahoma sky filled with glittering stars. Nala curled her head against my shoulder and was purring contentedly when I felt her entire body tense up.

"Nala? What's wrong with—?"

And I heard it. A single croaking raven that sounded like it was so close that I should be able to see it within the night-sleeping shadows of the nearest tree. His cry was taken up by first one, and then another and then another. That simple sound was indescribably terrifying. I understood why they were called mockers of ravens because, even though you could easily mistake them for regular birds, if you listened just a little more carefully, you heard in their suspiciously mundane call the echo of death and fear and madness. The breeze that had been warm and sweet-smelling was replaced by an icy nothingness, like I'd just entered a mausoleum. My blood went cold.

Nala hissed long and menacingly, staring back over my shoulder at the darkness surrounding the huge old oaks that were usually so familiar and welcoming. Not tonight. Tonight they housed monsters. I automatically started to walk faster, looking frantically around for the kids that had just moments ago seemed to be all around me. But Nala and I had turned a corner in the sidewalk, and we were totally alone with the night and all it shrouded.

The ravens cried again. The sound made the hair on my arms and the back of my neck stand up. Nala growled low in her throat and hissed again. Wings fluttered all around me, so close, I could feel the cold wind they were displacing. I smelled them then. They reeked of old meat and pus. A scent that was deadly, sickeningly sweet. I tasted the bile of fear in the back of my throat.

More croaking caws filled the night, and now I could see darkness within the darkness of stirring shadows. I caught glimpses of something flashing, sharp and hooked. How could they have beaks that shone glossy in the softness of the gaslights if they were just spirit? How could spirits smell like death and decay? And if they weren't just spirits anymore, what did that mean?

I stopped, unsure of whether I should run on or go back. And while I stood there, frozen with panic and indecision, the blackness within the nearest tree quivered and launched itself at me. My heart was hammering painfully, and I was on the verge of panic that was making me dumb with numbing fear. All I could do was pant with terror as it got closer. Its horrible wings displacing freezing, putrid air, it came at me. I could see it—I could see the man's eyes within the mutated bird's face . . . and arms . . . the arms of a man with twisted, grotesque hands held up in the shape of ragged, dirty claws. The creature opened its hooked beak and shrieked at me, forked tongue extended.

"No!" I cried, scrambling back from it, keeping a tight hold on my hissing cat. "Get away!" I turned and ran.

It caught me then. I could feel its horribly cold hands hook on my shoulders. I screamed and dropped Nala, who crouched at my feet, snarling up at the creature. Its horrible wings unfurled on either side of me, holding me there. I felt it lean into my back in a mockery of an embrace. Its head craned over my shoulder so that its beak hooked around my neck, resting against the place my pulse beat frantically in my throat. It stayed there, and its beak opened just enough to let the thing's red forked tongue slide out and taste my neck, like it was savoring me before it devoured me.

I was absolutely frozen with fear. I knew it was going to slice open my throat. Aphrodite's vision was coming true, only it was a demon who was going to kill me and not Neferet! *No! O Goddess, no!* My mind shrieked. *Spirit! Find someone to help me!*

"*Zoey?*" Damien's voice was suddenly in a questioning wind whirling around me.

"Damien, help me . . . ," I managed in a broken whisper.

"*Save Zoey!*" Damien shouted.

A violent blast of air knocked the creature from my back, but the thing was still able to slide its beak across my throat. As I fell to my knees, my hand went to my stinging neck, expecting to feel the wetness of my life's blood pouring hot and thick, but there was nothing there except a raised line that hurt like hell.

The sound of flapping wings regrouping behind me had me jumping to my feet and whirling around. But this time the wind that smoothed against my skin wasn't frigid and rank with death. It was familiar and filled with the strength of Damien's friendship. The knowledge that I wasn't alone—that my friends hadn't deserted me—cut through the paralyzing mist of panic that had clouded my thoughts like a goddess's avenging sword, and my frozen mind began to work again. Spirits or monstrous birds or minions of Neferet's twisted desires—it didn't really matter. I knew something that would handle all those things.

I quickly oriented myself, facing the direction I knew was east. Then I raised both my arms over my head, closed my eyes, and blocked out the evil mockery of twisted bird calls. "Wind! Blow hard—blow strong—blow true—and show these creatures what it is to attack someone who is beloved of a Goddess!" I hurled my hands outward toward the creatures that had overtaken the night. I saw the one closest—the one who had tried to slit my throat, caught first in the gale. The wind lifted it up and away and threw it against the stone wall that ringed the school grounds. It crumpled and then seemed to dissolve into the ground, completely disappearing.

"All of them!" I cried, my fear lending power and urgency to my voice. "Blow them all away!" I flung my hands out again and was grimly pleased when the mocking calls of the creatures that lurked in the trees turned to shrieks of panic and then died away completely. When I knew they were gone, I let my trembling arms drift down to my sides. "In the name of my Goddess, Nyx, I thank you, wind. I release you, and please tell Damien I'm fine now. I'm okay."

But before wind left me, it found my face, caressed it briefly, and then it was filled with more than Damien's presence. Within the lingering breeze there was suddenly a distinct warmth that reminded me of Shaunee with its hint of spice and sizzle, as well as the scent of a life-affirming spring shower, which I knew had been sent by Erin. The three elements of my friends joined together, and the wind became a healing breeze that circled around my neck like a silk scarf, soothing the stinging wound left by the Raven Mocker. When the pain around my throat had faded completely, the wind gently blew itself away, taking with it the warmth of fire and the healing touch of water, leaving only the peace of the night and silence.

I lifted my hand, letting my fingers run across my throat. Nothing. There was not a scratch there. I closed my eyes and sent a silent *thank you for my friends* prayer to Nyx. With their help, I'd overcome one of Aphrodite's death visions for me. One down . . . one to go . . .

I picked up Nala and, holding her close to me, hurried down the sidewalk, trying to stop the trembling that was still quaking through my body.

I was feeling shaky and ultrasensitive, and when my gut told me I really shouldn't be seen right now, I called spirit to me as I entered the quieting school building, and through it covered myself in silence and shadow. So I moved through the mostly deserted halls of school undetected. It was weird of me to do this inside our school building, and it made me feel detached, like I was hiding not just my body, but my thoughts, too, and gradually as I made my way to the Council Chamber, the fear and the triumph that trembled inside me stilled and I began to breathe more easily.

Though Neferet's hand hadn't literally tried to slit my throat, I knew deep in my gut that what I'd just avoided really had been my death, or at the very least a foreshadowing of it. Had Damien still been mad at me, I don't think I could have pushed through the terror the Raven Mockers washed over me and reached out to the elements for protection. And even though Neferet hadn't been holding a blade to my neck, I couldn't help but believe that she was somehow all tied up in what was happening.

Was I still scared? Hell yes!

But I was also still breathing and more or less in one piece. (Okay, I was currently invisible, but still.) Could I beat the Raven Mockers again? In their current form where they were part spirit, part body, yes—with the help of my friends and the elements.

Could I beat them if they were fully formed and had come into all their power?

I shivered. Just the thought of it terrified me.

So I did what any reasonable kid would do—I decided to think about it later. A snatched piece of a quote surfaced from my memory, *sufficient unto the day is the evil thereof,* and as I dived deeply into the lovely Land of Denial, I kept my mind busy trying to figure out where I'd read it.

Soundlessly, I floated up the stairs to the Council Chamber, across from the library, where I thought I would probably find Shekinah. It was in the hall outside the room that I heard the all-too-familiar voice, and I was very, very glad I'd followed my instinct to conceal myself.

"So you admit to feeling it, too? This sense of something being not right?"

"Yes, Neferet. I readily admit to sensing there was something wrong about the school, but if you'll recall, I was firmly against buying this campus from the Cascia Hall monks five years ago."

"We needed a House of Night in this part of the country," Neferet insisted.

"And that is the argument that won the Council over and convinced them to open this House of Night. I didn't agree with it then, and I don't agree with it now. The recent deaths simply prove we should not be here."

"The recent murders prove we need *more* of a presence here and all over the world!" Neferet snapped. I heard her draw a deep breath, as if she was working hard to control herself. When she spoke again, her voice was much more subdued. "This bad feeling of which we were speaking—it has nothing to do with being reticent about opening a school. It's different, more malevolent, and it's grown far worse in the recent months."

There was a long pause before Shekinah answered her. "I do feel a malevolence here, but I cannot name it. It seems hidden, shrouded in something I do not find familiar."

"I think I can name it," Neferet said.

"What do you suspect?"

"I have come to believe it is an evil hidden, shrouded, in the appearance of a child, and that is why it is going to be so hard to expose," Neferet said.

"I don't understand your meaning, Neferet. Are you saying one of the fledglings is hiding evil?"

"I don't want to say it, but I'm coming to believe it." Neferet's voice was filled with sadness, like what she was saying was so difficult to admit, she was almost on the brink of tears.

I knew it was absolutely, utterly, an act.

"Again I ask you, what do you suspect?"

"It isn't a what, but a who. Shekinah, sister, it grieves me to say it, but the deep evil I have been sensing, that *you* have been sensing, too, began to build and intensify with one student's entry to this House of Night." She paused, and even though I knew what she was going to say, it was a shock to hear her actually speak the words. "I'm afraid Zoey Redbird is hiding a terrible secret."

"Zoey! But she is the most gifted fledgling in history. Not only has no other fledging ever wielded the power of all five elements, but no other fledgling has ever been surrounded by so many gifted peers. Each of her closest friends can manifest one of the elements. How could she possibly be so gifted and be hiding evil?" Shekinah said.

"I don't know!" Neferet's voice broke, and I could tell she was crying. "I'm her mentor. Can you imagine how much it grieves me to even think these things, let alone say them aloud?"

"What evidence do you have for your belief?" Shekinah asked, and I was glad to hear that she didn't sound particularly convinced Neferet was on to something.

"A teenage boy who used to be her lover was almost killed by spirits she conjured just days after she was Marked."

I blinked in utter shock. Heath and I had been lovers? Not hardly! Neferet knew that. And I hadn't conjured those mean spirits—Aphrodite had. Yes, they'd almost eaten Heath—well, and also Erik—but with the help of Stevie Rae, Damien, and the Twins, I'd stopped them.

"Then not more than a month later, two more teenage boys, again humans who were, let's just say *intimate* with her, were abducted and brutally killed—drained of all blood. A third boy, another human close to her, was taken, too. The community was in a frenzy, and that is when Zoey *rescued* the boy."

Oh. My. Goddess! Neferet was twisting everything and lying

her butt off! It was the nasty undead dead kids who had killed the two Union football players, who I definitely had *not* been intimate with! Yes, I'd saved Heath (again—sigh), but I'd saved him from *her* disgusting, bloodsucking (not that there's anything wrong with it) minions!

"What else?" Shekinah said. I was glad to hear that her voice had remained calm and she still didn't sound like she was convinced Neferet was right about me.

"This last part is the most difficult for me to admit, but Zoey was special to Patricia Nolan. She spent quite a bit of time with her before she was murdered."

My head was buzzing. Sure, I'd liked Professor Nolan, and I think she liked me, but I definitely hadn't been special to her, and hadn't spent any extra time with her, either.

Then I knew what she was going to accuse me of next, even though I could hardly believe it.

"And I have reason to believe Zoey had become Loren Blake's lover just before he, too, was murdered. Actually, I'm sure the two of them had Imprinted." Neferet broke off, sobbing brokenly.

"Why did you not report any of this to the Council?" Shekinah asked sternly.

"What was I supposed to say? I *think* this most gifted of all fledglings has allied herself with evil? How could I bring such a charge against a young girl with no more proof than coincidence, supposition, and a feeling?"

Well, that was exactly what she was doing right now!

"But Neferet, if a fledgling gets involved with a professor, it is the High Priestess's duty to put a stop to it, and to report it to the Council."

"I know!" I could hear that Neferet was still crying. "I was wrong. I should have said something. Perhaps if I had, I could have prevented his death."

There was a long pause, and then Shekinah said, "You and Loren were lovers, were you not?"

"Yes!" Neferet sobbed.

"You realize your relationship with Loren could be clouding your judgment of Zoey?"

"I do." I heard her "valiantly" (barf!) try to pull herself together. "Which is another reason I was hesitant to tell anyone about my suspicions."

"Have you looked into her mind?" Shekinah asked.

I shivered while I waited for Neferet's answer.

"I've tried. I cannot read her mind."

"How about her friends? The other fledglings who have special affinities?"

Crap! Crap! Crap!

"I have looked within them periodically. I have not found anything disturbing. Yet."

I heard Shekinah's sigh. "It is good that I am staying on here for the rest of this semester. I, too, will watch and listen around Zoey and the other fledglings. There is always a chance, and a very good one at that, that Zoey only seems in the middle of these events because she is, indeed, a very powerfully gifted young woman. She might not be causing the events, but might have been put here by Nyx to help thwart evil that is not of her making."

"I sincerely hope so," Neferet said.

She was such a liar!

"But we shall watch her. Closely," Shekinah said.

"Be careful of the favors she asks," Neferet said.

Huh? Favors? I hadn't asked Neferet for any favors! And then, with a jolt, I realized what it was Neferet was doing. She was messing it up for me to ask that Grandma visit me and stay here on campus. Bitch!

And the jolt of understanding turned to a sick dread. How had Neferet known Grandma was coming?

Suddenly, a huge commotion from outside drowned Shekinah's response. I was listening from the hall, so it was easy for me to drift over to one of the large curtained windows. Because it was night, the drapes were open and I looked down on the front grounds of the school. What I saw made me press my hand against my mouth to keep from cracking up.

Duchess was barking her head off as she raced after a snarling, hissing, yowling white ball of Maleficent. Aphrodite was chasing after the dog, screaming for her to "Come! Stay! Be good, damnit!" Damien was close behind her, flailing his arms and yelling, "Duchess! Come!" All of a sudden the Twins' cat, the huge and very stuck-up Beelzebub, joined in the chase, only he was tearing around after Duchess.

"Ohmygod! Beelzebub! Honey!" Shaunee ran into my view, yelling at the top of her very healthy lungs.

"Beelzebub! Duchess! Stop!" Erin wailed, right behind her twin.

Darius suddenly burst into the hallway, and I stepped back behind the curtains, not sure if my shrouding could be detected by him. Apparently he didn't notice me, or anything else, because he ran into the Council Room. I peeked through the drapes and could hear him telling Neferet that she was needed on the school grounds—that there was an "altercation." Then Neferet was hurrying out of the room and down the hall, following Darius into the dog-barking, cat-yowling, kid-screaming craziness.

I noticed that through all of it I hadn't seen hide nor hair of Jack.

Talk about an excellent diversion!

CHAPTER TWENTY-SIX

Again I listened to my instincts, and instead of sending away my concealing spirit right outside the Council Room, I moved quickly down the hall, retracing my path until I was at the bottom of the stairs. Then I lifted the concealment, thanking spirit, and started back up the stairs completely visible and telling myself, *Be calm . . . be normal . . . Neferet is a liar and Shekinah is very, very wise . . .*

Outside the Council Chamber, I paused to knock twice on the door.

"You may come in, Zoey!" Shekinah called.

I tried not to wonder if she'd known I'd been outside before. Putting a smile on my face, I entered the room. I fisted my hand over my heart and bowed respectfully. "Merry meet, Shekinah."

"Merry meet, Zoey Redbird," she said. I didn't notice any weirdness in her voice. "So, how was your visit with the ladies at Street Cats?"

I grinned. "Did you know that Street Cats is run by Benedictine nuns?"

She smiled back at me. "I did not, though I did expect the charity to be run by women. Women have long had a strong connection with cats. Were the good sisters open to your volunteer work?"

"Definitely. They were really nice. Oh, and Aphrodite adopted a cat while we were there, although Maleficent adopting Aphrodite is probably a more accurate way to describe what happened."

"Maleficent? What an unusual name."

"Yeah, but it fits her. All that noise that's happening out there." I jerked my head back in the direction of the hallway and the front of the school. We both listened and could still hear dog barking, cat yowling, and kid shouting. "I think you'll find out that all of that was instigated by Maleficent."

"So what you're saying is the nuns have double cause to thank you. For your volunteerism and for helping them rid themselves of one very difficult feline?"

"Yes, that's exactly what I'm saying. Oh, and Sister Mary Angela asked me to check with you about a date that would work well for the flea market. She said she'd work their schedule around ours. Besides that, they're going to stay open late every Saturday night so that we can volunteer once a week."

"That sounds lovely. I will meet with Neferet about a date that works best for the school." Shekinah paused for a moment, and then added, "Zoey, Neferet is your mentor, isn't she?"

I heard warning bells inside my head, but I forced myself to relax. I was going to answer Shekinah as honestly as I could in everything she asked me. I hadn't done anything wrong!

"Yes. Neferet is my mentor."

"And do you feel close to Neferet?"

"I used to. We were very close when I first came here. Actually, my mom and I haven't been close for several years, and I kinda felt like Neferet was the mom I wish I'd had," I said truthfully.

"But that has changed?" she asked gently.

"Yes," I said.

"And why is that?"

I hesitated, choosing my words very carefully. I wanted to tell

Shekinah as much of the truth as I dared, and for an instant I considered telling her everything—the whole truth about Stevie Rae and the prophecy and what we were afraid was happening, but my gut told me not to reveal everything now. Shekinah would learn the truth tomorrow. Until then, I didn't want Neferet to have any inkling about what was going to happen—about the fact that she was going to have to face what she had done, and what she was becoming.

"I'm not one hundred percent sure," I said.

"What is your best guess?"

"Well, I think she's changed lately, and I'm not sure why. Some of it might have to do with some personal stuff that happened between us. I'd really rather not talk about that, if it's okay with you."

"Of course. I understand your need to keep things that are private to yourself. But, Zoey, you should know that I am here for you to talk with if you need me. Though it was long ago, I remember very well what it was to be a powerful fledgling and to feel like I was carrying so many responsibilities that the burden of them sometimes became too much to bear."

"Yeah," I said, suddenly having to fight back tears. "That's exactly what it feels like sometimes."

Her candid gaze was warm and kind. "It gets better. I can promise you that."

"I really hope so," I said. "Oh, and speaking of making things better—my grandma would like to come for a little visit. She and I are really close. I meant to spend some of winter break with her, but, well, you know that break was called off. So Grandma said she'd like to come here to spend some time with me. Do you think it would be okay if she stayed at the school?"

Shekinah studied me carefully. "There are guest rooms in the professors' building, but I believe they are all filled right now because of my visit and the influx of the Sons of Erebus."

"Could she maybe stay in my room with me? My roommate, Stevie Rae, died last month, and I haven't gotten a new one, so I have an empty bed and everything."

"I suppose I don't see any harm in that. If your grandmother is comfortable with being surrounded by so many fledglings."

I grinned. "Grandma likes kids. Plus, she knows a bunch of my friends here, and they all like her."

"Then I'll let the Sons of Erebus, as well as Neferet, know that you have permission for your grandmother to visit and to stay in your room. Zoey, you know that asking for special favors is not always wise, even if you have special abilities."

I met Shekinah's gaze steadily. "This is the first favor I have asked for since I came to the House of Night." Then I thought about it for a second and corrected myself. "No, wait. It's the second. The first favor I asked for was to keep a few of my roommate's things after she died."

Shekinah nodded slowly, and I hoped as hard as I could that she believed me. I wanted to yell: *Check it out with the other professors! They know I don't ask for special treatment!* But I couldn't say anything to let Shekinah believe that I'd overheard her conversation with Neferet.

"Well, good. Then you're already starting down the right road. Gifts from our Goddess don't mean privilege—they mean responsibility."

"I understand that," I said firmly.

"I think maybe you do," she said. "Now, I'm sure you have homework to catch up on and a ritual to prepare to lead tomorrow, so I will bid you a good night and hope that you will blessed be," she said.

"Blessed be." I saluted her formally again, bowed, and left the room.

Things really hadn't gone so bad. Sure, Neferet was lying her butt off about me and was clearly an evil-filled bitch, but I'd already known that. Shekinah wasn't stupid, and she certainly wouldn't be made into Neferet's fool (*like Loren had been*, my mind whispered). Grandma was on her way to the school, and she was going to stay with me while we figured out this whole prophecy thing. My friends finally knew everything, so I didn't have to constantly make excuses and evade them, and they had my back, even though just thinking about the Raven Mockers creeped me totally out. But I could handle the creeping-out part with my friends by my side. And tomorrow everyone would know about Stevie Rae and the red fledglings, and Neferet would lose the power of secrecy. Then maybe Stark wouldn't really be dead, and would come back himself. Things really were looking up! I was just opening the door to the front of the building and grinning like a fool when I ran smack into Erik.

"Oh, sorry I wasn't looking—," he began, automatically reaching out to steady me before he realized who he'd almost knocked over. "Oh," he repeated, this time in a much less nice-guy voice. "It's you."

I pulled my arm out of his hand and stepped back, brushing my hair from my face. Looking up into his cold blue eyes was like taking a nosedive into freezing water—and I'd just about had enough cold water splashed in my face by him.

"Look, I have something to say to you." I moved in front of him, blocking his way into the building.

"So say it."

"You liked kissing me today. You liked it a lot."

His smile was mocking and very well rehearsed. "Yeah, so? I never said I didn't like kissing you. The problem is too many guys have liked kissing you."

I felt my face go hot. "Don't you dare talk to me like that!"

"Why not? It's true. You were kissing your human boyfriend.

You were kissing me. And you were kissing Blake. As far as I'm concerned, that's a lot of guys."

"Since when you do turn into such a jerk? You knew about Heath. I never tried to hide him from you. You knew it was hard for me being Imprinted with him and caring about you at the same time."

"Yeah, what about Blake? Explain that."

"Loren was a mistake!" I yelled, finally tipping over that line of self-control. I was tired of Erik judging me for something I'd beaten myself up about more times than I could count. "You were right. He was using me. Only it wasn't for sex—that was just the way he got me to believe he loved me. You overheard the scene between Neferet and me. You know there's more going on here than everyone thinks. Neferet sent Loren, *her lover,* to seduce me—to make me believe he loved me because I'm special." I paused, wiping angrily at the tears that were somehow falling out of my eyes. "But really he was after me so that I could piss off all my friends and be alone and hurt and distracted so my powers didn't mean anything anymore. And it would have worked if Aphrodite hadn't stood by me. You sure as hell didn't take one second to give me a chance to explain."

Erik ran his hand through his thick dark hair. "I saw him making love to you."

"You know what you saw, Erik? You saw him using me. You saw me making the biggest mistake of my life. At least so far. That's what you saw."

"You hurt me," he said softly, all the anger and jerkness going out of his voice.

"I know and I'm sorry. But I guess we didn't have much together in the first place if we can't learn to forgive each other for this mess."

"You think you need to forgive me?"

He was starting to look like a jerk again. I'd definitely had enough of the jerk Erik. My eyes narrowed and I snapped, "Yeah! I need to forgive you. You said you cared about me, but you've called me a slut. You've embarrassed me in front of my friends. You've embarrassed me in front of a class of kids. And you did all of that because you had only part of the story, Erik! So, yeah, you're not totally spotless in this whole thing either!"

Erik blinked in surprise at my outburst. "I didn't know I had only part of the story."

"Maybe next time you should think before you vent without knowing the full story."

"So you hate me now?" he said.

"No. I don't hate you. I miss you."

We stared at each other, neither of us knowing where to go from there.

"I miss you, too," he finally said.

My heart made a little skip-beat.

"Maybe we could talk again," I said. "I mean, without the yelling part."

He looked at me for a long, long time. I tried to read his eyes, but they just reflected back at me my own confusion.

My phone rang, and I pulled it out of my pocket. It was Grandma. "Oh, sorry. It's my grandma," I told Erik. Then I flipped the cell open. "Hi, Grandma, are you here?" I nodded as she told me she'd just pulled into the parking lot. "Okay, I'll meet you there in just a few minutes. Can't wait to see you! Bye!"

"Your grandma's here?" Erik asked.

"Yeah." I was still smiling. "She's come to stay for a little while. You know, what with the whole winter break being cut short and all."

"Oh, yeah. That makes sense. Okay, well, I guess I'll see you around."

"Uh, want to walk with me to the parking lot? Grandma said

she was going to pack a little something, which means she probably brought one ginormic bag or ten little ones, and she could
definitely use a grown vamp to carry them for her, what with me
being just a little fledgling."

I held my breath, thinking I'd messed up (again) and gone too
far too soon with him. And, sure enough, the guarded look was
back in his eyes.

It was exactly then that a vamp in the Sons of Erebus uniform
came out of the door behind me.

"Excuse me," Erik said to him. "This is Zoey Redbird. A guest
of hers has just arrived. Are you available to help bring in her
luggage?"

The warrior saluted me respectfully. "I am Stephan, and it is
my pleasure to aid you, young Priestess."

I made myself smile and say thanks. Then I looked at Erik. "So,
I'll see you later?" I said.

"Of course. You're taking my class." He saluted me and then
went into the building.

The parking lot was just a short way around the side of the
main building. So, thankfully, I didn't have much walking with
the warrior in uncomfortable silence to endure. Grandma waved
to me from the middle of the very crowded parking lot. I waved
back, and Stephan and I headed toward her.

"Wow, there are a ton of vamps here," I said, looking at all the
unfamiliar cars.

"Many Sons of Erebus have been called to this House of
Night," Stephan said.

I nodded thoughtfully.

I could feel his eyes on me. "Priestess, you need not fear for
your safety," he said with quiet authority.

I smiled at him and thought, *If only you knew,* but I didn't say
anything.

"Zoey! Oh, honey! Here you are." Grandma enveloped me in her arms, and I hugged her hard, breathing in the familiar scent of lavender and home.

"Grandma, I'm so glad you're here!"

"So am I, honey. So am I." She squeezed me tight.

Stephan bowed respectfully to Grandma before he gathered up her mound of luggage.

"Grandma, are you planning on staying a year?" I asked, throwing a laughing look over my shoulder at her bulging luggage.

"Well, honey, one must always be prepared for all contingencies." Grandma Redbird wrapped her arm though mine, and we started back toward the sidewalk that would lead to the girls' dorm, with Stephan following behind us.

Soon she tilted her head close to mine and whispered, "The school is completely surrounded."

I felt a sizzle of fear. "By what?"

"Ravens." She said the word as if it left a nasty taste in her mouth. "They're all around the grounds, but none are actually inside the boundary of the school's wall."

"That's because I blew them out of here," I said.

"Did you?" she whispered. "Well done, Zoeybird!"

"They scare me, Grandma," I whispered back. "I think they're getting their bodies back."

"I know, honey. I know."

Shivering, we held tightly to each other as we hurried to my room. The night seemed to watch us go.

CHAPTER TWENTY-SEVEN

Not surprisingly, everydangbody was crammed into my dorm room.

"Grandma Redbird!" Damien cried, and hurled himself into her arms. Then there was a big flurry of him introducing Jack to her, the Twins saying their hellos, and finally, Aphrodite, looking uncomfortable but pleased, getting a very tight, very heartfelt hug from Grandma. During the commotion, Damien and the Twins cornered me.

"Z, are you okay?" Damien asked in a low voice.

"Yeah, we were worried," Shaunee said.

"Some scary crap is going on," Erin said.

"I'm fine." I threw a furtive look to where Jack was babbling something at Grandma about how much he liked lavender. "Because of your help, I'm fine."

"We're here for you, Z. You're not in this alone," Damien said.

"Ditto," said the Twins together.

"Zoey? Is that a dog?" Grandma had just noticed that the lump of blond fur stretched out on the end of my bed actually moved and caused every cat in the room to hiss at the same instant.

"Yep, Grandma. It's a dog. And it's a long story."

"Who does she belong to?" Grandma asked, giving Duchess a tentative head rub.

"Well, kinda me. At least temporarily," Jack said.

"Maybe this would be a good time to explain to your grandma about Stevie Rae and everyone," Aphrodite said.

"Stevie Rae? Oh, honey. Are you still grieving her loss?"

"Not exactly, Grandma," I said slowly. "There's really a lot to explain."

"Then you should get started. Something tells me we're getting ready to run out of the luxury of time," Grandma said.

"First, you should know that I haven't told you all of this, because Neferet is involved in it—in a bad way. And she's majorly psychic. So whatever I tell you, she may be able to pick out of your brain, and that's not good," I said.

Grandma thought about that while she pulled the chair away from my desk and made herself comfortable. "Jack, sweetheart," she said. "I would really like a glass of cold water. Do you think you could scare up one for me?"

"I have Fiji in the fridge in my room," Aphrodite said.

"That would be lovely," Grandma said.

"Go ahead and get it for her. But don't touch anything else," Aphrodite said.

"Not even your—"

"Not even."

Jack pouted, but he hurried out to get the water for Grandma.

"So, I'm guessing all the rest of you are up to date about the things Zoey is getting ready to tell me?" Grandma asked the group in general when Jack returned.

They all nodded, looking round-eyed and baby bird–like.

"And how are you all keeping Neferet from picking your brains?"

"Well, it's just theory right now, but we figure if we focus on thinking about shallow, silly, teenage things," Damien said.

"Like shoe sales and whatnot," Erin explained.

"Yeah, the whatnot being cute guys or homework stress," Shaunee added.

"Then she won't think to look any deeper," I finished. "But Neferet underestimates us. I don't think she'd make the same mistake with you, Grandma. She already knows you follow the Cherokee ways—that you're in touch with the spirit of the land. She might look deeper into you no matter what is buzzing around in the front of your mind."

"Then I will have to clear my mind and practice the meditation skills I have been using since I was a girl." Grandma's smile was confident. "She cannot force herself into my mind, not if I block her first."

"What if she's Queen of the Tsi Sgili?"

Grandma's smile faltered. "You truly believe that might be so, *u-we-tsi-a-ge-ya*?"

"We think she might be," I said.

"Then we are all in the gravest of dangers. You must tell me everything."

And so I did—with the help of Aphrodite, Damien, the Twins, and Jack, we caught Grandma up on everything, even though I will admit to glossing over the part about Stevie Rae not being totally herself. Aphrodite shot me a look during that part, but she didn't say anything.

As she heard all of it, Grandma's weather-lined face got grimmer and grimmer. I also gave everyone details about the latest Raven Mocker attack. Finally I concluded with explaining to her how Stark's death might not be permanent, and how Stevie Rae and Aphrodite and I had decided that, as morbid and disturbing as it sounded, we needed to keep an eye on his, well, corpse.

"And so Jack was supposed to have installed the nanny cam in the morgue," I said. "Did you, Jack? I saw some of your diversionary tactics." I gave Duchess a grin and ruffled her ears. She woofed softly and licked my face. Maleficent and Beleezebub, who were curled up together near the door (seems hateful cats attract each other—who knew?) lifted their heads and hissed in unison. Nala, who was sleeping on my pillow, barely opened her eyes.

"Oh, yeah, in all the excitement I almost forgot!" Jack jumped up and went over to where he'd laid his man purse—or "satchel," as he liked to call it—on the floor by the door. He carried it back to me and then pulled out a weird, mini TV-screen thing. He played with some knobs and then, with a grin of victory, handed it to me. "Voilà! Thus you can view the—hopefully—sleeping guy."

Everyone crowded around, peeking over my shoulder. Bracing myself, I pressed the ON button. Sure enough, the little screen showed a black-and-white picture of a small room with a big oven-looking thing at one end, a bunch of metal shelves lining all the visible walls, and a single metal table (body-sized), on which lay a human form covered in a sheet.

"Icky," the Twins said.

"Not pleasant," Aphrodite said.

"Maybe we should turn it off while the *d-o-g* is in here," Jack said.

I was all for that and turned the knob to OFF, not liking the feeling of spying on the dead.

"That's the boy's body?" Grandma asked, looking kinda pale.

Jack nodded. "Yep. I had to look under the sheet to be sure." His eyes turned sad, and he began petting Duchess a little frantically. The big Lab lay her head on his lap and sighed, which seemed to settle him down because Jack sighed, too, and hugged the dog before saying, "I just, you know, pretended he was sleeping."

"Did he look dead?" I had to ask.

Jack nodded again. He pressed his lips together and didn't say anything.

"You're doing the right thing," Grandma proclaimed firmly. "Neferet's power has a lot to do with secrecy. She is perceived as being a powerful priestess of Nyx—a mighty force for good. She's hidden behind that façade for quite a while, and it has allowed her the freedom to commit acts that, if you're right about the extent of them, are atrocious."

"So you agree that bringing Stevie Rae and the red fledglings out in the open tomorrow is what we should do?" I asked.

"I do. If secrecy is evil's ally, then let's break their allegiance."

"Okay!" I said.

"Okay!" everyone else chimed in.

And then Jack yawned. "Oopsie! Sorry. I'm not bored or anything," he said.

"Of course you're not, but it's almost dawn. You've had an exhausting day," Grandma said. "Perhaps we should all get some sleep? Besides, isn't it past curfew for boys to be in the girls' dormitory?"

"Uh-oh! We totally forgot about that. Like we need detention crap to worry about right now on top of everything else!" Jack said. Then, looking chagrined, he added, "Sorry, Grandma. I didn't mean to say *crap*."

Grandma smiled at him and patted his cheek. "No harm done, honey. Now, off to bed with you."

Not surprisingly, we all responded instantly to Grandma's mothering. Jack and Damien shuffled off with Duchess in tow.

"Hey," I called before they were out the door. "Duchess didn't get in any real trouble for being the central part of that diversion, did she?"

Damien shook his head. "Nope. We blamed it on Maleficent, and as insane as that cat was acting, no one batted an eye at Duchess."

"My cat is not insane," Aphrodite said. "She's just a really good actress."

The Twins headed out next, hugging Grandma and then picking up a sleepy Beelzebub. "See you at breakfast," they called.

That left Grandma and me alone with Aphrodite, Maleficent, and a totally asleep Nala.

"Well, I guess I should go, too," Aphrodite said. "Tomorrow's going to be major."

"Maybe you should sleep in here tonight," I said.

Aphrodite raised a perfect blond eyebrow and gave my twin beds a disdainful look.

I rolled my eyes. "You're so spoiled. You can sleep in my bed. I'll use a sleeping bag."

"Has Aphrodite ever stayed in your room before tonight?" Grandma asked.

Aphrodite snorted. "Not hardly. Grandma, if you saw my room, you'd know why I prefer to stay there."

"Plus, Aphrodite has a reputation for being a hateful hag. She doesn't do sleepovers." I failed to mention that she might do *guy* sleepovers—that would definitely be TMI for Grandma.

"Thank you," Aphrodite said.

"If she stays in your room, especially since I would guess that by now Shekinah has told Neferet I'm here, wouldn't it seem very unusual behavior for her?"

"Yes," I admitted reluctantly.

"It would be more than unusual—it would be utterly bizarre," Aphrodite said.

"Then you must return to your room so that we give Neferet no reason to look more closely at us than she already has,"

Grandma said. "But, you will not sleep unprotected." Grandma got up a little stiffly and went over to her pile of bags. She started digging through the pretty blue carry-on she liked to call her "overnight bag."

First she pulled out a beautiful dream catcher. It was a leather-wrapped circle with lavender-colored string webbed inside, and caught within the center of the web was a smooth turquoise stone, the breathtaking blue of a summer sky. The feathers that hung in three tiers from the sides and the bottom were the pearl gray of a dove. Grandma handed the dream catcher to Aphrodite.

"It's gorgeous!" she said. "Really. I absolutely adore it."

"I'm glad you like it, child. I know many people believe dream catchers do nothing more than filter good dreams—or maybe not even that. I've made several of them lately, and as I wove the protective turquoise within the center of each one, I thought about the need to filter more than bad dreams from our lives. Take this and hang it in your window. May its spirit protect your sleeping soul from harm."

"Thank you, Grandma," Aphrodite said sincerely.

"And one more thing." Grandma turned back to her bag, searched a little while, and then brought out a pillar candle that was a creamy white color. "Light this on your bedside table while you sleep. I spoke protective words over it last full moon and let it soak up the rays of moonlight all that night."

"Been a little obsessed with protection lately, Grandma?" I asked with a grin. After seventeen years, I was used to Grandma's weird way of knowing things she shouldn't know—like when guests were coming, or a tornado was brewing (long before Doppler 8 was invented)—or, in this case, when we would need protecting.

"It is always wise to be cautious, *u-we-tsi-a-ge-ya*." She took Aphrodite's face between her hands and kissed her lightly on her forehead. "Sleep well, little daughter, and may your dreams be happy ones."

I watched Aphrodite blink her eyes hard and knew she was struggling not to cry. "Night," she managed. Waving at me, she hurried from the room.

Grandma didn't say anything for a little while; she just gazed thoughtfully at the closed door. Finally she said, "I don't believe that girl has ever known the warmth of a mother's love."

"You're right again, Grandma," I said. "She used to be so awful, no one could stand her, especially not me, but I think most of it was an act. Not that she's perfect. She's majorly spoiled and shallow, and sometimes she can be seriously hateful, but she's . . ." I paused, trying to put Aphrodite into words.

"She's your friend," Grandma finished for me.

"You know, you're freakishly close to perfect," I told her.

Grandma grinned impishly. "I know. It runs in our family. Now, help me hang our dream catcher and light our moon candle—then you need to get some sleep."

"Aren't you going to sleep? I got you up in the middle of the night, and you said you'd already been up for hours."

"Oh, I'll sleep for a while, but I have plans. I don't get to town often enough, and while my vampyre family sleeps, I'm going to do a little shopping and take myself out to a lovely lunch at the Chalkboard."

"Yum! I haven't been there since last time you and I went."

"Well, sleepyhead, I'll let you know if it's as good as we remember, and then maybe the next really rainy day, you and I will revisit it together."

"So really you eating lunch there is just reconnoitering to be sure it hasn't gone downhill?" I pulled the chair over to the window and searched for someplace to hook the dream catcher Grandma handed me.

"That's exactly it. Honey, what do you want to do with the nanny cam?" Grandma held up one of the little viewscreens. Even though it was turned off, she handled it carefully, as if it might be an explosive device.

I sighed. "Aphrodite told me that there's an audio feed with it. Can you see a sound button?"

"Yes, I believe this is it." Grandma pressed a button, and a green light came on.

"Okay, well, why don't we just leave on the audio, *without* the video? I'll put it by my bedside. If anything stirs, I should be able to hear it."

"Much better than watching the dead all night," Grandma said grimly as she carried the little screen to my bedside table. Then she looked up at me. "Honey, why don't you open the curtains for a second and hang the dream catcher closer to the window? We're protecting from outside in—not inside out."

"Oh, okay."

I reached up with both hands to pull apart the thick drapes. They opened, and I felt a stab of raw fear as I looked directly into the hideous face of a gigantic black bird with terrible glowing red eyes shaped like a man's. The creature was clinging to the outside of my window with arms and legs that were human. Its dangerously hooked black beak opened, showing a forked red tongue. The thing let out a soft "*crooo-ak*" that sounded mocking and threatening at the same time.

I couldn't move. I was frozen by its mutated red eyes—human in the face of a terrible bird—a creature that existed only because of ancient rape and evil. I could feel cold spots on my shoulders where one of these creatures had clung to me earlier. I remembered the touch of its disgusting tongue and stinging pain its beak had caused as it had tried to cut my throat.

As Nala began hissing and yowling, Grandma rushed to be

beside me. I could see her reflection in the dark glass of the window. "Call wind to me, Zoey!" she commanded.

"Wind! Come to me—my grandma needs you," I cried, still trapped in the Raven Mocker's monstrous gaze.

I felt wind fluttering restlessly below and beside me, where Grandma stood.

"*U-no-le!*" Grandma cried. "Carry this with my warning to the beast." I watched Grandma lift her hands and blow what was cupped in her palms straight at the creature that crouched on the other side of the window. "*Ahiya'a A-s-gi-na!*" she cried.

The wind, conjured by me but commanded by my grandma, the Ghigua Woman, snatched up the sparkling blue dust that she had blown from her palms and whizzed it through the tiny cracks between the panes of beveled glass. The wind whirled the dust around the Raven Mocker so that it was caught in the vortex of the sparkling dust. The beast's too-human eyes widened as the specks surrounded him and then, as the wind whipped fiercely, pressing the dust into the creature's body, a terrible scream was wrenched from the open beak, and in a flurry of flapping wings, it disappeared.

"Send away the wind, *u-we-tsi-a-ge-ya*," Grandma said as she grabbed my hand to steady me.

"Th-thank you wind. I release you," I said shakily.

"Thank you, *u-no-le*," Grandma murmured. Then she said, "The dream catcher—be sure you hang it."

With shaking hands, I hooked it around the inside of the curtain rod and hurriedly closed the curtains. Then Grandma helped me off the chair. Scooping Nala up, the three of us wrapped together while we shook and shook and shook.

"It's gone . . . it's over now . . . ," Grandma kept murmuring.

I didn't realize that we'd both been crying until Grandma gave me one last squeeze and then went to find Kleenexes. I sank down on the bed, cuddling Nala.

"Thanks," I said, wiping my face and blowing my nose. "Should I call the others?" I asked.

"If you do, how scared will they be?"

"Terrified," I said.

"Then I think it would do more good if you called the wind again. Can you send it in a big burst around the dorms so that if anything is lurking around outside, it'll be blown away?"

"Yeah, but I think I should stop shaking first."

Grandma smiled and stroked the hair back from my face. "You did well, *u-we-tsi-a-ge-ya.*"

"I freaked and froze, just like I did last time!"

"No, you met the gaze of a demon without flinching and managed to conjure wind and commanded it to obey me," she said.

"Only because you told me to."

"But next time it won't be because I told you to. Next time you will be stronger and you will do what you must on your own."

"What was that blue dust you blew at it?"

"Crushed turquoise. I'll give you a pouch of it. It's a very powerful protective stone."

"Do you have enough to give the others, too?"

"No, but I'll put it on my shopping list. I can pick up some turquoise stones and a mortar and pestle to grind them with. The grinding will give me something constructive to do while you sleep."

"What was it you said?" I asked.

"*Ahiya'a A-s-gi-na* means 'leave, demon.'"

"And *u-no-le* is wind?"

"Yes, sweetheart."

"Grandma, did it have physical form, or was it just a spirit?"

"I think it's some of both. But it is very close to its physical form."

"Which means Kalona must be getting stronger," I said.

"I believe so."

"It's scary, Grandma."

Grandma pulled me into her arms and stroked my head like she used to when I was a little girl. "Do not fear, *u-we-tsi-a-ge-ya*. The demon's father will find that today's women are not so easy to subdue."

"You kicked butt, Grandma."

She smiled. "Yes, daughter, we certainly did."

CHAPTER TWENTY-EIGHT

With Grandma watching in approval, I called wind back and had it whip around campus, especially focusing on the dorms. We listened carefully for sounds of shrieking demons, but all we heard was the comforting whistle of the wind. Then, exhausted, I put on my pj's and finally got into bed. Grandma lit a full-moon protective candle for us, too, and I curled up with Nala, liking the sounds of Grandma brushing out her long silver hair as she went through her familiar nighttime rituals.

I was just drifting off when her soft voice caught me. *U-we-tsi-a-ge-ya,* I want you to promise me something."

"Okay, Grandma," I said sleepily.

"No matter what happens, I want you to promise me that you'll remember Kalona must not rise. Nothing and no one is more important than that."

A little trickle of worry made me wake up all the way. "What do you mean?"

"Exactly what I said. Do not let anything distract you from your purpose."

"You're sounding like you won't be around to keep me straight," I said, feeling a flutter of panic start in my chest.

Grandma came over and sat on the edge of my bed. "I plan to be around for a very long time, sweetheart, you know that. But

I still want your promise. Think of it as helping an old woman sleep well."

I frowned at her. "You're not an old woman."

"Promise me," she insisted.

"I promise. Now you promise me you won't let anything happen to you," I said.

"I'll do my best; I promise," she said with a smile. "Turn your head, and I'll brush your hair while you fall asleep. It will give you good dreams."

With a sigh I rolled over onto my side and fell asleep to the loving touch of my grandma and a softly hummed Cherokee lullaby.

At first I thought the muffled voices were coming from the nanny cam, and not even fully awake, I sat up and reached for the little viewscreen. Holding my breath, I clicked to ON the video button, and then I let out a big sigh of relief when the solitary table came into view with its unchanged, shrouded occupant. I turned off the video and glanced over at Grandma's now empty but tidily made-up bed. I smiled as I looked blearily around my room. Actually, Grandma had done a nice little bit of cleaning up before she'd gone out for her day of shopping and lunch. I looked down at Nala, who blinked at me sleepily.

"Sorry. Must have been my overactive imagination making me hear things." The full moon candle was still burning, though it was definitely smaller than when I'd fallen asleep. I glanced at my clock and smiled. It was only two o'clock in the afternoon. I had several good sleeping hours left before I had to wake up. I lay back down and pulled my quilt up around my neck.

Muffled voices, this time accompanied by several soft knocks on my door were definitely not my imagination. Nala grumbled a sleepy *mee-uf-ow*, which I couldn't help but agree with.

"If it's the Twins wanting to sneak off to a shoe sale, I'm going to strangle them," I told my cat, who looked pleased at the prospect. Then I cleared the sleep out of my throat and called, "Yeah! Come on in."

When the door opened, I was surprised to see Shekinah standing there, along with Aphrodite and Neferet. And Aphrodite was crying. I sat bolt upright, brushing my crazy bedhead hair out of my face. "What's wrong?"

The three of them came into my room. Aphrodite walked over to me and sat on the bed beside me. I looked from her to Shekinah and finally to Neferet. I couldn't read anything but sadness in any of their eyes, but I continued to stare at Neferet, wishing I could see past her careful façade—wishing everyone could.

"What's wrong?" I repeated.

"Child," Shekinah began in a sad, kind voice. "It's your grandmother."

"Grandma! Where is she?" My stomach clenched when no one said anything. I grabbed Aphrodite's hand. "Tell me!"

"She was in a car wreck. A bad one. She lost control as she was driving down Main Street because . . . because a big black bird flew into her window. Her car left the road and hit a light pole head-on." Tears were running down Aphrodite's face, but her voice was steady. "She's at St. John's Hospital in intensive care."

I couldn't say anything for a second. I just kept staring at Grandma's empty bed and the little lavender-filled pillow she'd placed there. Grandma always surrounded herself with the scent of lavender.

"She was going to the Chalkboard for lunch. She told me so last night just before—" I broke off, remembering how Grandma and I had been talking about her going to the Chalkboard for lunch just before I opened the curtains to find the horrible Raven Mocker. It had been listening to us, and it had known exactly where Grandma was going today. Then it had been there to run her off the road and cause her accident.

"Just before what?" To the uninformed observer, Neferet's voice would have seemed concerned—that of a friend and mentor. But when I looked up into her emerald eyes, I saw the cold calculation of an enemy.

"Just before we went to bed." I was trying hard not to show how much Neferet disgusted me—how truly vile and twisted I knew she was. "That's how I know what she was doing driving that way. She told me what she was going to be doing today while I slept." I looked away from Neferet and spoke to Shekinah instead. "I need to go to her."

"Of course you do, child," Shekinah said. "Darius is waiting with a car."

"May I go with her?" Aphrodite asked.

"You already missed all of your classes yesterday, and I don't—"

"Please," I interrupted Neferet, appealing directly to Shekinah. "I don't want to be alone."

"Don't you agree that family is more important than academics?" Shekinah said to Neferet.

Neferet hesitated just for a second. "Yes, of course I do. I was just concerned about Aphrodite falling behind."

"I'll take my homework with me to the hospital. I won't fall behind." Aphrodite gave Neferet a big reassuring smile that was as fake as Pamela Anderson's boobs.

"Then it is decided. Aphrodite will accompany Zoey to the hospital, and Darius will look after the both of them. Take your time there, Zoey. And be sure to let me know if there is anything the school can do for your grandmother," Shekinah said kindly.

"Thank you."

I didn't so much as glance at Neferet as the two of them left my room.

"Fucking bitch!" Aphrodite said, glaring at my closed door. "Like she's *ever* been concerned about me falling behind in anything! She just hates it that the two of us are friends."

Okay . . . okay. I have to think. I have to go to Grandma, but I have to think and make sure everything is taken care of here, first. I have to remember my promise to Grandma.

I wiped tears from my face with the back of my hand and rushed over to my dresser, pulling out jeans and a sweatshirt. "Neferet hates that we're friends because she can't get inside our heads. But she can get inside Damien, Jack, and the Twins' heads, and I can promise you she'll be sniffing around them today."

"We have to warn them," Aphrodite said.

I nodded. "Yes, we do. This nanny cam thing won't reach all the way to St. John's, will it?"

"Probably not. I think the range is only a few hundred yards."

"Then while I'm getting dressed, take it to the Twins' room. Tell them what's happened, and also tell them to warn Damien and Jack about Neferet." Then I took a deep breath and added, "Last night, there was a Raven Mocker clinging to my window."

"Oh my Goddess!"

"It was horrible." I shuddered. "Grandma blew crushed turquoise at it, and I had wind help her out, and that made it disappear, but I don't know how long it had been listening to us."

"That's what you started to say. The Raven Mocker knew your grandma was going to the Chalkboard."

"It caused her accident," I said.

"It or Neferet," she said.

"Or the two of them together." I went to my bedside table and grabbed the nanny cam monitor. "Get this to the Twins. Wait." I stopped her before she'd left the room. I went to Grandma's blue overnight bag and search through the zippered compartment that she'd left open. Sure enough, just inside it was a deer hide pouch. I opened it up to double-check and then, satisfied, I handed it to Aphrodite. "This is more turquoise dust. Have the Twins split it with Damien and Jack. Tell them it's powerful protection, but we don't have much of it."

She nodded. "Got it."

"Hurry. I'll be ready to go when you get back."

"Zoey, she's going to be okay. They said she's in intensive care, but she had her seat belt on and she's still alive."

"She has to be," I told Aphrodite as my eyes filled with tears again. "I don't know what I'd do if she wasn't okay."

The short ride to St. John's Hospital was a silent one. It was, of course, an obnoxiously sunny day. So, even though we all had on sunglasses and the Lexus had heavily tinted windows, it was uncomfortable for us. (Well, us being Darius and me—Aphrodite looked like she was having a hard time not hanging out the window and basking in the sun.) Darius dropped us off in the ER drive-through and said he'd park the car and meet us in intensive care.

Even though I hadn't spent much time inside a hospital, the smell seemed to be an innate memory, and one that wasn't positive. I really hated the antiseptic-covering-disease sense of it. Aphrodite and I stopped at the information desk, and a nice old lady in a salmon-colored smock pointed us to intensive care.

Okay, it was *really* scary in intensive care. We hesitated, not sure whether we could actually go through the swinging double doors that had INTENSIVE CARE emblazoned in red across them. Then I remembered that they had my grandma in there, and I marched resolutely through the intimidating doors into Scaryville.

"Don't look," Aphrodite whispered as I started to stumble because my eyes were automatically being drawn to the glass windows of the patient rooms. Seriously. The walls of the rooms weren't walls at all. They were windows—so that everyone could gawk at the dying old people using potty pans and such. "Just keep walking to the nurses' station. They'll tell you about your grandma."

"How do you know so much about this stuff?" I whispered back.

"My dad's OD'ed twice and ended up here."

I gave her a shocked look. "Really?"

She shrugged. "Wouldn't you OD if you were married to my mom?"

I suppose I would, but I thought it best not to say so. Plus, we'd come to the nurses' station.

"How may I help you?" said a blonde who was built like a brick.

"I'm here to see my grandma, Sylvia Redbird."

"And you are?"

"Zoey Redbird," I said.

The nurse checked a chart, and then she smiled at me. "You're listed here as her next of kin. Just a moment. The doctor is with her now. If you wait in the family room just down the hall there, I'll let him know you're here."

"Can't I see her?"

"Of course you can, but the doctor needs to finish with her first."

"Okay. I'll be waiting." After I'd taken just a few steps, I stopped. "She's not left alone, is she?"

"No, that's why all the rooms have windows for walls. None of the patients in intensive care are ever left alone."

Well, peeking through a window wasn't going to be good

enough for what was going on with Grandma. "Just be sure the doctor gets me right away, okay?"

"Of course."

Aphrodite and I went to the family room, which was almost as sterile and scary as the rest of intensive care.

"I don't like it." I couldn't sit, so I paced back and forth in front of a really ugly blue-flowered love seat.

"She needs more protection than nurses looking through a window every once in a while," Aphrodite said.

"Even before what's happened recently, Raven Mockers had the ability to mess with old people who were on the verge of death. Grandma's old, and now she's—she's . . ." I stumbled over my words, not able to speak the frightening truth.

"She's been hurt," Aphrodite said firmly. "That's all. She's just been hurt. But you're right. She's vulnerable right now."

"Do you think they'll let me call in a Medicine Man for her?"

"Do you know one?"

"Well, kinda. There's this old guy, John Whitehorse, who's been a friend of Grandma's for a long time. She's told me he's an Elder. His number is probably in Grandma's cell. I'm sure he'd know a Medicine Man."

"Might not hurt to try to get one here," Aphrodite said.

"How is she?" Darius asked as he strode into the family room.

"We don't know yet. We're waiting for the doctor. We were just talking about maybe needing to call one of Grandma Redbird's friends to get a Medicine Man in here to sit with her."

"Wouldn't it be easier just to ask Neferet to come? She's our High Priestess and also a Healer."

"No!" Aphrodite and I said at the same time.

Darius frowned, but the doctor's entrance saved us from having to explain further to the warrior.

"Zoey Redbird?"

I turned to the tall thin man and held out my hand. "I'm Zoey."

He took it and shook hands with me solemnly. His grip was firm, and his hands were strong and smooth. "I'm Dr. Ruffing. I've been taking care of your grandmother."

"How is she?" I was surprised I sounded so normal, because my throat felt like it was completely clogged with fear.

"Let's have a seat over here," he said.

"I'd rather stand," I said. Then I tried to give him an apologetic smile. "I'm too nervous to sit."

His smile was more successful, and I was glad to see such kindness in his face. "Very well. Your grandmother has been in a serious accident. She sustained head injuries, and her right arm is broken in three places. The seat belt bruised her chest, and the airbags deploying burned her face, but both saved her life."

"Is she going to be okay?" I was finding it hard to speak above a whisper.

"Her chances are good, but we'll know more after the next twenty-four hours," Dr. Ruffing said.

"Is she awake?"

"No. I've induced a coma so that—"

"A coma!" I felt myself sway. I was suddenly flushed and hot, and there were bright little specks around the edges of my vision. Then Darius's hand was under my elbow, and he was guiding me to a seat.

"Just breathe slowly. Concentrate on catching your breath." Dr. Ruffing was crouched in front of me, and he had my wrist between his large fingers, taking my pulse.

"Sorry, sorry. I'm okay," I said, wiping the sweat that was beading my forehead. "It's just that a coma sounds so terrible."

"It's actually not so bad. I've induced the coma to give her brain a chance to heal itself," Dr. Ruffing said. "Hopefully, we'll be able to control the swelling that way."

"And if you can't control the swelling?"

He patted my knee before he stood up. "Let's just take this one step at a time—one problem at a time."

"Can I see her?"

"Yes, but she needs to be kept quiet." He started leading me toward the patients' rooms.

"Can Aphrodite come with me?"

"Just one at a time right now," he said.

"It's okay," Aphrodite said. "We'll be right here waiting for you. Remember—don't be scared. No matter what, she's still your grandma."

I nodded, biting the side of my cheek so that I didn't cry.

I followed Dr. Ruffing to a glass room not far away from the nurses' station. We paused outside the door. The doctor looked down at me. "She's going to be hooked up to a lot of machines and tubes. They look worse than they are."

"Is she breathing on her own?"

"Yes, and her heartbeat is good and steady. Are you ready?"

I nodded, and he opened the door for me. As I entered the room, I heard the distinctly frightening sound of bird wings.

"Did you hear that?" I whispered to the doctor.

"Hear what?"

I looked into his completely guileless eyes and knew beyond any doubt that he had not heard the sound of the Raven Mockers' wings.

"Nothing, I'm sorry."

He touched my shoulder. "It's a lot to take in, but your grandmother is healthy and strong. She has an excellent chance."

I walked slowly over to the side of her bed. Grandma looked so small and frail that I couldn't keep the tears from slipping from my eyes and washing down my cheeks. Her face was terribly bruised and burned. Her lip was torn, and she had stitches in it and in another place on her chin. Most of her head was covered by bandages. Her right arm was completely swathed in a thick cast that had weird metal screw things sticking out of it.

"Do you have any questions I can answer?" Dr. Ruffing asked softly.

"Yes," I said without hesitating and without taking my eyes from Grandma's face. "My grandma is a Cherokee, and I know she'd feel better if I called in a Medicine Man." I did pull my gaze from Grandma's broken face to look up at the doctor then. "I don't mean to be disrespectful to you, and it's not for the medicine part. It's for the spiritual part."

"Well, I suppose you could, but not until later, when she's out of intensive care."

I had to stifle the urge to scream at him, *It's while she's in intensive care that she needs the Medicine Man!*

Dr. Ruffing was continuing to speak quietly, but he sounded very sincere. "You have to understand that this is a Catholic hospital, and we really only allow those—"

"Catholic?" I interrupted, feeling a flood of relief. "So you'd allow a nun to sit with Grandma."

"Well, yes, of course. Nuns and priests often visit our patients."

I smiled. "Excellent. I know the perfect nun."

"Good, well, are there any other questions I can answer for you?"

"Yeah, could you point me to a phone book?"

CHAPTER TWENTY-NINE

I don't know how many hours passed. I'd sent Darius and Aphrodite back to school—under protest—but Aphrodite knew I needed her to be sure everything was okay there, so I didn't have to worry about it while I was here, worrying about Grandma, and reminding her of that was how I finally got her to leave. And I promised Darius I wouldn't leave the hospital unless I called him for a ride, even though the school was less than a mile down the street, and it would be mega-easy for me to walk back.

Time passed weirdly in ICU. There were no outside windows and, except for the sci-fi thrums and beats and clicks of the hospital machinery, the rooms were dark and quiet. I imagined it was a kind of waiting room for death, which completely creeped me out. But I couldn't leave Grandma. I wouldn't leave her, not unless someone ready to battle demons would take my place. So I sat and I waited and I kept watch over her sleeping body as it fought to heal itself.

I was sitting there, just holding her hand and softly singing the words of one of the Cherokee lullabies she liked to sing me to sleep with when Sister Mary Angela finally breezed into the room.

She took one look at me, one look at my grandma, and then she opened her arms. I hurled myself into her arms, stifling my sobs against the smooth material of her habit.

"Shh, now. All will be well, child. She is in Our Lady's hands now," she murmured while she patted my back.

When I could finally talk, I looked up at her and thought I'd never been so happy to see anyone in my life. "Thank you so much for coming, Sister."

"I was honored that you called me, and I'm sorry it took me so long to get here. I had a lot of fires to put out before I could get away from the abbey," she said. Still keeping an arm around me, she walked back to Grandma's bedside.

"That's okay. I'm just glad you're here now. Sister Mary Angela, this is my grandma, Sylvia Redbird," I said in a choked little voice. "She's been my mother and my father. I love her very much."

"She must be quite a special woman to have the devotion of such a grandchild."

I looked quickly up at Sister Mary Angela. "The hospital doesn't know I'm a fledgling."

"It shouldn't matter what you are," the nun said firmly. "If you or your family needs succor and care, they should provide it."

"It doesn't always work out that way," I said.

Her wise eyes studied me. "Unfortunately, I must agree with you."

"Then you'll help me without telling them who I am?"

"I will," she said.

"Good, because Grandma and I need your help."

"What can I do?"

I glanced at Grandma. She seemed to be resting as peacefully as she had been ever since I sat down next to her. I'd heard no more bird wings, and felt no premonitions of evil. And yet I was reluctant to leave her alone, even if it was for just a few minutes.

"Zoey?"

I looked into the wise, kind eyes of this amazing nun and told her the utter truth. "I need to talk to you, and I don't want to do it in here, where we could be interrupted or overheard, but I'm scared to leave Grandma alone and unprotected."

She gazed back at me calmly, not at all perturbed by my weirdness. Then she reached into one of the front pockets of her voluminous black habit and drew out a small but beautifully detailed statue of the Virgin Mary.

"Would it ease your mind if I left Our Lady here with your grandmother while you and I speak?"

I nodded. "I think it would, Sister," I said, not trying to analyze why I should be so reassured by an icon of the mother of Christianity that a nun had brought with her. I was just grateful my gut was saying that I could trust this nun and the "magic" she carried.

Sister Mary Angela put the little statue of Mary on Grandma's bedside table. Then she bowed her head and clasped her hands. I could see her lips moving, but her words were so soft that I could not hear them. The nun crossed herself, kissed her fingers, and touched the statue lightly, and then she and I left Grandma's room.

"Is it still daylight outside?" I asked.

She looked at me with surprise. "It hasn't been daylight for hours, Zoey. It's after ten o'clock at night."

I rubbed at my face. I was utterly exhausted. "Do you mind if we walk outside for just a little while? I have to tell you a lot of hard stuff, and it'll be easier if I can feel the night air surrounding me."

"It's a lovely, cool night. I'd be happy to walk in it with you."

We wound our way out of the maze of St. John's and finally exited on its west side, facing Utica Street and the beautiful fountain that cascaded across the street from the hospital at the corner of Twenty-first and Utica.

"Wanta walk over by the fountain?" I asked.

"Lead the way, Zoey," Sister Mary Angela said with a smile.

We didn't talk while we walked. I looked all around us, watching for twisted bird images hiding in shadows, listening for the mocking sound that passed too easily for simple ravens. But there was nothing. The only thing I sensed in the night around us was waiting. And I didn't know if that was a good or bad sign.

There was a handy bench not far from the fountain. It faced the white marble statue of Mary surrounded by lambs and shepherd boys that decorated the southwest corner of the hospital. There was also a really pretty statue of Mary in full color, wearing her famous blue shawl, right inside the door to the ER. Strange how I'd never noticed how many statues there were of Mary around here before now.

We'd been sitting on the bench for a little while, just resting in the cool silence of the night, when I drew a deep breath and turned on the bench so that I could face Sister Mary Angela.

"Sister, do you believe in demons?" I decided to go right for the jugular. There was just no point in messing around. Plus, I really didn't have the time or patience for it.

She raised her gray brows. "Demons? Well, yes, I do. Demons and the Catholic church have a long and turbulent history."

Then she just looked steadily at me, waiting like it was my turn. This is one of the things I liked best about Sister Mary Angela. She wasn't one of those adults who felt like it was their job to finish a sentence for you. She also wasn't one of those adults who couldn't stand to be quiet and wait while a kid got her thoughts in order.

"Have you ever known any personally?"

"Not any real ones, no. I've had some close calls, but all of them turned out to be either very sick people or very dishonest people."

"How about angels?"

"Do I believe in them or do I know any?"

"Both," I said.

"Yes and no, in that order. Although I'd much rather meet an angel than a demon, should I get the choice."

"Don't be so sure."

"Zoey?"

"Does the word *Nephilim* sound familiar to you?"

"Yes, they're referenced in the Old Testament. Some theologians surmise that Goliath was either a nephilium, or the offspring of one."

"And Goliath wasn't a good guy, right?"

"Not according to the Old Testament."

"Okay, well, I need to tell you a story about another Nephilim. He wasn't a good guy, either. It's a story that comes from my grandma's people."

"Her people?"

"She's Cherokee."

"Oh, then proceed, Zoey. I enjoy Native American tales."

"Well, hold on to your wimple. This one is no bedtime story." Then I launched into an abbreviated version of what Grandma had told me about Kalona, the Tsi Sgili, and the Raven Mockers.

I ended the story with Kalona's imprisonment and the lost song of the Raven Mockers that prophesied their father's return. Sister Mary Angela didn't say anything for several minutes. When she did speak, it was eerie how she echoed my first reaction to the story.

"The women made what was little more than a clay doll come alive?"

I smiled. "That was what I said to Grandma when she told me the story."

"And how did your grandmother respond?"

I could tell by the serene expression on her face that she expected me to laugh and say Grandma had explained that it was a fairy tale, or maybe a religious allegory. Instead I told her the truth.

"Grandma reminded me that magic is real. And that her ancestors, who were really my ancestors, too, weren't any more or less believable than a girl who can summon and command all five of the elements."

"Are you saying that is your gift and why you are important enough to require a warrior escort to Street Cats?" Sister Mary Angela said.

I could see in her eyes that she didn't want to call me a liar and break our newly formed friendship, but she didn't believe me. So I stood up and took one short step back from the bench so that I was out of the abrasive light of the streetlamp. I closed my eyes and breathed deeply of the cool night air. I didn't have to think long to find east. It came to me naturally. I faced St. John's, which was across the street and directly east of where I stood. I opened my eyes and, smiling, said, "Wind, you have answered my call often in the past days. I honor you for your loyalty and I ask that you answer to me once again. Come to me, wind!"

There had been virtually no night breeze, but the moment I invoked the first element, a sweet, teasing breeze began to whip around me. Sister Mary Angela was close enough that she felt the wind obey me. She even had to put a hand up to her wimple to keep it from blowing off her head. I waggled my eyebrows at her stunned look. Then I turned to my right, facing south.

"Fire, the evening is cool and, as always, we have need of your protecting warmth. Come to me, fire!"

The cool wind suddenly went warm, hot even. I could hear the crackling of a blazing fireplace surrounding me, and it felt like Sister Mary Angela and I were getting ready to roast weenies on a balmy summer night.

"My goodness!" I heard her gasp.

I smiled and turned to my right again. "Water, we need you to cleanse us and relieve the heat fire brings. Come to me, water!"

It was with more than a little relief that I felt the heat instantly doused in the scent and touch of a spring rain. My skin didn't get wet, but it should have. It was like being dropped down in the middle of a rainstorm and washed, cooled, and renewed.

Sister Mary Angela tilted her face up to the sky and opened her mouth, as if she thought she could actually catch a raindrop.

I continued to my right. "Earth, I always feel close to you. You nurture and protect. Come to me, earth!"

The spring rain metamorphosized into a newly cut field of summer hay. The rain-cooled breeze was now thick with alfalfa and sun and the happy sounds of playing children.

I looked at the nun. She was still sitting on the bench, but she'd pulled off her wimple so that her short gray hair blew around her face as she laughed and breathed deeply of the summer breeze, making her look like a pretty child again.

She felt my gaze on her and she met my eyes just as I raised my arms over my head. "It is spirit that unites us, and spirit that makes us unique. Come to me, spirit!"

As always the sweetly familiar sensation of my soul lifting caught me and filled me as spirit answered my call.

"Oh!" Sister Mary Angela's gasp didn't sound freaked or angry. It sounded awed. I watched as the nun bowed her head and pressed the rosary beads that she wore around her neck to her heart.

"Thank you, spirit, earth, water, fire, and wind. You may depart now with my thanks. I appreciate you!" I cried, throwing wide my arms as the elements swirled playfully around me and then dissipated into the night.

Slowly, I walked back to the bench and took my seat beside Sister Mary Angela, who was smoothing her hair and reaffixing her wimple. Finally she looked at me.

"I've long suspected it."

That was so not what I'd expected her to say. "You suspected that I can control the elements?"

She laughed. "No, child. I've long suspected that the world is filled with unseen powers."

"No offense, but that's weird for a nun to say."

"Really? I don't think it's so weird when you remember I'm married to what is in essence a spirit." She hesitated, then continued, "And I have felt the stirrings of these powers—"

"Elements," I interrupted. "They're the five elements."

"I stand corrected. I have felt the stirrings of these elements often before at our abbey. Legend has it the abbey is built on an ancient place of power. You see, Zoey Redbird, fledgling Priestess, what you have shown me tonight is more validation than shock."

"Huh, well, that's good to hear."

"So, you were explaining how the Ghigua Women created a maiden from clay who entrapped the fallen angel, and the Raven Mockers sang a song about his return, and then turned into spirit? Then what happened?"

I grinned at her matter-of-fact tone before my expression got serious again. "Apparently nothing much happened for a bunch of years—like a thousand or so. Then, just a few days ago, I started hearing what I thought were crows cawing obnoxiously at night."

"You don't think they're crows?"

"I know they're not. First of all, cawing is not really what they did—they croaked."

She nodded. "Ravens croak. Crows caw."

I nodded. "So I've recently learned. Second, not only have I been attacked by two of them, but I saw one last night. It was listening in at my window when Grandma was saying where she'd be driving to today while I was asleep. It was while she was driving that she had her weird, and almost fatal, 'accident.'" I made air quotes around *accident*. "Witnesses said it was caused by a huge black bird flying directly at her car."

"Mother of God! Why were the Raven Mockers after your grandmother?"

"I think they were after her to get to me and to be sure she didn't help us any more than she already has."

"Help you and who else with what?"

"Help me and my fledgling friends. Most of them have single affinities for the elements, and one of my friends sees visions that warn about bad things that are going to happen—usually death and destruction, you know, the standard vision stuff."

"Would that be Aphrodite, the lovely young woman who—thankfully—adopted Maleficent yesterday?"

I grinned. "Yeah, that's Vision Girl. And no, none of us are thrilled about the Maleficent adoption." Sister Mary Angela laughed, and I went on. "Anyway, Aphrodite saw what we think is the Raven Mockers' prophecy in her last vision, and she wrote it down."

Sister Mary Angela's face paled. "And the prophecy foretells the return of Kalona?"

"Yes, which appears to be happening now."

"Oh, Mary!" she breathed, crossing herself.

"That's why we need your help," I said.

"How can I help keep the prophecy from coming true? I do know a few things about the Nephilim, but nothing specific to this Cherokee legend."

"No, I think we have most of it figured out, and tonight we're setting into motion some stuff that's seriously going to mess with his ability to fulfill the prophecy. What I need your help with is Grandma. See, the Raven Mockers were right. By messing with her, they messed with me. I won't leave her alone so that they can torment her. The folks at St. John won't call in a Medicine Man because they don't like the whole Pagan thing. So I need someone who is spiritually powerful, and who believes me."

"So that is where I come in," she said.

"Yes. Will you help me? Will you stay with Grandma and protect her from the Raven Mockers while I try to set the prophecy back another thousand years or so?"

"I would love to." She stood up and started walking resolutely to the crosswalk. She glanced back at me. "What? You thought you'd have to conjure wind again to blow me back up there?"

I laughed and crossed the street with her. This time when she paused before the statue of Mary in the foyer, bowing her head and whispering a quick prayer, I didn't wait impatiently. This time I took a good long look at the statue of the Virgin, noticing for the first time the kindness of her face and the wisdom in her eyes. And as Sister Mary Angela genuflected, I whispered, "Fire, I need you." When I felt the heat begin to build around me, I cupped it into my hand and then flicked my fingers at one of the votive candles that sat, unlit, at the statue's feet. Instantly it, along with half a dozen others, burst into happy flame. "Thank you, fire. You can go play now," I said.

Sister Mary Angela didn't say anything; she just picked up one of the lit votives and looked at me expectantly. When I didn't say anything, she prompted, "Do you have a quarter?"

"Yeah, I think so." I dug into the pocket of my jeans and pulled out the change I'd gotten from the Coke machine earlier that day. There were two quarters, two dimes, and a nickel in my hand. Not sure what she wanted me to do with any of it, I held the change out to her.

She just smiled and said, "Good, put all of it in place of this candle, and let's go upstairs."

I did as she told me and then we walked back to Grandma's room while she shielded the flickering flame of the votive with her hand.

The flutter of wings did not greet us as we entered Grandma's room. And there weren't any dark shadows that flitted suddenly at the edge of my vision. Sister Mary Angela went to the statue of Mary and placed the votive in front of it; then she took a seat in the chair I'd been sitting in all day and took her rosary from around her neck. Without looking at me, she said, "Hadn't you better be going, child? You have your own evil to battle."

"Yeah, I do." I hurried to the side of Grandma's bed. She hadn't moved, but I tried to believe that her color looked a little healthier and that her breathing was a little stronger. I kissed her on the forehead and whispered, "I love you, Grandma. I'll be back soon. Until then, Sister Mary Angela will stay with you. She won't let the Raven Mockers take you away."

Then I turned to the nun who looked so serene and otherworldly sitting in the hospital chair, fingering her rosary in the small flickering light of the votive that danced shadows on her and on her goddess. I was just opening my mouth to thank her when she spoke first.

"You don't need to thank me, child. This is my job."

"Sitting with the sick is your job?"

"Helping good keep evil at bay is my job."

"I'm glad you're good at it," I said.

"As am I."

I bent and kissed her soft cheek, and she smiled. But there was one more thing I had to say before I left. "Sister, if I don't do it . . . If my friends and I don't get Kalona stopped and he does rise, it's going to be bad for people around here, especially female people. You'll need to get somewhere underground. Do you know someplace, like a basement or a cellar or even a cave, that you can get to quickly and stay for a while?"

She nodded. "Under our abbey there is a large cellar that was once used for many things. Including hiding illegal liquor during the twenties, if old stories are to be believed."

"Well, that's where you should go. Take the other nuns—hell, take all the Street Cats, too. Just get underground. Kalona hates the earth, and he won't follow you there."

"I understand, but I am going to believe you will be victorious."

"I hope you're right, but promise me that you'll go underground if I'm not, and that you'll take Grandma with you." I looked into her eyes, expecting her to remind me that getting a wounded old woman out of intensive care and into the cellar or a nunnery wouldn't be particularly easy.

Instead she just smiled serenely. "You have my word on it."

I blinked at her in surprise.

"Did you think that you were the only one who could wield magic?" The nun raised gray brows at me. "People rarely question the actions of a nun."

"Huh. Well, good. Okay, then, I have your cell phone number. Keep it close. I'll call you as soon as I can."

"Don't worry about your grandmother or me. Old women know how to take care of ourselves."

I kissed her cheek again. "Sister, you're just like Grandma. You two will never be old."

CHAPTER THIRTY

I didn't want to wait for Darius when I could have practically walked the short distance to the school in the time it would take him to get to his car, start it, and drive to the hospital, but I couldn't make myself. The night had gone from being a friend to a frightening, elusive enemy. While I waited for him, I dialed Stevie Rae's number.

But she didn't answer. It didn't even ring, and instead went straight to her voice mail. And again I wondered just what kind of message I was supposed to leave. *Hi, Stevie Rae, big prophecy and ancient evil I wanted to chat with you about before you walk into the middle of it tonight, but I guess I'll catch you later.* Somehow I didn't think that would be very smart. So while I waited for Darius, I chastised myself for not calling Stevie Rae earlier, but Grandma's accident had consumed me.

Which is exactly what the Raven Mockers had intended.

Darius's black Lexus pulled up to the curb by the ER entrance, and he hopped out to open the door for me.

"How is your grandmother?"

"There's really no change, which the doctor says is a good thing. Sister Mary Angela is sitting with her tonight, so I can go ahead and lead the cleansing ritual."

Darius nodded and swung the car around so we could head

the short distance back to the school. "Sister Mary Angela is a powerful priestess. She would have made an excellent vampyre."

I smiled. "I'll tell her you said so. Anything happen today at school I should know about?"

"There was some talk about postponing the ritual when news of your grandmother's accident got out."

"Oh, no! We shouldn't do that," I said quickly. "It's too important to postpone."

He gave me a curious look, but said only, "That is what Neferet said. She convinced Shekinah to go ahead with tonight's schedule."

"Did she?" I mused aloud, wondering why it was so important to Neferet that I go ahead with the ritual tonight. Maybe she had some inkling that Aphrodite had lost her earth affinity and so she was looking forward to what she hoped would be a major embarrassment for her and for me. Well, Neferet was in for a big surprise if that's what she expected.

"You are cutting it pretty close, though," Darius said, glancing at the digital clock on the dash. "You have barely enough time to change your clothes and get to the east wall."

"That's okay. I'm great under time-crunch pressure," I lied.

"Well, I do believe Aphrodite and the rest of the group have everything prepared for you."

I nodded and smiled at him. "Aphrodite, huh?"

He smiled back at me. "Yes, Aphrodite."

We pulled up to the sidewalk, and Darius got out to open my door for me. "Thanks, boyfriend," I teased. "See you at the ritual."

"I would not miss it for the world," he said.

"Ohmigod! Is your grandma okay? I was so upset when I heard!" Jack burst like a little gay tornado into my dorm room, practically choking me in an exuberant hug. Duchess crowded to me with him, wagging her tail and panting a doggy welcome.

"Yeah, we're really freaked about Grandma," Damien said, coming in right behind Jack and Duchess and taking his turn hugging me. "I lit a lavender candle for her and kept it burning all day."

"Grandma would like that," I said.

"So, what's the word? Is she gonna be okay?" Erin asked.

"Yeah, Aphrodite wouldn't tell us shit," Shaunee said.

"I told you everything I knew," Aphrodite said, following everyone else into my room. "And that was we wouldn't know anything for sure for a day or so."

"That's still all we know," I said. "But it seems good that she's not getting any worse."

"Was it really the Raven Mockers who caused her accident?" Jack asked.

"I'm sure of it," I said. "There was one in her room when I got there."

"Are you sure you should leave her there all alone? I mean, can't they hurt her?" Jack said.

"I'm sure they can, but she's not alone. Remember the nun Aphrodite and I told you about who runs Street Cats? She's there with her, and she's not going to let anything get Grandma."

"Nuns freak me out," Erin said.

"They scare me, that's for sure. I spent five elementary school years in a private Catholic school, and I can promise you they are some meeeeean women," Shaunee said.

"Sister Mary Angela can definitely handle herself," Aphrodite said.

"And any Raven Mockers who try to mess with Grandma," I said.

"So the nun knows about Raven Mockers?" Damien said.

"She knows about all of it—the prophecy and everything. I had to tell her so that she'd know why it's so important she doesn't leave Grandma alone." I paused, and decided to admit all of it. "Plus, I trust her. I feel a great force for good whenever I'm with her. Actually, she reminds me a lot of Grandma."

"Besides that, she thinks Nyx is just another version of their Virgin Mary, which means she doesn't see us as evil and going straight to hell," Aphrodite added.

"That's interesting," Damien said. "I'd like to meet her—as soon as this Kalona craziness is taken care of."

"Oh, speaking of craziness. Have you guys been keeping an eye on the nanny cam?" I asked.

Jack nodded and patted his ever-present satchel. "Yep, I sure have, and all is still totally, well, dead quiet." He giggled and then slapped his hand over his mouth. "Sorry! I didn't mean to sound so disrespectful of the maybe *d-e-a-d,*" he spelled.

"Honey, it's okay," Damien put an arm around him. "Humor helps in these kinds of situations. And you're really cute when you giggle."

"Okay, before I get sick and perhaps barf on my lovely new dress, can we go over the basic plan for the ritual and then get going? Being late tonight would not be a good thing," Aphrodite said.

"Yeah, you're right. We should get this going. But you guys really do look good," I said, grinning at all of them. "We are one pretty group."

Everyone smiled and took turns curtseying, bowing, and making cute little spins. It had been the Twins' idea that we should all wear new clothes to this cleansing ritual. They said to symbolize the new year and the newness of a newly cleansed school we all needed new things. I'd thought that was a lot of "new," but I'd been too busy to care one way or another. So while

I'd been at Grandma's bedside, the Twins had been shopping. (I didn't ask how they'd skipped class—some things are better if I don't know the details.) We were all wearing black, but each outfit was different. Aphrodite's dress was black velvet, with a teardrop neckline and a totally short skirt. It looked killer with her black stiletto boots. My guess was she was going with her motto of *No matter what happens, if you look good, everything's better.* Damien and Jack were wearing black boy clothes. I don't know crap about boy clothes, but they definitely looked cute. The Twins were wearing short black skirts and those blousy black silk tops that I can't figure out if I think are cute or just pregnant-looking. Of course I'd never mention that to the Twins. I was wearing a new dress Erin had picked out for me. It was black, but it had little red glass beads sewn around the neckline and the long tight sleeves, as well as dangling from the skirt that ended just above my knees. It fit me perfectly, and I knew when I lifted my arms to invoke the elements, the moonlight would shimmer like blood off the decorative glass. In other words, it would look majorly cool.

Of course, we were all wearing our triple moon Dark Daughters and Sons pendants. Mine was trimmed in red stones that sparkled like my dress.

I grinned at my friends, feeling proud and confident. Grandma was in excellent hands with Sister Mary Angela. My friends were beside me—this time with no secrets between us. The ritual would go well, and Stevie Rae and the red fledglings would be out in the open, which meant Neferet would no longer be able to hide, whether she admitted her part in their existence or not. Erik had sorta started to talk to me again. And, speaking of guys, I was even feeling hopeful about Stark undeading. This time a kid coming back from death would be witnessed by the vamp power of Shekinah. And I wasn't going to worry about the possibility of being interested in two guys at the same time (again). Or at least not right now I wasn't going to worry about that.

Basically, I was feeling good and we were ready to take on any stupid ancient evil that tried to mess with us.

"Okay, so the ritual will go pretty much like it always does. I'll come in to whatever music Jack plays."

Jack nodded enthusiastically. "I'm ready! The best parts of the *Memoirs of a Geisha* soundtrack mixed with something else is what you're gonna come in to. But I'll wait and surprise you with the something-else part."

I frowned at him. Like I needed a surprise tonight?

"Don't worry," Damien said. "You'll like it."

I sighed. It was too damn late to change whatever it was now anyway. "So then I'll cast the circle with the elemental invocations. Aphrodite, let's be sure you're standing right in front of that huge oak by the east wall."

"Already taken care of, Z," Erin said.

"Yeah, we set up the candles and the ritual table when Jack and Damien did the audio stuff. So we put the earth candle right next to the tree."

"Uh, you guys didn't catch sight of Stevie Rae, did you?"

"Nope," the Twins, Damien, and Jack all said.

I sighed again. She'd better show.

"Don't worry about it. She'll be there," Damien said.

Aphrodite and I exchanged a quick look. "I hope so," I said, "or I don't know what the hell we're gonna do about the earth candle being zapped from your hands when I try to invoke it."

"Aphrodite could always put the candle down while you light it and do an interpretive earth dance," Jack said helpfully.

Aphrodite rolled her eyes, but I said, "Let's consider that a Plan B we hope never happens. So once Stevie Rae appears and all of the elements are invoked and the circle cast, I'll make some kind of general announcement about the red fledglings and how their appearance should help cleanse the school of secrets."

"That's an excellent point to make," Damien said.

"Thanks," I said. "And what I'm expecting is that there will be a lot of explaining that will need to go on after the ritual, so I'm going to cut it pretty short."

"Then we watch Neferet deal with the fallout," Aphrodite said.

"And if she's Queen Tsi Sgili, like we think she might be, she's going to be way too busy trying to squirm her way out of how pissed Shekinah is going to be to do anything about fulfilling Kalona's prophecy," I said. *And if the very worst happens, and Queen Tsi Sgili is Stevie Rae or one of her kids, I'll trust Shekinah and Nyx to handle that, too.* Out loud I added, "Damien, keep an eye open for those Raven Mockers, though. If you think you see, or even hear one, zap him with wind."

"Will do," Damien said.

"So are we ready?" I asked my friends.

"Yes!" they yelled.

Then we all hurried out of the dorm and, with confident hearts, headed straight into our last moments of innocence.

CHAPTER THIRTY-ONE

It seemed like the whole school was already there waiting for us. By prepositioning the tall pillar candles, the Twins had already set the stage, so fledglings and vampyres made a huge circle around the appointed area, with the big oak serving as the focal point and head of the soon-to-be-cast circle.

I was glad to see all the Sons of Erebus. The warriors had situated themselves all along the outside of the circle, but they'd also taken up positions on top of the big stone-and-brick wall that surrounded the school. I knew it was probably making it a pain in the butt for Stevie Rae and the red fledglings to get onto the school grounds, but between the Raven Mockers, Kalona, and whoever had been killing vampyres—they made me feel safe.

Jack and I stood off to the side while Damien, the Twins, and Aphrodite took their places facing inward with the colored candles representing their elements in their hands. If I stood on my tiptoes, I could just make out Nyx's feast table that we sometimes put in the center of the circle. Tonight I imagined it held dried fruits and pickled vegetables, as would be right for deep winter, along with the ritual goblet of wine and such. I thought I also saw someone standing beside the table, but there were too many people in the way, and I couldn't be sure.

"Merry meet!" Shekinah greeted me.

"Merry meet." I smiled and saluted her.

"How is your grandmother?"

"She's holding her own," I said.

"I considered canceling the ritual, or at least postponing it, but Neferet was adamant it should go on as planned. She seemed to believe it would be important to you."

I fixed my expression so that I looked interested but neutral about what she'd said.

"Well, I think the ritual is important, and I wouldn't want to be the cause of it being cancelled," I said. I looked around. Weird that Neferet herself wasn't here to jab at me. I was sure the only reason she'd been pushing for this to go on tonight was because she knew I'd been hurt and distracted by Grandma's accident. "Where is Neferet?" I asked.

Shekinah glanced behind her, and then I saw her frown and send a quick look around the crowd. "She was just here behind me. Odd that I can't find her now . . ."

"She's probably already part of the circle." I hoped my face didn't betray any of the warning bells that had started to bong in my head. I looked over at where Jack was tinkering with the audio equipment. "Well, I should probably get started."

"Oh, I almost forgot to mention this to you. Actually I expected Neferet to tell you." Shekinah paused and looked around for Neferet again. "No matter, I can let you know just as easily. Neferet mentioned that you'd never performed such a large cleansing ritual before and that perhaps you didn't know, because you are such a very young fledgling, that during a ritual of this type you must mix the blood of a vampyre with the sacrificial wine you'll offer to the elements."

"What?" I couldn't have heard her right.

"Yes, it's quite simple, actually. Erik Night has volunteered not only to call you into the circle, taking our poor Loren Blake's place, but Erik will also play the traditional role of priestess's consort and offer his blood to you as sacrifice. I hear he's an excellent actor, so he'll do quite well tonight. Just follow his lead."

"That was the surprise I was talking about!" Jack said, popping up beside Shekinah. "Well, the part about Erik calling you into the circle, I mean. The blood part is just whatever." Said the kid who was still a young enough fledgling not to be deeply affected by blood like, say, *I was*. "Isn't it cool that Erik volunteered!"

"Oh, yeah, cool," was all I could make myself say.

"I shall take my place now," Shekinah said. "Blessed be."

I muttered a "Blessed be" at her back, then I turned on Jack.

"Jack," I whispered violently. "Erik playing Loren's part tonight is *not* what I'd call a good surprise!"

Jack frowned. "Damien and I thought it would be. It just shows that you guys can maybe try to talk to each other."

"Not in front of the whole school we're not!"

"Oh. Um. I didn't think about it like that." Jack's lip started to quiver. "Sorry. If I'd known you'd be mad, I would have told you first thing."

I wiped a hand across my forehead, brushing my hair out of my face. The last thing I needed was Jack breaking down into tears. No, the last thing I needed was having to face seriously hot Erik and his delicious blood in front of the entire school! *Okay, okay, just breathe . . . you've gotten through more embarrassing situations than this.*

"Zoey?" Jack sniffled.

"Jack, it's okay. Really. I was just, well, surprised. Which is what a surprise is all about. I'll be fine now."

"O-okay. Are you sure? Are you ready?"

"Yes and yes," I said before I could run screaming in the opposite direction. "Start the music for me."

"Knock 'em dead, Z!" he said, and ran back to the audio equipment, keying the beginning of the music.

I closed my eyes and began the deep breathing that would help me clear my mind and prepare myself for calling the elements and casting the circle—and because of the Erik surprise, totally forgetting to tell Jack he should check the nanny cam.

As always, I was a ball of nerves until I started toward the circle and the music filled me. Tonight the soundtrack of *Memoirs of a Geisha* was haunting and beautiful. I lifted my arms and let my body move gracefully to the orchestra. Then Erik's voice joined with the music and the night, creating magic.

> *Beneath the shining stars,*
> *Beneath the gleaming moon,*
> *When night has healed the scars*
> *Of burning noon . . .*

The words of the poem caught me, carrying me on a tide of Erik's voice. I flung back my head and let my hair fall around me as I moved slowly into the circle, weaving words with music and dance and magic.

> *. . . And so, I say to you,*
> *If hate possess your heart,*
> *When day's hot strife is through*
> *Bid hate depart . . .*

I moved unerringly around the circle, loving the perfection of the poem Erik was reciting. It felt so right, and I knew that before, when Loren had called me into the circle, he'd used it as an opportunity to seduce and dazzle me. He hadn't thought about what the ritual should mean to me, or the rest of the fledglings, or even to Nyx. Loren's motives had always been self-serving. I could see that so easily now that I wondered how he could have ever fooled me so completely. Erik was as unlike him as the moon was unlike the sun. The poem he'd chosen was about forgiveness and healing, and though it would be nice to think he meant some of it for me, I knew that his first thought had been what would be best for the school and the kids who were trying to heal from the deaths of two professors.

The disappointing day,
Whenever wrong, or how,
Is something passed away,
Is ended now.
Forget, forgive, the scars,
And sleep will find you soon
Beneath the shining stars,
The gleaming moon.

The poem ended as I joined Erik in the middle of the circle in front of Nyx's table. I looked up at him. He was tall and heart-stoppingly handsome dressed all in black, which complemented his dark hair and intensified the blue of his eyes.

"Hello, Priestess," he said softly.

"Hello, Consort," I replied.

He saluted me formally, bowing deeply with his right fist closed over his heart; then he turned to the table. When he came back to me, he was holding Nyx's ornately decorated silver goblet in one hand, and a ceremonial knife in the other. Okay, by "ceremonial" I don't mean it was for play. It was sharp, wicked sharp, but it was also beautiful and had been carved with words and symbols that were sacred to Nyx.

"You'll need this," he said, handing me the knife.

I took it, disturbed by how the moonlight glinted off the blade, not having a clue what to do next. Thankfully, the music was still playing and the watching horde of people were swaying gently to the mesmerizing *Geisha* melody. In other words, they were watching us, but only with easy anticipation, and as long as we kept our voices low, they couldn't hear us. I did glance at Damien, and he waggled his brows at me and winked. I looked away fast.

"Zoey? You okay?" Erik whispered. "You know it's not going to hurt me much at all."

"It's not?"

"You haven't done this before, have you?"

I shook my head slightly.

He touched my cheek for just a second. "I keep forgetting how new you are to all of this. All right, it's easy. I'm going to hold my right hand out, palm up, over the goblet." He lifted the goblet, which he had already shifted to his left hand. I could smell the red wine that almost filled it. "You lift the dagger over your head, salute all four directions with it, then slash my palm."

"Slash!" I gulped.

He smiled. "Cut, slash, whatever. Just run the blade along the meaty part under my thumb. It's seriously sharp, so it'll do the work for you. I'll turn my hand and while you thank me in the name of Nyx for my sacrifice to her, some of my blood will run into the wine. After a little while I'll close my fist, and that's when you take the goblet and walk to Damien so you can start casting the circle. Tonight you give each of the representatives of the elements a drink of the wine, ritualistically cleansing the elements before you do the big school cleansing part. Got it?"

"Yeah," I said shakily.

"Better get going then. Don't worry. You'll do fine," he said.

I nodded, and lifted the dagger over my head. "Wind! Fire! Water! Earth! I salute you!" I said, turning the blade from east to

south, west, and north as I called each element's name. My nerves
stated to fade as I could already feel the power of the elements
building around me, eager to answer my coming summons.
While I could still feel the echo of my salute, I brought the dagger
down. I pressed the tip of it against the base of Erik's thumb,
which he held steadily for me, and then with one quick motion,
sliced the deadly sharp blade across his palm, exactly where he'd
told me to cut.

The scent of his blood hit me immediately, warm and dark and
indescribably delicious. Transfixed, I watched it bead, like ruby
jewels, and then Erik turned his hand so that they could fall into
the waiting wine. I looked up into his clear blue eyes.

"In Nyx's name, I thank you for your sacrifice tonight and for
your love and loyalty. You are blessed by Nyx and beloved of her
Priestess." And then I bent and gently kissed the back of his bleeding hand.

When I met his eyes again, I saw that they were unusually
bright, and I thought his face was tender, his expression intimate,
but I couldn't tell if he was just acting the part of Nyx's consort,
or if he was really experiencing the feelings he was showing me.
He fisted his hand and saluted me again saying, "I am now, and
always will be, loyal to Nyx and to her High Priestess."

There wasn't any more time for me to wonder whether he was
talking about me, or whether he was just acting out the rest of his
part. I had a job to do. So I took my goblet of blood-spiked wine
and walked over to stand in front of Damien. He lifted his yellow
candle and smiled at me.

"Wind, you are as dear to me and familiar as the breath of life.
Tonight I need your strength to cleanse the stagnant breath of
death and fear from us. I ask that you come to me, wind!" This
ritual was a little different, and Damien had obviously been more
forewarned than I had been, so he was ready with a lighter to

touch it to his candle. The moment it lit, we were surrounded in a mini-tornado of exquisitely controlled wind. Damien and I grinned at each other, and then I held the goblet up so he could sip from it.

I moved clockwise, or deosil, around the circle to Shaunee, who was already holding her red candle up and smiling eagerly.

"Fire, you warm and cleanse. Tonight we need your cleansing power to burn the darkness from our hearts. Come to me, fire!" As per usual, no one needed to touch Shaunee's candle with a lighter, the wick burst into glorious flame all by itself as we were filled with warmth and the light of a guiding hearth fire. I lifted the goblet for Shaunee, and she took her drink.

From fire I moved to water and Erin holding her blue candle.

"Water, we go to you dirty and rise from you clean. Tonight I ask that you wash us free of any lingering taint that might want to cling to us. Come to me, water!" Erin lit her candle, and I swear I could hear the rush of waves against a beach and feel the coolness of dew against my skin. I lifted the goblet for Erin, and after drinking, she whispered, "Good luck, Z."

I nodded and moved resolutely to Aphrodite, who was looking pale and tense as she held the green candle she knew would zap her if we tried to call earth. "Where is she?" I whispered, without hardly moving my lips.

Aphrodite made a nervous little shrug.

I closed my eyes and prayed. *Goddess, I'm counting on you to make this work. Or at least if I make a fool out of myself, I'm hoping you'll somehow get me out of it. Again.* When I opened my eyes, my mind was made up. It didn't really change things if Stevie Rae didn't show. I was going to tell everyone anyway. Some would believe me without proof. Some wouldn't. I'd take my chances on how things came down. I knew I was telling the truth, and so did my friends.

So instead of beginning my invocation of earth, I winked at Aphrodite and whispered, "Well, here we go," and turned around to face the circle and the questioning crowd of watchers.

"I need to invoke earth next. We all know that. But there's a problem. You all saw that Nyx gifted Aphrodite with an affinity for earth. And she did. But it turns out the gift was just a temporary one because Aphrodite was keeping the element safe for the one who really represented earth, Stevie Rae."

As soon as I said her name, there was a fluttering movement in the big oak and the night-darkened boughs that spread over our heads, and then Stevie Rae dropped gracefully from the branch above us.

"Dang, Z, it took you long enough to get to me," she said. Then she walked over to Aphrodite and took the green candle from her. "Thanks for keeping my place warm."

"Glad you could make it," Aphrodite said, and stepped aside so that Stevie Rae could move into her place.

Stevie Rae took the earth position, turned, and shaking her curly blond hair back from her face, grinned out at everyone while the intricate pattern of vines and birds and flowers that made up her scarlet tattoo blazed as brightly as her smile. "Okay, *now* you can invoke earth."

CHAPTER THIRTY-TWO

Naturally all hell broke loose then. Sons of Erebus shouted and started forward toward our circle. Vampyres were crying out in shock, and I swear some girl started screaming.

"Ah, oh," I heard Stevie Rae whisper. "Better fix this, Z."

I whirled around to face Stevie Rae. With no time for niceties I said, "Earth, come to me!" For a second I wanted to freak because I didn't have a lighter and neither did Stevie Rae, but Aphrodite, cool as ever, leaned over, flicked the lighter she still held, and lit the candle. The scents and sounds of a summer meadow instantly surrounded us. "Here, have a drink." I lifted the goblet, and Stevie Rae took a big gulp. I frowned a little at her.

"What?" she whispered. "Erik's yummy."

I rolled my eyes at her and jogged back to the center of the circle, where Erik was gawking at Stevie Rae. I raised one arm over my head. "Spirit! Come to me," I said without any preamble. As my soul quickened within me, I took the ceremonial lighter from Nyx's table and lit the purple spirit candle that waited there. Then I, too, took a big gulp of the blood-spiked wine.

And what an amazing rush that was! Stevie Rae had a point, Erik was yummy, but then I already knew that. Filled with the exhilaration of wine and blood and spirit, I strode out. I couldn't have been prouder of my friends. They'd held steady to their places in the circle, lifting their candles and keeping control of their elements so that our circle stayed strong and unbreachable. Pacing around the circumference of the glistening thread of circle I'd just cast, I raised my voice and began to shout over the pandemonium that surrounded us.

"House of Night, listen to me!" Everyone fell silent when they heard the power of the Goddess magnifying my voice. I almost fell silent, too, as shocked as I was by it. Instead I cleared my throat and began again, this time not having to Goddess-shout over a screaming horde. "Stevie Rae did not die. She went through another kind of a Change. It was hard for her, and it almost cost Stevie Rae her humanity, but she made it through, and now she is a new kind of vampyre." I made my way slowly around the inside of the circle, trying to meet as many of the eyes as I could as I explained. "Nyx never abandoned her, though. As you can see, she still has her affinity for earth, a gift given to her, and then given to her again by Nyx."

"I do not understand. This child was a fledgling who died and then was resurrected?" Shekinah had stepped forward and was standing near Stevie Rae, staring hard at her.

Before I could answer, Stevie Rae spoke. "Yes, ma'am. I did die. But then I came back, and when I did, I wasn't the same anymore. I'd lost myself, or at least most of myself, but Zoey, Damien, Shaunee, Erin, and especially Aphrodite, helped me to find myself again, and when I did, I also found I'd Changed into a different kind of vampyre." She pointed to her beautiful red tattoo.

Aphrodite stepped forward, actually moving into the glowing silver thread that held our circle as one. I expected to see her get zapped or bounced back or something terrible, but instead the thread gave, allowing her to walk through to me. When she joined me, I could see her body was outlined in the same glowing silver thread that still held our circle.

"When Stevie Rae Changed, I did, too." Aphrodite lifted her hand and with a quick swipe, she wiped off the blue crescent that had been outlined there. I heard several gasps as she continued. "Nyx Changed me into a human, but I'm a new kind of human, just like Stevie Rae is a new kind of vampyre. I'm a human who has been blessed by Nyx. I still hold the gift of visions Nyx gave me when I was a fledgling. The Goddess has not turned her face from me." Aphrodite lifted her head proudly and faced the House of Night, as if daring anyone to say anymore crap about her.

"So we have a new kind of vampyre and a new kind of human," I said. I glanced at Stevie Rae and she grinned and nodded. "And we also have a new kind of fledgling." As soon as I finished speaking, the oak seemed to rain fledglings. I made a mental note to ask Stevie Rae later how the hell she'd hidden all of those kids up there, because I easily counted half a dozen or so of them. I recognized Venus, who I knew had been Aphrodite's old roommate, and wondered briefly if the two of them had had words yet. I also saw that obnoxious Elliot kid, who I swear I still wasn't going to like. They were all standing there, inside the circle, spreading out on either side of Stevie Rae as they looked more than a little nervous, with their bright red crescent outlines plainly visible on their foreheads.

I could hear some of the kids outside the circle crying and calling the names of red fledglings they were recognizing as dead roommates and friends, and I felt for them. I knew what it was like to think your friend was dead, and then see her walking and talking and breathing again.

"They're not dead," I said firmly. "They're a new kind of fledgling—a new kind of people. But they're *our* people, and it's time we found a place for them with us and learned why Nyx has brought them to us."

"Lies!" The word was a shriek, so loud that I could almost feel it battering my ears. There was a murmuring in the crowd, and then the people outside the southernmost part of the circle parted to let Neferet through.

She looked like an avenging goddess, and even I was struck speechless at her raw beauty. Her smooth white shoulders were bared by an exquisite black silk dress that molded to her graceful body. Her thick auburn hair was free, tumbling in waves down around her slim waist. Her green eyes flashed—her lips were the deep red of fresh blood.

"You ask us to accept a perversion of nature as something the Goddess made?" she spoke in her deep, beautifully modulated voice. "Those creatures were dead. They should be dead again."

The anger that spiked within me shattered her magnetism. "You should know about these *creatures,* as you call them." I squared my shoulders and faced her. I might not have her well-trained voice, or her incredible beauty, but I had truth and I had my Goddess. "You tried to use them. You tried to twist them. It was you who kept them as prisoners until through us Nyx healed and then freed them."

Her eyes widened in a perfect look of surprise. "You blame me for these monstrosities?"

"Hey, me and my friends aren't monstrosities!" came Stevie Rae's voice from behind me.

"Silence, beast!" Neferet commanded. "Enough is enough!" Neferet turned so that her gaze swept the stunned crowd. "To-night I discovered another of the creatures Zoey and her people were raising from the dead." She bent and picked up something that lay at her feet, tossing it into the circle. I recognized Jack's satchel as it landed, opening to spill out the nanny cam monitor and the camera itself (which should have been safely hidden in the morgue). Neferet's eyes scoured the crowd until they found him; then she snapped, "Jack! Do you deny that Zoey made you plant this in the morgue, where you locked the body of the recently dead James Stark, so that she could watch to see when her wicked spells would resurrect him?"

"No. Yes. It wasn't like that," Jack squeaked. Duchess, who was pressed against his legs whined pitifully.

"Leave him alone!" Damien shouted from his place in the circle.

Neferet rounded on him. "So you continue to be blinded by her? You continue to follow her rather than Nyx?"

Before he could answer, Aphrodite spoke from beside me. "Hey, Neferet. Where's your Goddess insignia?"

Neferet looked from Damien to Aphrodite, and her eyes narrowed in anger. But everyone was now looking at Neferet and noticing what Aphrodite had said—that Neferet's exquisite black dress had no badge of Nyx over her breast. And then I noticed something else. She was wearing a pendant I'd never seen before. I blinked, not sure if I was seeing it correctly, and then, yep, I decided, I sure was. Dangling from a golden chain around her neck were wings—big, black, raven wings carved from onyx.

"What's that around your neck?" I asked.

Neferet's hand moved automatically to stroke the black wings hanging between her breasts. "The wings of Erebus, Nyx's consort."

"Um, excuse me, but, no, they're not," Damien said. "Erebus's wings are made of gold. They're never black. You taught me that yourself in Vamp Soc class."

"I have had enough of this meaningless babble," Neferet snapped. "It is time this little charade came to an end."

"You know, I think that's a darn good idea," I said.

I was just starting to scan the crowd to find Shekinah when Neferet stepped aside, crooking her finger at a shadowy shape that seemed to materialize behind her. "Come to me and show what it is they created tonight."

Duchess's howl of agony and her pitiful whines that followed will be forever be imprinted in my mind with my first sight of the new Stark. He moved forward like a ghost. His skin was eerily pale, and his eyes the red of old blood. The crescent on his fore-head was red, too, like the fledglings who filled my circle, but he was different than they were. The thing Stark had become stood there beside Neferet, glaring, madness shining in his eyes. Looking at him, I felt like I was going to be sick.

"Stark!" I meant to call his name loud and strong, but it came out of my mouth as little more than a broken whisper.

Still he turned his face in my direction. I saw the blood color in his eyes fade, and for just a moment I thought I glimpsed the boy I knew.

"Zzzzoey . . ." He said my name in something like a hiss, but it gave me an instant of hope.

I took a stumbling step toward him. "Yes, Stark, it's me," I said, trying hard not to cry.

"Ssssaid I'd come back to you," he murmured.

I smiled through the tears that were filling my eyes as I moved closer and closer to where he stood just outside the circle. I had opened my mouth to tell him it'd be okay, that somehow we'd fig-ure out a way for it to be okay, but suddenly Aphrodite was there beside me. She grabbed my wrist, pulling me back from the edge of the circle.

"Don't go to him," she whispered. "Neferet is setting you up."

I wanted to shake her off, especially when Shekinah's voice came from the other side of the circle. "What has been done to this child is quite horrible. Zoey, I must insist that you close this ritual for this evening. We shall take the fledglings inside, and contact the Council of Nyx to come and judge these events."

I could feel the red fledglings stir restlessly at my back, drawing my attention from Stark. I turned and met Stevie Rae's eyes. "It's okay. That's Shekinah. She'll know the difference between lies and truth."

"I know the difference between lies and truth, and I carry a judgment with me greater than some distant Council." I heard Neferet speak and turned to face her again.

"You've been found out!" I yelled at her. "I didn't do this to Stark, or to the other red fledglings. You did, and now you're going to have to face what you've done."

Neferet's smile was more of a sneer. "And yet the creature calls your name."

"Zzzzzoey," Stark called me again.

I stared at him, trying to see the guy I'd know within his haunted face. "Stark, I'm so sorry this has happened to you."

"Zoey Redbird!" Shekinah's voice was a whip. "Close the circle now. These events must be reviewed by those whose judgment can be trusted. And I will take this poor fledgling into my care."

For some reason, Shekinah's command made Neferet begin to laugh.

"I have a bad feeling about this," Aphrodite said, pulling me back toward the center of the circle.

"Me, too," Stevie Rae said from her northernmost position in the circle.

"Don't close the circle," Aphrodite said.

Then in the middle of everything, Neferet's voice whispered across the circle to me, *Don't close the circle and you'll look guilty. Close it and you'll be vulnerable. Which do you choose?*

I met Neferet's eyes across my circle. "I choose the power of my circle and the truth," I said.

Her smile was victorious. She turned to Stark. "Aim for the true mark—the one that will make the earth bleed. Now!" Neferet commanded him. I saw him pause, as if he was fighting against himself. "Do as I command, and I will give you your heart's desire." Neferet whispered the words for Stark's ears alone, but I read them on her ruby lips. The effect they had on him was instantaneous. Stark's eyes blazed red and with the swiftness of a striking snake, he lifted the bow I hadn't noticed he was holding at his side, sighted an arrow, and shot. Slicing the air in a deadly line, it struck Stevie Rae in the center of her chest with such force that it buried itself to the dark feathers on the end of its shaft.

Stevie Rae gasped and fell to the ground, crumbling in on herself. I screamed and ran toward her. I could hear Aphrodite yelling at Damien and the Twins not the break the circle, and I silently blessed her for her cool head. I reached Stevie Rae and dropped to the ground beside her. Her breath was coming in painful little gasps, and her head was bowed.

"Stevie Rae! Oh, Goddess no! Stevie Rae!"

Slowly she raised her head and looked at me. Blood was pouring from her chest—more blood than I thought any one person could hold. It was soaking the ground around her, which was lumpy from the roots of the big oak. The blood mesmerized me. Not because of its sweet, intoxicating smell, but because I realized what it looked like. It looked like the earth at the base of the great oak was bleeding.

I stared over my shoulder at Neferet, who stood smiling triumphantly just outside my circle. Stark had fallen to his knees beside her, and he was staring at me with eyes that were no longer red, but were now filled with horror. "Neferet, you are the monstrosity, not Stevie Rae!" I shouted.

My name is no longer Neferet. From this night on call me Queen Tsi Sgili. The words were spoken in my mind just as plainly as if Neferet had been standing beside me whispering them in my ear.

"No!" I cried, and then the night exploded.

CHAPTER THIRTY-THREE

The ground beneath my feet, soaked through with Stevie Rae's blood, began to shudder, rippling like it was no longer solid earth but had suddenly turned to water. Through panicked cries, I heard Aphrodite's voice again, as calm as if she was only yelling at Damien and the Twins about their fashion choices.

"Move in to us, but don't break the circle!"

"Zoey." Stevie Rae gasped my name. She looked up at me with pain-filled eyes. "Listen to Aphrodite. Don't break the circle. No matter what!"

"But you're—"

"No! I'm not dying. I promise. He's just taken my blood, not my life. Don't break the circle." I nodded, then stood up. Erik and Venus were closest to me. "Get on either side of Stevie Rae. Hold her up. Help her keep the candle, and no matter what, don't let it go out and don't let the circle be broken."

Venus looked shaky, but she nodded and moved to Stevie Rae. Erik, white-faced with shock, just stared at me.

"Make your choice now," I said. "You're either with us or with Neferet and the rest of them."

Erik didn't hesitate. "I made my choice when I volunteered to be your consort tonight. I'm with you." Then he hurried to help Venus lift Stevie Rae.

Stumbling over the shifting ground, I staggered to Nyx's table and caught my purple spirit candle just before it fell over and went out. Clutching it close to me, I turned my attention to Damien and the Twins. They were following Aphrodite's calm instructions and, in the midst of the screaming chaos that was outside our circle, they were walking slowly together, tightening the circumference of the silver thread toward Stevie Rae, until we were all of us, Damien, the Twins, Aphrodite, Erik, the red fledglings, and me clustered together around Stevie Rae.

"Start moving her away from the tree," Aphrodite said. "All of us, without breaking the circle. We need to head to the trapdoor in the wall. Now."

I stared at Aphrodite, and she nodded solemnly. "I know what's going to happen next, and it's not going to be good."

"Then let's get out of here," I said.

We started to move as a group, taking small steps over the bucking earth, having to be ultra-careful with Stevie Rae and the candles and the circle that seemed so important to maintain. You'd think fledglings and vampyres would be in our way. You'd think at least Shekinah would have said something to us, but it seemed we existed in a weird little bubble of serenity amidst a world suddenly awash in blood and panic and chaos. We kept moving away from the tree, following the wall, slowly and carefully making progress. I'd noticed that the grass underneath our feet was smoother and completely dry of Stevie Rae's blood when Neferet's terrible laughter floated across the grounds to me.

The oak, with a horrible ripping sound, tore apart. I had been walking backwards, helping to prop Stevie Rae up from the front, so I had a clear view of the tree when it split. From underneath the middle of the destroyed oak a creature rose. At first all I saw were huge black wings that completely enfolded something. Then he stepped from the destroyed oak, straightening his mighty body and unfurling his night-colored wings.

"Oh, Goddess!" The cry was ripped from me at my first sight of Kalona. He was the most beautiful thing I had ever seen. His skin was smooth and completely unmarred, and was gilded with what looked like the kiss of the sun's loving rays. His hair was as black as his wings, and fell loose and thick around his shoulders, making him look like an ancient warrior. His face—how can I ever fully describe his beautiful face? It was like a sculpture come to life, and it made even the most handsome mortal, be he human or vampyre, look like a sickly, unsuccessful attempt at imitation of his glory. His eyes were the color of amber, so perfect, they were almost golden. I found myself wanting to get lost in them. Those eyes called to me . . . he called to me . . .

I had stumbled to a stop, and I swear I would have broken the circle right then so that I could run back and fall at his feet, had he not raised his gorgeous arms and called in a voice that was deep and rich and full of power, "Arise with me, children!"

Raven Mockers burst from the hole in the ground and filled the sky, and it was the fear that filled me at the sight of their terribly familiar misshapen bodies that broke the spell Kalona's beauty had cast on me. They shrieked and circled their father, who laughed and held his arms up higher so that their wings could caress him.

"We have to get out of here!" Aphrodite hissed.

"Yes, now! Hurry," I said, totally myself again. The ground was no longer shaking, so we were able to increase our pace. I was still moving backwards, so I watched in fascinated horror as Neferet approached the newly freed angel. She stopped before him and swept a low, graceful curtsey.

He inclined his head regally, his eyes already glinting with lust as he looked at her. "My Queen," he said.

"My Consort," she said. Then she turned to face the crowd that had stopped milling around in panic and was instead staring in fascination at Kalona.

"This is Erebus, come to earth finally!" Neferet proclaimed. "Bow to Nyx's consort, and our new Lord on earth."

Many of the watching crowd, especially the fledglings, instantly dropped to their knees. I looked for Stark, but didn't see him. I did see Shekinah begin to stride forward, picking her way around worshipful fledglings, her wise face guarded, her expression fixed in a deep frown. As she walked, many of the Sons of Erebus joined her, looking alert, but I couldn't tell if they were questioning Kalona, as Shekinah obviously was, or if they thought to protect him from the High Priestess. Before Shekinah could break through the crowd and confront the risen angel, Neferet lifted her hand and made a slight flicking motion with her wrist. It was a gesture so small and insignificant that had I not been watching for it, I would not have seen it.

Shekinah's eyes went wide, she gasped, grabbed her neck, and then crumpled to the ground. The Sons of Erebus rushed to her body.

It was at that moment that I took the cell phone out of my pocket and keyed up Sister Mary Angela's number.

"Zoey?" she answered on the first ring.

"Get out. Get out now," I said.

"I understand." She sounded utterly calm.

"Take Grandma! You have to take Grandma with you!"

"Of course I will. Look after yourself and your people. I shall look after her."

"I'll call you when I can." I flipped the phone shut.

When I looked up from the phone I saw that Neferet had turned her attention to us.

"We're there!" Aphrodite said. "Get that damn door open now!"

"It is already open," said a familiar voice. I glanced behind me at the wall to see Darius standing beside a cracked trapdoor that seemed to appear magically in the bricks and rock. And, with a huge rush of relief, I saw that Jack was standing beside the warrior, bawling his eyes out, but in one piece with Duchess close to his side.

"If you're with us, you have to be against them," I told Darius, jerking my chin back toward the House of Night and the Sons of Erebus who filled the school grounds and who were not making one move against Kalona.

"I've made my choice," said the warrior.

"Can we please get out of here? She's looking at us!" Jack said.

"Zoey! You've got to buy us some time," Aphrodite said. "Use the elements—all of them. Shield us."

I nodded and closed my eyes, centering myself. Vaguely in the back of my mind I knew Aphrodite was ordering around the red fledglings and telling them to stay close, stay inside our circle, even if it was mushed and not really circle-shaped anymore as we crammed ourselves through the trapdoor. But I was only partly there. The rest of me was commanding wind, fire, water, earth, and spirit to cover us, protect us, to blot us from Neferet's view. As they hurried to obey me, I felt a drain on my strength like I'd never known before. Of course I'd never tried to command all five of the elements at once to do such powerful work for me—it felt as if my mind, my will, was trying to sprint a marathon.

I gritted my teeth and held on. The elements swarmed above and around us. I could hear the wind and smell the salt of ocean as a strong breeze swirled a thick mist around us. Then thunder rolled in the suddenly cloudy sky and with a *crack!* a shard of lightning sizzled down, hitting a tree a few yards in front of us. The tree seemed to expand as earth magnified it, so that I opened my eyes as one of the red fledglings was guiding me backwards and through the trapdoor to see our little group completely shielded by the fury of the elements. In the midst of that chaos, I heard the wonderful sound of *"mee-uf-ow!"* and I looked through the trapdoor to see Nala sitting on the ground outside the school at the head of a bevy of cats, including the horrible and very disheveled-looking Maleficent, who was staying close to the Twins' hateful Beelzebub.

I got one last glimpse of Neferet as she looked wildly around, clearly not wanting to believe that we had somehow escaped her. And then the trapdoor closed, sealing us out of the House of Night.

"Okay, reform up the circle. Tighten it up. Twins! You're too close together. You're making it lopsided. Cats! Stop hissing at Duchess. We don't have time for it." Aphrodite was calling orders like a drill sergeant.

"The tunnels." Stevie Rae's weak voice seemed to slice through the night.

I looked at her. She couldn't stand up. Erik had lifted her in his arms, and he was holding her like a baby, careful not to touch the arrow that was sticking out of her back. Her face was completely chalk white except for her red tattoos.

"We have to get to the tunnels. We'll be safe there," she said.

"Stevie Rae's right. He won't follow us there, and neither will Neferet, not anymore," Aphrodite said.

"What tunnels?" Darius asked.

"They're under the city, old Prohibition hiding places. The entrance is through the depot downtown," I said.

"The depot. That's a good three miles or so away, through the heart of the city," he said. "How are we going to—?" His words broke off as we heard terrible screams coming from all around us outside the House of Night. Bright balls of fire were blossoming in the sky like terrible, deadly flowers.

"What's happening?" Jack asked, moving closer to Damien.

"It's the Raven Mockers. They have their bodies back, and they're hungry. They're feeding on humans," Aphrodite said.

"They can use fire?" Shaunee asked, looking supremely pissed.

"They can," Aphrodite said.

"Like hell they can!" Shaunee started to lift her arm, and I felt heat begin to swirl in the air around us.

"No!" Aphrodite yelled. "You can't call attention to us. Not to-night. If you do, we're finished."

"You've seen this?" I asked.

She nodded. "All this and more. Those who don't get under-ground will be their prey."

"Then we get to Stevie Rae's tunnels," I said.

"How?" one of the red fledglings I didn't recognize said. She sounded young and very afraid.

I braced myself, already exhausted by manipulating all five of the elements to such an extent. I didn't want them to know how draining I was finding all of this. They had to believe I was strong and sure and in control. I drew a deep breath. "Don't worry. I know how we move without being seen. I've done it before." I smiled wearily at Stevie Rae. "*We've* done it before." My gaze took in Aphrodite. "Haven't we?"

Stevie Rae managed to nod weakly.

"Yep, we sure have," Aphrodite said.

"So what's the plan?" Damien asked.

"Yeah, let's get with it," Erin said.

"Ditto. I'm getting a cramp from smooshing so close to everyone," Shaunee muttered, obviously still pissed she couldn't fight fire with fire.

"Here's the plan. We become mist and shadows, night and darkness. We don't exist. No one sees us. We are the night and the night is us." As I explained it, I felt that familiar shiver of my body and saw the red fledglings gasp, and knew when they looked at me, they were seeing nothing but mist covered with darkness, steeped in shadow. I thought how weird it was that blending with the night felt easier now that I was exhausted . . . it was like I could just fade away and finally sleep . . .

"Zoey!" Erik's voice shook me out of my dangerous trance.

"Fine! I'm fine," I said quickly. "Now you guys do it. Concentrate. It's no different than when you used to sneak out of the House of Night to meet boyfriends or go to off campus rituals, only you're going to focus even more. You can do it. You are mist and shadow. No one can see you. No one can hear you. Only night is here, and you are part of night."

I watched my little group shimmer and begin to dissolve. It wasn't perfect, and Duchess was still solidly a big blond Lab—unlike our cats she couldn't blend with the night—but the kid she stuck close to was little more than a shadow.

"Now let's go. Stay together. Hold hands. Do not let anything mess with your concentration. Darius, lead the way," I said.

We moved out into what had become a city of living nightmare. I wondered later how we ever made it, and realized the answer even as I wondered. We made it because the guiding hand of Nyx was on us. We moved in her shadow. Covered with her power we became the night, even though the rest of the night had become madness.

The Raven Mockers were everywhere. It was just after midnight New Year's Eve, and the creatures had their pickings of tipsy, celebrating humans who poured out of clubs and restaurants and beautiful old oil mansions because they'd heard the crackle and pop of the creatures' inhuman fire and, thinking the city had set off fireworks, rushed out to watch the show. I wondered with oddly detached horror how many of them looked up at the sky only to have their last sight be terrible red eyes of men looking out at them from monstrous faces.

Before we'd reached the halfway point near Cincinnati and Thirteenth I started hearing police and fire sirens, along with gunshots, which made me smile grimly. This was Oklahoma, and us Okies did love our guns. Yep, we exercise our Second Amendment right with pride and vigor. I wished I had a clue if modern weapons would make any difference to creatures born of magic and myth, and knew I wouldn't have to wonder long. Soon we'd all find out.

Within a block of the abandoned Tulsa depot, it began to rain a cold, miserable misty wetness that chilled us to the bone, but it did help to hide our little group even more from probing eyes— whether they were human or beast.

We hurried into the basement of the abandoned Tulsa depot, gaining entrance easily by swinging open a metal grate that looked deceptively well barred. As soon as the darkness of the basement swallowed us, we gave a group sigh of relief.

"Okay, now we can close the circle."

"Thank you spirit, you may depart," I began. I turned to Stevie Rae, still in Erik's arms. "I am grateful to you, earth, you may depart." Erin was on my left, and I smiled through the darkness to her. "Water, you did well tonight. You may depart." Still turning to my left, I found Shaunee. "Fire, thank you, please depart." Then I closed the circle with the element that opened it. "Wind, you have my gratitude as always. You may depart." And with a little pop and sizzle, the silver thread that had bound us and saved us, disappeared.

I gritted my teeth against the exhaustion that threatened to overwhelm me, and I think I would have fallen had Darius not grabbed my arm to steady my wobbly knees.

"Let's get down there. We're still not completely safe," Aphrodite said.

We all moved toward the rear of the basement to the drainage entrance I knew hid a wide system of tunnels. Reentering these tunnels was as surreal an experience as the night had become. The last time I'd been here had been in the middle of a snow-storm. I was struggling to save Heath from Stevie Rae and a bunch of the fledglings I was now struggling to save.

Heath!

"Zoey, come on," Erik said when I hesitated. He had passed Stevie Rae to Darius, so he and I were the last of the group left aboveground.

"Gotta make two phone calls first. There's no reception down there."

"Then make it quick," he said. "I'll tell them you're coming."

"Thanks." I smiled wearily at him. "I'll hurry."

He gave me a tight nod and then disappeared down the steel ladder into the tunnels.

I was surprised when Heath picked up on the first ring. "What do you want, Zoey?"

"Listen to me, Heath, I have to be quick. Something terrible has been released at the House of Night. It's going to be bad, re-ally bad. I don't know for how long because I don't know how to stop it. But the only way you'll be safe is if you get underground. It doesn't like to be under the earth. Do you understand?"

"Yes," he said.

"Do you believe me?"

He didn't even hesitate. "Yes."

I sighed in relief. "Get your family and anyone else you care about and get underground. Doesn't your grandpa's house have a big ol' basement?"

"Yeah, we can go there."

"Good, I'll call you again when I can."

"Zoey, are you going to be safe, too?"

My heart squeezed. "I am."

"Where?"

"In the old tunnels under the depot," I said.

"But they're dangerous!"

"No, no—it's not like that anymore. Don't worry. You just stay safe, too. 'Kay?"

" 'Kay," he said.

I hung up before I said something both of us would regret. Then I dialed the second number I had to call. My mom didn't answer. The phone went to voice mail after five rings. Her overly perky voice said, "This is the Heffer residence, we love and fear the Lord and wish you a blessed day. Leave us a message. Amen!" I rolled my eyes and when the beep came I said, "Mom, you're gonna think that Satan has been let loose on earth, and for once you're close to right. This thing is bad, and the only way you can be safe from it is if you get underground, like in a basement or a cave. So get to the church basement and stay there. Okay? I do love you, Mom, and I've made sure that Grandma is safe, too, she's with the—" Her answering service cut me off. I sighed and hoped that she would, for the first time in a long time, listen to me. Then I followed everyone else into the tunnels.

My group was waiting for me near the entrance. I saw lights begin to flicker on down the tunnel that stretched, dark and intimidating, in front of us.

"I sent the red fledglings ahead to get the lights on and stuff," Aphrodite said, then she glanced at Stevie Rae. "The 'and stuff' being hustling to get some blankets and dry clothes."

"Good. That's good." I forced myself to think through my exhaustion. The kids had already lit a few oil lanterns, the old-fashioned kind that could be carried around by swinging handles, and put them on hooks at about eye level, so it was easy to see the expression on my friends' faces when they looked up at me. The same thing was on all their faces, even Aphrodite's. They were afraid.

Please Nyx, I sent up one fervent, silent prayer, *give me strength and help me to say this right because how we begin here is going to set the tone for how we live here. Please don't let me mess up.*

I didn't get a wordy answer, but I did get a rush of warmth and love and confidence that made my heart take a little stutter beat and filled me with a burst of strength.

"Yeah, it's bad," I began. "There's no denying that. We're young. We're alone. We're hurt. Neferet and Kalona are powerful and, as far as we know, they might have all the rest of the fledglings and vampyres on their side. But we have something they'll never have. We have love and truth and each other. We also have Nyx. She's Marked each of us, and in some special way, Chosen each of us, too. There has never been a group like us—we're completely new." I paused, trying to meet everyone's eyes and smile confidence to them. Into my pause, Darius spoke.

"Priestess, this evil is like nothing I've felt before," he said. "Nothing I've even heard of before. It is an untamed thing seething with hatred. When it burst forth from the earth, I felt as if evil had been reborn."

"But you recognized it, Darius. And lots of the other warriors didn't. I watched their reactions to it. They didn't grab their weapons or get the hell out of there, like you did."

"Perhaps a braver warrior would have stayed," he said.

"Bullshit!" Aphrodite said. "A stupider warrior would have stayed. You're here with us, and now you have a chance to fight it.

For all we know those other warriors were either mowed down by those damn bird things, or are under some weird spell like the rest of the fledglings."

"Yeah," said Jack. "We're here because there's something different about us."

"Something special," Damien said.

"Damn special," Shaunee said.

"I'm with you on that one, Twin," Erin said.

"We're so special, when you look in the dictionary under *short bus*, there's a group picture of us," Stevie Rae said, sounding weak but definitely alive.

"All right. So what do we do next?" Erik said.

They all looked at me. I looked at them.

"Well, uh, we make up a Plan," I said.

"A Plan?" Erik said. "That's it?"

"Nope. We make up a Plan, and then we figure out how to take our school back. Together." I stuck my hand out in the middle of them, like I was a softball-playing dork. "Are you guys with me?"

Aphrodite rolled her eyes, but hers was the first hand to cover mine. "Yeah, I'm in," she said.

"And me," said Damien.

"Me, too," said Jack.

"Ditto," said both of the Twins together.

"I'm in, too," said Stevie Rae.

"I wouldn't miss it for the world," said Erik, putting his hand on the top of the pile and smiling into my eyes.

"All right, then," I said. "Let's go get 'em!" And as they all yelled dorkishly after me, I felt an awesome tingle spread from my fingertips to cover the palms of my hands, and I knew when I pulled them out of the hand pile I'd find brand-new intricate tattoos decorating each of my palms, like I was an exotic ancient priestess who had been henna-Marked as special by her Goddess. So, even in the midst of craziness and exhaustion and life-changing chaos, I was filled with peace and the sweet knowledge that I was walking the path my Goddess wanted me on.

Not that that path was smooth and pothole free. But still, it was my path, and like me, it was bound to be unique.